One Passionate Night

She belongs to him - for one
unforgettable night!

Three exhilarating, contemporary
romances from three beloved
Mills & Boon authors!

In December 2008 Mills & Boon bring
you two classic collections, each
featuring three favourite romances
by our bestselling authors…

ONE PASSIONATE NIGHT

His Bride for One Night by Miranda Lee
One Night at Parenga by Robyn Donald
His One-Night Mistress by Sandra Field

BLACKMAILED BY THE RICH MAN

In the Millionaire's Possession
by Sara Craven
Blackmailed Into Marriage
by Lucy Monroe
Bedded by Blackmail by Julia James

One Passionate Night

HIS BRIDE FOR ONE NIGHT
by
Miranda Lee

ONE NIGHT AT PARENGA
by
Robyn Donald

HIS ONE-NIGHT MISTRESS
by
Sandra Field

MILLS & BOON
Pure reading pleasure™

*Harlequin Mills & Boon Limited,
Eton House, 18-24 Paradise Road, Richmond, Surrey TW9 1SR*

ONE PASSIONATE NIGHT
© by Harlequin Enterprises II B.V./S.à.r.l 2008

His Bride for One Night, One Night at Parenga and *His One-Night
Mistress* were first published in Great Britain by Harlequin
Mills & Boon Limited in separate, single volumes.

His Bride for One Night © Miranda Lee 2005
One Night at Parenga © Robyn Donald 2002
His One-Night Mistress © Sandra Field 2005

ISBN: 978 0 263 86139 6

05-1208

*Printed and bound in Spain
by Litografia Rosés S.A., Barcelona*

HIS BRIDE FOR ONE NIGHT

by

Miranda Lee

100 Reasons to Celebrate

We invite you to join us in celebrating Mills & Boon's centenary. Gerald Mills and Charles Boon founded Mills & Boon Limited in 1908 and opened offices in London's Covent Garden. Since then, Mills & Boon has become a hallmark for romantic fiction, recognised around the world.

We're proud of our 100 years of publishing excellence, which wouldn't have been achieved without the loyalty and enthusiasm of our authors and readers.

Thank you!

Each month throughout the year there will be something new and exciting to mark the centenary, so watch for your favourite authors, captivating new stories, special limited edition collections…and more!

Miranda Lee is Australian, living near Sydney. Born and raised in the bush, she was boarding-school educated and briefly pursued a career in classical music before moving to Sydney and embracing the world of computers. Happily married, with three daughters, she began writing when family commitments kept her at home. She likes to create stories that are believable, modern, fast-paced and sexy. Her interests include meaty sagas, doing word puzzles, gambling and going to the movies.

Don't miss Miranda Lee's exciting new novel,
The Billionaire's Bride of Vengeance,
available in January 2009
from Mills & Boon® Modern™.

CHAPTER ONE

DANIEL stared down through the plane window at the panoramic beauty of the city and coastline below. The captain had just announced a slight delay in landing at Mascot Airport and was doing a sweeping circle over Sydney to give his mainly tourist passengers a good look at the city which reputedly had the best harbour—and the best beaches—in the world.

Not an exaggerated claim, in Daniel's opinion. He'd flown over some pretty spectacular cities in his time. New York. San Francisco. Rio.

But Sydney was in a class of its own.

Maybe it was the early-morning light which made its beaches look whiter than white, and the water bluer than blue. But just the sight of that dazzling harbour with its famous icons of the bridge and the opera house—each one sparkling in the summer sunshine—lightened Daniel's spirits.

Beth had been right to insist he come home, even if only for a visit.

Home…

Funny how he always thought of Sydney as home. True, he'd been born here. And yes, he'd gone to school here from the age of twelve to eighteen, which was why he didn't have much of an American accent. But most of his life had been spent in the States. In

5

Los Angeles, to be precise. The city of angels. Or devils, depending on your point of view.

LA could be one tough city. Usually, Daniel could handle its toughness. One could say he'd thrived on it.

But life had finally got the better of him. This last Christmas had been particularly bleak and lonely, with his mother having died earlier that year.

A shudder rippled down Daniel's spine. It was eight months since his poor mom had passed away, but it felt like yesterday.

He still didn't know how he'd controlled himself when his father showed up at her funeral with his new wife on his arm. His fourth. Blonde, of course. And young. They were always blonde and young. And his father was what now? Sixty-five, ten years older than his mother would have been next month. Still, successful producers never seemed to have trouble attracting—and marrying—ambitious young starlets.

His own mother had had stars in her eyes when she'd first met the handsome Ben Bannister on a star-finding trip to Sydney. He'd been a very experienced thirty whereas she was a naive twenty.

Daniel often wondered why his father had married his mother. The pretty little brunette from Bondi didn't seem his style. OK, so he'd got her pregnant, but was that reason enough to marry? Far better that he'd gone back to America and left her to raise her son by herself here in Australia.

None of his father's marriages lasted very long. A few years at the most. But they always produced a child or two. Daniel had several half-brothers and -sisters whom he barely knew. His father no longer lived in Los Angeles, having moved to New York after he left Daniel's mother when Daniel was six. Or had he been seven?

Must have been seven, Daniel mused. He was six years older than his little sister, Beth, who'd just begun to walk at the time.

Whatever, he'd been old enough to be almost as hurt as his mother, his sweet, soft-hearted mother, who had never got over her husband's betrayal. Before his father stormed out of the front door, he'd callously told his weeping wife that he'd been unfaithful to her all along. She'd turned to pills for comfort at first. Then drink. And finally other men, younger men who used her body and spent her settlement money like water.

When things became really bad, Daniel's maternal grandfather stepped in and took Beth and himself back to Australia to live with him, making sure they got a good education and a more stable upbringing. Both children loved life in Sydney with their widower grandfather, Beth especially. Within months, she was saying she wanted to stay forever. Daniel liked the life too, but he was older and couldn't help worrying about his mother. She sounded OK in her letters, claimed she'd stopped drinking and had a job, but she always had some excuse why she couldn't fly out and visit.

Once he'd completed high school, Daniel felt compelled to return to Los Angeles, where he'd been relieved to see that his mom *had* stopped drinking, but oh…how she'd aged. Yes, she did have a job, but it didn't pay much and she was living in a dump. Unable to convince her to return to Australia with him—a warped form of pride, in his opinion—Daniel borrowed some money from his grandfather, found somewhere better for them both to live, then enrolled at a local university to study law. He worked three part-time jobs to pay his fees, and to make sure his mother wanted for nothing.

When he graduated top of his class, the prestigious LA law firm of Johansen, O'Neill and Morecroft snapped Daniel up and he soon found his feet as their most aggressive and successful divorce lawyer. Soon he was able to repay his grandfather every cent he'd borrowed, plus interest. When his impressive first-year bonus came in he put down a deposit on a maintenance-free condominium for his mother, and a nearby bachelor pad for himself. As much as he adored his mother, Daniel felt it was high time he had his own space.

In the first few years of his career as a divorce lawyer, Daniel represented both men and women, but when he made partner shortly after his thirtieth birthday he announced that in future the only clients he would represent were women. The men he left to someone else.

Daniel found great satisfaction in preventing sleazebag husbands with more money than morals from weaseling their way out of paying what was due to their ex-wives. He was ruthless in his quest to gain financial security for the discarded, disillusioned and distressed women who trailed through his office. Women who were no longer young enough, or pretty enough, or exciting enough for the husbands who'd once promised to love, honour and cherish them forever.

Daniel was particularly vicious in his pursuit of justice if there were children involved, especially when the men in question didn't want to face their responsibility regarding hands-on child-rearing. And there were plenty of those.

Men who abandoned their children had to be made to pay.

'But not all men are like that,' his more optimistic little sister had recently said to him over the phone during her weekly call from Sydney. Beth never had returned to America, even after her beloved grandfather passed away. 'If my marriage ever broke up, Vince would never abandon our child. Or children. I'm not sure how many we'll have. But more than one.'

Beth was currently seven months pregnant with her first child.

'Not that our marriage is ever going to break up,' Beth had added quickly. 'We have our ups and downs but we're still very much in love with each other.'

In love, Daniel mused as the jumbo jet banked and began its descent into Sydney.

What was being *in love*, exactly?

He'd never felt it, he was sure. Not once. Thirty-six years old, and he'd never fallen in love.

He'd liked lots of women. And lusted after them. And made love to them.

But that wasn't the same as being in love. He'd never been so overcome by mad passion that he'd do anything for the object of said passion, such as ask her to marry him. Even if he did fall in love one day, Daniel couldn't see himself marrying. He'd seen far too many divorces!

'You're a cynical, cold-blooded bastard,' his last ladyfriend had flung at him just before she'd flounced out of his office—and his life—a couple of weeks before Christmas. 'I refuse to waste any more time on you, Daniel Bannister. You obviously don't love me. I doubt you even know what love is.'

All true, he'd finally agreed after she'd stormed out, her fury forcing him to have a long, hard look at himself.

What he'd discovered had been sobering.

He'd always condemned his father for being a serial husband, but he wasn't much better when it came to relationships. He'd become a serial lover, going from one woman to another, never committing himself, never losing much sleep when these relationships—such as they were—were terminated.

Yep. He was a cynical, cold-blooded bastard all right. Not quite the noble, knight-in-shining-armour type he'd always imagined himself to be.

Two months later he was in a plane circling Sydney, still trying to come to terms with this revised character assessment of himself, trying to justify his past behaviour. Not very successfully. OK, so he hadn't ever lied to his ladyfriends, or promised anything serious, or betrayed any vows, or abandoned any children. But he'd still hurt the women he'd dated, and who had probably wanted more from him than what he'd been prepared to give.

Daniel understood that he was a good catch, as the saying went. Physically attractive, professionally successful, financially secure. The kind of guy that his married acquaintances were always trying to set up with their single, female, husband-hunting friends.

To give himself some credit, Daniel always steered clear of the more obvious traps, sticking to women whom he'd mistakenly believed were dedicated career girls.

Only in hindsight did he realise that thirty-something girls who'd devoted their lives to their careers often had a change of heart when their biological clocks started ticking. Suddenly, some of them began to want wedding bells and baby bootees, whereas in the beginning all they'd wanted was some stimulating conversation over dinner and some satisfying sex at the end of the night.

Which he was more than happy to provide.

As Daniel stared through the plane window, his eyes glazed over and he started wondering if men ever suffered from the biological-clock syndrome. He'd turned thirty-six last month.

Maybe one day soon, he'd meet some girl and suddenly feel things he'd never felt before. Maybe he'd lose his head through love and desire and uncontrollable passion.

Daniel uttered a small, dry laugh.

Dream on, Daniel. This is *you* we're talking about here. That cynical, cold-blooded bastard. You'd be the last man on earth to lose his head over a woman!

The plane's wheels making contact with the tarmac startled Daniel. He'd been so wrapped up in his thoughts that he'd stopped following their descent.

His gaze focused again through the window to take in the view of Sydney from the ground.

A large bay of water stretched out before him on the plane's left, fringed by sand. Directly opposite was an industrial area. To his right, a residential suburb. Airports were usually on the outskirts of cities but Mascot wasn't far from Sydney's city centre.

His sister's house was in the eastern suburbs, at Rose Bay, also near the city centre. She'd promised to meet him, despite the early hour and her advanced pregnancy.

Daniel knew it would do him good to spend a couple of weeks here in Sydney with his sister and her husband. Australians were wonderfully easygoing, and Beth was Australian through and through now.

People blamed the hot weather, but Daniel didn't believe it had anything to do with the weather. He believed it had something to do with their isolation. They lived so far away that they hadn't yet been contaminated with the rest of the world's mad and bad habits. In his experience, Australians didn't seem to live to work as a lot of Americans did. They worked to live.

Daniel hoped to embrace some of that philosophy during his visit here. He was in danger of becoming a serious workaholic.

All work and no play made Daniel a very dull boy.

A fortnight of total relaxation would do him a power of good.

CHAPTER TWO

CHARLOTTE responded to the annoying beep-beep of her clock alarm as any person would at five a.m. on a Friday morning, especially one who'd only got to bed at two. She flung an arm over her duvet, cut the irritating noise off by hitting the snooze button, then rolled over and curled up again for ten more minutes' precious sleep.

But before she could return to the bliss of oblivion, Charlotte suddenly remembered why she'd set her alarm at such a God-forsaken hour.

Gary's flight was due in at six-twenty.

Although it was not a long drive from Bondi to Mascot at that hour of the morning, Charlotte had known in advance that she'd need extra time to make herself look tippy-top to meet her fiancé. Hence her early alarm.

Throwing back the duvet, Charlotte leapt out of bed, swearing when she banged her leg on the corner of her bedside chest. Rubbing her thigh, she limped to the bathroom.

'Aaah!' she squawked when she finally saw herself in the mirror above the vanity.

Her screech of alarm was followed by the appearance of an equally dishevelled Louise in the bathroom door. 'What's all the noise about?' her flatmate asked blearily.

'Look at me!' Charlotte proclaimed with a despairing groan. 'This is all your fault, Louise. You should never have insisted on having my hen night only two days before my wedding, and the night before Gary's arrival. You know what even a few drinks do to me. Not to mention lack of sleep. My God, I look a positive fright!'

Louise snorted. 'You couldn't look a positive fright if your life depended on it. You even look good with dark roots.'

Charlotte groaned again. Louise had to be blind! Her hair was nothing short of appalling.

Maintaining herself as the long-haired, golden-locked blonde whom Gary had met and fallen instantly in love with up on the Gold Coast last year had taken its toll. All Charlotte and Louise's skills as hairdressers could not prevent the damage which had been done to her naturally thick, dark brown hair by continual bleaching.

She'd only gone blonde for that holiday in a fit of pique after her break-up with Dwayne. His new girl-friend was a blonde. Charlotte had never intended to keep it that way. She'd been planning on cutting it short afterwards and returning to her natural colour.

But her plans had changed on meeting Gary, and eight months later she was still a blonde. A blonde with dark roots and split ends.

Charlotte wished now she hadn't put off doing the roots till the day of her wedding. She should have had them done yesterday. And had a trim. *And* put in a treatment.

'I have to use the bathroom,' Louise said with a

yawn. 'Why don't you go make me some coffee, in exchange for which I'll blow-dry your hair for you?'

'Do you think you could give me a quick trim and an instant treatment as well?' Charlotte pleaded.

'What am I, your fairy godmother? OK, OK, just go get that coffee.'

One hour later Charlotte looked as good as she could, under the circumstances. But, truly, if she kept bleaching and blow-drying her hair so ruthlessly it would start breaking off, as Louise had pointed out.

'If Gary really loves you,' Louise had added drily, 'he wouldn't care if your hair's long or short. Or if you're a blonde or a brunette.'

Louise's words echoed in Charlotte's mind during the short drive to the airport.

If Gary really loves you...

It wasn't the first time Louise had expressed doubts over the reality of Gary's love for her. And vice versa.

Charlotte could understand her friend's misgivings. Most of her relationship with the good-looking American lawyer *had* developed over the internet, which was a trap in itself. Exchanging emails wasn't the same as actually spending time with each other. It was easy to put your best foot forward with words, rather than action. Charlotte did understand that.

But theirs hadn't been a strictly email romance. Their initial meeting had been in the flesh. Unfortunately, their time together had been brief. It had been the last night of her holiday on the Gold Coast. The last night of Gary's trip to Australia as well. He had been due to return to LA the next day.

Gary had spied her across a crowded room—actually, it was a smoke-filled club—and zeroed in on her straight away. He'd asked her to dance and the rest, as they say, was history.

They'd spent the whole night together. Not in bed or anything like that. Charlotte had never been the sort of girl to jump into bed at the drop of a hat, especially with some smooth-talking American out here on holiday. There was no doubt Gary wouldn't have minded, but he'd seemed impressed when she'd resisted his advances to have sex. Instead, they'd walked along the beach for hours, hand in hand, just talking. As they'd watched the sun come up together, he told her she was the girl he'd waited for all his life.

Later that day she'd accompanied Gary to the airport, where he'd promised to call her as soon as he got home. His passionate goodbye kiss had sent her head spinning, repairing some of the damage Dwayne had perpetrated on her battered self-esteem.

Louise had warned her when she came back to Sydney that men met on holiday rarely contacted you afterwards. But Gary had. He'd called Charlotte as soon as he'd returned to Los Angeles and they'd been in constant contact ever since, sometimes by phone, but mostly by email.

Charlotte felt she knew Gary much better than she'd even known Dwayne, the rat on whom she'd wasted the previous two years of her life. He'd eventually dumped her for some gym bunny, whom he'd got pregnant.

When Gary asked her to marry him last November, Charlotte hadn't hesitated to say yes.

Maybe she would have hesitated if he hadn't been prepared to marry her here in Sydney, and make his life here.

Or if you weren't thirty-three, another nasty little voice whispered in her head. *And beginning to believe that you would never find a husband.*

Charlotte swiftly brushed that no longer relevant thought aside.

She *was* getting married. Tomorrow. And in considerable style.

Charlotte hoped Gary wouldn't mind. He'd requested a simple wedding. No church. Just a celebrant, and only a small guest list. He himself had no close family; his parents had been killed in a tragic house fire when he was a teenager.

But Charlotte's father hadn't waited thirty-three years to give his youngest daughter away in anything less than a white wedding with all the trimmings.

Secretly, Charlotte had been glad her father had insisted on this. Her two older sisters had both been beautiful brides with white wedding gowns, and Charlotte hadn't really wanted to settle for anything less. The church part she'd managed to skirt around, her parents reluctantly agreeing to a celebrant. But everything else was to be very traditional, complete with a proper reception, a three-tiered wedding cake, the bridal waltz. The lot!

Charlotte hadn't informed Gary of any of this. She reasoned that once he was here, she could explain that it wasn't her doing. It was her parents' idea. And it wasn't as though he had to pay for any of it. Her father had footed the bill, dear sweet man that he was. All Gary had to do was be fitted with a rental tux today—a fitting had been arranged for this afternoon—then show up in it tomorrow.

Charlotte didn't think that was too much to ask. Not of a man who really loved her. And he did. He must really love her, otherwise he wouldn't be coming all this way to marry her. Or have sent her such a lovely sapphire and diamond engagement ring.

Just the sight of it on her ring finger was reassuring.

Half an hour later, Charlotte was pacing back and forth outside the arrivals gate to which Gary's flight had been allotted, her eyes darting continuously to the ramp down which her fiancé would walk any moment now. His plane had only touched down ten minutes earlier—it had been late landing—but business class passengers were rarely held up in Customs.

She couldn't stand still. Nerves had her stomach in knots. But was she excited or afraid, afraid that she was about to rush into marriage with a man she hadn't even been to bed with?

Still, maybe that was a good thing. She'd eventually slept with most of her other boyfriends and none of them had proposed marriage. Perhaps because she'd always ultimately disappointed them, sexually. Her lack of enjoyment seemed to bother her boyfriends more than it did her.

She'd been totally honest with Gary and he'd reassured her he wasn't marrying her because she was a sexpot, but because she was beautiful and warm and sweet and wanted what he wanted. A family. At the same time, he seemed extremely confident that everything would turn out fine on their wedding night.

Charlotte hoped so, hoped that this time she would feel the earth move the way Louise was always talking about.

If she didn't? Well…as Gary said, they would work on it together.

There! There he was!

She started jumping up and down, waving and smiling.

'Here! Here! Over here!'

When he turned his darkly handsome head from where he'd been looking over to one side, Charlotte's hand froze mid-air, her smile instantly fading.

Because it wasn't Gary at all. Just someone who looked like him. In broad strokes, that was. About the same height. Gary was over six feet. Similar hair. Dark brown. Short. No parting. Rather similar in profile as well. High forehead, strong nose, square jaw.

But when this man stared straight at her, Charlotte could see his eyes were nothing like Gary's. This man's were deeper set, and very penetrating. Not blue, either, but brown. Almost black when they narrowed underneath his dark straight brows.

They were narrowed right now. On her.

Never in her life had Charlotte been looked at the way this man was looking at her. The focused intensity in his gaze was nothing short of blistering.

When he started pushing his luggage trolley towards her, Charlotte's arm dropped back down to clutch her shoulder bag across her chest in a strangely defensive fashion. Despite her stomach curling with embarrassment, she found she could not look away from him, but kept on staring back into those darkly magnetic eyes.

'Did Beth send you to meet me?' he asked as he ground to a halt in front of her, his accent not dissimilar to Gary's.

Dear God, *Gary*! In her fluster, she'd forgotten all about him.

'I'm sorry, no,' she apologised swiftly, dragging her eyes away from the disturbing stranger to see if Gary had made an appearance. 'I don't know anyone named Beth. I...I thought you were my fiancé for a moment,' she rattled on, her eyes agitatedly searching the now constant line of exiting passengers.

But Gary wasn't amongst them.

She glanced back at the American, who was still standing there. He was still staring at her as well, but now with an air of curiosity, whereas before his eyes had carried...what, exactly?

She wasn't sure.

'You...um...look like him. Sort of.' In truth, Gary was not quite in this man's league. Gary was good-looking. This man was heart-thumpingly handsome.

'Aah,' he said. 'I see.'

The obvious disappointment in his voice and eyes rattled Charlotte. What had he been thinking? Or hoping?

'We're getting married tomorrow,' she added, for goodness knew what reason. She'd already explained why she'd waved and smiled at him.

'Lucky man,' he murmured, his gaze moving slowly over her from head to toe.

Suddenly she knew what she'd seen in his eyes earlier, and why he'd sounded disappointed just now.

Charlotte had encountered desire in lots of men before, but never had the message been delivered with such high voltage, and by such incredible eyes. They weren't just beautiful, but intelligent and intriguing, and very sexy.

Her feminine antennae quivered as his message was received once more, the current charging through her veins heating her body from the inside out.

Charlotte could not have been more shocked when her face actually flamed. Why, she hadn't blushed in years!

'If you'll excuse me,' she said, and forced her legs to carry her away from his disturbing presence. But even as she went back to searching for Gary, her mind still lingered on the handsome stranger. Who was he? *What* was he? And what was he doing here in Sydney?

CHAPTER THREE

DANIEL was almost grateful when she gave him the brush-off. What on earth had he been doing, staring at her like that?

Hitting on women had never been his style. On top of that, she was a blonde. One of the bottled variety. Daniel had an aversion to bottled blondes.

To be fair to himself, she wasn't the usual bottle blonde, the kind his father married. The kind Daniel often met in LA, the ones whose over-bleached, over-teased hair was not the only thing false about them.

Despite the dark roots, this girl's hair was sleek and simply styled, falling in a straight curtain half-way down her back. There was nothing even re-motely false about her face, either, which was as beautiful as it was refreshingly natural. If she was wearing make-up, it had been applied with a light hand. Her skin didn't need enhancement, anyway, being fine and clear and olive-toned. Her eyes were just as naturally beautiful. Big and blue as the Pacific, with the longest, darkest lashes.

She did have lip gloss on. Her lips had definitely looked extra shiny when he'd stared at them. Shiny and wet and full. The kind of lips made for kissing, and for being kissed by, and for…

Daniel pulled himself up sharply and whirled away

from where he'd been standing, still staring after her. It had been a long time since he'd been knocked for six by a woman at first sight. And an even longer time since he had no chance at all in being successful with one he fancied as much as he'd instantly fancied this one.

An intelligent man had to know when a female target was worth pursuing, and when she was not. This girl was getting married tomorrow. He couldn't expect her to fall at his feet. Couldn't expect her to respond to him in any way.

Which perhaps was what was still bothering him. Because she *had* responded to him, hadn't she? He'd seen the flash of sexual connection in her eyes. He'd spotted the telling tension in her body language. Sensed that she'd been as startled by her attraction to him as he'd been by his for her.

The way she'd blushed when he'd looked her up and down might have been embarrassment. But he suspected not. She was a woman, not some naive young girl.

No, she'd responded to him all right, which was a source of great irritation.

Daniel was not a man who liked to lose at anything in life. But this time, he had to accept defeat gracefully. Had to ignore the signs of mutual attraction and move on. Literally.

With a sigh, he started searching the crowded arrivals area for his sister, deliberately making sure he didn't go back the way the blonde had gone. The last thing he wanted was to see her throwing her arms around some other man. His male ego was still smarting. His male body wasn't feeling crash hot, either.

But Beth was nowhere to be found. Yet she should have been here. The plane had been late enough landing.

If Beth had one flaw it was chronic tardiness.

The beeping of his cellphone had Daniel pulling it out and putting it to his ear.

'Yes, Beth,' he said drily.

'I'm sorry, Daniel, but I overslept. I was so excited to see you today that I couldn't sleep at first last night. So I lay down on the sofa to watch TV and I must have drifted off there. So I wasn't in my bed to hear the alarm and Vince, of course, would have just banged the button down and gone back to sleep.'

'Fine. I'll catch a taxi.'

'No, no, don't do that. I *am* on my way. Have some breakfast in the coffee shop down the far end of Arrivals and I'll be there in around twenty minutes, OK?'

'OK,' he agreed, resignation in his voice.

'You're not mad at me?'

'No.'

'I'm amazed!'

'I decided on the plane to be more relaxed in future,' he informed her with a somewhat ironic smile. Relaxed was not how he was feeling at this moment. Clearly, he needed more practice at being laid-back. And in handling sexual frustration.

'No kidding. That'll be a first. Look, I have to hang up. I can't risk being booked talking on my mobile whilst driving. I've already lost three points on my licence for speeding. See you soon. Bye.'

'Bye,' Daniel replied into an already dead phone.

Smiling wryly to himself, he slipped the phone into his pocket, then pushed his luggage trolley down to the coffee shop Beth had directed him to. Once he'd ordered a mug of flat white at the counter— he'd had breakfast on the plane—he settled himself at a clean table, stretched his legs out, crossed his arms and started surveying the world passing by.

Bad idea.

For who should be coming towards him but the gorgeous blonde, *without* a fiancé by her side? She was walking very slowly, with a cute little pink cell-phone clamped to her ear, totally unaware of him, her lovely head down, her concentration on the conversation she was having.

Once again, Daniel could not take his eyes off her. Not her face so much this time, but her body, which in slow motion was a sight to behold. His first visual port of call were her breasts—especially in that tight pink top. Full and lush, with perky nipples which even the confines of a bra could not hide. There was nothing wrong with her lower half, either. Small waist. Womanly hips. Flat stomach. Long legs. Slender ankles.

Daniel liked shapely girls in tight jeans, especially hipster jeans that hugged their legs all the way down. He hated flares on a female. He liked to see their ankles. And their feet.

He noticed that she had pretty little feet, shown to advantage in open-toed, high-heeled sandals, her toenails painted the same candy-pink as her top. And her phone.

As she came closer he saw that she was looking pale. Pale and somewhat shaken. Clearly, she was receiving some bad news.

She ground to a halt within listening distance of Daniel's table. 'I don't believe it!' she cried out. 'Life couldn't be that cruel to me!'

Oh-oh. Something serious must have happened to her missing fiancé. As much as Daniel would like the blonde to be footloose and fancy-free, he wasn't selfish enough to hope her boyfriend had had an accident, or anything horrible like that.

'The bastard!' the blonde suddenly spat, and Daniel's eyebrows shot up.

Nope. Not an accident. The cad just hadn't shown up. By the sounds of things, he wasn't about to, either.

Despite his feeling sorry for the girl, all sorts of sexual vistas suddenly opened up before Daniel's eyes. When his conscience pricked, he ignored it. He was a normal, red-blooded male, after all, not a saint.

'No, I'll be all right,' the blonde said in clipped tones. 'No, I'm tougher than that. No, of course I'm not going to start crying. I'm in public, for pity's sake. I'll wait till I get home first. Or at least in the car.'

But she didn't wait till she got home. Or even in the car. No sooner had she said goodbye to whoever she was talking to than she burst into tears. Not quiet tears, either. Great, shoulder-racking sobs.

He could understand why the person on the other end of the phone had been worried about her crying.

Thanking fate, Daniel jumped to his feet and rushed to the rescue.

'Is there anything I can do to help?' he asked as he laid a firm, but gentle hand on one of her shaking shoulders.

Charlotte stiffened, then glanced up through her sodden lashes.

It was *him*, the handsome American she'd encountered earlier, the one she'd mistaken for Gary, the one who'd stared at her with hot, hungry eyes.

But they weren't hot, or hungry at the moment. They were looking at her with kindness and concern.

'Bad news, I gather.'

'You could say that,' Charlotte mumbled as she pulled a tissue out of her bag and dabbed at her nose.

'Look, why don't you come over and have some coffee with me?' the American invited, indicating a nearby table. 'I'm stuck here, waiting for my sister to arrive, and wouldn't mind a bit of company. Meanwhile, you can tell me why your fiancé didn't show up.'

Shock made her blink, then blink again. 'How on earth did you know that?'

'You told me yourself you'd mistaken me for your fiancé back at the exit gate,' he explained. 'There's no man by your side and you were just crying. It doesn't take much intelligence to put two and two together.'

'Oh. Yes, I see,' she said as she wiped her nose again, then took a deep, gathering breath.

'So, have you been temporarily stood up?' he asked. 'Or fully jilted?'

'Fully jilted, I'm afraid,' she said dully, her earlier distress gradually being replaced by despair. How *could* fate be so cruel? And what on earth was she going to tell her parents?

'Some men are bloody fools,' the American said.

Charlotte might have been flattered, if she hadn't been feeling so devastated.

'Come on. A cup of coffee will do you the world of good.'

Charlotte was beyond protesting when he took her elbow and led her over to the table. The many-times-bitten part of her knew the American probably had his own agenda in being nice to her. But she wasn't too worried. They were in public. She was quite safe. If he wanted to buy her a cup of coffee, then he could. She was in no fit state to drive home just yet, anyway.

But she had no intention of telling him a single personal detail. He was a perfect stranger, for heaven's sake!

The next couple of minutes passed in a blank blur. Charlotte just sat there in a daze whilst the American ordered her a cappuccino. When it arrived soon after his own mug of coffee, he heaped in a couple of spoonfuls of sugar and pushed it over in front of her.

'Drink up,' he advised. 'You need a sugar hit. You're in shock.'

She did, and soon began to feel marginally better.

'Thank you,' she said at last. 'You were right. I needed that.'

'Aren't you going to tell me what happened?'

'Why on earth would you be interested?' she countered, just a tad stroppily. Charlotte knew he didn't really give a damn about her personal pain. He was just trying to pick her up.

His knight-to-the-rescue act. The coffee. His seemingly kind questions. All weapons to get what he wanted. *Her.*

She'd met his kind before. Overseas visitors who were always on the look-out for female company whilst they were away. He probably had a wife at home, or a live-in lover, or at least a girlfriend. Men who looked and dressed like him were rarely unattached. That suit he was wearing was not of the off-the-peg variety. His gold watch looked expensive as well, as did his gold and diamond dress ring.

He smiled, the gleam in his eyes carrying amusement and admiration. 'I see you're already on the road to recovery. That's good. You'll survive, then.'

'That depends on what you mean by survive,' she retorted. 'I have my parents driving down to Sydney today to meet my fiancé. Then the rest of my entire family will be arriving tomorrow to attend my wedding. Sisters. Aunts. Uncles. Nieces. Nephews. Cousins. All of them have been dying for me to get married for years. They're country, you see, and country people think marriage and motherhood is the only true career for a female. At last, I was going to be a success in their eyes...'

Tears threatened again, but she valiantly blinked them back.

'Tell me what happened with your fiancé,' he insisted.

She stared hard at him and wondered if she'd been wrong about his intentions. Those expressive eyes of his did seem genuinely sympathetic this time.

'Nothing much to tell,' she said with a weary shrug. 'He's not coming. The wedding's off. End of story.'

Again, she had to reach for a fresh tissue. Sympathy always set Charlotte off when she was upset.

He didn't press her to talk whilst she mopped her eyes once more, and this time she gathered herself more quickly. But as she sat there in wretched silence, having the occasional sip of coffee, Charlotte was suddenly filled with the urge to give vent to her feelings. What did it really matter if he was a stranger? she reasoned as anger started to simmer inside her. Probably better than his being a friend. Most of her friends were sick and tired of hearing about her relationship disasters.

'Louise was right,' she bit out, the coffee-cup clattering as she dropped it back into the saucer. 'He didn't really love me.'

'Who's Louise?'

'My best friend. We share a flat together.'

'She was the one on the phone to you just now, I presume.'

My, but he was a very observant man! And extremely intuitive.

She nodded her agreement. 'Apparently, Gary rang last night and left a message saying he wouldn't be on the plane and that he'd sent a long email, explaining everything, but we were out very late and didn't check the answering machine when we came in. Louise saw there was a message after I left this morning. She rang Gary to find out what was going on, but he didn't answer. I guess it's the middle of the night over there. So she rang me and I had her have a look at the email he sent.'

'That would be your missing fiancé's name? Gary?'

'Gary Cantrell. And he's not missing,' Charlotte ground out bitterly. 'He's in LA, with his *PA*. His *pregnant* PA, the one who somehow miraculously discovered she was having Gary's baby the same day he was supposed to be leaving to marry *me*!'

'Aah,' the American said knowingly.

'Yes. Aaah.'

'So how long has it been since you and Gary were together?'

'I haven't seen him since last June.'

'That's eight months ago!' His shocked tone carried a none too subtle message. Eight months was too long to leave any man on his own, in his opinion.

'I was faithful to *him*,' Charlotte snapped.

'That's commendable. But men are not renowned for their faithfulness when their fiancées—or wives—are a world away for such an extended period of time.'

'Tell me something new.'

'Why *were* you apart for so long?'

Charlotte sighed, then gave him a brief run-down on her romance with Gary, leaving out the fact she hadn't been to bed with him, but including her stupidly going against Gary's wishes and secretly planning a traditional wedding at a top Sydney hotel.

'I suppose you don't know the Regency Royale, being an American,' she said at this point.

'The name does ring a bell,' he replied.

'It's one of the plushest hotels in Sydney. Everything there is so expensive. I should be able to cancel the suite I booked for the wedding night, but the reception is a done deal. Know anyone who might want a three-tiered wedding cake and a designer wedding gown? Not to mention a five-day pre-paid package holiday up at the Hunter Valley?'

Her father wasn't the only one who'd wasted a small fortune.

'Not at the moment. Maybe you can advertise them on the internet. You seem to be able to sell anything there.'

Charlotte groaned. 'Don't talk to me about the internet.'

'Just trying to be practical.'

'I know what you're thinking.'

'What am I thinking?'

'That internet romances are often little more than fantasies being played out by both parties. They're not real. Our love for each other wasn't real.'

'That is a widely held opinion,' he said.

'Maybe that was the case for Gary, but it wasn't for me. I loved him,' Charlotte cried. 'And I was going to marry him tomorrow.'

But even as she proclaimed the depth and sincerity of her love for Gary, Charlotte suspected there had been more than a touch of romantic fantasy about their whole relationship. A touch of desperation on her part as well.

Maybe it was all for the best that she wasn't marrying Gary.

But that didn't make her dismay or disappointment any easier to bear.

'Tomorrow is going to be the worst, most humiliating day of my life,' she declared, then grimaced. 'Actually no, *today* will probably take that prize. I'm supposed to be having lunch with my parents today, to introduce my fiancé in the flesh. I'd do anything in the world not to have to tell my father that the wedding's off. He's spent such a lot of money on this wedding, and he's not a rich man. Just a farmer. I'll pay him back, of course, but it will take me years on a hairdresser's pay.'

If only she hadn't treated herself to a new car last year, or that stupid honeymoon holiday. Her savings account was less than zero, once you factored in her credit-card debt.

With a sigh Charlotte went back to drinking the last of the coffee, her heart sinking lower than it ever had before.

'Would you like to go out to dinner with me tonight?'

Charlotte's head shot up, blue eyes widening. 'Are you serious?' she said disbelievingly. 'Haven't you been listening? I've just been jilted. My heart's been broken. The last thing I want to do is go out with another good-looking, smooth-talking American who's out here on holiday and who'll say and do anything to get a girl into bed!'

'I'm not American, actually,' he informed her coolly. 'I'm Australian.'

'Huh?'

'I know I sound American,' he elaborated. 'That's because I've been living and working in LA for some years. But I was born in Sydney. My mother married an American, you see, and took us there when I was just a baby. My sister, Beth, was born in the States, but we both went to school here in Australia. Beth stayed on afterwards and is now happily married to a Sydney doctor. Speak of the devil, here she is.'

Charlotte glanced up to see a very pregnant lady waddling towards them. She was not unlike her brother in looks, being tall and striking-looking, with dark hair and eyes. At a guess, Charlotte would have put her age at around thirty, with her brother a few years older.

'I see you haven't changed, brother dear,' she said in a decidedly Australian voice before her laughing eyes went to Charlotte. 'Leave him alone for more than a minute and invariably he'll zero in on the best looking girl for miles. But be warned, darling. He's the love 'em and leave 'em type.'

'Thank you for the recommendation, sister dear,' her brother said drily as he rose to kiss his sister on the cheek. 'I'd introduce you if I knew the lady's name, but she forgot to mention it.'

Charlotte decided this was her cue to escape before she did something stupid, like tell him her name and agree to go to dinner with him tonight. She'd had enough of the love 'em and leave 'em types to last her a lifetime.

Rising to her feet, she hooked her bag over her shoulder and flashed a somewhat brittle smile at him. 'Thanks for the coffee, but I should be going.' And she was off in the direction of the exit, striding out as quickly as she could in her high-heeled, backless sandals.

She should have known he would not let her get away that easily.

'Wait!' he called out, and raced after her. 'Don't take any notice of my sister. She was only joking.'

She stopped and threw him a cynical glance. 'Are you saying you're not of the love 'em and leave 'em variety?'

Charlotte glimpsed the flash of guilt in his eyes before he could hide it.

'Right,' she said, and went to move on again.

'At least tell me your name.'

She stopped again to stare up into his handsome face.

Bad mistake.

His eyes had gone back to hot and hungry. Suddenly, she wanted to tell him her name *and* her phone number; wanted to say yes, I'll go out to dinner with you. But to do so would be the ultimate of foolishnesses. At thirty-three, it was time she stopped being a fool where men were concerned.

'I...I don't think so,' she said, but unconvincingly.

Before she could say boo, he'd whipped out a business card and Biro.

'The numbers on this are irrelevant whilst I'm here,' he said as he balanced the card in his left palm and wrote something on it. 'But I'll put my new mobile number on the back. Or you can call me at my sister's place. Her name's Beth Harvey. She's married to Dr Vincent Harvey. He's an orthopoedic surgeon. They live in Rose Bay and I'll be staying with them for the next fortnight. They're in the phone book. Call me if you change your mind,' he said, and pressed the card into her hand. 'You're upset at the moment, but you know and I know that you didn't really love that Gary guy.'

Their eyes clashed again. Her feminine antennae didn't just twitch this time. They twanged.

'What do you mean?' she asked breathlessly.

'You know what I mean, beautiful,' he returned.

Charlotte opened her mouth to deny any such knowledge. But she couldn't. Because she knew exactly what he meant. How could she have been in love with Gary when *this* man could make her more aware of being a woman than any man ever had? Her heart was racing and the entire surface of her skin felt as if it was on fire.

She glanced down at the card he'd given her, partly out of curiosity, but mostly to escape those unnervingly magnetic and seductive eyes.

His name was Daniel Bannister. And he was a lawyer, with offices in LA.

Charlotte laughed. She couldn't help it. Oh, the irony of it all!

'What's so funny?' he asked.

She looked up, her expression quite cynical. 'Gary

was from LA as well. I think I've had enough of LA lawyers, don't you?'

And, shoving the card back into his hand, she whirled on her high heels and fled.

CHAPTER FOUR

'LOOK, I'm truly sorry, OK?' Beth apologised. 'I didn't mean any harm. I didn't lie, either. You *are* the love 'em and leave 'em type. Or so you keep telling me.'

Her brother had hardly spoken to her during the drive back from the airport. Or in the two hours since. As soon as they arrived at the house, he'd taken himself off to the guest suite, where he'd showered and changed, after which he'd settled himself on the back terrace and read the morning paper from beginning to end in frosty silence.

Vince had already left for the surgery by their return, and wouldn't be home till at least seven tonight, so Beth had the unpleasant prospect of entertaining Mr Grumpy all day by herself. She was almost grateful that she had an appointment with her obstetrician later on.

Meanwhile, she refused to put up with her brother's sulking any longer.

'For pity's sake, Daniel, what did you expect, anyway?' she went on when he didn't respond to her apology. 'That the girl would fall from her fiancé's arms into yours in a few minutes flat? You're not that irresistible.'

But as Beth lowered herself gingerly into one of the deck chairs she recalled that even when Daniel had been at school, the opposite sex had found him decidedly irresistible.

Yet he was a much more impressive individual now. His shoulders had filled out and his chest had broadened. His hair, still thick and lustrous, was better groomed these days. His features had sharpened and strengthened. There were a few lines at the corners of his eyes, but they didn't detract from his looks. His face now had a stronger, more lived-in look, and his dark, deeply set eyes carried a wealth of intelligence and worldliness in their depths which women would find mysterious and sexy.

'The trouble with you, Daniel Bannister,' she pronounced irritably, 'is you're too used to getting your own way with the women that take your eye.'

Daniel knew Beth was right. But it didn't make this morning's fiasco any easier to bear. And it didn't really explain why he was so upset.

'I just can't get her out of my mind,' he said, surprising himself when he realised he'd made this admission out loud.

Beth looked startled, too. 'But you only spoke to her for a few minutes.'

'I know.'

'On top of that, she was a blonde.'

Daniel smiled a wry smile. 'Yes, I know. But I really liked this one. She was sweet.'

Beth laughed. 'She was sexy.'

'Not in an obvious way.'

'Oh, come on. With *that* figure?'

Daniel frowned. Yes, he supposed she *was* sexy, and yes, he'd like nothing better than to have the chance to make love to her. But in the time since she'd walked out of his life this morning, it wasn't sex that was on his mind so much as just wanting to be with her again.

'I have to find her,' he pronounced.

'How? You don't even know her name.'

'I know she booked a wedding reception at the Regency Royale hotel tomorrow. I could get her name and number from them.'

'They won't give it to you.'

Daniel nodded determinedly. 'Oh, yes, they will.'

Beth sighed. He was right. They probably would. Daniel had the gift of the gab. He could talk anybody into anything.

'You said you had to go into the city to see your doctor at twelve, didn't you?' he asked.

'Yes.'

'Anywhere near the Regency Royale?'

'A good ten to fifteen minute walk.' Her doctor's rooms were up in Macquarie Street. The Regency was down near the Rocks.

'I'll pop down there whilst you're in the surgery. How long do you think you'll take?'

'Could be anything up to an hour or two if the doctor's called away to deliver a baby. That seems to happen quite a bit.'

'We can keep in touch by phone.'

'Are you sure this is such a good idea, Daniel? I mean, that poor girl would have to be extra-vulnerable right now.'

'I have no intention of hurting her, sis. I just want

to take her out to dinner. Get to know her a bit better.'

Beth rolled her eyes. There was no point in arguing with Daniel. There never was. Once he decided he wanted something, nothing stood in his way.

'I'll book a taxi for eleven-thirty, then. No point in driving into town. Parking is a pain.'

Charlotte pulled up at the entrance to the Regency Royale just after noon. Although twelve-thirty was the time she'd arranged to meet her mum and dad for lunch, she knew that her ultra-punctual, always-leave-plenty-of-time-to-spare parents were sure to have arrived in Sydney early, and would already be sitting there in the lobby, waiting for her. She had contemplated being late but then decided it was far better to get her bad news over and done with as soon as possible.

The hours since returning home from the airport had been difficult, with recriminations and regrets. But mostly filled with tears.

Maybe if Louise had been there, she'd have been able to maintain her equilibrium by having a bitching session about Gary's betrayal. But Louise had had to go to work. Whereas *she* was on a week's holiday from today, courtesy of her supposed wedding tomorrow. They virtually passed each other in the foyer of their old apartment building, with Louise giving her a quick hug before making Charlotte promise not to ring that bastard, Gary. An easy promise to give, and to keep. She couldn't have borne to even talk to him, let alone listen to his pathetic excuses and apologies.

The effect of their empty flat was undermining in the extreme, a huge wave of depression descending within seconds of Charlotte letting herself in through the front door. The silence was awful—plus the sight of the snaps of herself and Gary taken at the airport which she kept on the bookcase in the hallway. She threw them all in the bin, then threw herself on her bed and wept in a wild mixture of bitterness, anger and despair.

After an hour or so, she pulled herself together to have some breakfast and to send an email back to Gary telling him what she thought of him and that he was to never, ever contact her again!

The moment she sent it, however, she burst into tears again.

This time, she pulled herself together reasonably quickly and made a few necessary cancellation calls. The formal-clothes hire place. The celebrant. The florist. And finally, the suite she'd booked for their wedding night.

By this point, she was too upset to cancel the whole reception as well. She decided to do that later in the day, in person, after she'd talked to her parents. Maybe she could talk the hotel into giving her father some kind of refund.

The physical damage of her three crying jags had not been easy to repair. An ice pack had helped, plus some carefully applied make-up. She'd changed her clothes as well, her outfit this morning having been chosen with Gary in mind. Now she was wearing tailored cream trousers and a red shirt with three-quarter-length sleeves. Fawn pumps. Straw bag. Red lipstick.

'Will you be booking into the hotel, ma'am?' the parking valet asked when she climbed out of her car.

Charlotte suppressed a groan over the 'ma'am'. Since when had she become a ma'am and not a miss? Still, the valet attendant looked all of nineteen, if that, so she supposed, at thirty-three, she was a ma'am to him.

Depressing, though, and not what she needed today.

'No,' she said, forcing a smile as she handed the fellow the keys to her silver Kia Rio. 'Just meeting someone here for lunch,' she added.

'You'll need a parking ticket, then, ma'am.'

Taking the ticket from him, she whirled and pushed through the revolving glass doors into the huge, airy arcade which led to the hotel proper.

A right trap for tourists and guests, this arcade, Charlotte thought as she strode past the exclusive boutiques which sold designer clothes, fabulous jewellery and the sexiest of lingerie. A trap for brides-to-be as well, she recalled with a sigh, thinking of the money she'd spent in the lingerie shop the last time she'd been in here.

Charlotte promptly veered to the other side of the arcade, where there was nothing to provoke depressing memories, just a couple of doorways. The first led into the Rendezvous bar, a trendy bar she'd visited once or twice with Louise. The second led into the bistro-style bar and grill called the Tavern, which she'd checked out the last time she'd been here and where she intended taking her parents for lunch. They served good old-fashioned pub and club meals, just the thing for a country couple who weren't partial to à la carte cuisine.

'Can't stand fancy food,' her father always said.

Charlotte's stomach churned as she thought of her father. More so when she reached the end of the arcade and stepped from the marble floor onto the plush carpet of the hotel lobby. Just the sight of the decor in there reminded her how expensive a wedding reception here was, even one which was only having fifty guests. The cake alone had cost a bomb!

Charlotte's only comfort was that she'd decided on only the one bridesmaid. If one of her sisters hadn't been pregnant there would have been two more!

But oh…how she wished she'd taken notice of Gary when he'd requested a really small wedding. That would have made what she was about to do a little easier. Bad enough that she had to tell her parents she wasn't getting married. Worse that her dad had wasted all that money which he could have put to far better use.

The ongoing drought over the last decade had not hit the family as hard as some, but things were still tough. The money her wedding had cost would have replaced the breeding stock her dad had been forced to sell this past year. Or put in an extra dam. Or taken her parents on that cruise they were always talking about going on but which they never got round to having.

She'd thought how tired and old they were looking at Christmas.

Charlotte glanced around the lobby with an ever-tightening stomach. But her parents weren't there. She turned full circle, her gaze checking every corner of the reception area. The place wasn't remotely crowded at this time of day. Too late to be booking out. Too early to be booking in.

No. They definitely weren't there.

She might have rung them if they'd had a mobile phone, check if they'd become lost once they hit the city. But of course her parents hadn't come into the twenty-first century yet. Probably never would.

Charlotte settled herself down on one of the deep, velvet-covered armchairs to wait, her body facing the entrance from the arcade. That was the way her folks would come.

She almost didn't recognise him at first. He wasn't wearing the same clothes he'd been wearing this morning. His expensive grey suit had been replaced by dark blue jeans and a navy polo shirt trimmed with white. A pair of sunglasses was perched on top of his head. Navy and white trainers covered his feet.

It had taken an effort of will for Charlotte to put Mr Daniel Bannister out of her mind after she'd left the airport this morning, though once she arrived home more immediate and pressing events had overtaken her. Now, suddenly, there he was again, as disturbingly sexy as ever.

Charlotte's jolt of shock had her sucking in air, and immediately his head turned in her direction. He seemed just as startled to see *her*. But pleased.

Oh, yes, definitely pleased.

Charlotte's back stiffened against the armchair as he started walking towards her. At the last moment, she rose to her feet, rather than stay seated. Too awkward having to look up so far into those incredible eyes.

He whipped the sunglasses off his head during his approach, folding and popping them into his chest pocket, his mouth broadening into a dazzling smile at the same time, showing perfectly straight white teeth and a dimple in one cheek.

As if he wasn't attractive enough already.

'I don't believe it!' he exclaimed. 'I came here hoping to pry your name and number out of the hotel staff, and here you are in the flesh.'

All the breath rushed out of Charlotte's lungs at his admission. This wasn't an amazing coincidence. He was actively pursuing her.

Fury warred with flattery till she was simply flustered.

'I told you I was meeting my parents here for lunch,' she said, her face going hot once more. What was it about this man that made her act and feel like some silly teenager in front of her favourite pop star?

'Really? Can't say I recall you mentioning it. If you had, I would have remembered. But no matter. You're here. Now I have the opportunity to redress the bad impression my sister must have given you of me this morning.'

'You just don't know how to take no for an answer, do you?' she threw at him.

He grinned. 'Beth said as much when I told her I

had to find you. She's here in town, seeing her doctor, so I set out on my mission to uncover the identity of the lovely lady I met this morning, and whom I haven't stopped thinking about since.'

'You are the most annoying man,' Charlotte declared, even as she coloured some more. Couldn't he understand that the last thing she wanted and needed today was more evidence of how stupid she'd been, thinking she was in love with Gary?

It was mortifying, the way her eyes kept gobbling him up. Dear heaven, but he *was* gorgeous.

She couldn't help wishing that it had been *this* LA lawyer she'd run into on the Gold Coast last year. Because he wouldn't have taken any notice of her romantically. He'd have seduced her on the spot, then happily dumped her the next day. He wouldn't have lied to her and betrayed her and jilted her.

Men like Daniel didn't have to con women to get them into bed. The silly fools would be only too ready to do whatever he wanted without a single promise, herself included.

This was the most flustering part of her feelings right now. That she, Charlotte Gale, a just-jilted woman, could be wanting any man the way she was suddenly wanting the man standing right in front of her.

'I'm still not going out to dinner with you tonight,' she pronounced tartly.

'That's OK,' he replied without missing a beat. 'Tomorrow night will do just as well. Or the next night. I'm here in Sydney for a fortnight.'

'You're not listening again. I said no. Now I'm

saying it again. I don't want to go out to dinner with
you. Ever.'

'You don't mean that.'

She did. But he wasn't getting the message.

'Some things are meant to be, beautiful. Otherwise
why would fate have put you here, just waiting for
me?'

Charlotte groaned. 'I wasn't waiting for *you*. I was
waiting for my parents. I told you. They… Oh—'
She broke off, her head still spinning with the effort
of trying to gain some control over herself and the
situation. 'They're here.'

CHAPTER FIVE

DANIEL turned to see a couple who had country written all over them coming across the lobby in their direction. Both looked in their mid to late sixties, the woman plump with short grey hair, the man also grey-haired, but rake-thin with a weather-beaten face and kind blue eyes. Both had probably once been quite handsome. They had good features. Both were wearing suits and looked uncomfortable in them.

'Charlotte!' the woman exclaimed as she hurried forward to give her daughter a peck on the cheek.

Daniel smiled. At least now he knew her name. Charlotte. Great name for a great girl. She was going to take some talking around, he could see. But he was *not* going to take no for an answer.

Daniel was well versed in body language. And in the contrariness of women. Charlotte was as attracted to him as he was to her. Her relationship with that pathetic Gary guy had been one big romantic illusion. And she knew it. He'd seen the realisation in her eyes this morning.

Of course, he understood she was still upset. No woman liked to be dumped, especially the day before her wedding. She also clearly loved her parents and didn't want to disappoint them. Or tell them that they'd wasted a whole heap of cash on a wedding which wasn't going to take place. Once she broke the bad news to them, she was going to need some comforting.

'And dear Gary!' Charlotte's mother suddenly whirled to give him a big bear hug before putting him from her at arm's length and looking him over from top to toe. 'My, but you're even better looking than in your photos. Of course, you had sunglasses on in those so I couldn't see your eyes. You didn't tell me Gary had such beautiful eyes, Charlotte.'

Charlotte, Daniel could see, was dumbstruck. He was pretty flabbergasted himself.

But of course, it was a logical mistake for her mother to make. Charlotte had made it herself this morning. Which was another reason he knew Charlotte was attracted to him. She must have a certain physical type she liked.

'The thing is, Mum,' Charlotte finally blurted out, 'he's n—'

'He's a damn fine-looking man all round,' her father broke in, taking Daniel's hand and pumping it enthusiastically in both of his. 'Tomorrow is going to be the happiest day of my life, seeing my baby girl finally married to a man worthy of her. I have to tell you, Gary, that her last boyfriend was a right drongo. But she's finally come up trumps!'

'Dad, for pity's sake!' Charlotte wailed.

'You told me there were no secrets between you and Gary here. You said you'd told him all about Dwayne. Do you know he even wore an earring?' he directed at Daniel with a truly pained expression. 'Real men don't wear earrings!'

'I certainly don't.' Daniel had tried one once but he thought he looked a right prat.

'I noticed that. You're my kind of man, Gary. Welcome to the family.' And he pumped his hand some more.

Daniel wished at that moment that he *were* Gary. He hated having to disappoint them almost as much as Charlotte did.

When a wild but brilliant idea popped into his mind, Daniel embraced it immediately. It would kill two birds with one stone.

'It's a pleasure to meet you at last, sir,' he said. 'And you too, Mrs—er...' Damn it all, he didn't know their surname. 'Would you mind if I called you Mum and Dad?' he improvised.

'Not at all, my boy!' Charlotte's father beamed. So did her mother.

Charlotte just stared at him, her mouth still dangling open a little. But she didn't make a move to tell them the truth, he noticed.

'Always wanted a son-in-law to call me Dad,' her father raved on, having at last returned Daniel's hand. 'John—that's Lizzie's husband—he at least calls us Peter and Betty. But Keith—that's Alice's husband—he still calls us Mr and Mrs Gale.'

Daniel absorbed all this information for future reference.

'Ga-ry.'

Daniel was startled when Charlotte spoke up, the sweet smile on her face belying the dark irony in her eyes, and in her voice. 'Could I have a moment?

Mum. Dad. There's something I need to discuss privately with Gary. Would you mind?'

'That's all right, love,' her father said. 'We'll be back shortly. Give you two lovebirds time enough to sort out whatever it is you have to sort out.'

'What in hell do you think you're doing?' Charlotte hissed under her breath as soon as her parents were far enough away.

'I guess I'm going to marry you tomorrow,' Daniel returned evenly, unable to stop a smile from pulling at his mouth.

'Don't be ridiculous!'

'Look, it won't be legal,' he reassured her calmly. 'But it'll stop your parents from having a really rotten day today. And tomorrow. You might feel a whole lot better, too. You look seriously stressed out, Charlotte.'

She was shaking her head in continued disbelief.

'You're insane!'

'Absolutely not. I'm a lot of things but insane is not one of them.'

'But we can't possibly get away with it!'

'Yes, we can. Your parents already believe I'm Gary. Everyone else will, too.'

'Louise won't. She knows Gary didn't show up.'

Louise. Daniel searched his excellent memory bank and retrieved Louise from their conversation this morning. 'Isn't she supposed to be your best friend?'

'Yes.'

'Then tell her the truth and ask her to go along with it.'

'But…but I've already cancelled things!' she protested.

'What things?'

'The celebrant for starters, and the flowers, and the tux rental, and…and…'

'Nothing that can't be sorted out.' Though the celebrant could stay cancelled, Daniel decided. He'd find someone else to act as a celebrant. As a lawyer, he couldn't risk being guilty of any kind of fraud.

Vince would probably do it. For a doctor, he was somewhat of a thrill-seeker. Went skydiving for fun.

'You haven't cancelled the reception yet, have you?' he rapped out.

'No.'

'Where's the ceremony itself taking place? Not a church obviously, if you were having a celebrant.'

'Here, in the hotel.'

'No problems there, then.'

'You *are* crazy,' she muttered under her breath.

'Crazy about you, beautiful.'

She stared up at him, stunned by the speed with which he'd arranged things, and taken advantage of his similarity to Gary.

Not that he was really like Gary.

'I've never met a man like you,' she said dazedly. 'I'll bet you wouldn't romance a girl over the internet, ask her to marry you and then not show up.'

'No, Charlotte, I definitely wouldn't. Aside from being allergic to real marriages as opposed to pretend ones, I can't stand the internet. Waste of time except for business reasons, and *very* bad for the eyes.'

She laughed. She couldn't help it. This whole situation was bizarre. And it was whilst she was laughing that he pulled her into his arms and kissed her, right there, in the hotel lobby. In front of everyone.

At thirty-three, Charlotte had been kissed many times before. But this man kissed the same way he'd looked at her at the airport this morning. With a passion and intensity that was mind-blowing. His arms were wrapped tightly around her, his mouth white-hot on hers. She could feel herself dissolving under the sizzling brand of his lips. Not just her body, but also her mind. When his tongue joined in, every ounce of will-power she owned melted right away, replaced by the desire to surrender herself totally to what he wanted.

He wanted to pretend to marry her tomorrow?

Fine.

He wanted her to go to dinner with him tonight?

OK.

He wanted to take her to bed afterwards?

Yes, please.

Her father noisily clearing his throat had Charlotte finally surfacing from her liquid state to the real world. Once she stepped back out of Daniel's arms, some semblance of common sense returned. But the smouldering inner heat he'd generated remained, teasing her with the thought that maybe this man could do for her what no man ever had before…

Charlotte tried not to blush at this thought, whilst Daniel looked highly satisfied with the situation. His mission had been accomplished.

Charlotte knew he wasn't doing this for her parents' happiness. Or for hers. He was doing it to put her in his debt, and in his bed.

Not that he had to go to such amazing lengths. She would have gone to bed with him, anyway.

Twenty-four hours ago, Charlotte would have scorned anyone who said she would ever be a push-over. The fact she was prepared to say yes to Daniel Bannister within hours of meeting him was as shock-ing to her as it was intriguing.

Why him?

Was it his movie-star looks? His charm? His in-telligence? Or was it the power of *his* desire that was seducing and compelling her? Men had desired her before but never quite like this. This was something else.

Her cheeks continued to burn as her eyes met his, her heart-rate having not yet calmed. If she felt like this after a kiss, then how would she feel once she was in bed with him, their bodies totally naked, his flesh inside hers?

A quiver rippled down her spine at the thought, her heart flipping right over when he slid an intimate arm around her waist and pulled her back against him.

Daniel resumed the conversation. 'Charlotte was confessing to me that you'd all organised a bigger wedding for us than we'd originally planned.'

'Yes, well, I couldn't give my youngest daughter a lesser wedding than my other daughters, could I?' her father pronounced proudly, reminding Charlotte why she'd been sick with worry over disappointing her darling dad. She would be forever grateful to

Daniel that she didn't have to now, regardless of his ulterior motives.

Of course, it was still going to be awkward at a later date, explaining why her loving husband had to go back to the States, then extremely disappointing for her to confess that their marriage hadn't worked out.

But she would cross that bridge when she came to it.

For now, her mum and dad were smiling. That was all that mattered.

'Do you think we might get along to the restaurant, daughter?' her dad said. 'Haven't had a bite since breakfast.'

'I'm hungry too,' Daniel said with a wicked glance at Charlotte.

The man was a devil, no doubt about it. But it was impossible not to like him, as well as want him. He must have cut a right swathe through the ladies in LA these past few years, Charlotte reckoned. That combination of magnetism, machismo and manners was lethally attractive.

'I hope we're not going to one of those places where they take hours to serve you,' her father said with a frown.

'Amen to that,' Daniel agreed. 'When I'm hungry, I have to be fed quickly.'

Charlotte cocked an eyebrow, just to show him she was well aware what he was up to with his *double entendres*. Then she shot him a sickeningly sarcastic smile. 'I had a feeling you'd say that. Don't worry, Dad, the bistro is just a short walk away. You boys could have a beer while we're waiting for our meal. And, Mum, you could have a sherry. Or some white wine, if you'd prefer.'

'A sherry would be lovely,' her mother said, the warm approval on her face giving Charlotte a real buzz.

Charlotte rarely received her mother's approval, unlike her two older sisters, who hadn't put a foot wrong in their lives. They'd both done well at school. Both had married their childhood sweethearts, sons of local farmers. Both had produced children.

Charlotte, by contrast, hadn't finished school, had never learned to cook, couldn't take up a hem, regularly forgot important dates and, till recently, was yet to find a husband.

As a child, she'd often been described as difficult. And a dreamer.

'Her head is always in the clouds,' she had heard her mother say to Aunt Gladys one day when she was about thirteen. 'I don't know what's going to become of her.'

What became of her was she bolted for the city when she was a couple of months shy of her sixteenth birthday, having secretly applied for and secured a hairdressing apprenticeship advertised in the *Sydney Morning Herald*. Her distraught parents weren't able to force her to return home, or to finish her school certificate, because she was able to support herself. In the end, they stopped trying to convince Charlotte she was too young to live away from home in the big city.

Actually, hairdressing was just a means to an end.

Her heart's desire was to see what the world had to offer outside of farm life and country boys. Sydney was an eye-opener but soon it too was limiting. So when Charlotte finished her apprenticeship, she began a series of jobs on ships that cruised all over the world.

By the time she was twenty-five, she'd been everywhere an ocean liner could take her. By then, she'd grown a bit bored with ship life and decided to try working in some of the world's luxury resorts.

Over the next few years, Charlotte worked mostly in Asia, but also in the South Pacific, on various tropical islands. She then did a brief stint in a top hotel in London, but had found the climate not to her liking. She also found herself suffering, surprisingly, from homesickness, something which astounded her.

So, shortly before her thirtieth birthday, Charlotte returned to Australia, where she spent a few wonderfully restful weeks with her folks on the farm before realising, rather reluctantly this time, that country life was still not for her. What she *was* craving, she discovered, was a more settled existence. She wanted to put down roots. Wanted a boyfriend who lasted longer than a few months. She wanted marriage, and children. Possibly even a house with a garden.

Charlotte was blown away by this last bit. Miss Wanderlust herself wanting what most Australian girls wanted. Amazing!

Not one to ever shirk from a goal, Charlotte set about achieving what she wanted with a passion. She returned to Sydney, got herself a job and a flat, then set about doing what girls of her age did when they were on the lookout for Mr Right. She made friends with all the single girls she worked with—networking was crucial. She went to all the right bars with them on a Friday night. She smiled at every available-looking guy. And—most important of all—she joined a gym.

Which was where she met Dwayne, one of their personal trainers. Dwayne made it obvious right from the start that he fancied her. Within two weeks they were dating. Within four he coerced her into bed with words of undying love. Within six they were living together.

But that was where their relationship stagnated for the next two years. Dwayne was not ready, he said, for marriage and kiddies just yet. He was only twenty-eight. But he hinted a proposal was definitely on the cards once he reached thirty. So Charlotte clung on, despite becoming aware that they rarely talked any more, their sex life had dwindled to once a week, and Dwayne was working late more nights than ever.

She should not have been shocked by his dumping her for another girl. What shocked her was the speed with which he married his new, already pregnant girlfriend.

Charlotte was left to wonder what the gym bunny had that she didn't have. She couldn't help thinking that the answer wasn't the other girl's blonde hair, but her sexual know-how.

'Charlotte. Is this the place you were talking about?'

Her mother's voice cut through Charlotte's reverie, shocking her back to the present. Blinking a bit blankly for a second or two, she discovered they were standing outside the entrance to the bistro. She must have walked there on automatic pilot whilst she daydreamed.

'Yes, yes, it is. Sorry. Just wool-gathering as usual.'

Her mother smiled indulgently. 'That's all right. A girl's allowed some wool-gathering the day before her wedding. Most brides are a bit nervous.'

Her father laughed. 'Nervous? Our Charlie? That'll be the day. She's just excited.'

Excited…

Charlotte glanced up into Daniel's dark eyes, which glittered back down at her.

'Just a tad,' she confessed with considerable understatement. 'Come on, let's get you in here to eat.'

Taking her mother's elbow, she ushered her into the bistro. Daniel and her dad trailed after them, chatting away as if they'd been best mates for years.

'Have you decided what you might like to eat yet?' she asked her mother after the woman had spent several minutes perusing all the options. Daniel and her dad had already ordered steaks, medium rare. Men, Charlotte had always found, were more decisive with food than women. She herself didn't feel like eating at all. Stress always doused her appetite. Excitement, too.

She'd had more than enough of both for one day.

Her mother continued to dither whilst Daniel proceeded to the bar to order the drinks. Beer for the men. Cream sherry for her mother and a dry white wine for herself.

Meanwhile, her dad claimed a booth-style table for them next to one of the wide windows that overlooked the city street outside.

In the end, both her mother and Charlotte ordered the same as the men, though they chose smaller steaks and ordered them well done. Their drinks had arrived by the time they sat down. Charlotte immediately swooped up her glass and was having some soothing sips of the crisply chilled wine when a mobile phone started ringing.

Charlotte knew it wasn't hers. Wrong tune.

It was Daniel's.

CHAPTER SIX

'EXCUSE me, everyone,' Daniel said as he fished his slimline cellphone out of his back pocket, flipped it open and put it to his ear.

Charlotte gave him a slight dig in the ribs, reminding him he'd have to be careful what he said.

'Hi there,' seemed safe enough.

'Beth here. I'm finally finished with the doc. Everything's fine, though I've put on another damned kilo. So where are you and how did things go? Did you find out her name?'

'I'm having lunch with Charlotte and her folks right now,' he replied, hoping that would floor his sister into silence.

He was right. It did.

'Don't worry about me,' he went on hurriedly. 'I'll take a taxi back to your place after we're finished, though that might not be for a while. Arrangements to make, et cetera. Thanks for calling. See you later. Ciao.'

Turning his mobile right off to stop any further awkward calls from Beth, he slipped it in his pocket, vowing to give her a call back as soon as he had the chance.

'Sorry about that,' he said brightly. 'It was the lady whose place I'm staying at tonight. She and her husband are friends of friends of mine. I didn't think it would be right to stay at Charlotte's place. Not the night before the wedding, anyway.'

'Are these people coming to the wedding tomorrow, Charlotte?' Betty Gale asked her daughter.

'Er—'

'No, they're not,' Daniel jumped in. 'I didn't ask them. I didn't realise it was going to be such a big wedding, remember?'

'But that's not right,' Mr Gale said. 'They should come. Charlotte, surely something could be arranged.'

Charlotte groaned inside. 'I don't think so, Dad. The numbers for the reception were finalised a couple of days ago.' The last thing she wanted was to cost her dad *more* money.

'Please don't concern yourselves,' Daniel said swiftly. 'They really wouldn't expect to come.'

'If you say so, Gary.'

Charlotte winced. How she hated hearing them call him Gary! Daniel was a much nicer name.

Their meals arrived. Charlotte only picked at hers, her mind drifting back to names.

Daniel. Daniel Bannister. *Mrs* Daniel Bannister.

'You're not dieting, are you, darling?' Daniel suddenly asked her.

Her sharp intake of breath reflected the shock produced by her own foolish thoughts, *not* by his calling her darling. She knew he was only acting. No way was she really his darling, or anything close. Yet there *she* was, fantasising about being married to him.

God, she was hopeless. Hadn't this fiasco with

Gary taught her anything? Talk about jumping from the frying pan into the fire. If she started imagining she was falling for Daniel, she needed her head read. OK, so he was utterly gorgeous-looking and incredibly sexy, with the kind of powerful and dynamic personality you usually only read about.

Charlotte had no doubt he would be very good in bed.

But he wasn't good at love. Or commitment. He couldn't have made his intentions clearer. He said he was allergic to marriage, and his own sister had called him the love 'em and leave 'em type.

Common sense demanded she not weave any romantic fantasies around him. He was not some knight in shining armour. His aim hadn't been rescuing her damsel in distress, but seducing her.

She had to keep that fact in the forefront of her mind during the next couple of days or she'd end up crying a whole lot more than she had about Gary.

'Charlotte never eats much when she's nervous,' her mother answered for her, which brought a grateful smile from Charlotte. She put down her knife and fork, picked up a chip with her fingers and nibbled on it.

'I'm just the opposite,' Daniel said. 'I eat like a horse when I'm nervous.' And he forked a large piece of steak into his mouth.

'I can't imagine you ever being nervous,' Charlotte said with a dry laugh.

'You'd be surprised,' he returned.

Charlotte wouldn't mind betting he'd never suffered a crisis of confidence in his entire life, whereas she'd spent most of hers not even knowing what she wanted out of life. Even when she thought she did, her life had still lurched from one disaster to the next.

'Everyone gets nervous occasionally,' her father joined in. 'Caring makes any man nervous. I was nervous when I married your mother. And each time she was expecting. I dare say I'll be nervous again when you and Gary have a little one.'

The threat of tears came out of nowhere. Charlotte knew she would not be able to explain them, so she had to get out of there. At least for a minute or two.

She dropped the rest of the chip and stood up abruptly. 'Sorry. Have to go the ladies'. The wine.'

Bolting for the powder room did the trick. Not only did it stop the tears, but it also gave her the opportunity to call Louise.

'Goodness knows what she's going to say,' Charlotte muttered as she raced into a cubicle and punched in Louise's work number.

The owner of the hairdressing place Louise worked at didn't like her taking personal calls, especially on a Friday, but this was an emergency. It took a while before she came on the line, during which Charlotte's already over-active stomach did the tango.

'Yes?' Louise asked agitatedly.

'Louise, it's Charlotte. You haven't told anyone about what happened with Gary this morning, have you?'

'No. Why?'

'Not even Brad?' Brad was Louise's boyfriend and the best man.

'Haven't had the opportunity. I was going to tell him tonight. We're meeting for drinks after work.'

'Thank heaven, because the wedding's back on.'

'What? *How?* Did Gary ditch the PA and take a later plane or something?'

Charlotte told her what had transpired in broad strokes.

'Now, don't say a single word,' Charlotte warned before her friend could launch into a torrent of protest. 'This is a done deed and nothing you say will stop me, so don't waste your breath.'

'Fine by me. It's your life. Besides, this Daniel sounds a darn sight more interesting than Gary. He really came gunning for you, huh? Must be seriously smitten. I suppose he has to be reasonably good-looking, if he looks like Gary. Not that I thought Gary was all that hot in his photos.'

'Makes Gary look lukewarm.'

'Oho, he's not the only one who's smitten. I always said you didn't love Gary. And vice versa.'

'Yes, I know. But this isn't love, Louise.'

'Don't tell you've finally fallen in *lust* with a man?'

Louise had a way of cutting to the chase about things, especially on the subject of sex. Lust was not a word Charlotte liked but *lustful* certainly described most of the thoughts Daniel engendered in her.

'Possibly.'

'About time too. Look, we'll talk more tonight. Alvira is looking daggers at me, so I'd better go. You will be coming home some time tonight, won't you?'

'Yes, of course,' Charlotte said, and meant it.

Daniel was going to have to wait till tomorrow night to have his wicked way with her. No way was she going to jump into bed with him tonight, no matter how much she might want to. A girl had to have some pride!

Her return to the table was greeted by a questioning glance from Daniel. But she could hardly tell him anything till the lunch was over and her parents had checked into their room in the hotel.

Fortunately, after lunch her mum and dad were happy enough to look after themselves for the rest of the day.

Charlotte sighed a rather weary sigh as soon as the lift doors shut on her parents.

'You sound tired,' Daniel said.

'I *am* tired.'

'In that case I'll let you off dinner tonight. Far better you go home and have a good night's rest.'

'I never said I'd *have* dinner with you tonight,' she reminded him tartly.

'The girl who kissed me in the lobby would have come to dinner with me if I'd asked again.'

'*You* kissed *me*!'

'Don't be pedantic. You liked me kissing you. A lot.'

'Good grief, you're impossible!'

'And you're irresistible.'

She laughed. 'Not according to my last two boyfriends.'

'They were fools. I'm not.'

'I only have your word for that. So why *are* you doing this for me tomorrow, Daniel?' she asked him, determined to have him put his cards on the table. 'Or perhaps more to the point, why did you chase after me the way you did? The truth, please. I've had enough of men telling me lies.'

He shrugged. 'Impossible to analyse some things. When I first saw you this morning, it was like being struck by a bolt of lightning. I've never felt that way about a woman before, especially a blonde.'

Charlotte was both flattered and taken aback. 'You don't like blondes?'

'Let's just say they usually set off bad memories for me. After my father left my mother, his subsequent wives have all been blondes.'

'His *wives*! How many has he had?'

'Five, including my mother, at last count. But what the heck? He's only sixty-five. Plenty of time yet for a few more.'

The bitterness in Daniel's voice brought some understanding as to why he might be allergic to marriage, whereas Charlotte had had nothing but good examples of people being married. Her parents. Her aunts and uncles. Her sisters. All happy with their partners. Divorce was unheard-of in her family.

Suddenly she wanted to know more about the man who was going to pretend to marry her tomorrow. A whole lot more.

'How about we go for a cup of coffee somewhere?' she suggested. 'We really need to talk.'

He smiled that sexy smile of his. 'We really need to do a whole lot of things. But you're right. Talking would be a good idea for now. But somewhere very public, please. So that I can keep my hands off you.

Kissing you before did dreadful things to me. If I hadn't been able to distract myself with food I don't know what I would have done.'

Charlotte found herself laughing again. 'You're a wicked man, do you know that?'

Daniel didn't know that. He had his shortcomings but he'd never thought of himself as wicked. Still, her comment made him try to do what he'd just said couldn't be done. Analyse his feelings for Charlotte.

Was it just sexual desire for her which had propelled and compelled his actions today? Was he going through with this pretend wedding, just to get her into bed?

Absolutely not. He could have got her into bed anyway. The way she'd responded to his kiss had told him that. He was doing what he was doing because he genuinely liked her. And genuinely liked her folks. They were the warmest, nicest family he'd ever met and he hated to think of them in distress.

But perhaps it was for the best if he didn't tell her that. Best she think he *was* wicked. The thought seemed to amuse her. And turn her on. Turning her on was good. Having her fall in love with him on the rebound was not.

Daniel didn't want to take up where Gary had left off.

That would be cruel.

Charlotte had to be extra-vulnerable right now. Still, she wasn't some young naive girl. She was a woman, a beautiful sexy woman with needs. It had been eight months since she'd been with a man. Daniel had been without a woman in his bed too.

High time they both had some comfort.

The prospect of spending their 'wedding night' together tomorrow was going to keep him awake tonight, that was for sure. Thinking of their wedding night, however, brought another idea, one which he would attend to before leaving the hotel.

'Where do you want to go for coffee?' he asked.

'We could walk down to one of the cafés on the quay. Then I could take you to the clothes-hire place on the way. It's not far from here. We need to rent a tux for you.'

'No need. I have a tux. Never go anywhere without one.' He'd been caught short once when he'd gone to Boston to visit friends.

Charlotte frowned. 'What kind?'

'Black. Single-breasted. Satin lapels. A white dress shirt and a black bow-tie. Will that do?'

'Perfect,' she said. 'That's one less expense. And one less job to do. Now all I have to do is let the florist know the wedding's back on, plus the celebrant.'

'You can call the florist but forget the celebrant. We can't have a real one, Charlotte. Too risky, legally. I'll get someone to stand in and play the part. My brother-in-law will do it. The bridal suite can be real, though.'

'The bridal suite?' she choked out.

Their eyes locked, hers wide, his narrowed.

Daniel was momentarily thrown by the sudden

panic he glimpsed there. Surely she must have realised that was where tomorrow would end.

'You said you'd cancelled it,' he reminded her.

'I…I didn't actually book one of the bridal suites,'
she said, clearly flustered. 'They have several here in
the hotel, each one decorated with a different theme.
They're all terribly expensive. I couldn't afford any
of them so I booked one of the ordinary suites.'

'I see. Well, you don't have to worry about the
expense any more. My treat. You ring the florist
whilst I go organise one of those suites. Then we'll
have that coffee. I think a walk in the fresh air would
do us both good.'

Ten minutes later they were walking together down
George Street towards the quay. The day had become
a little hotter, but not unpleasantly so. Charlotte had
had no trouble re-booking the florist, with Daniel
looking similarly pleased.

She didn't dare ask him what suite he'd booked.
She didn't want to think about tomorrow night. She
would think about that tomorrow.

'You handled the situation with your parents very
well,' Daniel complimented when they stopped at a
corner for a red light. 'No one would have known
you were upset. Which you must be. I'm not that
insensitive that I don't realise today has been very
difficult for you.'

Difficult in more ways than one. How often did
one man dump you and another bewitch you within
the space of a few hours?

'Training,' she said brusquely, which led to her

telling him about her work history and how she'd learned not to wear her heart on her sleeve.

'Except when I've just been jilted,' she added as the light turned green and they walked on. 'I always lose it on occasions like that. Especially when I find out the man who's supposedly in love with me has made some other girl pregnant. Would you believe this isn't the first time this has happened?'

'That's incredibly bad luck.'

'I agree,' she said drily, and launched into her sad tale about Dwayne.

Daniel nodded sympathetically at all the right moments.

'Men can be right bastards at times,' he pronounced when she finished.

She stared at him, then smiled. 'You'd know, I guess.'

By this time they'd reached the quay area and weren't far from the open-air café Charlotte was taking him to.

'On the plus side,' she said as they strolled along together, 'you are a wonderful listener.'

'Aah, now, that's *my* training. I'm not just any old lawyer, you see. I'm a divorce lawyer. With female-only clients. A good proportion of my job is just listening to women rave on. I have to confess I'm used to hearing the sexual shortcomings of the male sex. Frankly, some of the horror stories I've heard make me ashamed of being a man at times.'

'But why do you have only female clients? Surely men want you to represent them sometimes.'

'Aah, now, that's a long story.'

Charlotte refused to let him fob her off with that old chestnut. 'You must tell me all about it over coffee,' she said firmly.

Daniel had no intention of doing any such thing, but oddly enough, within ten minutes of their sitting down together at one of the very pleasant alfresco tables, he found himself telling her in minute detail all about his father's desertion and subsequent marriages.

'Mom never recovered from his betrayal,' he said as he stirred his coffee. 'And I guess neither did I. Beth was too young to hate him. She never even knew him. But I despise the man for what he did, and what he's done since. When I first started practising law and handling divorces, I did have male clients. But I couldn't put my heart into representing them. It felt like I was representing my father. When I became a partner in the practice a few years back, I decided enough was enough. I've only had women clients from then on.'

'I fully understand,' Charlotte sympathised. 'And your mother? How is she coping these days?'

Daniel's chest tightened. 'Mom passed away last year.'

'Oh, how dreadful for you!' Charlotte exclaimed with genuine sympathy in her gorgeous blue eyes. 'I don't know what I'd do if my mother died. I'd be devastated. And of course so were you. I can see it in your face.'

Daniel blinked his amazement. He'd always prided himself on never showing his emotions to the outside world. Maybe he wasn't as self-contained as he thought. Or maybe Charlotte was extra-observant when it came to people's body language. He'd read somewhere that hairdressers had to be good counsellors and therapists as well. They spent as much time talking to their clients as he did.

'So is this why you've come out here to visit your sister?' she went on. 'Because she's the only one who understands how you've been feeling?'

Daniel was once again taken aback at the accuracy of Charlotte's observation. He wasn't used to being read so well.

'Partially,' he replied. 'But I also had the urge to come home for a while. I've lived in LA for many years, but I always think of Sydney as home. There's no place like it,' he said as he glanced around.

Their table was less than ten metres from the harbour, which he was facing. To his left loomed the magnificent coat-hanger-shaped harbour bridge. To his right, the truly splendid opera house with its white sail roof and absolutely perfect setting. Right on a point that jutted out into the harbour.

'I fully agree,' she said. 'I know exactly what you mean about that urge to come home. I lived overseas for years, but in the end all I wanted to do was come home to Australia.'

When she picked up her coffee he did likewise, sipping and soaking in some of the sunshine whilst he admired the beautiful city he had been born in.

'Daniel…'

'Yes?' He put down his cup and looked over at her.

'I want to thank you. For everything. Regardless of your motives. You were wonderful with my parents at lunch-time. And very agreeable about the food. I know it was pretty simple fare.'

'I enjoyed it immensely.'

'Oh, come, now. A big-shot divorce lawyer from the Hollywood hills would be used to the best of wine and food, *and* the most sophisticated of company.'

Used to them. And bored silly with them. 'I much prefer the company I had today. And the company I'll have tomorrow.'

'What about after that, Daniel? I mean…you're going back to the States in a fortnight, aren't you?'

'That's my plan,' Daniel said. 'Meanwhile, I thought you might like some company on that honeymoon you've already paid for. The one up at the Hunter Valley.'

Her eyes widened. 'Did I tell you about that?'

'You certainly did.'

'Good old blabbermouth me.'

'So how about it?'

She stared at him, her expressive eyes betraying her. She wanted him to come with her. He could *feel* it.

'I don't think so, Daniel,' she replied, stunning him. 'As much as I find you a very attractive man, I don't want to risk becoming emotionally involved with you. You've made your position on marriage quite clear so to spend more time with you would be foolish. The reason I was marrying Gary was because he said he wanted what I wanted. Marriage. And children. I'm thirty-three years old. I haven't got enough time to waste on another man who won't give me what I want. I'll spend tomorrow night with you. But come the following morning, that will be it for us.'

Her stance both impressed and sobered Daniel. All his adult life, it had been him laying down the law about what he wanted and didn't want in a relationship. He'd finally come across a woman who was capable of telling him what *she* wanted, right from the start. Usually, in the beginning, his girlfriends were more than willing to go along with his sex-only demands, perhaps because they hoped to trap him into more.

Charlotte was willing to give him one night. But only that one night. After that, she was sending him off with a flea in his ear.

Wow. What a woman. The kind of woman a man would be crazy not to want for much more than one night. The urge to pull her into his arms and tell her he was already emotionally involved was incredibly strong.

But he stopped himself. Such an action would be counter-productive at this stage.

Past hurts had made Charlotte very determined. And extremely wary. If he told her he just might have changed his mind about lots of things since meeting her, she would think he was lying; conning her so that he could have his wicked way with her for more than a night.

He had to pretend to go along with her wishes.

But as much as she was determined to resist him, he was determined to have her.

For a lot longer than their 'wedding' night. Not marriage, of course. Daniel would never embrace that unrealistic and unreliable institution.

But marriage was not the only alternative for a future relationship.

'Fair enough,' he said, pleased to see she looked disappointed by his easy agreement. 'So what are you going to tell your family about us?'

'That's my problem. I'll drive you back to your sister's place the morning after the wedding, then go up to the Hunter Valley on my own. That should give me time enough to decide when and how to tell my parents that our marriage didn't work out.'

'Speaking of our marriage,' Daniel said, 'perhaps you'd better fill me in on all the details about to-morrow. Times, places, et cetera. And then, if you don't mind, could you give me a lift back to Beth's house? It might be easier if we explained what we're going to do tomorrow together.'

'Oh, no, do I have to?'

Daniel wasn't worried. He knew Beth was going to like Charlotte. A lot.

'Yes, Charlotte,' he said firmly. 'You have to.'

CHAPTER SEVEN

'ARE you absolutely sure about this, Charlotte?' Louise asked. 'It'll be too late afterwards.'

Charlotte, who was sitting on one of their wooden kitchen chairs with a plastic cape around her shoulders, took a moment to snap out of her daydreaming. For a split-second, she thought Louise was talking about her decision to go through with the fake wedding later that day. But then she realised Louise was giving her one last chance to back out of her decision to get rid of her blonde hair.

'Absolutely,' she said.

Changing her hair was one thing she *was* sure about. Her going through with the fake wedding—whilst impossible to back out of now—was still causing her concern.

She should have told her parents the truth straight away. She could see that now. Pretending to marry Daniel, then spending the night in the bridal suite as his bride, was asking for trouble.

The man was dynamite. And she…she was a silly fool.

Already she could feel herself being drawn into his web, into wanting more than one night with him. Who knew how she'd feel tomorrow morning if he was as good in bed as she suspected he was going to be?

And maybe he was bargaining on that. He'd been all too ready to agree to her saying he couldn't come on the honeymoon with her. She wouldn't mind betting he still hoped to persuade her otherwise. *She* could only hope that when the time came, she would have the courage—and the character—to say no to him.

'Be it on your head, then,' Louise said blithely, and began applying the deep-walnut-brown colour.

'Well, it will be, won't it? On my head, that is.'

'Very funny.'

'Come, now, Louise, you always said my being blonde was not my best look. Underneath, I agreed with you. Now that I don't have to please Gary any more, I can't wait to go back to being a brunette.'

'So who are you trying to please this time? Not this Daniel, I hope. You haven't fallen for him, have you?'

Charlotte should not have hesitated in answering.

'Oh, you have!'

'No, no, I haven't,' she denied. 'But he's the sort of man a girl could easily fall for. You haven't met him, Louise. Wait till you do. Then you'll understand. He had Mum and Dad eating out of his hand in no time flat. It was almost embarrassing. But impressive.'

'Sounds like another empty charmer to me. Like Gary. And Dwayne. They both had the gift of the gab. You always go for the guys with the silver tongues.'

'He's nothing like Gary or Dwayne,' Charlotte said. He was far more dangerous than either of them.

Charlotte could see now that neither Gary nor Dwayne had *meant* to betray her. They'd just been weak.

There was nothing remotely weak about Daniel.

'You'll see when you meet him,' she repeated.

'I can't wait. Neither can Brad.'

'I wish you hadn't told Brad the truth.'

'You didn't really expect me not to tell him, did you? He has to get dressed with this guy at the hotel today and hold his hand till you show up and pretend to marry him. Brad can smell a rat a mile away. He'd have known something was up.'

'I suppose so.'

'Don't worry. He really liked the sound of Daniel. Brad admires the go-getters in this world.'

Charlotte shivered inside. The last thing she needed to hear today was how much of a go-getter Daniel was. She was trying not to think too much about him at all. She had a wedding to prepare for and get through.

Which rather made a mockery of her decision to revert to being a brunette. If she was strictly honest with herself, Charlotte had to confess she wanted to blow Daniel away today with how she looked.

Her so-called pride had given way to sheer vanity. She would pay the price, she knew, if he fancied her even more as a brunette. But she simply couldn't resist the temptation to eliminate the one thing about her he probably liked the least.

Her fake blonde hair.

'You are going to look fab with this colour hair,' Louise said. 'Blonde hair was so not you. Daniel is going to flip when he sees you, especially wearing that sexy wedding dress. Who knows? Maybe he'll fall in love with you and the next thing you know, you'll be having a real wedding.'

'Dream on, Louise. He's a divorce lawyer with a dad who's been married five times. Daniel's dead against marriage, except when it gets him into the pants of the bride.'

'Charlotte! You're sounding as cynical as I do.'

'You get that way eventually.'

'True. But I hate to see you like that. I always liked your sweet, country-girl optimism.'

'Huh. That's just a nice way of saying I was naive and stupid. Well, I don't intend being naive and stupid any longer. I'm going to spend one night with Daniel, just to see if he's as hot in bed as he looks, and the next day I'm off.'

'You're not taking him on the honeymoon with you?'

'Absolutely not.'

'But why not? I bet he'd go.'

'I'm sure he would. But I can't use men like you do, Louise. I'm not cut out for it. I'd fall in love and have my heart broken all over again.'

'You're right. You would.'

Both girls fell silent for a while.

'You really think I use men?' Louise asked finally.

Charlotte sighed. She loved Louise. The girl had been a good friend to her. But she was awfully hard on the opposite sex. She believed none of them were capable of true love, only true lust, which Louise estimated had about a six-month shelf-life. She and Brad had been together for just on six months.

'Brad really loves you, Louise.'

Louise snorted. 'I know what Brad loves. That's why I'm dating him. Man, but that guy is good in bed. And he can go all night.'

'*Really? All* night?'

'He's awesome,' Louise said with feeling in her voice.

'If Daniel doesn't work out, maybe you could lend me Brad for a night,' Charlotte quipped.

'Over my dead body, girl.'

'See? You love him,' Charlotte said, and glanced up at her friend. 'It's not just sex.'

Louise stopped painting on the colour for a second. 'Yeah. I probably do. But I don't intend telling him that. Not yet, anyway. I want to see what he does after the gloss wears off. Which should be any day now. But back to you, lovey dovey. Why don't I fix you up with one of Brad's mates in a week or two? He's got plenty.'

Charlotte didn't doubt it. Brad was a very outgoing guy with loads of energy and a great sense of humour.

'I don't think so, Louise. I think I'll just forget about dating for a while.'

'Don't leave it too long. You know what they say. When you fall off a horse, you should get right back on again.'

Charlotte didn't respond to this advice. She suspected that Daniel would be the straw that broke her back where men were concerned. She sat there in

silence, fiddling with the diamond and sapphire engagement ring Gary had given her, and which she
was forced to keep wearing, at least till after the wedding.

The wedding…

A wave of depression suddenly swamped her as
she realised the utter futility of today. And tonight.
Any silly hope that she was going to suddenly blos-
som seemed ludicrous. Blonde or brunette, she was
the same girl who'd been consistently dumped and
cheated on by her boyfriends in the past. The same
clueless Charlotte.

By tomorrow morning, Daniel would be relieved
that he wasn't coming on the honeymoon with her.
He'd probably be bolting for the bridal-suite door
before breakfast, only too happy to leave her to her
misery.

Charlotte's sucked-in sobs had Louise dropping the
brush back into the basin and running round to kneel
in front of her friend.

The sight of her best friend's flooded eyes brought
a huge lump to her throat. Truly, she could be such
a fool at times. She should have anticipated how
fragile Charlotte would be this morning.

'There there,' she said softly. 'I'd give you a hug,
except I'd end up with a walnut-coloured face. You
don't want your chief bridesmaid looking like she
bought a cheap tanning product, do you?'

A watery smile broke through Charlotte's tears. 'I
guess not.'

'Look, I know today is going to be hard for you,

Charlotte, but just keep remembering why you're doing it,' she said encouragingly. 'You said you couldn't bear to hurt your folks. Nothing else matters today, does it? Not really.'

'You're right,' Charlotte returned, dashing her tears away with her hands. 'I'm being pathetic. And so typically female. Don't worry, Louise. I'll be fine. Get back to my hair. I want to be the most beautiful bride I can be today. I want my mum and dad to feel nothing but pride.'

'Atta girl!' Louise said, thinking privately that that wouldn't be too hard.

Dear Daniel was in for one big surprise when he saw Charlotte. He might have lusted after her yesterday. But today, the bride was going to lift the groom's desire to another level entirely!

CHAPTER EIGHT

'So, Gary, is this the first time you've been married?'

Daniel stopped tying his bow-tie to give his supposed best man a thoughtful glance.

Brad was in his mid-twenties, a tall, lean guy with sandy hair and a cheeky grin. A real-estate assessor, he'd been dating Charlotte's best friend for about six months, despite being a decade younger. He seemed intelligent, and highly amused by something. It didn't take a genius to figure out what.

'OK, *Brad*,' Daniel returned, 'let's cut the crap. You obviously know the real deal here, so you can forget calling me Gary. In private, that is. My name is Daniel,' he said, extending his hand for the second time. 'Daniel Bannister.'

Brad grinned as he shook it. 'Great to know you, Dan. Sorry about the charade. I can never resist a laugh. But for what it's worth, I think what you're doing for Charlotte is real neat. She's a great girl. You sure you don't want to marry her for real?'

Daniel smiled. 'Apart from the legalities which could not be overcome at such short notice, I don't think that would be a very sensible thing to do. I only met Charlotte yesterday,' he finished, and went back to tying his tie.

'So what? I knew within minutes of meeting Lou

that she was the girl for me. What a hot babe!
Trouble is she's a tough cookie. Been burnt a few
times. But I'm going to marry her one day, no question about it.'

'Have you asked her?'

'Sure. The very first week. Lou laughed so hard
and for so long that I decided not to ask again for a
while. She says younger guys are good for only one
thing and it's not marriage.' He grinned again. 'But
I'm making headway. We sometimes spend time together out of bed now.'

Daniel had to laugh. But the word 'bed' propelled
his mind to tonight. A lot rested on tonight. Frankly,
he'd never felt such sexual pressure. Today was
proving to be much more stressful than he had anticipated.

'To answer your first question,' he said, undoing
his slightly lopsided tie and starting again, 'no, I've
never been married before.'

'So you're on the market, eh, Dan?'

'I'm a bachelor, yes.'

'How old are you, exactly?'

'Thirty-six.'

'Girlfriend back home?'

'Not at the moment.'

'Lou says you're a lawyer. A well-heeled one by
the look of you.'

'I'm comfortably off.'

Rather an understatement of his financial status.

'Comfortably off' would have been an accurate
description of Daniel's wealth prior to his investing
in a movie four years earlier. At the time, one of his

female clients—a middle-aged actress—had just been dumped by her producer husband. When she showed him this script she'd bought and which she claimed would revitalise her career, Daniel had read it more out of sympathy than anything, but found himself totally engrossed. He'd invested as much as he could find in it, and talked all his partners into putting up the rest.

The independently made thriller had gone on to be a huge hit and the money had been rolling in ever since.

'I've made a few wise investments over the years,' he added.

Brad chuckled. 'You're a cool dude, aren't you? What a pity you don't want to marry our Charlotte for real. You'd make her a good husband, I reckon. Not that Lou agrees. She thinks you're only interested in getting into Charlotte's pants.'

'What?' Daniel whirled round, his abrupt action reefing his tie back undone.

Brad shrugged. 'That's Lou for you. If she can believe the worst of a bloke, she will. Personally, I can't see anything wrong with your wanting to get Charlotte into bed. That girl's a looker all right. And she could do with being laid by a guy who knows how.'

Daniel tried not to look too shocked. But shocked he was. 'I don't think we should be discussing Charlotte's private life, do you?' he said somewhat stiffly.

Brad was taken aback by the reproof. 'Oh. Er— yeah. Right. If you say so. It's just that Lou said you were going to spend the night with her in some fancy honeymoon suite here in the hotel so I thought I'd better warn you up front.'

'Right. Thanks.'

'No sweat.'

Daniel went back to tying his bow-tie, Brad's astonishing news revolving in his mind. Who would have imagined that the girl who'd kissed him so passionately was so sexually inexperienced. Perhaps she just hadn't had the right partner yet.

He tried tying his bow-tie for the third time but it ended up crooked again.

'You're not too good at that, are you?' Brad said.

Daniel's sigh carried frustration. 'Normally I am.'

'Maybe you're more nervous than you look.'

'What's there to be nervous about?' he retorted, his clumsiness having irritated him. 'This is just pretend.'

'The speeches aren't pretend, mate.'

'Speeches? You mean, I have to give a *speech*?'

'Yep. You're the groom. Haven't you been to any weddings?'

'I avoid them.' Difficult to share in the joy of a wedding when you were a divorce lawyer, and when your father had been married five times. He would have happily gone to Beth's wedding, but Beth and her husband had eloped.

'You must have seen movies with weddings in them,' Brad said with a touch of exasperation in his voice. '*My Best Friend's Wedding. Four Weddings and a Funeral.* There was a cracker of a speech in that flick. But I don't think it was the groom's speech,' Brad said, stroking his chin. 'It was the best man's. That's me. I have to give a speech about you. *You* have to give a speech about the bride. Nothing funny. Mushy stuff. Like how you felt when you first met her. What you think of her family. How much you love her. Stuff like that.'

Daniel grimaced. This was going to be more difficult than he'd imagined. Speeches were his stock in trade, but this was totally different from addressing a jury.

'Take some advice from an old hand at this kind of speech,' Brad said, stepping forward and doing Daniel's bow-tie for him. 'Kiss is the answer.'

Daniel blinked. 'Huh?'

'Don't you know that saying in America? Kiss? K I S S. Keep it simple, stupid. Just say how gorgeous she is, how much you love her, and how you would go to the ends of the earth for her. Which you have,' Brad added with a guffaw. 'Can't go much farther than Australia, mate. Unless you want to live with the penguins down in Antarctica. Right! Your tie's done. You're all set.'

'Thanks,' Daniel said before scooping in a steadying breath and telling himself he could handle this.

A glance at his watch revealed that it was thirteen minutes to four. The wedding was scheduled for four. Time to get out there. But first of all, he checked the breast pocket of his jacket for something. Yes. It was there.

'Have you got the rings?' he asked the best man.

Brad patted his jacket pocket. 'Yep. Both there,

safe as houses. I've done this before, mate. Trust me.'

Daniel nodded. 'I can see that. You've been a great help. To be honest, I don't know what I'd have done without you.' His tie would have been crooked for one.

Brad looked chuffed at the compliment. 'You know, for an American lawyer, you're OK. I thought you were all supposed to be bastards.'

Daniel laughed. 'Don't believe everything you see on television.'

'I was thinking of Gary.'

'Yes, well, the Garys of this world are everywhere,' he pointed out. 'Not just in America. And not just in the legal profession. But for your information, I'm not American, despite the accent. I was born here in Sydney. Went to school here, too.'

'Well, stone the crows! Now I know why I like you so much.'

Daniel smiled. 'The feelings are mutual. Shall we go?'

Both men turned as one and headed for the door.

Daniel had checked out the setting for the wedding ceremony with Vince earlier in the day, Vince having agreed last night to act as celebrant. It was to be held on the ground floor of the hotel, in a conservatory that was in keeping with the old-fashioned and very romantic decor of the Regency Royale.

There was a huge domed glass ceiling, reminiscent of bygone eras, plus a circular flagstone floor fringed by lots of exotic flowering plants and palms. All the walls of the hexagonal structure were made of glass, except for one section opposite the entrance. It looked as if it was made of rock, and a constant stream of water ran down the façade to an ornamental pool at the base.

The wedding ceremony was to take place in front of this pool and waterfall.

When Daniel had been shown the conservatory this morning, the flagstone floor had been dotted with black wrought-iron furniture. The conservatory was usually used as a beer garden. He'd been assured the furniture would all be cleared away and replaced by clean white chairs, neatly arranged in two curved rows on each side of the circular floor to give all the guests a perfect view. A strip of rich red carpet would bisect these rows, ending in a T shape in front of the waterfall. An elegantly carved wooden podium would be provided for the celebrant to stand behind, as well as a white linen-covered table for the signing of the marriage documents.

'Wow!' Brad exclaimed as they walked through the entrance to the conservatory.

Daniel was equally surprised. The transformation in the conservatory was much more than had been described to him that morning. They had said nothing of the masses of added flowers. Or the wonderful music. Or the two splendidly uniformed men standing to attention on each side of the entrance, like footmen of old.

But it was the atmosphere that struck Daniel the most, the excited energy that was coming from the well-dressed guests, most of whom were already seated. At Daniel's appearance on the red carpet, all heads had jerked up and around, everyone either smiling or staring at him.

Of course, Daniel didn't know a single face amongst them, except Charlotte's mother. Betty— dressed in pink—was beaming over at him. Beaming and waving a gloved hand.

A banging sound behind him made Daniel whirl round. The two uniformed attendants had shut the doors, which, Daniel noticed for the first time, were not clear glass but heavily stained. Impossible to see through them.

'That's so you don't see the bride till the time is right,' Brad explained. 'Brides like to make an entrance.'

'I see,' Daniel bit out, wishing now that he'd thought to have a couple of glasses of something intoxicating and soothing. He hadn't appreciated till this moment just how much of an ordeal this would be.

'This way, mate,' Brad said with a wry smile, and gave Daniel a nudge.

They proceeded along the red carpet towards the spot where Vince was waiting for them, looking suitably dignified and older than his thirty-seven years in a dark grey suit with a crisp white shirt and muted grey tie. His dark wavy hair, which was usually on the long side and decidedly wayward, had been cut this morning to make him look less like a Bohemian and more like a marriage celebrant. They'd already planned not to act as if they knew each other, Daniel shaking Vince's hand as though they'd just met. Brad did likewise after winking slyly at both of them.

As they turned together to face the stained-glass doors, the music suddenly changed from the softly romantic number currently being piped into the room to the more robust and stirring *Wedding March*.

Charlotte, it seemed, was not going to be late.

The stained-glass doors were flung open and a hush came over the guests as necks craned to get a view of the bride.

Daniel felt his chest tighten.

But it was the bridesmaid who appeared first, walking slowly along the red carpet. Louise, he presumed.

Tall and slender, she was elegantly gowned in a strapless blue dress that draped around her bust then fell in soft Grecian folds to the floor. Her hair, which was almost as red as her bouquet, was straight and sleek, and swung around her face as she walked. Her face was equally angular, but her mouth was full and sultry. Her eyes, which were possibly set too close for real beauty, were, nevertheless, striking in their blueness. Or was it their boldness?

Daniel concluded rightly that Louise would be a handful for any man. Brad had his work cut out for him if he was to succeed in his goal to marry her.

'Wow,' Brad enthused by Daniel's side. 'See what I mean? She's hot, man.'

As she drew closer, those bold blue eyes narrowed on Daniel in an assessing fashion, making him squirm a little.

Poor Brad. This female would run rings around him.

'Mmm,' she murmured in an unnervingly droll fashion when she was close enough for him to hear. 'I see what Charlotte means.'

Daniel would have liked to ask her what *that* meant, but this was hardly the time or the place. Later, maybe. Instead, he plastered a cool smile on his face and said a soft hello.

She gave him a killer look in return, then turned a full-wattage smile Brad's way.

'You look gorgeous, lover,' she whispered to Brad, before taking her place on the other side of Daniel, leaving plenty of room for Charlotte.

Daniel's focus returned to the entrance to the conservatory, where he could see a cloud of white in the dimmer light just beyond the open doors.

The bride, waiting to make her entry.

Daniel's throat suddenly went bone-dry. He swallowed, then swallowed again. Was Charlotte as nervous as he was? Was that why she was taking so long to appear?

'What's she doing?' he whispered over to the redhead.

'Taking off the small face veil, I think. She thought it didn't look right with her new hairdo.'

The words 'new hairdo' barely registered before the cloud of white came into focus and Daniel was confronted by a Charlotte he could never have envisaged.

If his throat had been dry before, it felt like parchment now.

She wasn't just beautiful. She was devastatingly beautiful. A fairy-tale princess of a bride in a dress designed to make any husband-to-be go ga-ga.

Daniel complied with a raw rush of desire.

Like Louise's, Charlotte's gown was strapless, but, where her friend's bodice was draped, this one was smooth and tight, bolstering up Charlotte's already impressive breasts whilst constricting her waist into hand-spanning size. The skirt, by contrast, was full and frothy, brushing against her father's legs as he accompanied her down the red carpet.

But her crowning glory was her hair.

Gone was the long, straight curtain of blonde hair, replaced by soft, glossy, shoulder-length waves in a glorious dark brown that glinted red when the light hit it. The rich walnut shade was a perfect foil for the dazzling whiteness of the dress and the honey-coloured skin of her bare shoulders and arms. Framing her striking face and hair was a short but very feminine veil, which was anchored on top of her head by an exquisite tiara decorated with dia-mantés and pearls. She wore no jewellery around her elegant throat. She didn't need any.

The sight of her literally took Daniel's breath away.

He was barely aware of the camera flashes going off, or the video man off to one side filming every-thing. His eyes were riveted on his bride, his heart pounding in a way it hadn't pounded in his entire life.

CHAPTER NINE

A WAVE of emotional confusion swamped Charlotte as she started to walk down that red carpet on her father's arm, her eyes dropping agitatedly to the bouquet she was holding.

Was she happy or sad? Regretful or resentful? Nervous or excited?

All of those things, she realised.

Happy that her hair had turned out brilliantly. But sad that she'd spent so long as a blonde, trying to please Gary. Regretful that she was wasting so much of her dad's money today, and resentful that Gary didn't give a damn. Nervous over pretending to marry Daniel, but also appallingly excited.

All day, one overriding thought had dominated Charlotte's mind.

Tonight.

Difficult to think of anything else.

Was Daniel as excited as she was?

Her eyes lifted at last to look at him.

Her step faltered. Her heart as well.

Had there ever been a more handsome groom?

People said brides always looked beautiful in their wedding dresses, even the plain ones. But the same could be said for grooms, in Charlotte's opinion. There was something about a tuxedo which made the most of any man. It gave him stature, and styling, and sophistication.

Daniel had been handsome in a business suit and impossibly sexy in jeans. In the elegant black tuxedo he was wearing today, he was *so* handsome and sexy, it was criminal.

Just looking at him was a turn-on. Being with him was going to be incredible. She could feel it in every fibre of her being.

Her resolve not to take him with her to the Hunter Valley tomorrow immediately went a bit wobbly. If the earth moved in Daniel's arms tonight, how could she possibly give him up after just one night?

But if she prolonged their affair, wouldn't that make losing him later on all the more terrible? And wasn't she just making the same mistake again, going from one relationship disaster to another, this time in a shockingly short space of time? After Dwayne it had at least been a few weeks before she met Gary. It had been less than two days since Gary had jilted her.

'Are you all right, love?'

Charlotte's head turned slowly to find her father frowning at her.

It was a defining moment for Charlotte, a moment when she realised she was sick and tired of fighting her feelings for Daniel.

She wanted to be with him. OK, so they might only have a few days together. But those few days would probably be better than a lifetime with another man.

'Yes, Dad,' she said, resigning herself to the fact

she was setting herself up for some serious heart-break this time. But what she felt was too powerful to ignore.

'I'm fine,' she added. And forced a smile to her mouth.

Her smile reassured Daniel. Till he saw her eyes.

There was sadness in her eyes.

Was she wishing it were Gary standing here, waiting to marry her?

Surely not. She didn't love Gary any more than Gary had loved her.

Daniel supposed *that* might be what was making her sad, her having been so mistaken, not only about Gary's feelings but also her own. No one liked to feel a fool.

Did Charlotte feel a fool?

He hoped not. Because she was far from foolish. She was sweet and brave and loving, and that stupid bloody Gary didn't deserve her. As for that Dwayne guy... Daniel would have liked to punch his lights out, the miserable jerk.

Still, Charlotte was better off without either of those two. Hell, they couldn't even make her happy in bed! The least a man could do was make his woman happy in bed.

He smiled back at her as she approached, determined that he wouldn't let her down. Tonight could not come quickly enough.

'You look so beautiful,' he whispered when her father handed her over to him.

Her blue eyes sparkled this time. 'Thank you. So do you.'

Vince cleared his throat, bringing their attention back to the moment at hand.

'We are gathered here today,' he started, his having decided on a very traditional ceremony, chiefly because that was the only one he'd been able to find a copy of last night, 'to celebrate the marriage of...'

Daniel's mind drifted away from the words to concentrate on Charlotte. She was wearing more make-up today. But her glorious dark hair and the glamorous white wedding dress demanded it. With blue eye-shadow and black eye-liner, her eyes looked so big and blue. And that red gloss on her mouth made Daniel long to kiss her.

When his eyes dropped to her cleavage, he had some difficulty keeping his thoughts from straying to her beautiful breasts and the many ways in which he wanted to make love to her tonight.

Daniel determined to make it impossible for her to send him on his way tomorrow. He might not be good marriage material but he was a good lover.

He was working out his sexual strategy when he heard Vince ask who gave this woman in marriage.

Her father answered, 'I do,' proudly and then the ceremony began in earnest.

Daniel winced over being called Gary Cantrell, but swallowed his pride and said 'I do' at the right moment. Charlotte made them all suffer with a heart-stopping hesitation before *she* said 'I do'. At least she didn't have to promise to obey.

The exchange of rings carried more tension,

mainly because his was a tight fit. How was he ever going to get the darned thing off afterwards?

Daniel breathed a sigh of relief when they got to the 'I now pronounce you man and wife' part. The worst was over. Now he got to kiss the bride.

They were already facing each other, with Charlotte gazing up into his eyes with an expression Daniel found extremely flattering. No, she certainly hadn't loved Gary.

A sudden panic zoomed into her face. She didn't want him to kiss her, that much was evident.

Daniel felt put out, till he realised she might be worried he was going to kiss her as he had kissed her yesterday in the hotel lobby. That had been some kiss!

He decided he could wait till he had her behind closed doors before he unleashed his still smouldering passion. Though damn it all, controlling himself once his lips were on hers was not going to be easy.

Steeling himself, he took her face gently between his hands and gave her the softest, sweetest kiss on the mouth. No pressure. No pushing open her lips. Daniel suspected embarrassing things might happen if he did that.

But he wanted to. Hell, he wanted to desperately.

The reception loomed ahead as a far bigger trial than this wedding, because it was longer. Hours, maybe. But there was no getting out of it.

Meanwhile, he would have had to be careful not to let his frustration show. And not to drink. He had to be stone-cold sober to perform as he wanted to perform tonight.

'Love the hair,' he complimented after his mouth lifted. '*And* the dress.'

He could have added *love what's in it*, but he didn't, of course. That would have been crass. And Daniel was not crass.

Aroused, but not crass.

She stared up into his eyes with the oddest expression. Kind of dazed.

'Better than blonde?' she asked with a charming tilt of her head.

'Much,' he said. 'You made a beautiful blonde, but you're a ravishing brunette.' He certainly wanted to ravish her. Right now.

She smiled. A happy smile. No, a *dazzling* smile.

Daniel stifled a groan and managed to smile back. 'I've always been partial to brunettes,' he said truthfully.

Vince stopped any further conversation with a touch to Daniel's elbow. He led them over to the table to sign the pretend papers, which they did, along with Brad and Louise. Cameras continued to flash. The video rolled on. Daniel murmured a discreet 'thank you' to Vince, who said he would be going straight home to tell Beth all about it.

Beth, it had been obvious last night, thought this whole pretend wedding thing was *so* romantic. There again, Beth had always been an incurable romantic.

'Smile, please,' the photographer ordered. 'The groom! *Smile*, please.'

Daniel smiled.

CHAPTER TEN

'EXCUSE me a moment, please, Charlotte,' Daniel said, and pushed back his chair.

Charlotte's eyes followed him as he stood up and walked to the table where her father was seated. There was an empty chair next to her dad, her mother having temporarily vacated it.

The reception had been in full swing for over an hour, with the entrée and the main meal having been served. Charlotte had chosen the menu herself, but hadn't really enjoyed any of the food. In fact, she'd just picked at it.

From the moment Daniel had said she was ravishing, her hunger hadn't been for food.

Her eyes were still glued to him when he suddenly glanced back over his shoulder at her. Embarrassed at being caught staring, she pulled her eyes away and picked up her glass. She might not have eaten much but she'd been downing the wine. Chardonnay. Her favourite.

'See what I told you would happen?' Louise whispered to Charlotte. 'He can't take his eyes off you.'

'More like the other way around. I...I've never wanted a man like I do him. I think I will take him away on my honeymoon holiday after all.'

Louise gave a softly knowing laugh. 'Aah, so you

know now what I feel when I'm with Brad. Nothing like a bit of good old-fashioned lust, is there?'

'Lust...' Charlotte frowned. 'How can I be sure that's all this is?'

'What else, at this early stage? Goodness, don't go thinking what you feel is *love*, girl. I have to admit, if I wasn't so taken with Brad, I might bat my eye-lashes in Daniel's direction as well.'

'Did I hear someone mention my name?' Brad said from his seat on the other side of Daniel's vacant one.

Louise rolled her eyes. 'Amazing how his ears al-ways prick up every time he hears his name. That's men for you. Yes, Brad, we were both talking about you and how yummy you look in your tux.'

'I was thinking the same about you, babe.'

'What, how good I'd look in your tux?'

Brad laughed. 'You're a crack-up, Lou. You really are. Aah, here's Dan back again. Ready for your speech, mate? We're on soon.'

'Ready as I'll ever be,' Daniel replied as he sat down. 'Your dad tells me he's up first, Charlotte.'

'What were you talking to him about?' she asked, her mind still pondering Louise's assertion that what she felt for Daniel was just lust.

'Nothing for you to worry about.'

The MC's announcement that the father of the bride was going to speak had Charlotte falling silent, but her head was still spinning. She supposed Louise was probably right. Louise knew what she was talk-ing about where lust was concerned, whereas Charlotte was a right novice.

But even if it was just lust stirring her, Charlotte still worried that several days spent with Daniel could make her feelings for him deepen. Louise was made of tougher stuff than she was. She didn't appreciate the risk.

But Charlotte couldn't see herself resisting the temptation. Not unless tonight was a disaster.

Her father's tapping the microphone cut into her thoughts, bringing her back to the present. The speeches. It was not a moment she'd been looking forward to.

'I'm not one for giving speeches, as you probably all know,' her father began. 'I'm a farmer and farmers are at their best with their backsides on a tractor and their mouths shut.'

Everyone laughed. Everyone except Charlotte. She was too aware of Daniel sitting next to her, too strung up with nerves.

'We're best left in the country, too. But I'm not just a farmer. I'm a father, too. And a father will do anything for a daughter. So here I am in this fancy city hotel, eating fancy food and drinking fancy wine. But I can tell you right now that I've never had a happier day in all my life.'

Charlotte jumped in her seat when Daniel suddenly picked up her hand and squeezed it. 'Do try to look a little happier,' he whispered. 'You're supposed to be wildly in love with me. Smile a bit more.'

Somehow she found another smile, though her mouth was beginning to ache with all the smiling.

'Yes, that's it,' he said, giving her hand another squeeze. 'Not long to go now. Hang in there.'

'Of course, we all know that Charlotte has not followed the usual path of a country girl,' her dad continued. 'There were moments where I thought I would never see her as she is today. As a bride. And for that I have to thank Gary. I only had to know my future son-in-law for ten seconds before I understood why our Charlotte had fallen head over heels with a man I thought she hardly knew. As for Gary…have you ever seen a man so handsome, or so much in love?'

Everyone clapped and cheered. Charlotte wanted to cry.

'They say you can tell a man by his actions more than his words. Gary told me to keep this a secret but I want to tell you that just now, my new son-in-law is going to pay for this wedding.'

More clapping and cheering.

Charlotte, however, was speechless.

'Oh-oh,' Daniel said out of the corner of his mouth. 'You don't look pleased. I thought you'd be happy that your father wouldn't be out of pocket.'

'But it wasn't your place! I would have paid him back after I told him we'd separated. Every single cent.'

'Hey, hush up, you two,' Brad said.

They hushed up, leaving Charlotte to simmer in silence. If he'd been her real groom, it would have been an incredibly generous gesture. As it was, she suspected it was more a corrupting gesture, a type of advance payment on services to be rendered.

The thought infuriated her. But it also flattered her. Right from the start, Daniel's pursuit had been incredibly aggressive. Clearly, he would stop at nothing to have her.

What woman wouldn't thrill to a man being so taken by her charms? What she had to keep remembering, however, was that it was just a sexual interest. Wealthy playboys like Daniel didn't want women for anything else. They might pretend to value other things in their partners, but the bottom line was sex. Plus the challenge of the chase. Charlotte suspected that once she'd capitulated and he'd had her a few times, Daniel's passion would begin to wane.

His own sister had warned her that his girlfriends came and went.

Charlotte tried to stay angry with her logical, if somewhat cynical, thoughts. But it was impossible. She just felt more and more excited. Louise was right. This was just lust on her part. She couldn't think about anything else.

Her father spoke for another couple of minutes, giving them some advice over the tolerance necessary for a happy marriage then wishing them all the happiness in the world before offering the official toast to the bride and groom.

Charlotte plastered a plastic smile on her face and willed for the reception to be over. She couldn't wait to be alone with Daniel, and to have him kiss her once more. Not the way he'd kissed her after the ceremony. The way he'd kissed her in the lobby yesterday.

After her father sat down, it was Brad's turn to speak. Charlotte winced as he stood up. Lord knew what he was going to say. Something embarrassing, that was for sure.

'My job as best man today,' he began, 'is a little awkward. A best man is usually the groom's best mate, or his big brother. Someone who has known him for yonks. But I only met this good-looking fella a couple of hours ago. The other times I've been best man at a wedding, it's been dead easy to tell some naughty stories about what the groom has been up to over the years. I have those kind of mates,' he added, grinning. 'But I can't do that with Gary here. But you know what? I reckon there *are* no naughty stories in Gary's past. Pete said he knew straight away what kind of bloke was marrying his daughter. I felt the same way. This man here,' he said, resting a hand on Daniel's shoulder, 'is one of the good guys. True blue, in our Aussie language. I told him when we were getting dressed that he'd made a fantastic husband for our beautiful bride here and I meant it. By the way, she is beautiful, don't you agree?'

More clapping and cheering. Charlotte groaned. Talk about torment!

'But it's not my job to gush over the bride. That's Gary's. My job is to gush over the bridesmaid. Not a hard job to do, considering we're an item,' he added with a wink Louise's way. 'I might be biased but I've never seen a better-looking bridesmaid. And that dress… Wow, babe. You should wear blue more often. Although I'd really like to see you in white.'

More clapping and cheering and shouts of, 'Hear! hear!'

Louise blushed furiously, which was a first for Louise.

Brad proposed the toast to Louise, Charlotte grateful for another swallow of the delicious champagne.

Daniel, she noticed, barely sipped his.

She didn't look up at him when he stood up, but kept her eyes focused on the back part of the room.

'Brad might have been to a good few weddings,' were his opening words. 'But strangely, I've never been to one. So forgive me if my speech doesn't follow the norm. Firstly, I want to thank my best man for doing such a sterling job today, and the lovely Louise for all the help and friendship she has given Charlotte. I also want to thank the Gales for the wonderful way they have welcomed me into their family. I can honestly say that I have never met their like before. Charlotte is very fortunate to have such exceptionally loving parents. Very fortunate indeed.'

Charlotte resisted the temptation to roll her eyes, but heavens to Betsy, did he have to lay it on that thick? Clearly, he was relishing the role of man of the moment. Every single person in the room was smiling at him. Of course, all her relatives already thought he was the ant's pants because he was taking troublesome Charlotte off the single shelf. If they only knew!

She sighed, then made the mistake of glancing up at Daniel.

When he smiled back down at her, she found she could not look away. Her gaze remained locked to his, her insides dissolving. She was helpless when he smiled at her like that. Helpless and hopeless.

'What can I say about Charlotte?' he said quietly, his eyes caressing hers. 'She *is* beautiful, there is no doubt about that. But she is beautiful on the inside as well as the outside. That might sound clichéd but with Charlotte, nothing is clichéd. She is a remarkable woman and any man would be lucky to have her as his wife. No, not lucky. Privileged. My life hasn't been the same since the first moment we met. Actually, Brad was wrong when he said there were no naughty stories to be told about me. There have been. Quite a few. But no longer. I'm a changed man. Charlotte has changed me.'

At last he looked away from her, and all the breath suddenly rushed out of her lungs from where she'd been holding it.

Louise leant close to her right ear. 'If I didn't know better, I'd think he meant all that.'

Charlotte almost laughed. She wished.

He was a good actor, that was all. A polished performer. He'd be dynamite in the courtroom.

Dynamite in the bedroom, too, an insidious voice inserted.

'I've been told I have to propose a toast to my bride. So raise your glasses, everyone. To my lovely Charlotte...' And he looked down at her again.

Daniel was taken aback by the sarcastic light that glittered in Charlotte's eyes as he drank to her.

What on earth was going on in that girl's head?

He'd expected her to be a bit unhappy today.

Maybe even bitter. But with Gary, not him. He was trying to be a good guy, as Brad had said.

She hadn't liked him paying for the wedding. Pride, he supposed. Charlotte was proud.

Well, that was too bad because he'd liked giving the Gales that money. He could well afford it and it had made both of them very happy. If Charlotte chose not to see it in that light, then that was her problem.

Frankly, he was getting just a tad irritated with her. She should have been grateful for all he'd done, not looking daggers at him.

When he sat back down, Brad gave him a poke in the ribs. 'You have to go cut the cake now.'

Daniel sighed. Would this ever end?

They stood up together with Daniel putting his hand on Charlotte's elbow as they made their way round to the table that housed the three-tiered wedding cake. More smiles. More photographs.

'And now,' the MC boomed, 'the bride and groom will take the floor for the bridal waltz.'

Daniel winced. He'd actually heard of the bridal waltz and always thought it sounded schmaltzy. Suddenly, it seemed hazardous as well. He would have to take Charlotte in his arms and hold her close, and God only knew what would happen after that.

Daniel hesitated, despite the music having started up.

'Surely you know how to dance,' his bride said, again with that caustic gleam in her eye.

Right. He'd had enough of this.

With no further ado, he swept her into his arms

and onto the dance floor, twirling her round with elegant ease.

His fears over dancing with Charlotte, however, proved correct. No sooner had one hand been clamped to the small of her back and the other curled round her hot little hand than he felt the none too subtle stirrings of his flesh.

Thank goodness for the bridal gown, with its huge skirt and masses of petticoats. No way would Charlotte be able to feel a thing, he soon realised, smiling ruefully as he danced on, masochistically enjoying his arousal.

'You're looking very pleased with yourself,' she tossed at him.

'I'll be a lot more pleased when this reception is over,' he replied, and pulled her just a little closer.

That shut her up.

'Did you give the porter your overnight bag like we arranged?' he asked, his mind now solidly on the aftermath of this reception.

'Yes,' she replied a bit breathlessly.

'Good.' Daniel didn't want anything going wrong tonight. He had everything planned, and arranged.

'Er—which one of the bridal suites did you book?' she asked.

There'd only been the one available. The most expensive one.

'The Arabian Nights suite,' he replied, and listened, with a surge of triumph, as she gasped.

CHAPTER ELEVEN

CHARLOTTE gasped, then gulped. The Arabian Nights suite!

Oh…my…God…

Somehow Charlotte got through the bridal waltz, and the rest of the reception. She smiled at all her relatives when they came up to congratulate her and thanked them for their gifts, which were piled up on a huge table at the back of the reception room.

Charlotte had known not to bother with that bridal-register idea at any of the department stores where guests could order presents from a list and have them delivered to the bride's house beforehand. Country folk liked to bring their presents to the actual wedding.

Louise kept asking her if she was all right and she kept saying she was fine.

But she wasn't fine. In her head, she was already in that decadent bridal suite, in that decadent bed, gazing up at the decadent, mirrored ceiling.

Charlotte had been shown all the themed bridal suites when she'd first made enquiries here at the hotel, so she knew exactly what the Arabian Nights suite entailed. Not only was it the most expensive, but it was also the most exotic—and erotic—in decor.

By the time her mother hugged her goodbye,

brushing a tear from her eye, Charlotte's already strung-out nerves were stretched tight as a drum.

'Look after her for us, Gary,' her father said as he pumped Daniel's hand, then turned to hug his daughter.

'And you look after your husband, Charlotte,' he advised.

'I will, Dad,' she choked out.

'Now, off you go, you two, and have a great honeymoon. And don't worry about your wedding presents. Louise and Brad said they'd take them home for you and look after them. Mother and I will be taking off pretty early in the morning so this is goodbye from us for now. Give us a call after you get back from your honeymoon, OK?'

Daniel said they would.

Thankfully, there was a bank of lifts just outside the reception-room doors into which the 'honeymooners' raced to the cheers and claps of the happily intoxicated guests.

Fortunately, the lift they caught was empty. It whisked them up to the tenth floor, Charlotte only then realising she'd possibly drunk too much wine on her mostly empty stomach. She'd only managed a bite or two of the dessert, and none of the coffee and mints afterwards.

'You all right?' Daniel asked when the doors whooshed open and she stayed clasping the brass railing that ran around the lift wall at hand-height.

'I think I had a bit too much to drink.'

'I noticed you didn't eat much. Are you feeling sick?'

He looked worried, Charlotte noticed.

'I'll be all right. Just a slight dizzy spell from the lift.'

'Here. Take my arm.'

She smiled a wry smile as she did so. 'Is this you looking after me?'

He grinned. 'Absolutely. You can look after me later.'

Suddenly, Charlotte was overcome with panic. Because she knew what Daniel meant. Without a doubt, he was expecting her to be a woman of the world, experienced and confident.

'Daniel, I… There's something I have to tell you,' she said. She had to warn him; had to explain that she was not the sexy piece she seemed.

'There's nothing you have to tell me, beautiful,' he said softly, pulling her round into his arms. 'Tonight is my responsibility, not yours. You don't have to do a thing. Just lie back and enjoy.'

His words brought a rush of relief, Charlotte realising that if she'd told him she was bad—or boring—in bed, everything would have been spoilt in advance. This way, she had a chance to become the wanton woman she was in her fantasies.

'But I don't think I should kiss you just yet,' he said ruefully. 'Better we get behind closed doors first.'

A shudder rippled down her spine. 'Closed doors sounds good,' she agreed. 'Have you—er—got the passkey to the suite?'

'Right here.' And he patted his pocket.

'Did you come up to see this particular suite before you booked it?'

'No. Should I have? Is there something wrong with it?'

'Not at all,' Charlotte denied.

But he was in for a surprise. She hoped he liked it. She certainly had, despite being initially startled.

Daniel saw the gleam in her eyes and wondered what was waiting for him. Whatever it was, he was sure he would approve. Anything that pleased Charlotte this much would please him.

The Arabian Nights suite was the first one along the carpeted corridor, its name outlined in gold on the door. Shoving the plastic card into the lock, Daniel waited for the green light, turned the brass handle then pushed the rather heavy door open. The darkness inside was soon dispelled when he slid the card into the slot by the door, the lights coming on automatically.

'Good God!' he couldn't help exclaiming.

'You think it's over-the-top?' she asked, sounding disappointed by his reaction.

'No, no, it's fabulous.'

Her face beamed with more happiness than it had all night.

'Come and see the rest,' she said excitedly, taking his hand and pulling him across the black, marble-floored foyer and under a very ornate Moroccan-style archway. There, the marble gave way to thick, velvety red carpet that sank underfoot further than any carpet he'd ever encountered.

'This carpet is amazing,' he said. Just made for making love on.

And so were the sofas!

There were three of them. Low and wide and colourful, they were slightly curved, arranged around a circular, black-lacquered coffee-table on which rested a huge platter of fresh fruit, and a gilt ice bucket holding a magnum of champagne.

Beyond the sofas, curtains the colour of the water around Tahiti framed a floor-to-ceiling window that showed a panoramic view of the city skyline. There was no overhead lighting. Only lamps and wall lights. All gold. All exotic-looking.

'Look up at the ceiling,' she said.

His eyes moved up the deep blue walls to the very high ceiling above, which was draped in black silk shot with gold.

Wow. He now understood why this place had cost so much.

'Fit for a sheikh,' he remarked.

'That's the idea. It's supposed to tap into people's fantasies.'

'Do you have a sheikh fantasy?' he asked, reaching to pull her into his arms once more.

She gasped as their chests made contact. 'Only if you're the sheikh.'

He liked the sound of that.

'So tell me,' he murmured as he set about removing her tiara and veil, 'how does that fantasy go?'

Charlotte shivered at the touch of his fingers in her hair.

'You have your wicked way with me all night,'

she confessed breathlessly. 'And I love every single moment.'

'That's not fantasy, my beautiful Charlotte. That's going to be reality.' He tossed her veil and tiara onto the nearest sofa, before suddenly quirking an eyebrow at her. '*All* night?'

'See? I told you it was a fantasy.'

'No, no. I'm sure I can rise to the challenge. But I have only limited protection with me. I will have to be inventive when they run out. Do you mind inventive, beautiful Charlotte?'

'I don't think I'd mind anything with you,' she told him truthfully as her heart thundered behind her ribs.

Daniel suppressed a groan. There went his intentions to be a caring, considerate and conservative lover tonight.

Still, she clearly didn't want a caring, considerate and conservative lover tonight. She wanted the sheikh fantasy, where the dark and dangerous desert prince carried her off by force, thereby wiping away any sense of shame or guilt if she just happened to enjoy herself. She wanted him to take total responsibility for what happened here tonight. She wanted him to play the sheikh.

Fine. He could do that. Especially here, in this incredibly erotic setting. He'd already glimpsed the bedroom through another archway and it made the exotic living room look almost sedate.

'Come,' he said in a masterful tone. 'We shall retire to the boudoir.'

'Wait till you see it!'

Daniel tried not to ooh and aah.

But talk about harem territory. This was full-on.

'I'm sure honeymooners love it,' Charlotte said with a nervous little laugh.

Not just honeymooners, Daniel thought as he looked from the raised, black-lacquered four-poster bed with its filmy white curtains up to the mirrored ceiling above. Once again, the carpet underfoot was lush and thick, though this time it was green. Emerald-green. Everything else in the room, however, was black, white or silver.

'Lots of silver,' he commented. The wallpaper was silver, and so were the edges of the mirrors, and the thread running through the white satin quilt. 'I would have expected gold.'

'The bathroom has gold fittings,' she said. 'To go with the black marble, I guess.'

'They said it had a spa bath.'

'Yes, a huge one.' She flushed at the mention of the bath.

Surely not from shyness, Daniel reasoned. No woman who'd chosen the wedding dress she was wearing was shy about her body.

'Good,' he said.

Daniel decided any more delay would be counterproductive. 'I think it's time to check out that bathroom,' he said, reaching for her. 'But first, let's get you out of that dress.' And he turned her round.

CHAPTER TWELVE

CHARLOTTE sucked in sharply when his hands started work on the laces that anchored the bustier top to her body. Louise had tied them very tightly so that her waist was pulled in as far as it would go, the compression pushing her ribs in and her breasts upwards, giving her an extreme, hourglass shape.

She wore no bra. None had been needed, the top of her gown heavily boned and lined. Once Daniel got the laces undone, Charlotte knew that the top would fall from her body, leaving her naked from the waist up.

Just the thought turned her on.

She'd never been this eager to be naked before. Or to have a man's hands on her body.

'Aah, now I get it,' Daniel said as the bodice went slack around her. 'The top's separate from the skirt.'

The freeing of her breasts from the skin-tight constriction brought with it a wave of melting heat. When he removed the top right away from her body, she swayed.

'Hey!' he said softly, his arms sliding around her just underneath her breasts. 'Don't go fainting on me.'

Her answer was a soft moan, her eyes fluttering shut as she leant back against him in blissful surrender.

When his hands moved upwards to cup her breasts she almost cried out, her nipples stabbing at the centre of his palms. As though he knew what they wanted, he spread his hands out flat and rotated his palms slowly over the taut peaks.

Charlotte gasped, then groaned.

He kept up the rotating motion till her breasts were swollen and her nipples so sensitive that the sensations he created were close to pain.

Just when she felt she could bear it no longer, he stopped. Perversely, she opened her mouth to protest. But before she could utter a word, he spun her in his arms and covered her mouth with his own.

His lips were hard, and hungry, his hands on her back just as demanding. He clamped her to him, kept her lips open and drove his tongue deep. Charlotte had thought he'd kissed her with passion in the lobby. But this…this was more than a kiss. This was total ravishment.

His reefing away both startled and dismayed her. Her eyes flew open to find him taking a backward step from her and running an agitated hand through his hair. His face was flushed and his breathing ragged.

'What's wrong?' she asked.

He stared at her, before shaking his head, then smiling a rather wry smile.

'I was going way too fast.'

'But I liked you going fast.'

'You wouldn't in the end.'

'How do you know?'

'I know.' He smiled another of those wry smiles.

'Sheikhs know these things. Now I suggest you go get the rest of that dress off by yourself. Take a shower. And put on something more comfortable. Both our bags should be in the dressing room leading off from the bathroom. Or so I was told.'

Charlotte didn't want to do any of those things. She wanted to stay with him and have him kiss her some more. And play with her some more, then just take her, without too much preamble. Her nipples were still hard but the rest of her body was in melt-down mode. She wanted him.

But she would not beg.

'I won't be long,' she said, hurrying into the bathroom and shutting the door behind her.

The sight of herself in the huge vanity mirror was a shock. How decadent she looked standing there, half-naked. Spinning away, she hurried into the adjoining dressing room, where she stripped off the rest of her clothes, not returning to the bathroom till she was totally naked.

As she walked over to the vanity to get one of the complimentary shower caps, she glanced at herself in the mirror again.

Louise always said she had a fabulous body. Charlotte thought it was good, but not fabulous. Her hips were a bit wide. But she looked in proportion and she'd never felt ashamed of it.

But she'd been brought up in a modest household where you didn't flaunt yourself. Being totally naked in front of *anyone* had always been a problem with her, but especially the opposite sex. Mostly, in the past, she would undress then dive into bed and keep under the sheets.

Charlotte had long ago realised her inhibitions were a contributing factor in the ultimate failure of all her relationships, especially the one with Dwayne.

Strangely, though, she did not feel any of her usual shyness with Daniel. She wanted him to see her naked. Wanted him to make love to her, to be inventive.

Her hands lifted to lightly touch her nipples, producing a delicious quiver. She did it again, then cupped her whole breasts as Daniel had.

Her responses rocked Charlotte. Daniel wasn't even here and she was finding pleasure in her body.

Louise was right. This had to be lust, not love.

It was a liberating realisation, because she didn't want to love Daniel. She did, however, want to make love with him.

The bathroom door suddenly opening behind her had her snatching her hands away from her still throbbing breasts and whirling round.

'I didn't hear the shower,' Daniel said as he entered and walked towards her, seemingly unaware of being totally naked. Not so Charlotte. Her mouth went dry at the sight of him.

'Why don't we share?' he asked, and with one smoothly sweeping action scooped her up into his arms.

Charlotte didn't object. How could she? She was having enough trouble just breathing.

He held her with one hand whilst he turned on both taps in the made-for-two shower, adjusting the temperature and the shower heads till he was satisfied. Then he lowered her carefully to that spot where the two sprays met in the middle.

'My hair,' she did protest when the warm water started streaming down over her head.

'Don't worry about your hair,' he commanded, and pulled her against him again, not quite so roughly as the last time. But there was still an intensity in his body language which Charlotte found incredibly exciting. She liked to think he wasn't quite as cool as usual, that she had rattled him today.

She could feel his hardness pressed against her stomach, evoking wild images in her imagination.

'Are we going to do it here?' she asked him breathlessly.

He frowned down at her. 'Do you want to?'

'Yes.'

'Hell, Charlotte.'

'What?'

'You have to stop doing this to me.'

'Doing what?'

'Making me lose the plot. I'm the sheikh here. You're the captive bride. You do as *I* say.'

'Do I have to? I mean…I don't want to wait.'

'You might not have noticed but I'm not wearing a condom. They're back in the bedroom. Can't you wait a few minutes?'

She really couldn't.

'Unless there's some other reason why you have to use protection,' she blurted out, 'I—er—I'm on the Pill.'

'On the Pill,' he repeated, and a shudder ran

through him. 'You shouldn't have told me that, Charlotte.'

'Why not?'

'Because men will often say anything not to use condoms. Men can be very selfish. And stupid. I've always used protection myself. I'm somewhat paranoid about getting a girl pregnant. But you only have my word for that.'

'Your word is fine by me,' she said. 'I know you wouldn't lie about something as serious as that.'

'God, woman.'

'What?'

'Nothing.' He shook his head, splashing water all over the place. 'This is going to be a new experience for me.'

'What is?'

'Being with someone like you.'

'What does that mean? What's different about me?'

'Everything. Now shut up and let me kiss you.'

She shut up and let him kiss her and kiss her till she was squirming against him. Once again, his mouth burst away, his eyes flashing her a warning.

'Enough of that,' he growled, and spun her in his arms so that her back was to him. The water splashed down over her head and body, forming rivulets that streamed down.

'Wind your arms back around my waist,' he told her.

It was an incredibly exciting position, leaving her entire front totally accessible to his hands whilst hers were linked behind him as if she was, indeed, a captive bride. She could feel her heart thudding behind her ribs, her chest rising and falling.

Her heart raced even more when he dribbled shower gel over her breasts then started to caress them. The slipperiness of the liquid soap made everything more sensual and sensitive. Soft little sounds of pleasure escaped her lips every time he grazed one of her nipples.

When he abandoned her breasts and moved southward, Charlotte sucked in her stomach. When he passed beyond her navel, her whole belly started quivering. He was going to touch her down there. Her breath caught in anticipation and then his hand was sliding into the slickened folds of her sex. Every internal muscle she owned tensed, and waited. Waited and craved. His fingers slowly slid inside, moving as deep as they could before withdrawing a little then pushing deep again.

And again. And again.

Her breath began coming in short, sharp pants. Something was happening inside her. He kept touching something with each inward push, then sweeping over another highly sensitive part as he withdrew. Blinding pleasure mingled with an escalating frustration, a need for something that remained just outside her reach. Her muscles tightened further. Her mouth fell open. She wanted to scream. Or sob.

'Oh,' she cried out when the first spasm hit. 'Oh…'

Charlotte had always tried to imagine what an orgasm felt like. Nothing in her mind, however, matched the reality of the experience.

But how *could* you describe such feelings? Or the sensations? They were beyond words.

'Good?' he whispered in her ear when it was over.

'Mmm,' was all she could reply. Suddenly she went all limp, her arms flopping back down to her sides.

'Too tired to continue?'

'Not at all,' she shot back, snapping out of her momentary exhaustion in a hurry. No way was she going to waste any of tonight. Not if she could help it.

'In that case, I think we should adjourn to the bed.'

She swung round to face him. 'But I don't want to go to bed.' As much as the bed out there looked incredibly romantic and erotic, bed had never been a place where sex for her had been all that successful. She liked being in this shower with him. It excited her. 'I'd much prefer to stay here for a while.'

'Actual sex in the shower is not always a good idea, Charlotte,' he said. 'Not unless…' His black eyes glittered momentarily. But then he shook his head. 'No. No, I don't think so.'

'But I want to,' she insisted, her hands lifting to rest on his chest. 'Tell me what to do. *Show* me.'

Show her.

Daniel groaned. Didn't she know he was already close to the point of no return?

His male ego had been pleased with having made her come. But it demanded more. He wanted her to climax whilst he was making love to her. But that was unlikely if he proceeded at this stage. He'd come himself in no time and she'd be left in no man's land.

But he was tempted. Cruelly tempted.

'It's too soon,' he told her. 'For *you*.'

'But not for you,' she returned, her eyes dropping to where he was still erect.

'No,' he said ruefully. 'Not for me.'

He almost jumped out of his skin when she reached down and curled both her hands around him.

'No, don't,' he warned her. But she was already caressing him, moving her soft hands up and down his aching shaft. When she moved a thumbpad over the velvety tip, he groaned.

'Good?' she whispered, an echo of what he'd asked her earlier.

'Yes,' he bit out.

He grimaced when she reached for the shower gel and poured some over him. Hell on earth!

Now her hands slid so easily up and down. Up and down. Up and down.

'Charlotte,' he choked out.

She looked up into his eyes. Hers were big and gleaming with a wild excitement. She was genuinely enjoying what she was doing, this realisation shattering what little was left of his control.

He still tried to stop himself. This was not what he intended. He'd been going to be the master here, and she the pupil. It was clear, however, that she was not as inexperienced as Brad had intimated, for she sure as hell had done this before.

'Yes,' she ground out with elation in her eyes when he started to tremble. 'Yes...'

CHAPTER THIRTEEN

'How do you take your coffee?' Charlotte asked, glancing over at Daniel.

He was sprawled out on one of the sofas, eating grapes, his upper torso bare, a bath sheet slung low around his hips.

Charlotte was wearing one of the hotel's white towelling bathrobes. She'd spotted her overnight bag in the dressing room when she'd stripped off earlier, but hadn't bothered to open it yet.

'Black. One sugar,' he replied.

'I wish I had a rubber band,' she muttered as she made them both coffee. 'I'd like to get this hair out of my face.' Still damp, her hair was a heavy mass of wayward waves that fell across one eye all the time. She pushed it back and tried to anchor it behind her ear, not altogether successfully.

'Don't be silly. Your hair looks great like that. Very sexy. Like you.'

Charlotte flushed. 'You honestly think I'm sexy?'

'Do you doubt me?'

'I'm different from usual with you,' she confessed as she carried over the two mugs and placed them down on the black-lacquered coffee-table. 'I don't make a habit of doing what I did in the shower. In fact, I've never done anything like that before.'

But she'd wanted to. That was the most shocking

thing of all. She didn't just feel sexier with him, she felt wicked. Lust had turned her from her usual reserved self into a vamp.

'You are constantly surprising me, Charlotte,' he said as he picked up his coffee mug, his eyes meeting hers over the rim.

Lord, but he had incredible eyes. His body wasn't too bad, either.

Not too hard. Not too soft. Just right.

Like baby bear's bed.

Charlotte smiled at this unlikely simile. There was nothing babyish about Daniel.

'What's so amusing?' he asked.

'Nothing.'

'Don't go all mysterious on me. I like it that you're so honest and open.'

'I was thinking what a great body you have,' she confessed.

He actually looked surprised by her compliment.

'It's adequate enough. The person in this room with the really great body is you.'

She flushed. 'Flatterer.'

'Don't be coy. You must know you look great in the buff.'

'My bottom's too big,' she protested.

He laughed. 'I don't think too many men would agree. I certainly don't. You have a delicious bottom. And beautiful breasts. And fabulous legs. Or so I recall,' he added, a devilish smile playing around his mouth. 'Why don't you take off that robe so that I can see it all again, make sure I wasn't mistaken?'

She froze, the mug at her lips. 'Out here?' she choked out, her heart stopping in its tracks.

OK, so the lighting was soft and romantic, but the curtains were wide open, and whilst it didn't look as if anyone could see in, how could she be sure? There were lots of high-rise buildings down this end of town, and lots had lights on in the windows.

'Why not out here?'

'M…maybe when I finish this coffee,' she stammered.

'Now would be better. Then I could look at you whilst we drink.'

Her hands shook as she lowered the mug to the coffee-table. Did she dare? Had she become *that* wicked?

It seemed she had.

Her thighs trembled as she stood up, but a second glance over at the tinted window reassured her that no one could see anything at that distance.

The looped sash of her robe undid with the slightest of pulls, the sides falling apart. His eyes narrowed but he didn't stop sipping his coffee. In fact, he leant right back against the sofa in an attitude of total relaxation.

Charlotte was far from relaxed. This was what it must feel like, she imagined, just before diving off one of those high boards.

She sucked in a deep breath, then shrugged the robe off her shoulders. It fell to the floor, leaving her feeling more naked than she ever had in her life.

Not just her body but her very soul. Both were

naked before him, this man who could make her do things and feel things that no man had before.

He put his mug down and just drank her in. Slowly.

'Beautiful,' was all he said, but it left her shaken.

Because she knew in that telling moment that she would do anything he asked her to do.

'Why don't you sit down and finish your coffee?'

His suggestion—delivered oh, so coolly—confirmed what Charlotte already suspected, which was that Daniel was far more sophisticated than any man she'd ever been with. Clearly, he was used to playing erotic games like this, in having women do his bidding in the bedroom.

Maybe that was what was turning her on so much. Not just his handsome face and great body but also his suave know-how; that air of supreme confidence that clung to him in everything he did.

Hadn't Louise said this was what she needed, to have an older man teach her everything?

Daniel wasn't all that much older than her in age but he sure was in experience.

Silly of her to waste a moment of the time she spent with him.

'I don't think I'll be wanting any more coffee,' she said, her voice sounding determined.

He raised one eyebrow before putting down his own coffee, then stripping the towel from around his hips. 'Best come over here, then, don't you think?' he said, tossing the towel aside and lightly slapping one of his muscular thighs.

Her knees felt like jelly but she went, mouth dry

and heart racing, her belly tightening as she settled her shapely bottom across his lap and wound her arms around his neck.

'No, this way,' he instructed, and lifted her round till she was straddling his thighs, their faces almost level. His eyes held hers as he took hold of her hips and eased her up onto her knees.

Charlotte sucked in air sharply.

His hands slid round behind her knees, gently drawing them forwards, causing her to slowly sink downwards and take him in, inch by glorious inch.

She could have wept with pleasure. He was buried very deep inside her, filling her entirely. She loved the feeling, but was anxious for more.

'What now?' she asked tautly.

His brows drew together. 'Are you saying you haven't done this before either?'

'Not on a sofa. And never very well.'

'Use your knees to lift your bottom up and down, like you're riding a horse. Have you ever ridden a horse?'

'Please. I'm country.'

Charlotte could not believe she could sound so calm and casual at such a moment. No doubt she was keen to impress him, if not with her sexual expertise, then her willingness to learn.

Her hands curled over his shoulders, her nails digging in as she started to rise and fall.

What had felt wonderful inside her in repose, now felt incredible. She could not get enough of the sensation of being filled by him, over and over. Those frantic feelings returned, stronger this time and more compelling. She began to move faster.

His raw moan brought her to a fearful halt. She'd hurt him. Oh, she was hopeless.

'No, don't stop.' His voice was hoarse, his face anguished. 'Just keep doing what you're doing. It feels fantastic. *You're* fantastic.'

She happily obeyed, closing her eyes in an effort to concentrate. But it became increasingly difficult to focus on anything but the tension building inside her. Her belly tightened. Her thighs quivered. Her heart stopped. Then suddenly she was there, splintering apart around him, practically sobbing with the intensity of her release.

He cried out at the same time and for the first time Charlotte understood what it meant to be as one. They were fused together, flesh within flesh, both shuddering in ecstasy at the same time. She was still contracting around him when his hands cupped her face and drew her gasping mouth down to his, kissing her till their mutual pleasure died away.

Only then did his lips leave hers.

'*More* than fantastic,' he murmured, his eyes heavily hooded with spent passion.

When he gathered her close to his heart, she sighed a deeply contented sigh, her mind and body already beginning to shut down.

'Enough for now,' he said as he smoothed his hand up and down her spine. 'Go to sleep, sweet Charlotte.'

'I don't want to sleep,' she mumbled.

'Don't worry. I'll wake you up later.'

'Promise?'

'Cross my heart and hope to die.'

'Don't take me to bed,' she told him, sounding for all the world as if she was drugged.

'Why not?' He sounded startled.

'Not the bed. Not yet. Promise.'

'Crazy girl. All right. I promise.'

'Good.'

CHAPTER FOURTEEN

CHARLOTTE woke slowly, drifting out of a deep haze of sleep that seemed to want to drag her back and cocoon her forever. She yawned. Stretched. Then, finally, opened her eyes.

The first thing she saw was herself in the ceiling mirror. And Daniel next to her. Still fast asleep.

He was sprawled face down, the white satin sheet covering him up to the waist, his arms folded under the pillow on which his head rested.

Charlotte caught herself smiling. She should have felt wrecked. Instead, she felt wonderful.

A glance at her wrist-watch showed that it was twenty past ten. Not all that late considering she'd been awake most of the night.

And what a night!

If she hadn't been at this moment looking at Daniel's real-life reflection, she might have thought it was all a dream. Rolling over, Charlotte placed a kiss of gratitude on his nearest shoulder, rubbing her lips lightly back and forth across his skin.

He didn't stir. Understandable. The man had to be exhausted.

He'd been incredible last night. The kind of lover women fantasised about but rarely ever experienced. He knew exactly what to do to turn her on, and to keep her there. He'd made love to her in ways she hadn't even read about.

He made a better sheikh than she could've ever imagined. Dominating and demanding at times, but wonderfully tender at others. He seemed to know exactly what she needed to obliterate her sexual history. With him, there'd been no sign of the rather timid, fearful lover she'd become over the years. Any tension she felt with Daniel had been strictly sexual. She did so love the way he had mercilessly taken her to the edge, wickedly leaving her there till she begged him for deliverance from her torment.

But it was a delicious torment. She loved it, really.

Charlotte would have liked to stay there in the bed, reliving every delicious moment in her mind, but nature was calling, and so was their lack of time. Of course, Daniel had suggested again at one particularly satisfying moment that he come with her up to the Hunter Valley today. And of course this time she'd said, yes, please.

If she was still worried at the back of her mind that her newly discovered desire might deepen to something else, her worry was not as strong as her need. Having Daniel make love to her some more was worth the risk of some heartbreak afterwards. Worth just about any risk, to be honest. Such was the power of her passion for him, and the pleasure he could deliver.

Charlotte wasn't sure what time checkout was, but even if it was late checkout at twelve, that didn't give them all that much time. Besides, she wanted to make herself perfect for Daniel before he woke.

Careful not to disturb him, she climbed out of the bed and tiptoed to the bathroom.

Daniel woke to the sound of the shower running. With a groan, he rolled over and checked the time on his watch, which was lying on the black-lacquered bedside table. Ten-thirty.

Checkout wasn't till twelve. Time enough for a decent breakfast. He was sure Room Service would organise something. This was the bridal suite, after all.

And it was worth every penny, he thought with a satisfied smile as he lifted the phone next to the bed. Charlotte had finally agreed to his coming with her up to the Hunter Valley today, giving him a few more days to convince her that he wanted her for more than a holiday fling. He wondered if she would consider coming back to America and living with him...

'Housekeeping,' a woman's voice answered when he punched in the number six.

'This is Mr Bannister in the Arabian Nights suite. We'd like to order some breakfast.'

'Yes, of course, Mr Bannister. What would you like? Lots of newlyweds opt for the champagne breakfast.'

'I don't think so.' They'd had more than enough champagne last night. 'We need something far more substantial this morning. We'll have muesli, freshly squeezed orange juice, bacon and eggs, wholemeal toast and brewed coffee.'

'Yes, Mr Bannister. And when would you like that delivered?'

'Make it eleven.' That gave him time to shower and shave.

'Very good, sir.'

Daniel hung up, got up and glanced around for something to put on, but there was nothing but the clothes he'd worn the day before. His bag was in the dressing room and the only access to that was through the bathroom. Not wanting to burst in on Charlotte again, he strode out to the sitting area, where he knew he'd left a towel during the night.

As he swept it up from where it was spread over the coffee-table, images flashed back into his mind of an abandoned Charlotte spread out across that table whilst he'd made love to her.

Daniel's chest contracted at the memory of how it had felt, taking her like that. It had been wild. *She'd* been wild.

For a girl with so little experience, Charlotte had been very quick to embrace the delights of the flesh. If Daniel had any worries this morning, they lay in the fact that sex might be the only thing Charlotte would ever want from him. However, she'd been quite adamant the other day about wanting marriage and children, and having no intention of settling for less.

Which rather left Daniel in a dilemma. Because no way was he marrying any woman, no matter how much he loved her!

Daniel froze, with the towel dangling in front of him.

Love. He *loved* her.

Well, of course you do, you idiot, came the ex-asperated voice of long-ignored logic. Why else do you think you've been acting the way you have? Pursuing her like some madman. Going through with that pretend wedding. Turning yourself inside out last night to make her feel fulfilled.

No man does all that if he's not in love!

Daniel slumped down on the nearest sofa, stunned. Somehow, admitting that he loved her changed everything. And forced him to face a fear far greater than his fear of marriage.

What if Charlotte never loved him back? What if, after the next few days were over, she said 'Goodbye, Daniel. Thanks for all the great sex. Off you go, lover. No, sorry, I don't want your love and I don't want you. I want a man capable of true caring and commitment, not some man who has no confidence in himself being a good husband and father'?

Daniel bristled at these imagined insults. Of *course* he could make a good husband and father. Now that he realised he was capable of love, he was capable of anything!

His sigh carried relief. That felt better. Much better. In fact, once the idea of marrying Charlotte took hold, Daniel liked it a lot. He even liked the idea of having children with her. She'd make a wonderful mother.

One problem still remained, however. Getting Charlotte to fall in love with him. Lusting after him was one thing, love something entirely different. He knew that now.

Daniel might have succumbed to a crisis of confidence if his male ego hadn't galloped to the rescue.

You've had no trouble getting women to fall in love with you in the past, he was reminded. You have a hell of a lot going for you.

Still, it might help to tell Charlotte he'd fallen in love with her, and that he'd changed his mind about getting married.

He would have to pick his moment, however. Not too soon. She might not believe him. No, he would have to wait. Meanwhile…

Daniel stood up, wrapped the towel around his hips and headed for the bathroom. The sound of water running had stopped. Hopefully Charlotte was dressed by now. Still, he would knock and make sure.

Charlotte was about to start blow-drying her hair when a firm tap came on the bathroom door.

'Yes?'

'I've ordered breakfast for eleven,' Daniel called through the door. 'I need to shower and shave before then. Are you finished in there?'

She wasn't. Not even remotely. But the hair-dryer wasn't one of those connected to the wall, so she could finish her face and hair elsewhere. There was a carved wooden desk in the sitting area, she'd noted last night, with a gilt-edged mirror on the wall above it. That could serve as a dressing table.

But she was disappointed that Daniel would see her as Louise did most mornings. She'd wanted to be all made up for him, with her hair looking as if she'd just stepped out of a salon.

Oh, well. At least she had a new outfit on, one of the ones she'd bought to wear on her honeymoon. Crisp white hipster jeans—the stretch kind that clung and didn't crush—teamed with a buttercup-yellow halter-necked top and white slip-on sandals. Strappy ones with sexy little heels.

Thinking of sex brought Charlotte's mind to her underwear, which was very sexy but not altogether comfortable. Her bra was a silky cream push-up number she'd bought in that expensive lingerie shop. There was a matching G-string with a lace edging, which looked great.

Picking up the hair-dryer and her toilet bag, Charlotte reluctantly clip-clopped across the black marble floor and opened the door.

Daniel tried not to stare at her. Love, they often said, was blind. In his case, however, it was anything but. As he looked down into her freshly washed face and clear blue eyes, he was overcome with emotion.

He almost told her he loved her right then and there.

Instead he swore, which brought a startled glance to her beautiful eyes.

'Sorry,' he apologised rather grumpily. 'But you have no right to look so damned gorgeous this morning. You should be all bleary-eyed. Like me.'

Bleary-eyed! Was he kidding? He looked scrumptious, that designer stubble on his chin only adding to his sex appeal. As did his only having a towel draped around his hips. Daniel had a great upper body, with broad shoulders, well-defined pecs and a flat, hard stomach.

Charlotte knew she was staring at the man quite shamelessly. But she didn't care. She was totally besotted.

'I've been thinking,' she said. Anything to get her mind off ripping that towel off him, right here and now. 'What's your sister going to say to your going away with me today? I mean…she's the one you've come all this way to visit, after all.'

'She won't mind,' he returned abruptly. 'I can always extend my visit.'

Charlotte's heart jumped at this news. 'Really? I thought you had to return to LA in a fortnight.'

He shrugged. 'I'm my own boss.'

'Oh. I see. Good. I wouldn't want you getting into trouble because of me.' And with a supreme effort of will she pushed past him. 'All yours,' she said blithely over her shoulder as she walked off.

Once the bathroom door was safely shut behind her and she heard the shower taps snap on, Charlotte bolted for the other room, dropping her things on one of the sofas and picking up the phone. Once she had an outside line she punched in her home number. She simply had to talk to Louise, had to have some common sense talked to her. And fast!

'Yes,' a foggy voice answered.

'Louise, it's me. Wake up.'

'Charlotte! Brad, it's Charlotte!'

'I don't want a three-way conversation, thanks,'

Charlotte said sharply. 'I want to talk to you and only you.'

She heard some muffled sounds in the background before Louise came back on the line.

'I'm on my way to the kitchen right now. Shoot!'

'Tell me again it's only lust.'

'Oooh. That good, eh?'

'Yes.'

'Then it's definitely only lust. A specially addictive kind. There'll be no going back now, sweetie.'

'So you don't think I've fallen in love with the man?'

'Nah. What's to love?'

Charlotte could think of many things to love about Daniel. He wasn't just a stud. He was kind, and intelligent, and sensitive, and successful, and generous.

Her heart contracted as she thought of how he'd given her father all that money. Thousands, it must have been. He needn't have done that. She'd been angry at the time but that had been *her* problem, not Daniel's. She must have seemed awfully ungrateful to him.

'Hey there!' Louise said. 'Why so quiet all of a sudden?'

'No reason. Louise, could you do me a favour?'

'Anything.'

'Pack a bag for me. There's a navy sports bag in the bottom of my wardrobe. Throw in all those new clothes I bought for my honeymoon. And whatever accessories you think I'll need. I already have my make-up, perfume and toiletries with me, so you don't have to worry about those. I'll be by to pick it up around twelve-thirty.'

'I won't be here by then. Brad's taking me to his house for a barbeque.'

'Oh…'

'Don't worry, I'll pack it and leave it near the front door. Gosh, I'm so glad last night was a success, but I can't stay and chat. Not if I have to pack you a bag and get ready myself. Brad's just come in and given me strict orders to hurry.'

'That's fine. Thanks, Louise.'

'No sweat. Take care.'

Louise hung up with Brad still looking impatiently at her. He came forward and pulled her into his arms. 'Forget the coffee and come back to bed.'

'I can't. I have to pack Charlotte a bag before we go.'

'Why can't she pack her own bag?'

'Because she wants to get lover-boy up to the Hunter Valley as soon as possible, I guess. Have some more of whatever she had last night.'

'And you don't?' He looked offended.

'I would have thought after six months of continual sex you'd have had enough by now.'

'I'll never have enough of you, babe. When are you going to realise that?'

Louise didn't reply. Impossible with Brad's mouth clamped solidly over hers. But underneath his kiss, her heart was doing strange things. Damn that wedding yesterday. It made a girl want things. And think things. And feel things.

Maybe the time had come to give love another chance.

CHAPTER FIFTEEN

'I'M SORRY about this, sis,' Daniel said as he hastily repacked the clothes he'd unpacked a couple of days earlier. 'I know you must be disappointed.'

'Yes, and no,' Beth replied.

Daniel flicked her a questioning glance. 'Meaning?'

'I *had* been looking forward to your stay. I won't deny it. I've been lonely since I gave up work to have this baby. But I'm willing to sacrifice the immediate pleasure of your company for the long term.'

Daniel zipped up his natty travelling case then glanced up at his sister again. 'Meaning?'

She smiled. 'I know my big brother well enough to know when he's finally fallen in love.'

Daniel's smile was wry. 'Have I been *that* obvious?'

'Afraid so. Vince said it was written all over your face at the wedding. Says he's never seen a groom so much in love with a bride.'

'It took *me* a while to realise the truth. But when I did, I have to tell you, Beth, I was blown away. True love's pretty powerful, isn't it?'

Her eyes went all soft. 'Yes, Daniel. It is.'

'I'd do anything for her.'

'I can see that.'

He sighed. 'I'm worried Charlotte might never feel

145

the same way. I mean…this could all be rebound stuff.' He didn't like to say he thought it might be just sex.

'Could be,' Beth replied. 'She must have at least *thought* she was in love with that other man, if she was going to marry him. But she's obviously very attracted to you. The girl I met on Friday would not be taking you with her on her honeymoon if her own feelings weren't pretty powerful. She didn't strike me as the promiscuous type.'

'She's not,' Daniel agreed, feeling marginally better with Beth's reminder of Charlotte's good character.

'Then be careful, Daniel. She has to be confused right now. She's going to need time to sort out her feelings.'

'How much time?'

'You'll have to play it by ear, darling. Just be your usual confident, charming self and I'm sure she'll be yours in the end.'

Daniel wasn't so sure. Charlotte was different from every woman he'd ever been with. She didn't seem all that impressed with his charm. Or his wealth. She only seemed interested in his body.

Which was certainly putting the boot on the other foot. In the past, that was all he'd been interested in when it came to women. Sex. Most of them hadn't liked being reduced to sex objects. He could now understand exactly how they felt.

'Charlotte inferred over breakfast that after this honeymoon holiday was over, we were over.'

'Maybe she's protecting herself. She thinks you're

the love 'em and leave 'em type, so she's getting in
first.'

Daniel glared at Beth. 'She wouldn't have thought
that if you hadn't said as much.'

'Come, now, Daniel, you have playboy written all
over you. Any man who looks like you, has money
and is still a bachelor at thirty-six is automatically
tagged by women as a good-time guy. Your
Charlotte is no dummy. She's been around. She
would make her own assessment of you.'

Daniel grimaced. 'Yeah, you're right. I even told
her myself I was allergic to marriage.'

'You certainly dug your own grave with that one.
The girl wants marriage above all, and children. Most
of us do, eventually. You have to let her know
you've changed your mind about commitment and
marriage. Give her a chance to fall in love with you.'

Daniel pulled a face. 'I want her to fall in love
with me for myself. Not because I'm dangling the
carrot of marriage.'

Beth sighed. 'You always did want it all, Daniel.'

'No, Beth, I just don't want what Dad has these
days. I want the real thing. Charlotte is the real
thing.'

'Then go get it.'

Charlotte sat in the car outside Beth's house, waiting
impatiently for him to reappear. She'd refused to ac-
company him inside whilst he packed some things
for their trip. She would have felt awkward in front
of his sister and her husband.

What must they be thinking of her?

It was one thing to go through with a pretend wedding, quite another to take the pretend groom away with her on her honeymoon.

Charlotte had never condoned casual sex. Or fast women. Yet here she was, being faster than fast. And loving it.

After talking to Louise this morning, she'd momentarily wondered again if she had fallen in love with Daniel. But when he emerged from the bathroom, looking sinfully sexy in cool beige trousers and a wine-coloured silk shirt, Charlotte had accepted the reality that desire was the main catalyst propelling her uncharacteristic behaviour.

She could not wait to go with Daniel to the resort. To have him all to herself. For five whole days!

Despite not wanting to face his sister right now, Charlotte steadfastly refused to let guilt, or shame, or worry spoil her excitement. She would keep all those negative emotions till the honeymoon was over. Meanwhile, she was going to enjoy every incredible moment.

Her heart leapt when the gate in the high security wall surrounding Beth's house swung open and Daniel walked through, pulling a compact black travelling case behind him.

Flicking the lock on her hatchback, she leapt out from behind the wheel and hurried round to open it for him.

He smiled one of his heart-stopping smiles as he joined her. 'I must have the most beautiful chauffeur in Sydney,' he complimented, swinging his case in beside hers before bending to kiss her on the mouth.

Just a light kiss but it sent her heart racing.

Their eyes met, with his seeming to search hers.

'What?' she said.

'Nothing. Shall we go?'

'What did your sister say?' she asked once they were on their way. 'Was she angry?'

'No. A little disappointed. But I promised to make it up to her.'

'How?'

'Like I said before, I'll stay on a while longer.'

Charlotte wasn't sure she liked the sound of that. What if he wanted to keep seeing her? She knew she could not help falling for him if things went on, and on, and on.

Just keep concentrating on the sexual side of things, she advised herself, a task that was all too easy at the moment. Just having Daniel sitting beside her in this car focused her mind on the physical. She could smell his tangy aftershave, feel the heat emanating from his body. She kept glancing over at his beautiful hands with their long, strong fingers and thinking of the places she wanted them to stroke and explore and…

'Better watch the road,' he warned sharply when the car drifted towards the next lane. 'Or let me drive.'

'Absolutely not,' she returned, quickly pulling herself—and the car—into line. 'You don't know the way.'

'I'm not a total stranger to Sydney, you know.'

'Maybe, but it's been a while. And you told me

over breakfast you'd never been up north to the Hunter Valley.'

On top of that, she didn't want him tired when they arrived.

'Why don't you lie back and have a rest?' she suggested. 'Not much to see till we get out of the city. Not much then, either, to be honest. The freeway is not renowned for its scenery. It's pretty when we cross the Hawkesbury River but that's about it.'

'Why can't we just talk?' he counter-suggested.

Talk? She didn't want to talk to him. She didn't want to get to know any more about him. She already liked what she knew too much.

'What about?' she asked warily.

He shrugged. 'Anything and everything.'

Her chest tightened. 'I find it hard to concentrate on the traffic and talk.'

'It's Sunday. There's not that much traffic.'

'Yes, well, I'm a nervous driver.'

'Your dad said you weren't the nervous type.'

'Well, I am around you, OK?' she snapped, then wished she hadn't. Keep it cool, Charlotte. 'Look, I'll put the radio on and you can listen to that.'

She turned the car radio on to the BBC, which had a lot of news and chat shows as opposed to music.

'Will that do?'

'It'll have to, I guess.' And he settled back with arms crossed, his eyes half-shut.

Charlotte almost sighed with relief. Though any real relief was short-lived, her mind swiftly back on what was to come later in the day. The clock on the dash said one-fifteen. Check-in time at the resort was three. With a bit of luck they should arrive shortly after three.

And shortly after that?

Charlotte quivered inside at the prospect of being behind closed doors with Daniel once more. She'd been excited yesterday, but nothing like this. Knowing the pleasure in store for her was turning her crazy. She could think of nothing else.

Her hands tightened around the wheel to stop them trembling.

The next two hours, Charlotte suspected, were going to be the longest two hours in her life!

CHAPTER SIXTEEN

DANIEL didn't listen to the radio. His mind was firmly on analysing Charlotte's actions and reactions to him just now.

She was nervous. That much was clear.

What was it her dad had said? Caring makes a person nervous. Did Charlotte's nervousness mean she cared? Or was she just turned on?

Maybe he shouldn't have kissed her back behind the car. But every time he saw her, he was overcome with the need to do something physical.

Damn it all, now *he* felt nervous, which wasn't his usual state of mind. But there was just so much at stake here. Winning Charlotte's heart was going to be a much more difficult mission. Yet giving her good sex was all he could do for a while.

Not that this prospect was unpleasant. Hell, he couldn't even *think* about making love to Charlotte without getting aroused. She was just so responsive. And so obviously delighted that she'd finally found the joy of sex. It was only natural that she'd want to experience everything.

A surreptitious sidewards glance showed she was quite pink in the cheeks. Possibly nervous *and* excited.

And so damned beautiful.

He really loved the way she'd done her hair today,

yet it was totally different from yesterday at the wedding. This time it was scraped back very tightly from her face and secured in a high ponytail. The ponytail wasn't at all girlish, or wavy. It was sleek and chic and very sexy, the style exposing her elegant neck and drawing his eye to her dangling earrings.

They were silver, and diamond-shaped, with small pearls hanging off each point. Every time the car went round a corner, they swung from side to side.

Daniel had read a book once on the various erotic zones on a woman's body. The earlobes were one of them. Women since the days of the Pharoahs had drawn attention to their earlobes with earrings to attract the male. And turn him on.

The tactic worked.

'Will you stop staring at me?' she said sharply.

Daniel noted the frustration in her voice, plus her knuckles showing white on the wheel. Plus something else.

'You've taken off Gary's ring,' he pointed out.

'What?'

'Your engagement ring. You've taken it off.' Left the wedding ring on, though, he noted. His was still firmly jammed on *his* finger.

'Oh, yes. The ring. I put it in a drawer when I picked up my things.'

'Are you going to send it back to Gary?' Keep her talking, Daniel.

She sighed. 'I probably will. I know what he did was weak and wrong, but I'm not proving much better, am I?'

'I wouldn't say that.'

She laughed. 'No, you wouldn't. You probably do things like this all the time. But I don't. Still, I'm not going to beat myself up over it. I'm here with you because I want to be. Nobody's twisting my arm.'

'You make it sound like what we're doing is sordid. You're free as a bird, Charlotte. You have a right to be with whoever you want to be.'

'You don't think people might think I'm shallow and promiscuous to go from wanting to marry Gary one day to sleeping with you the next?'

Daniel frowned. Beth was right. Charlotte was feeling very mixed-up. And not totally comfortable with her decision to come away with him.

'That's over-simplifying what is really a more complex situation than that,' he said carefully. 'You didn't love Gary, for starters.'

'No. But I thought I did. I'm always thinking I'm in love with men when I'm not.'

Daniel's heart missed a beat. Was that a slip of the tongue? Did she mean him? He sure hoped not. But this was not the right time to press. All he could do was soothe her conscience, and her fears over looking shallow or promiscuous.

'Lots of people think they're in love when they're not,' he began. Hell no, he shouldn't have said that.

Her laugh was dry. 'I've finally realised that. If I'd met you at any other time in my life, I might have thought I'd fallen for you. At least I've grown up enough now to know it's just a sex thing, like it is for you with me.'

Oh, terrific! Now what could he say? But it's not

just a sex thing with me, Charlotte. I love you. I've loved you from the first moment I saw you.

She'd laugh, or accuse him of lying.

'A lot of successful relationships start with sexual attraction,' he remarked instead.

'Obviously not with you. I'll bet you've never even lived with a girl.'

'You're right. I haven't. But maybe that's because I hadn't met the right girl before.'

She shot him a dry look. 'Oh, please, not that old chestnut. You said you liked it that *I* was open and honest. Well, I like it when you are. You're a good-time guy, Daniel. You admitted as much. Which is fine by me, because I want a good time for the next few days. With you.'

Daniel decided then and there to stop rushing things. It was clear he was going to have to be very patient in his mission to marry Charlotte. But that was all right. He had time. She wasn't going any-where.

'Well, if you want a good time later today,' he said nonchalantly, 'I think I might have to lie back and have that rest you suggested. I'm still a bit knackered from last night.'

CHAPTER SEVENTEEN

CHARLOTTE could not believe it when he not only put his seat right back, but he actually seemed to go to sleep, leaving her with nothing to distract her from her X-rated thoughts but the road and the radio.

After what seemed like an eternity, Charlotte turned off the freeway onto the side-road that led to Cessnock and the lower Hunter Valley. The clock on the dash said two forty-five. If Charlotte had been made to guess the time, she would have said it was much later.

She bitterly resented Daniel's sleeping, which was perverse, since that was what she'd suggested. But she hated him being so cool about everything when she felt like a cat on a hot tin roof.

He suddenly stirred in the seat, popping his seat back up straight and glancing around. 'Where in hell are we?' he said. 'We seem to have been on the road for hours.'

His impatience pleased her.

'Not far now,' she said.

'Thank goodness. Boy, it looks dry out there,' he said, staring out at the countryside.

Actually, Charlotte thought it didn't look too bad for the last month in summer. The grass alongside the road was quite green. Admittedly, the paddocks beyond were somewhat brown in parts and the trees had that thirsty look they got at the end of a hot day, their leaves drooping towards the ground.

'If you think this looks dry, you should see my dad's place. Not a blade of grass in some of the paddocks. He's been hand-feeding his stock for months.'

'What's his water situation like? I was reading the paper at Beth's the other morning, and it said some of the smaller towns are having to ship in water.'

'Water's always a problem in the bush in a long drought. Fortunately, Dad does have a bore well, and a couple of dams. But he'll probably use some of the money you gave him to put in another dam. And replace some of the breeding stock he's had to sell.'

'You're not still angry with me about that money, are you?'

'No,' she said. 'To be honest, I feel bad about the way I reacted to that. You didn't have to do what you did. I realised later you must have known I'd go to bed with you without it.'

The expression on his face was priceless. 'Are you saying you thought I gave your father that money as a bribe to get you to sleep with me?'

'It did cross my mind.'

'But I told your dad not to tell anyone! It's not my fault that he did.'

'I appreciate that now, Daniel. I wasn't thinking straight at the time. I was under a lot of stress. I'm sorry.'

'Apology accepted,' he grumbled, though still not looking too happy. 'But *try*, in future, not to jump to hasty conclusions about me, or judge me so harshly. I am not some depraved roué, Charlotte. I don't even like the term *good-time guy*. I'm just a normal red-blooded man who wants to spend time with a woman he thinks is very beautiful and very special.'

'If you say so,' Charlotte said noncommittally, determined not to be swayed too much, or seduced too far, by Daniel's silver tongue. 'Special, am I? That's sweet.'

'*Sweet!* You make me sound about as substantial as candy floss.'

Charlotte laughed. 'You said that. I didn't. Aah, here we are. Cessnock. Not far to go now. Know anything about Cessnock?'

'Not much.'

He sounded as if he didn't want to know anything, either. But being a tourist guide was nicely distracting.

'Mines, wines and people,' she read aloud from the road sign as they entered the outskirts of Cessnock. 'That just about sums Cessnock up. It was a mining town first. The vineyards came afterwards. In the past few years, that side of this area has boomed.'

'It looks prosperous enough,' he said as they drove slowly down the wide main street.

'It is. Real estate here has gone through the roof. But it *is* a hot spot, especially in the summer. Wait till you get out of this car. The heat outside will take your breath away.' The forecast for the Hunter Valley today had been thirty-eight degrees, much hotter than Sydney's milder climate.

'We're not stopping here, though, are we?'

'No,' she replied.

'How far to go now?' he asked.

'Not far.' The resort had emailed her a map to follow. Which she'd memorised. 'About ten minutes out of town,' she told him. 'Provided I don't take a wrong turn.'

She didn't take a wrong turn and soon they'd left Cessnock behind and were travelling along the winding, tree-lined road that led to Peacock Park.

'According to the map they sent me,' she said, 'it should be on the right. And soon.'

The road dipped down into a gully then began a steep rise. Suddenly, there it was, on their right, a grand-looking assortment of colonial-style buildings perched on the crest of the hill.

'Impressive,' Daniel said as she drove through the large black wrought-iron gates.

'It was actually built over twenty years ago, according to their website, but it's recently been refurbished and is now considered one of the top five resorts in the Hunter Valley. There's everything here you could possibly want,' she told him as she angled the car into one of the parking bays outside the building marked 'Reception'. 'A five-star restaurant, a bar, an indoor solar-heated pool. Tennis courts. Walking trails. A gym. The luxury rooms—where we'll be staying—have spa baths and private verandas with views over the valley.'

'And air-conditioning, I hope,' Daniel said as they both climbed out of the car. 'I see what you mean. This is seriously hot.'

'I did warn you. But it looks like a storm is on the way,' she said, glancing over to the horizon, where a mass of white thunderheads loomed over the mountain range.

But it wasn't only in the sky that a storm was gathering. Now that they had finally arrived, Charlotte felt herself being swept into a maelstrom of fierce longing. The heat in the air was nothing to the heat inside her.

'I think we should get out of this sun,' Daniel said, taking her arm and propelling her towards Reception.

The booking was in her name, thank heavens, so there was no trouble with the formalities. Within five minutes they had their passkey, along with directions to their room. When asked if they wanted a reservation in the restaurant for tonight, Daniel had briskly answered that no, they would be having Room Service.

Charlotte didn't argue. Room Service was exactly what she wanted. Amongst other things.

It took them another couple of minutes to move the car to the parking bay allotted to their room, which was housed in a block some distance from Reception.

'There's no one in the room next to you, so you will have total privacy,' the receptionist had informed them. 'And the best view. You're also quite close to the pool and the gym. Just follow the signs along the path.'

Their room was the end one in a rectangular block that had a high-pitched roof and verandas front and back.

'Would you like to go for a swim till the air-conditioning kicks in?' Daniel asked as he dropped their bags on the veranda outside the room and un-locked the door.

'Would you?' she returned, hating the idea.

'No. A shower would do just as well. If that's all right with you.'

She looked at him, unable to hide the need in her eyes any longer.

'I think you know the answer to that,' she said in a quiet voice, which was all the more powerful for its underlying intensity.

'I feel exactly the same.'

Charlotte would have liked to believe that. But she knew in her heart that Daniel felt nothing even close to what she was feeling. This was a first for her in so many ways. He'd obviously been here, done this before.

He pushed the door open and held it there for her whilst she walked in, rather stunned all of a sudden. It was as though her mind had reached overload. She glanced around the room, superficially noting its style—spacious and country described it best.

'They must have good insulation in here,' Daniel said as he closed the door behind her. 'Has to be ten degrees cooler than outside. But some air-conditioning is still called for.'

He busied himself as men did with all things me-chanical and functional, checking out the air-conditioning and the TV which was hidden in a huge wall cabinet across the way from the equally huge bed.

'Great bathroom,' he said after a brief visit there. 'Go check it out.'

She did and he was right. It was fabulous, with a corner spa bath, large shower, double vanities. And every toiletry supplied that any visitor could possibly want.

When she emerged, Daniel had pulled back the curtains that covered the sliding glass doors leading out onto the veranda. He was standing there with his back to her, his legs apart, his hands in his pockets.

'Great view,' he said. 'You can see for miles. Pity we can't go out there yet. Maybe later this evening.'

'Daniel,' Charlotte choked out, unable to bear any further delay.

He turned slowly, his body language showing an odd reluctance to face her.

'Yes, Charlotte?'

'Stop tormenting me.'

He smiled. 'I'm not tormenting you, my darling. I'm tormenting myself.'

His calling her his darling brought a soft moan to her lips. He misinterpreted it, of course, thinking it was an expression of frustration when it was actually a cry of despair. One miserable 'my darling' and all the rubbish about this being nothing but lust was stripped away, leaving her heart raw and bleeding.

He covered the distance between them with three long strides and pulled her roughly into his arms.

She welcomed his lack of gentility. If he'd been tender with her, she might have broken down. Instead, he clamped his mouth over hers quite brutally whilst his hands yanked at her clothes. She helped him, happy to dispense with any actions that smacked of love.

They were naked within no time, naked yet still clawing at each other's flesh. He pushed her back across the bed, spread her legs and drove in deep with a groan.

Suddenly he stopped, staring down at her with strange eyes, as though what he'd just done had shocked him. And maybe it had. Last night he'd been demanding, but never rough.

'Don't stop,' she begged.

Swearing, he hooked her legs high around his back and began to thrust into her.

Charlotte gasped, then groaned, her nails digging into his buttocks as he surged into her over and over. Sweat beaded on his forehead and on hers.

'God, Charlotte,' he moaned at one stage.

'Don't stop,' she replied.

He muttered another four-letter word, and kept on going. But not for long, his face grimacing with something akin to self-disgust as he climaxed.

But he needn't have worried. She came with him, her own face twisting with ecstasy. Or was it agony?

No, no, she refused to go down that self-pitying, self-destructive path, *refused* to believe this was love, no matter how much her silly, romantic soul wanted to believe it was. This was what Louise had told her it was, and nothing more.

Don't look for more. Don't hope for more.

For your sanity's sake, *don't*!

CHAPTER EIGHTEEN

CHARLOTTE stirred to the sound of thunder. The room was almost dark, although the bedside clock showed it was only five-twenty. A flash of lightning was swiftly followed by another rumble of thunder. The storm was very close.

Daniel was not beside her in the bed, but she could see him through the open sliding door. He was sitting out on the veranda, dressed in one of the complimentary bathrobes, sipping a glass of white wine.

The second complimentary robe was draped across the foot of the bed, waiting for her. Daniel must have put it there whilst she'd been asleep. He must have picked her clothes up off the floor as well, because they were lying on a nearby chair, neatly folded.

How kind of him. There again, Daniel *was* kind. Being a good-time guy didn't mean he couldn't be kind.

What a shame that he didn't want marriage. He would make a wonderful husband. Her heart twisted at this last thought, reinforcing what she'd suspected earlier on and which she'd been trying to convince herself wasn't so ever since.

She *did* love the man. Ridiculous to keep denying it.

For a moment, she let her eyes linger lovingly on him.

If only they were really married, and on their real honeymoon. If that were true she could go out there, sit on his lap, share his drink, run her fingers through his hair, tell him he was the handsomest, kindest, sexiest man she'd ever met. There would be no need for *any* pretence. No lies. No embarrassment.

Embarrassment consumed her now as she recalled how she'd clawed at him that first time. But she'd been so desperate with desire.

She still was, despite what had happened afterwards.

Her need for him seemed insatiable, perhaps because sex was her only means of expression. She could not be her natural self with him, or tell him how much she loved him. If she did, he would think her a fickle fool, going from one man to the next all the time, always thinking she was in love with them.

The trouble was this time she really was in love. Sometimes, you had to experience the fool's gold version a couple of times to recognise the real thing when it hit you.

And hit her it had. Like a bulldozer.

Charlotte might have sunk back down under the sheet and pretended to sleep a while longer if nature wasn't calling. With a sigh she rose, slipped into the white towelling robe and padded off to the bathroom, where her eyes inevitably went to the shower cubicle.

The glass walls were still wet from their shower together, Charlotte's stomach clenching down hard at the memory of how utterly shameless she'd been in there. Daniel hadn't had to seduce her into anything, either. She'd been more than willing to go down on her knees before him.

She would never be truly satisfied with just sex. She wanted Daniel to love her as well as make love to her. But that wasn't going to happen, so making love was the next best thing.

As she washed her hands, her reflection in the mirror mocked her private misery. She looked great. Glowing, in fact. Eyes bright. Lips pink. Glossy hair still tidy in its sleek ponytail, though it was slightly damp. She was even still wearing her earrings.

Shaking her head again at the irony of it all, she took the earrings off and left them on the vanity top before heading for the veranda. And Daniel. Her heartbeat quickened immediately, her nipples hardening against the soft cotton of the bathrobe. Already, she craved for him to make love to her again. Slowly this time.

'So you're still alive,' he said with a warm smile when she stepped out onto the veranda. 'I was just about to come in and check. Come on. Sit down. I'll get you a glass of wine, and top up mine at the same time. There were a couple of bottles of white already chilled in the fridge with a welcome note on them. And a couple of bottles of red in the cupboard above.'

'They'd be the four complimentary ones that came with the holiday package,' she said as she sat down at the white wrought-iron table and leant back, trying to relax.

A laughable exercise.

'You must have been tired after your long drive

up here,' Daniel said on his return. 'Feeling better now?'

Their eyes met as he handed her the wine. 'Much,' was all she could manage.

The darkening sky suddenly lit up with a sheet of lightning, a loud clap of thunder only a second behind.

'It's going to pour down any minute,' Daniel said, and settled himself back in the chair on the other side of the table. 'I love watching rain, don't you?'

'When I get the chance,' she replied, and took a sip of the chilled wine. 'What is this, a Verdelho?'

'Spot-on. From the Hunter Valley, of course. I read the label. It's damned good. We'll have to go round some of the local vineyards tomorrow and buy some wine.'

'All right,' she agreed. She supposed they couldn't stay in this room doing nothing but make love for the next four days and nights. Though she wouldn't have minded.

'Here comes the rain,' he said excitedly as large drops began falling on the colour-bond roof.

She found herself staring at his suddenly boyish face and wondering what kind of man he might have been if his father hadn't betrayed his mother. Would he have still become the love 'em and leave 'em type? Or would he have wanted marriage and children?

At least Gary had wanted marriage and children. No doubt he was already planning to marry his PA, whereas what was *she* doing? Wasting some more of her life on a man who would never give her what she wanted.

Daniel glanced over at her.

'You're thinking,' he said, his dark eyes glittering. 'Nothing good comes of thinking too much. Why don't you come over here? Bring your wine with you.'

It was close to what she'd thought about doing, sitting on his lap, making loving small talk and sipping wine together. But not quite.

Within no time Daniel put his glass down, his right hand slipping inside the top of her robe.

'I love your breasts,' he murmured as he teased her already erect nipples into points of the most exquisite sensitivity. When he pinched one of them, some of Charlotte's wine spilt into her lap.

He took the glass from her hand and put it down before returning his attention to her burning nipples, covering her left ear with his mouth at the same time and blowing softly inside.

'Daniel,' she choked out pleadingly as she squirmed against him.

'Tell me what you want,' he replied in that low, sexy voice which thrilled her.

Daniel seemed to like talking when he made love, liked complimenting and commanding her, liked making her give voice to her desires.

'You,' she groaned.

'Out here?'

'Yes,' she answered shakily.

Within no time he'd twisted her round. The air was thick, the storm about to break in earnest.

Lightning lit up the dark sky as he entered her, his hands gripping her hips once he was safely inside and pulling her back down onto him. The breath she was holding rushed from her lungs, her moan of pleasure silenced by another crash of thunder.

'Good?' he asked huskily.

Charlotte could only nod, emotion welling up within her.

I love you, she longed to say. But did not dare. Instead, she cupped his face with her hands and kissed him. Not wildly, but slowly and sensuously. She licked his lips. Sucked on the tip of his tongue. Teased the roof of his mouth with her own tongue, all the things he'd done to her.

The sudden sound of a door banging had her head jerking up, her eyes darting nervously around.

'You...you don't think someone could walk round and see us, do you?' Their veranda was reasonably private, but overlooked the extensive grounds, with several paths winding their way through the lawns and gardens.

'Not in this storm,' he reassured her. 'Everyone will be staying safely indoors.'

The rain was coming down heavily now, beating noisily against the roof.

He cupped her face and kissed *her* this time, showing her she still had a lot to learn. She whimpered when he stopped.

'I think we can dispense with this, don't you?' he murmured, undoing the sash on her robe.

Charlotte's head spun as he slowly pushed it back

off her shoulders till it fell down her arms, leaving her totally naked.

The air, cooler now with the rain, made her shiver, goose pimples breaking out all over her skin.

'I hate wasting wine,' he said, and, picking up his glass, trickled the rest of the contents over one of her throbbing breasts. She was still gasping when he picked up her glass and doused the other breast. When he leant forward and licked at her wet nipples, her gasps swiftly turned to groans. She started rocking back and forth on him, creating even more electric sensations than what was happening with her breasts.

'Yes,' he urged when she pressed her toes down and used them to lever her body up and down. He grabbed her hips and helped her, pushing her body upwards then pulling her back down onto him.

'Yes,' he ground out. 'Yes. That's the way, my darling. Aaah…'

Was it his hotly delivered endearment which tumbled her over the edge? Or his own flesh exploding within her?

Whatever, she came with a rush, bringing her wild ride to an abrupt halt. Her spasms froze her mid-movement, her mouth falling open as her head tipped back, her lungs dragging in much-needed air.

For a few seconds she just shook. And then she started dissolving around him. Disintegrating, really. She sank back down onto his lap, her head now falling forward. His arms moved to wrap around her, holding her close. Only then did she hear his breathing, which was even more ragged than her own.

Charlotte stayed that way for a long time, with no sense of time, or place. She was just there, all soft and sated and spent.

The ringing of her cellphone dragged her back to partial reality.

She groaned. Why, oh, why did phones ring at the most inopportune time?

'Don't answer it,' Daniel muttered, his arms tightening around her.

For about thirty seconds she obeyed him, wanting to do nothing but wallow in the comforting cocoon of his body. But the phone didn't stop, forcing her further out of her dream world and evoking anxious thoughts.

Not many people had her mobile number. Work. Her parents. Louise. It wouldn't be work, she reasoned logically. Which left her parents or Louise.

Charlotte couldn't imagine her parents ringing her on the first night of her supposed honeymoon, not unless it was an emergency. She hoped and prayed they hadn't had an accident driving home today. She couldn't bear it if anything had happened to her parents.

'I have to answer it,' she said at last. If it was Louise, wanting to gossip, she was going to kill her.

'If you must,' Daniel said, pulling the robe gently up onto her shoulders then lifting her even more gently off him. Charlotte threw him a slightly embarrassed smile before wrapping the robe around herself and dashing inside.

Her still ringing phone was resting just inside her carry-all, which she'd dropped on the small writing desk in the corner. Scooping it up, she pressed the button then put the tiny pink instrument to her ear.

'Yes?' she said anxiously.

'It's me, Charlotte. Louise.'

'Louise. I think I'm going to kill you.'

'Did I interrupt something? Oh, dear, I'm so sorry. But I knew you'd want to hear my news.'

'What news?' Charlotte said wearily.

'You'll never guess.'

'Then I suggest you just tell me.'

Daniel was thoughtful as he sipped his wine and waited for Charlotte to return.

Their lovemaking since arriving here, he realised, had been different from the previous night. More intense.

In some ways, the sex was more exciting. Mind-blowing, really. But there was an air of wild desperation about Charlotte that bothered him.

Especially just now…

Daniel frowned. Just how far could he have pushed that episode? Was it *love* making her more co-operative and daring?

Daniel worried that he might not be helping his cause. He vowed to cool it a little, get back to making love more tenderly, and behind closed doors. He wanted her to learn to love him.

All his worries and resolves were momentarily forgotten when Charlotte walked back out onto the veranda, the robe now firmly sashed around her. She didn't return to his lap, but slumped down on the other chair, on the other side of the table.

'Is there anything wrong?' he asked.

'No, no, nothing wrong. That was Louise. She and Brad are engaged. She finally decided to marry him.'

'Brad will be thrilled. So why are *you* upset?'

'I'm not upset,' she denied. 'I'm very happy for them both.'

She didn't look happy. She looked sad. Daniel couldn't stand her looking sad.

She glanced over at him, her expression almost bitter. 'She said it was because of something *I* said.'

'And what was that?'

Charlotte shrugged disconsolately. 'I told her I couldn't use men as she used Brad. Apparently, it set Louise thinking. She said she realised she *did* love Brad, and that if she didn't marry him she'd really regret it. So today she told him she loved him and said yes, she would marry him. They're going out to celebrate tonight.'

'I'm pleased for them. Though they are an odd match.'

'Maybe, but Brad truly loves Louise,' she said.

Daniel began to see why this news might upset Charlotte. Her best friend was getting married, whereas she'd just been jilted. Her best friend had a man who truly loved her whereas all she'd ever had were men like Dwayne and Gary.

Till now.

He'd been going to wait a lot longer before telling her he loved her, but clearly the time had come.

'You *are* upset,' he said gently. 'It doesn't take a

genius to know why. But Charlotte, you are a beautiful, sexy girl, with a sweet and loving soul. Dwayne and Gary were both fools. Let me tell you that—'

'Don't you dare say that there's someone out there who'll truly love me one day, Daniel,' she snapped, jumping to her feet and whirling to face him. 'Don't you dare. What would you know about love, anyway? You've never been in love. You don't know what it's like to love someone and not be loved back. It…it breaks your heart. It… Oh…' she groaned, and burst into tears.

Daniel was on his feet in an instant, reaching forward in an attempt to draw her into his arms.

But she wrenched away from him, dashing the tears from her eyes as she staggered back a step.

'No, no more!' she proclaimed, clutching the robe up around her neck. 'No more tears. And no more of this. I can't bear it. It's stupid and futile. I'm going inside to get dressed,' she said feverishly. 'And then I'll be driving back to Sydney.' And she began to run inside.

Daniel dashed after her, grabbing her by the shoulders and spinning her round. Their eyes clashed, hers flashing with bitter resentment, his darkly desperate.

'I wasn't going to say that there was someone out there who would truly love you one day. I was going to say that there's someone right *here* who truly loves you right *now*!'

Charlotte stared up at him for a moment, stunned. But her shock was swiftly replaced by anger.

'I don't believe you! You're lying!'

'I have no reason to lie, Charlotte. I *love* you.'

'No,' she said, shaking her head at him. *'No!'*

Things like this didn't happen to her. Guys dumped her. Rejected her. Jilted her. *Used* her.

Daniel was just lying to get her to stay, so that he could keep on sleeping with her, which she'd been only too willing to let him do.

'I *do* love you,' he insisted. 'The only reason I didn't tell you earlier was because I was worried you wouldn't believe me. I wanted to give you time to get over Gary.'

'I was over Gary in a heartbeat,' she told him, then wished she hadn't when she saw the gleam of triumph in his eyes.

'That's because you fell in love with me,' he said, pulling her forcefully back into his arms. 'You did, didn't you? Admit it. Don't lie to me.'

'So what if I did?' she threw up at him. 'What good will it do me?'

She watched, amazed, when his head tipped back in a gesture that smacked of raw relief. 'Thank you, God.'

When his eyes returned to her they were no longer desperate, or distressed. Just very determined.

'No more nonsense, then. You love me. I love you. We'll get married for real next time.'

Charlotte's mouth dropped open. 'But you told me you were allergic to marriage!'

'You cured me.'

'How very convenient.'

'Don't be cynical. It doesn't suit you. You know I love you. You know it. In your heart.'

Maybe. But her heart had always steered her wrong. Both Dwayne and Gary had claimed to love her and they had both betrayed her. She had to listen to her head this time. 'I think you're saying what you know I want you to say.'

His face showed frustration. 'What do I have to do to convince you? I'm asking you to marry me. As soon as it can be arranged.'

'And how soon can a divorce be arranged, Daniel? I've heard you have some very speedy ones in America. You won't even have to pay for a lawyer!'

'I won't go back to America. I mean, I will temporarily. I'll have to wind things up there. But I'll come back and marry you here. We'll raise our children here.'

'Our…our children?' Her heart wobbled. He was promising her children as well?

'Of course. When true love strikes, a man changes his mind about a lot of things. I want to have children with you, my darling. I thought that was what you wanted, too.'

'I…I do. I just… Oh, Daniel, it's so hard to find trust after you've been hurt as many times as I've been hurt.'

'I know,' he said, holding her closer and stroking her hair. 'I know. Truly. But trust will come with time. You wait and see.'

She wasn't so sure. Time had often been her enemy. Would Daniel still love her when he went back to America? Were his feelings an illusion, as Gary's had been? She didn't doubt he thought he was in love with her. But male love was so often based on nothing but sex. He didn't really know her, did he?

'Tell me you love me,' he demanded. 'Go on. Tell me.'

'I love you,' she choked out with far too much feeling. Now he'd know she was crazy about him.

'And you'll marry me?'

'Please don't ask me that,' she said, pulling back far enough to look up at him. 'Not yet. It's too quick. Try to understand, Daniel. I mean, you…you might go home and change your mind and…and…'

'I won't change my mind.' His handsome face was quite serious, his eyes strong.

'I can't think straight when I'm in your arms.'

'Good.' He kissed her then, a long, seductive kiss that left her reeling.

'Now I'm asking you again,' he murmured against her mouth. 'Will you marry me?'

Charlotte stiffened her spine, and her resolve. 'I told you. *No,*' she repeated, feeling quite proud of herself. 'Not yet.'

'How long do I have to wait?'

'I don't know.'

'For pity's sake, Charlotte, I thought you were dying to get married and have kids. You're not getting any younger, you know, and neither am I!'

Charlotte could appreciate the logic in this, but she was past acting like some desperate. She'd been there, done that, and she wasn't going along that road again. It was clear men didn't respect women who fell in with their plans too easily. She wanted Daniel's respect as much as she wanted his love.

'I'm not going to be bullied into saying yes just because I love you. Marriage is a very big step for two people who've only known each other for a few days. Ask me again in a month.'

'A month! I'll probably be back in LA in a month!'

Charlotte refused to be swayed. 'You can ask me when you return to Sydney, then,' she said. 'I refuse to be proposed to by email, or by phone. I will want to see you face to face. With a ring in your hand.'

He looked totally exasperated for a few seconds. But then the clouds cleared from his face and he smiled. 'Fair enough. I can wait that long, provided we spend every minute of every day I have left here in Australia with each other.'

'I have to go back to work next week.'

He sighed. 'OK. Every minute of every day *this* week. And every minute of every night *next* week,' he amended. 'Is that a deal?'

'I suppose so.' See, Charlotte? It sounds as if all he's interested in is sex.

'Another thing. When I get back from LA I think we should start trying for a baby.'

'What? You *want* me to get pregnant?'

'The sooner the better. Then you'll know I'm serious.'

'But I can't have a baby without being married!' she protested. 'Mum and Dad will have a pink fit.'

'Have you forgotten? They think we're already married. We were married yesterday.'

'But we weren't. Not really.'

'*We* know that,' he said, 'but *they* don't know that.

My plan is that we'll get married quietly as soon as possible after you say yes. Hopefully, you'll say yes before you become pregnant. I'd like to think you're not just marrying me because I'm the father of your child. Of course, that does leave your folks thinking your name is Mrs Cantrell, which is something I couldn't stand. So then we tell your parents the truth. But they love you, and they seemed to love me when they met me. They'll accept it.'

Charlotte had to laugh. Because they probably would. 'You're arrogant and ruthless when you want something, aren't you?'

'No. I'm ruthless when I love someone. And I love you, Charlotte Gale.'

Charlotte couldn't help thrilling to his declaration. But she needed more convincing.

'What is it that you love about me?'

'I love it that you would ask such a question,' he said, and scooped her up into his arms.

Charlotte tried to keep her head as he carried her inside and lowered her down onto the bed. 'That's no answer,' she said, sounding far too breathless.

'Nothing I say at this moment would satisfy you, my darling,' he said as he began undressing her. 'Let me concentrate on the one area where I can.'

'You won't change my mind with sex, you know.'

His smile carried far too much confidence for her liking. 'Probably not,' he murmured, his lips busily making their way down her already tense body. 'But a man can try, can't he?'

CHAPTER NINETEEN

'THAT'S my boarding call,' Daniel said.

'Yes, I heard it,' Charlotte replied, struggling for composure. The moment she'd been dreading had finally arrived.

The past two weeks had gone far too quickly. The days up at the Hunter Valley had been incredible. Like a real honeymoon. They'd only left the room for breakfast and the occasional swim. Dinner was always ordered from Room Service. They hadn't made it round to the wineries till the morning they checked out.

The ten days since their return to Sydney had been just as wonderful, despite Charlotte having to return to work. Somehow, being away from Daniel during the day made the time spent with him each evening all the sweeter. He'd taken her home to his sister's place for dinner a couple of evenings. And they'd gone out with Brad and Louise, once to the movies and another time to a club. But most evenings they'd spent alone, making love and talking endlessly, with Daniel really opening up to her about his life.

She'd been startled to learn just how rich he was, but not at all unhappy. How could she be unhappy about his having the means to throw up his job in America and come back to her?

That was his plan, to be back with her as soon as possible.

Charlotte had been happy with this plan, in principle, but now that the moment was here she felt nothing but dismay. And panic. What if he never came back?

'I don't have to get on that plane, Charlotte,' he said, his eyes searching hers. 'Just give me the nod and I'll cancel my flight.'

Charlotte swallowed. How easy it would be to just say yes. Cancel it. Stay with me. But he had to go back some time, logic told her. It might as well be today. He'd already delayed his flight till the Sunday so that she didn't have to take a day off work to see him off. Any further delay would make his going all the harder.

She was grateful, however, that Brad and Louise were able to be here with her. Without them, she might have broken down and begged him to stay. This way, she had to keep herself together. Louise still didn't seem convinced that Daniel was the real deal. Brad was the only one to totally approve of their whirlwind romance. Oh, and Daniel's sister, Beth. She seemed to be all for them both, which was some comfort.

Charlotte shook her head.

'You're not going to cry, are you?' Daniel asked, squeezing her hand, the one that was now bare of all rings. She'd finally mailed Gary's ring back to him, and put the wedding ring in a drawer.

'No, no. I'll be fine,' she choked out. 'Just promise

to call me as soon as you arrive. It doesn't matter what time it is here.'

'I don't think she should stay and watch the plane go,' Daniel advised Louise and Brad. 'I think you should take her away right now. Go on. Off you go.'

'Aren't you going to kiss me goodbye?' she asked plaintively.

'I'm much better at kissing hello,' he said. 'So no, I'm not going to kiss you goodbye, because this isn't goodbye. Just *au revoir*. Brad,' he said, giving Brad a sharp nod in the direction of the exits.

'Right, mate. Come on, Charlotte. Time to go.'

Charlotte threw Louise an anguished look. But she wasn't getting too much sympathy there. Louise took her arm on one side, with Brad on the other. One last desperate glance over her shoulder caught a glimpse of Daniel heading for the boarding gate. But then she lost sight of him as a group of people moved to block her view.

He was gone.

She didn't get very far before her chin began to quiver.

Her suddenly jelly-like legs only carried her a few more steps before she burst into tears. Walking farther was out of the question. She just wanted to sink to the ground right where she was and cry and cry.

'I knew something like this was going to happen,' Louise muttered as she dragged her distraught friend over to a nearby row of seats. Charlotte collapsed into one of them, her head dropping into her hands, her shoulders shaking.

'There, there, honey,' Louise said as she patted

Charlotte's back. 'You'll be fine once he calls. He's not gone for good. I'm sure he loves you. I've just been a silly, cynical cow thinking otherwise.'

'No, *I'm* the silly, cynical cow!' Charlotte burst out, her tear-stained face jerking up. 'He told me he loved me. He asked me to marry him. And all I could say was not yet. I miss him so much already. I'd give anything in the world to go back in time and tell him that I don't want him to go. Oh, Louise, what have I done?'

New tears welled up and her head dropped back into her hands. So she didn't see Daniel walk slowly towards her.

Louise did, however, her mouth dropping open.

Daniel put his fingers to his lips in a shushing gesture. Louise's eyes swung to Brad, who was grinning.

Thank goodness, she thought as she quietly stood up and gave her seat to Daniel, who sat and slid his arm across Charlotte's still trembling shoulders.

'You promised not to cry,' he said softly.

Charlotte's head whipped up, her sodden eyes flinging wide with shock and joy. 'Daniel!' she cried. 'You came back.'

He smiled. 'My shortest plane flight ever. I didn't even get to my seat.'

Daniel reached to wipe the tears from her cheeks. 'I just couldn't bear to leave you, my darling.'

'Oh, Daniel!'

'When I do go—and I will have to at some time to tie things up in the States—would you quit your job and come with me?'

'In a heartbeat.'

'And if I asked you again right now to marry me, what would you say?'

She smiled through her tears. 'You really have to ask me that?'

'Yes, I do.' And he drew a ring box out of his pocket and flipped it open. 'I want to put this on your finger before you change your mind.'

Charlotte stared down at the huge diamond solitaire and tried not to cry.

'I bought it one day whilst you were at work,' he added. 'I wanted to always have it at the ready, if and when the opportunity came to ask you again. I hope you like it.'

'I love it. But…but I want us to tell my parents as soon as possible.'

'Charlotte, I'll drive up with you and we'll explain everything together. I'm sure your mum and dad will understand. All they ever wanted was for their darling little girl to be happy. And you are happy, aren't you?'

Her eyes flooded anew with happiness.

He smiled, and slipped the ring on her finger.

It was a perfect fit. Just as they were.

Daniel sighed a truly happy sigh of his own. 'Now I think it's time for that hello kiss.'

ONE NIGHT AT PARENGA

by

Robyn Donald

Robyn Donald can't remember not being able to read, and will be eternally grateful to the local farmers who carefully avoided her on a dusty country road as she read her way to and from school, transported to places and times far away from her small village in Northland, New Zealand. Growing up fed her habit; as well as training as a teacher, marrying and raising two children, she discovered the delights of romances and read them voraciously, especially enjoying the ones written by New Zealand writers. So much so, that one day she decided to write one herself. Writing soon grew to be as much of a delight as reading – although infinitely more challenging – and when eventually her first book was accepted by Mills & Boon she felt she'd arrived home. She still lives in a small town in Northland with her family close by, using the landscape as a setting for much of her work. Her life is enriched by the friends she's made among writers and readers, and complicated by a determined corgi called Buster who is convinced that blackbirds are evil entities. Her greatest hobby is still reading, with travelling a very close second.

Don't miss Robyn Donald's exciting new novel, *Innocent Mistress, Royal Wife*, available in January 2009 from Mills & Boon® Modern™.

PROLOGUE

'SO THERE'S nothing left,' Sorrel Maitland said almost soundlessly, her face a beautiful mask. New Zealand was a long way from New York, and she'd lived in the States for almost eight years, yet her low voice still carried the accent of her birth country.

The lawyer directed a keen glance at her, relieved when the huge gold-green eyes remained dry and tearless. 'Very little, I'm afraid.'

He saw her brace herself.

She said huskily, 'It was—a lot of money to lose. What happened to it?'

'It appears your father's a gambler, and that's a quick, easy way to lose money.' He glanced down at the documents on his desk. The several million Sorrel Maitland had earned over the past years had slipped through her father's fingers as easily as water cupped in a hand.

She scanned the figures he'd given her and asked a couple of pertinent questions.

Brains as well as beauty, he decided after he'd answered, admiring the magnificent red-brown sweep of hair pulled back in a sleek, sophisticated chignon.

Family loyalty could cause enormous problems, and sometimes outright disasters like this one. If she'd come to him at the start of her career he'd have warned her that parents are rarely the best protectors of their children's earnings, but what girl of eighteen would have believed that?

5

'I wish I had better news to give you,' he said.

He was even sorrier to shatter her illusions. It was difficult to feel much sympathy over the lost earnings, massive though they were. Although the woman seated on the other side of the desk wasn't one of the top ten supermodels, she was famous enough, and as she was only in her mid-twenties she had a few years yet to build up another nest egg.

Broken trust was another thing entirely.

He said, 'If gambling addicts don't get help they subordinate everything—honesty, faith, the people they love—to the compulsion. An alcoholic needs support and a huge amount of will-power to overcome the need to drink, and it's the same for a gambling addiction. Some people won't admit to a problem, and others try, but can't get it under control.'

Almost noiselessly she said, 'I knew he enjoyed a flutter at the casino, and that he bet on horses, but—' She stopped, then finished helplessly, 'I had no idea.'

'Usually the families don't, until something like this happens.' He leaned forward. 'Ms Maitland, you must put your affairs in other hands.'

'I will. I know you and your staff have put in impossibly long hours to untangle my father's and my affairs,' she said quietly, her voice even and unemotional. 'Thank you for working so hard.'

'You're very welcome,' he said awkwardly. 'If there's any advice I can give, all you have to do is ask.'

Tall and impossibly elegant, she rose in a fluid motion and held out her hand. The legendary smile lit up her face, its slow radiance barely dimmed.

'You're very kind, but I know what to do now.'

Afterwards he wondered why he'd shaken her hand so carefully—as though she might break. However, her grip had been steady and firm, only the chill of her long fingers revealing the turmoil behind the smooth, immaculately made-up features and the formal words.

A class act, he thought as he closed the door of his office behind her.

An almost bankrupt class act.

In the apartment she'd shared with her father, Sorrel took off her gloves and walked across to the window to stare down at the snow-covered spread of Central Park.

Swivelling away, she pressed the heels of her hands into her burning eyes, holding the tears back until coloured sparks danced against her lids. In the space of a month her life had splintered, its jagged fragments impossible to reassemble.

First her beloved godmother's death in New Zealand, and hard on that shock had come the stroke that had imprisoned her father in the wreckage of his own body. Cynthia's house, Parenga, was empty, but her father was still alive.

If you could call his existence living.

Sorrel dropped her hands and blinked for several moments to bring the world into focus. A rapid glance at her watch told her she had half an hour before it was time to go back to the very expensive nursing home that would be Nigel Maitland's home for the foreseeable future.

But, as one of the things he'd failed to do was set up medical insurance for himself, she had to ring her agent first.

'Louise,' she said briskly. 'About the Founiere offer—I'll take it.'

Louise gave a small, hastily silenced shriek. 'Honey,

that's great news. Belle Sandford got her start in one of their campaigns, and I just heard today she's a cert for an Oscar nomination. Founiere are a fabulous firm for publicity—they're really proud of their reputation for exotic good taste.'

'Or tasteful exotica,' Sorrel said drily, thinking that *erotica* was a much better word for the perfume campaigns run by the world-famous cosmetic firm.

Her super-sharp agent snorted. 'Prissy, prissy, prissy, Sorrel! If you still think Founiere do soft porn, what changed your mind?'

The money from that campaign would keep her father in the clinic. Not that she was going to tell Louise that—the fewer people who knew about her situation the better.

'I just thought it might be fun—and different.' Her voice sounded thin and squeezed of emotion. She swallowed and forced a note of enthusiasm into her words. 'And, as you say, it might lead to—other things.'

'OK.' Louise's voice altered. 'I'm really glad you've made this decision—it's probably your last chance with Founiere. You're still gorgeous, of course, but I'd be failing as your agent if I didn't warn you that there are plenty ready to take your place.'

'A whole world of beautiful, hungry sixteen-year-olds,' Sorrel said lightly. 'It's all right, Louise, I know the life expectancy of models.'

'Well, you've got a few years in hand yet,' Louise reassured her. 'You take care, now. I'll be in touch.'

Sorrel hung up and looked around the apartment. It would have to go. Fortunately she had no emotional ties to the place—it had been her father's choice.

In the kitchen she poured a glass of water and drank it down before walking into the room her father called

his office. Like him, it was organised and tidy; he'd
kept the details of all his debts with compulsive neat-
ness.

She tried to reconcile the father she'd known and
loved all her life with the man who'd stripped her of
nearly every cent to feed his gambling habit, but her
brain couldn't cope.

Whatever, he was her father and he loved her.
Perhaps more important, he needed her; although he
could only move one eyelid, the nurses said his vital
signs improved when she came in and deteriorated
when she left. She had to find the money to pay for his
care until…

'Until he gets better,' she said sturdily, knowing that
he'd almost certainly never improve.

Her vital, energetic, vigorous father had nothing but
misery to look forward to. So, if keeping him comfortable and cared for meant posing half-naked in a
series of 'tasteful' perfume ads, she'd do it.

She couldn't afford the luxury of finer feelings.

CHAPTER ONE

LUKE HARDCASTLE strode across the forecourt outside Waimanu homestead, black brows drawing together in his hard, handsome face as his housekeeper looked at him with something like appeal. With her was the driver of a truck from the local carriers, and by her stance she appeared to be arguing with him.

'What's the problem?' Luke demanded.

Both turned to him with evident relief, speaking at the same time. 'Penn,' he decided, and the driver fell silent.

His housekeeper shot a disparaging look at the man. 'He says he has a box for Sorrel Maitland at Parenga, and I'm trying to tell him she doesn't live there.' She explained as though to a child, 'The Bannings rented the house for two years after Mrs Copestake died, but they shifted to Taupo a couple of weeks ago. Parenga's empty now.'

The driver said bluntly, 'I've been into Parenga and seen that nobody's living there now, but the directions on the box are plain—Sorrel Maitland, Parenga, Hardcastle Road—and that's where I have to leave it.'

Luke resisted the fierce clamour of sensation roaring through his big body. God, was it never going to end?

For ten years Sorrel had haunted him, filling him with frustration and anger. He'd despised himself for following her progress through the raffish world she'd made her own, relieved when the alluring, sexy photographs and the endless, titillating allusions in gossip columns had stopped two years ago, after hints of a marriage, of drug abuse, of pregnancy.

It had almost been a relief to think of her as married.

Nevertheless, he couldn't prevent a harsh note of authority to his voice. 'Can't you take it back to the depot until it's collected?'

In an aggrieved tone the driver told him, 'I've already rung the boss, but he says we haven't got the space to keep it until this Sorrel Maitland turns up. And I can't just dump it at Parenga—as far as I can see there's no place to store it out of the weather. Anyway, someone's got to sign for it.'

Crisply Luke said, 'I've got a key to Parenga—I'll follow you back there and we'll put it in the house.' From the corner of his eye he saw his housekeeper's mouth open. 'Thank you, Penn.'

She flushed a little, nodding before walking stiff-backed through the door and closing it with a slight bang behind her. Luke swung into his Land Rover and headed off behind the truck.

Was Sorrel planning to live in the house her god-mother had left her?

His mouth sketched a cold smile. Not if he had any say in it.

The Sorrel with whom he'd shared a magical, innocent summer years before was long gone, transformed into the woman whose face had smiled with sultry aloofness in hundreds of magazines, finally starring in a perfume campaign that had raised eyebrows world-wide.

Sometimes Luke dreamed he was the man she was looking at, her slanted, sleepy eyes half closed in slumbrous invitation, her mouth parted and expectant.

Despising himself for the jolt of pure lust that tightened every muscle, he turned the car onto the bridge at Parenga and swore as he took the corner too fast. The Land Rover coped, of course, clattering over the sideless wooden decking, but the lapse of concentration stung.

On the night before her eighteenth birthday she'd gazed up at him with exactly that smile. Goaded by the lash of a desire that had grown unbidden day after day, he'd kissed her.

And nothing had ever been the same since.

He'd known then that he had to get rid of Sorrel, and with ruthless determination he'd done it; he didn't regret his actions for a moment, even though she still had the power to fill his dreams with thwarted, hungry passion.

So was she bringing the husband with her, or had she left him? Was there a husband? The fact that she was still Sorrel Maitland indicated not, but plenty of women kept their maiden name.

Hell, what did he care?

He pulled up on the gravel forecourt behind the truck. Although a man came in twice a month to keep the place tidy, the big Edwardian house where he'd been born dreamed lonely, wistful dreams in a garden clouded by solitude.

The waiting driver thrust his clipboard at him. 'I know who you are, and so does the boss, but rules are rules. We need to prove delivery.'

Luke scrawled a signature along the bottom of the form. 'How big is this box?'

'Size of a tea chest,' the driver said cheerfully. 'Not too heavy, though. Probably clothes. She's a model, isn't she, Sorrel Maitland?'

There was nothing leering or suggestive about his

words or tone, but Luke had to deliberately rein in a brusque reply. 'She used to be,' he said neutrally.

The truck driver grinned. 'Must be a looker, then.' Abashed by the swift blue glitter in Luke's grey gaze, he hastily returned the clipboard to the cab of his truck, saying too heartily, 'Well, we'd better get this inside.'

Later that night Luke stood at the window of his sitting room, icy eyes seeing nothing of the river estuary below the wide stretch of lawn and garden.

On the edge of his vision glimmered the provocative, sophisticated smile he'd seen more times than he could count. Just to remind himself of what she was, he'd looked the magazine out when he'd come in after a hard afternoon drafting cattle—working off, he admitted reluctantly, the chaotic emotions caused by the prospect of Sorrel's return.

On the cover she was elegant and provocative in the sort of gown women wore to balls—a sensuous slither of amber silk; inside, the advertisement revealed a different Sorrel. With an exclamation of disgust Luke picked up his untouched glass of whisky.

Sometimes he thought he'd never be able to chisel that bloody picture out of his brain. Oh, it was tasteful and beautiful, brilliantly lit and photographed, air-brushed to perfection…and sinfully erotic. Two gleaming, apparently naked bodies pressed in a sultry embrace, the man's hand almost touching the woman's breast as he gazed possessively into eyes that beckoned with a gleaming, sensuous promise, pale eyes with soft gold-green centres set off by a thin, stark rim the colour of black jade.

Cat's eyes, set on a slant, smoky with the promise of passion…

Whisky slid with raw impact down Luke's throat. He set the half-empty glass in his hand on the coffee table with a sharp clink. Drinking wouldn't help; he'd seen what it had done to his father.

Sorrel's several well-publicised affairs—not to mention one definite engagement and a possible marriage—would have tarnished that innocence. The break-up of her engagement had been splashed across newspapers and magazines, the discarded lover blurting his pain to whoever would listen. Hailed as the singer/songwriter of the decade, he'd then used his heartbreak to produce his next album—the best he'd ever done, critics had raved.

Luke didn't give a damn about the man's songs, the broken engagement, or Sorrel's love life. He had accounts to check and businesses to see to.

Scooping up the magazine with its sexy, provocative advertisement, he carried it out of the room.

He'd almost reached the office when his housekeeper emerged from the kitchen, smiling, a little cautious. 'I'm off,' she said, her glance dropping for a puzzled moment to the magazine in his hand.

'Goodnight.' He nodded without breaking his stride, and closed the office door behind him with a decisive click before firing the magazine into the rubbish bin.

He had no idea why he'd kept it. Wilful stupidity, and an itch he'd refused to scratch once and wasn't going anywhere near again.

At fifteen, the day his young, greedy stepmother had tried to seduce him, he'd vowed he wasn't going to be like his father, letting a beautiful face and tantalising body rip his heart out. No woman was ever going to acquire that much power over him.

His father's early death, followed by the discovery

of a will he'd been seduced into making during one of his drunken bouts of self-pity, had reinforced Luke's determination to keep that vow.

Luke considered himself a normal man with normal needs, needs he'd never had any problem satisfying. He'd sometimes been smugly sure of himself, he admitted, remembering a lover who'd complained that so much charm was indecent and unfair. He'd kissed her out of her sulks, but he knew the worth of his power, and he exerted it with all the skill and subtlety he could command. Although he enjoyed women, finding intense pleasure in their sleek bodies, he'd never let one get under his skin.

Especially not Sorrel, who'd spent every school holiday at Parenga after he'd sold the house to her godmother. Very tall, and with the gangly awkwardness of a young filly, she'd been a bashful presence on the edge of his life, inconspicuous except for a startling swathe of chestnut hair and those huge, innocent eyes. She'd roused his inherent protectiveness and a sort of distant affection, but most of the time he'd been too busy dealing with the aftermath of his father's early, disillusioned death to notice her much.

And then, when he was twenty-five and she a few weeks short of her eighteenth birthday, she'd arrived for the summer holidays.

Luke bent to switch the computer on, and while it hummed and muttered into action he frowned at the screen. Somehow the schoolgirl Sorrel had metamorphosed into a serenely graceful creature, all clean lines and shy sweetness, with an unstudied allure more exciting than anything he'd ever experienced.

Later Luke had discovered that as a Christmas gift Cynthia had paid for a modelling course. At the time he'd taken one stunned look at her and that smug confidence in his ability to withstand any woman had splintered, replaced by an onslaught of primitive hunger that had eaten through his self-possession with taunting ease.

For the first time he'd understood what had persuaded his father to make two disastrous marriages.

Lips compressed in a stony face, he looked around his office. Things were different now—he was no longer the young man who'd been so cockily sure of himself, and she was certainly nothing like the lovely kid who'd blushed every time she set eyes on him.

'So who cares if Sorrel Maitland is coming back?' he said aloud, his voice harsh in the silent room.

He sat down at the computer desk and called up a file, long fingers drumming impatiently on the desktop. Sometimes he wondered whether he'd have reacted so violently to Sorrel if he hadn't been caught up in a vicious legal battle with a woman who'd borne a superficial resemblance to the much younger girl.

Furious when he'd contemptuously rejected her, his stepmother had done her best to cheat him out of Waimanu, his only inheritance from his father—unless you counted the lesson that love led to pain and despair. It had taken expensive lawyers and a court case to force her to accept defeat, and it had cost Luke a vast amount of money—money he'd needed to get Waimanu on its feet again.

Yet, in spite of that, over the four weeks of that long-ago summer he'd ignored every instinct, every mental warning. In the end neither his strength of will nor his coldly incisive brain had been able to save him from losing control. He'd looked once too often into Sorrel's face, and he'd kissed her.

It still rubbed him raw to admit that he hadn't been able to stop himself. Without even trying, with no sensual invitation, no conscious temptation, the girl had had the power to shatter his will-power and the control that had become second nature.

And, once done, there had been no going back. One kiss, and he'd already been in too deep to trust himself. He'd lifted his head and gazed into those tilted, exotic eyes, dilating with dawning awareness, and realised with coldly deliberate pragmatism that if he didn't do something to end this he'd be yet another Hardcastle in thrall to an utterly unsuitable woman. Despising himself for his weakness, Luke had cut her ruthlessly out of his life.

And he'd been right; that demure innocence had been a lie. Her subsequent career had revealed that Sorrel was every bit as self-indulgent as his stepmother.

He stared down at the letter he'd crushed—one his secretary had left for him to sign.

One day he'd marry, but he'd choose carefully. The woman he planned to marry would be nothing like his mother and his stepmother, greedy women who'd used their sexual power to exact financial and emotional tribute.

When was Sorrel coming back?

And why?

Sorrel resisted the instinct to stamp on the brake as the corner hurtled too quickly towards her. Calling on skills long unused, she eased her foot back onto the accelerator to steer the unfamiliar station wagon around the corner.

'Country roads, city driver,' she said mockingly, and peered through the streaming windscreen. The wipers were doing their best, but nothing could cope with this downpour, and the falling dusk wasn't helping.

Shaking the mane of red-brown hair back from her face, she relaxed her hands on the wheel. She'd learned to drive on this road, and Luke had taught her well.

In a cowardly way she almost welcomed the strain of navigating New Zealand's northern peninsula through a wild early-summer storm. Concentration took the edge off a deeper tension—one that screwed her nerves tighter and tighter as she approached Waimanu, the huge cattle station that had been home to the proud dynasty of Hardcastles for over a century and a half.

'It's been ten years, for heaven's sake,' she muttered, frowning into the lashing rain. 'He's probably forgotten you.'

A sardonic smile tugging at her mouth, she man-oeuvred the vehicle around the final corner. Her breath hissed through her teeth when at last she eased onto the two-kilometre straight that marked the end of the road.

Where was Luke now? 'It doesn't matter,' she muttered. 'Just so long as he isn't here.'

He wouldn't be. Cynthia had told her he spent most of his time away from Waimanu. 'Making his fortune,' she'd said, sighing. 'He works far too hard, but you have to admire him. He's already got Waimanu back onto its feet, and he's branching out into corporate farming—not just here, either, but in Australia and other places. He'll be a very rich man very soon.'

Even at fourteen Sorrel had been woman enough to recognise Luke's formidable determination and the steely intelligence that controlled his tough ambition.

Physically he was immensely impressive. At six foot four, broad-shouldered and lean-hipped, he'd generated enough raw power to drive the North Island. Sorrel's mouth twisted wryly. All that and a face like a fallen angel.

And he'd been five inches taller than she was! No wonder she'd developed a massive crush on him. He'd represented dangerous masculinity, a darkly dominant force that had prowled through her unsophisticated dreams, scaring and thrilling her equally.

A scatter of hailstones across the windscreen shocked her out of her memories. She switched the lights to full; hidden somewhere in the tunnel of trees ahead was the abrupt entrance to Cynthia's house. Her house now, and her home for the next six months.

Why had Cynthia made that condition in her will? There would have been a good reason—her godmother hadn't been one for whims—but Sorrel would never know it now.

Tears clogging her lashes, she squinted into the shadows beneath the great pohutukawas that linked rugged branches above the car. Hundreds of years old, staunch survivors from their hoary crowns to the wiry aerial roots that hung down like alien nets, the trees warmed Sorrel's heart. Even without Cynthia to welcome her, this still felt like coming home—the only home she'd ever really had.

Halfway along the straight, her headlights caught a flash of light—the reflectors at Parenga's gateway. Sorrel slowed to ease the car between two stone pillars and then over the little bridge—

'Oh, *no!*'

This time her foot hit the brake pedal hard, forcing the vehicle to skid to a halt with its rear blocking the narrow road.

Sorrel stared at the ominous, fast-flowing sheet of

thick brown water pouring across the bridge. How deep did floodwater have to be before it could wash away a vehicle?

'Not very,' she said aloud, hands clenched on the wheel.

Surely the car could cope? On the far side, beyond the massed plantings of cherry trees that had been Cynthia's joy each spring, the roof of the house beckoned.

'I should be able to get through this,' Sorrel muttered on a released breath, remembering television commercials where vehicles churned their way through rivers and streams. But her car was a middle-aged station wagon, and what if a surge came downstream when she was halfway across?

A short blast from a horn whipped her head around as every misgiving about this venture roared back to life. Heart thumping in her ears, she closed her eyes for a second; when she opened them again the rain had snapped off.

She knew who was behind the wheel of the muddy Land Rover a few inches from her rear bumper.

I'm not ready! she thought. Insides knotting in an intolerable, unexpected tangle of panic, apprehension and sharp excitement, she watched Luke Hardcastle get out.

He strode towards her like some grim god of the storm—sable head held high, striking, hard-featured face set in a mask of uncompromising authority that didn't alter by the quiver of a muscle when he bent to look at her.

Sorrel swallowed quickly to ease a dry mouth and throat and unclenched her hands, only to find they were trembling so much she had to leave them tensely looped around the rim of the steering wheel.

Black brows snapping together, Luke gestured for her to open the window. She fumbled for the handle, eventually finding it.

'You can't go across,' he said curtly before the glass was fully down. 'It's not safe. Back out and drive along to the homestead.'

Sorrel moistened dry lips. 'The homestead? This *is* the homestead.'

Luke directed a pointed smile her way. 'Not any more. I've built a new one at the end of the road.' And when she still stared into his icy grey eyes he said caustically, 'I didn't plan to live in that caravan all my life, Sorrel.'

'Well—no, of course not.' Think of something sensible to say, she instructed her brain. 'Surely I can take the car across? It doesn't look very deep, and I can see where the edges of the bridge are.'

'It's too dangerous—the water's more than halfway up the wheels. Get going. This weather's unpredictable and there'll be more rain any minute,' he ordered, straightening up. 'I'll follow you.'

'Hang on—'

But he'd already turned and was heading back to his own vehicle. Despite her irritation at his arrogant air of command, Sorrel's eyes feasted on his tall figure with its long, easy stride. How often had she watched him like this—so absorbed in him that nothing else mattered?

Hundreds of times, she thought sardonically. But she'd grown out of her adolescent obsession, although it was infuriating to discover her mind hadn't yet communicated this to her body.

She wasn't afraid of giving herself away. The iron control she'd acquired while modelling clothes for autocratic photographers had been reinforced by the past two years of caring for her father.

Not that she regretted either modelling or nursing her father. Once she'd realised he missed her enough to stop eating whenever she was away on a shoot, she'd given up work, rented a house, and settled down to be his constant companion. And somehow, in the ruins of his life, they'd forged a deeper love that went beyond words.

By the time he'd died almost all of the money she'd earned from the Founiere campaign had been used in his care. It didn't matter; she'd do the same again if she had the chance.

She put the car into gear, ready to back out. Alarming though this wild song in her blood was, it had nothing to do with emotions. For some reason her body wanted Luke Hardcastle. It always had; it still did. But, although he stirred her sexually, she could control her response to his dark magnetism. Time had worked its magic healing, and she no longer thought she was in love with him.

'It's inconvenient,' she told herself firmly, 'but not disastrous.'

From behind she heard the thud of a door, followed by the sound of a thousand needles of rain on the roof as the skies opened again—almost as though the deluge had waited for Luke to get under cover.

Perhaps he really is a rain god, she thought half hysterically, wincing when headlights in the rear-vision mirror dazzled her, his swift, instantly cut signal to get a move on.

Stomach churning, she flicked her own lights to tell

him she understood and began to reverse out onto the road.

Across the bridge, two glowing eyes reflected back at her. She stamped on the brakes and switched the beam to high again.

On the far bank, and precariously perched in the branches of a half-submerged cherry tree, a large, rain-drenched cat opened its mouth wide and yowled.

'Baggie!' Sorrel fought with the door handle. Surely he hadn't been living rough since Cynthia's death? Jerking the handle, she heaved against the door, almost falling out when it swung open.

She recovered her balance and slammed the door before racing onto the bridge. Ignoring Luke's shout, and the water tearing at her legs, she focused on the cat her godmother had cherished.

'Sorrel, stop!'

Luke's roar shocked her to a halt. And once she stopped moving she could no longer stay upright. Fast and deep, the water yanked ruthlessly at her legs and feet, surging up past her knees. Terror clawed at her as she staggered, arms flailing, and began to fall.

From behind, two hard hands seized her shoulders, supporting her in a grip of steel while Luke positioned himself upstream and pushed her forward.

'Keep *moving*, damn you!' he snarled, half-hauling her with him towards the other side.

The water was building up fast, and, big man though he was, and superbly fit, Luke too had difficulty staying on his feet against its terrifying force. Something large and hidden struck the bridge, its impact driving up through the soles of Sorrel's sodden shoes.

'I'm moving, I'm moving,' she muttered, exerting

every ounce of strength to take the final few steps with him.

Once on land, he yanked her out of the silty red floodwater, strong arms imprisoning her against him. Low and lethal, his voice reverberated through her. 'You crazy idiot! What the hell's the matter with you?'

Sorrel jumped as a branch thudded into the decking.

For a paralysing second Luke's powerful body tensed against her. And in spite of the rain, heat burned through their damp clothes, lighting forbidden fires— fires instantly doused by Luke's savage voice as he pulled her several more steps back from the brink.

'If that branch had been any bigger it would have caught you—presuming you'd still been on your feet, that is.' He released her abruptly.

She shivered, remembering the way the water had sucked at her legs. 'I was making it until you yelled!'

'Not for long. What the hell were you were doing?' Luke demanded.

'Baggie's stuck in a tree.' She pointed urgently towards the cat, no longer yowling but still ominously close to the water. 'Luke, I couldn't let him drown.'

'That cat is more trouble than any other animal in the district,' he ground out. 'He's perfectly capable of looking after himself.'

'He's stuck,' Sorrel said indignantly. 'He'll fall in the water if I don't get him down.'

By then the rain had soaked them both and was beginning to seep with nasty persistence down the back of her neck.

Even dripping wet, Luke knew how to intimidate. His grey eyes glittered with sharp blue fire. Speaking with biting authority, he said, 'You're not going anywhere near that tree. The water's already around its trunk. All Baggie has to do is jump from that branch to one in the tree behind, and then he'll be able to reach solid ground.' He looked up quickly as another thud announced the arrival of more debris. 'Get into the house,' he commanded in a voice that revealed how close he was to losing his temper.

He groped in his pocket and dragged out a key ring. Tossing it to her, he said, 'The big old-fashioned one opens the back door. Now go!'

She met his uncompromising gaze with determination and a hint of defiance. 'After I've got Baggie. It's all right—I know he scratches. I'll be careful.'

'Why the sudden interest in the cat?'

Sorrel's chin jerked upwards as he scanned her face with narrow-eyed antagonism. 'He's Cynthia's cat!'

'Your godmother's been dead two years,' he said caustically, boldly chiselled features clamping into contemptuous distaste. 'I haven't noticed much concern for the damned animal in all that time.'

Flinching, she shot back, 'How would you know? You don't live here any more.'

And could have bitten out her tongue.

He gave her a lethal, narrow-eyed stare. 'Who told you that?'

'Cynthia,' she snapped. 'She said you were more or less permanently living in Auckland.'

With Mari O'Neill. Or was she at Waimanu too, now? Had they married? For a horrifying second Sorrel fought the exhausted urge to sit down and bawl her eyes out.

'I live here,' Luke told her flatly, 'at Waimanu.' Where I belong, his tone indicated, and where you are an outsider.

If she'd known that, would she have returned to Parenga?

Yes; she had nowhere else to go.

Apparently tired of this, he turned away, saying, 'I'll get the cat.'

To reach Baggie he'd have to walk out into the flood-waters. 'No!' Sorrel said swiftly, adding, 'I'll get him—he's my responsibility now.'

'Don't be ridiculous. I'm not going to stand here and watch you drown,' Luke said on a scornful note, and set off.

Sorrel's heart rocketed into overdrive when she noticed another branch twisting down the creek, its splin-tered branches jagged and sharp. 'Watch out!' she yelled.

He avoided it with a combination of balance, strength and lethal grace that scrambled every brain cell she possessed.

She bit onto her lower lip, only relaxing when she saw him reach the tree. As he stretched a long arm to pluck the cat from the branch, Baggie rose and with offended dignity prepared to swarm across onto the branch Luke had pointed out, from which it was a small leap to safety.

Luke grabbed him, not flinching when the cat swiped an efficient claw across his hand. Only then, honour satisfied, did Baggie settle into his arms.

When they arrived back to safety she mumbled, 'Thank you. Only—don't ever do it again, all right? I'm sorry. I really thought he was in danger.'

'In danger of pushing his luck too far,' Luke stated, putting the cat onto the ground.

'I'll take him—'

'Sorrel,' he said, his level voice more intimidating than any other man's snarled threats, 'get into the house before I lose my few remaining shreds of patience. Incredible though it might seem, I've got better things to do than stand in the rain and admire your elegant, expensively maintained body in painstaking detail.'

This time the contempt was open and forceful. She looked down, colour stinging her skin when she saw the outline of her small pointed breasts through the thin wool of her shirt.

Furious with him for being so explicit, and herself for responding so obviously, she returned scathingly, 'And I'm equally pleased to see you again, dear Luke, after all these years.'

As a retort it lost much of its effect in a shiver that tumbled the words through her teeth.

His laughter was low and humourless, as cold as the ice-grey eyes that raked her face. 'Sorry, I'm all out of warm welcomes. Get going before you develop hypothermia!'

Pulses racing in the aftermath of adrenalin overload, she turned and ran up the drive to the back door, not caring whether he followed her or stayed out in the rain.

The key turned and the door yielded to her wet hand. In the big mud-room she switched on the light, watching as Luke rummaged in a cupboard and produced an old towel with which he proceeded to give Baggie a quick, effective rubdown.

Sorrel hovered, resenting the way the light picked out the tanned skin drawn over the strong, thrusting bone structure that would make him a striking man all his life. Her stomach performed a flip, and she began to shiver. No, she thought desperately. Not now—not ever again! Not Luke.

He looked up, guarded eyes forbidding as the iron-blue gleam on a sword blade. 'Welcome back,' he drawled.

CHAPTER TWO

SORREL blurted, 'We're stuck here, aren't we? It's too dangerous to go back over the bridge.'

'True,' Luke answered, the single derisive word setting her teeth on edge.

Marooned with the last man in the world she'd choose! And her clothes and make-up—horrors, even her toothbrush!—as inaccessible as the far side of the moon.

Flushing, she said between her teeth, 'I sent a box out from America—'

'It arrived a week ago—I put it in your bedroom.'

'Thanks.' So she had clothes. She hastily wrenched her gaze from Luke's soaked torso and broad shoulders. 'You can't stay like that without getting pneumonia or rheumatism or something.'

'We'll have to improvise,' he said coolly. 'When the box arrived I deduced you'd be following it, so I rang the power authority and Telecom, only to find you'd already arranged for the utilities to be switched on. A hot shower will ward off hypothermia, which is much more likely than either pneumonia or rheumatism.'

He stooped to put a wriggling Baggie onto the floor. Sorrel's mouth dried as she noted the smooth play of muscles beneath his shirt.

Indignation burned through her. She'd been so sure she was over Luke. Darn it, sometimes she went for a week at a time without thinking of him. And it hadn't ever been anything more than a crush—and one searing kiss. Now the years she'd spent away from Parenga might just as well not have happened! One glance into his grey eyes and she'd reverted straight back to pathetic adolescence.

It could stop right there. Falling in lust with Luke would be taking a direct route to misery. He seemed to despise her, and she—well, she was going to guard her heart too well for him to break it again.

Yawning, Baggie stretched voluptuously and, with a controlled self-possession that reminded Sorrel of the other male in the room, paced across to a bowl and looked up with regal expectancy. The cat's damp black fur stuck to a sturdy, far-from-starving body. Either someone had been looking after him or he was more than capable of fending for himself.

Sorrel could hear the reluctance in her husky voice as she said, 'There are towels in the box. I'm sorry, Luke. Dashing across to rescue Baggie was foolish of me.'

'Extremely,' he told her with brutal honesty. 'No animal is worth risking your life for.'

Pitched back into adolescence again, she demanded, 'What about the horse you saved from a cyclone one Christmas holiday? You *swam* across the river to bring it back. At least I had a bridge under my feet!'

He shrugged. 'I was young and stupid. Besides, the horse would have died. Baggie was perfectly safe. He's a con artist and saw a chance to get a ride back to Waimanu without getting his feet wet.'

She parried his sardonic survey with her most aloof expression. 'It was just the shock of seeing him. After—when Cynthia died I organised the vet to come and collect him. They told me he'd been taken in by a friend, and then—well, I was busy...' Busy fulfilling her contract for the wretched Founiere campaign, busy caring for her father.

She bit her lip. 'I just assumed Baggie was safe. I had no idea *you* were looking after him.'

Luke looked at her dispassionately. Even soaking wet and bedraggled, her rare, intoxicating beauty blazed forth, intensified now by an aura of controlled, poised sensuality. Savagely dismissing the image of her in another man's arms, he decided that she'd been a hugely successful model because she appealed to men's secret fantasies and women's insecurities.

'I told the vet to leave him here,' he said abrasively. 'Why didn't you ask me if I'd take care of him? You didn't need to have him put down—'

'Put down?' Long lashes shot up to reveal darkening gold-centred eyes as she stared accusingly at him. 'Who said anything about putting him down?'

She did it very well, he thought cynically—all outrage and hurt feelings. 'That's what the vet thought you wanted him to do.'

Almost she bared her teeth at him. 'I did not! They misunderstood. I wanted him safe in the vet clinic cattery, not living rough.' Gracefully she stooped to stroke the animal, her wet clothes moulding the feminine curves of her hips and breasts.

Luke cursed silently as his body began to harden.

But although he couldn't control this consuming, primitive response, he could certainly ignore it. Noting her shiver when she straightened up, he commanded curtly, 'Get upstairs and under a shower.'

'But what about you?'

'I'll shower in the downstairs bathroom.' When she didn't move he ran his gaze over her and asked in a soft, deliberately taunting voice, 'Do you need help to take off your clothes?'

It worked.

Sorrel stiffened. 'No!'

Halfway up the stairs she realised that he'd known exactly how she'd react. All right, she thought, setting her jaw; round one to Luke.

But this wasn't going to be a battle. Because she had to stay at Parenga for six months to fulfil Cynthia's wishes, and, as Luke was apparently living right next door, she'd have to establish a friendly relationship with him.

Friendly? an interested voice inside her head asked smoothly.

Yes, friendly! she snarled back. If she decided to set up Parenga as an exclusive bed and breakfast, she couldn't afford to antagonise Luke. Not only did he have a lot of clout in Northland, but as her closest neighbour he'd have input into the District Council's deliberations.

Leaning over the balustrade, she called, 'I'll open the box and bring down some towels.'

'OK.'

She ran up the rest of the stairs and pushed open the door of her old bedroom. Although the box had already been opened, a glance revealed that the contents were still sealed. Luke, no doubt. He thought of everything.

Slow rigors moved through her while she scrabbled through its contents. They didn't seem much to represent ten years of her life, yet this was all she'd salvaged—a few clothes, some soft goods, and the clothes in the car.

Sorrel sat back on her haunches and stared across the room; a rising wind was hurling vicious bullets of rain at the window, recalling the rain on the other side of the world when she'd packed the box after her father's death. She'd been weeping, and the house in which her father had died after a two years of misery had sighed heavily as it settled around her.

Yet, grief-stricken as she was, she felt only gratitude for his death; he had longed for it passionately since the day he'd been struck down.

Her shaking fingers found the towels; she got up and carried them out of the bedroom, stopping a few paces from the doorway when she saw Luke halfway up the stairs.

'There you go,' she said, handing the huge green bath sheets over to him. 'No soap, I'm afraid.'

She felt his regard, noted the way he paused a fraction of a second before answering, 'Thank you. You're starting to go pale. Get under the shower.'

He, of course, was entirely unaffected by his dousing!

Once in the bathroom Sorrel fumbled with the buttons of her shirt, her cold fingers making it difficult. By the time she got it off the shivers had turned to shaking; she had to clench her teeth as she unzipped her trousers, stepped out of them and turned on the shower.

She could cope with living next door to Luke. She had to. She had nowhere else to go and no other assets than Parenga.

'All you need to do is stay cool and make sure you don't fall in lust with him,' she said on a faint, humourless smile.

Blocking the memories, she let the water play over her sensitised body.

*   *   *

As Sorrel was coming back down, barefoot but warm again, in jeans and a long, loose shirt unearthed from the box, she heard the door to the laundry open and close. Relief whispered through her. Of course, the drier was functional, which meant Luke could dry his clothes. Like the stove and the washing machine and the fridge, the drier was part of the leased chattels.

She'd spent her time under the shower using calming techniques she'd mastered during the past years. As always, they had centred her and soothed her, so she really thought she was ready for Luke.

But when she saw him coming along the passage, naked except for the bath sheet wrapped around his lean hips and muscular thighs, her carefully manufactured composure evaporated, ambushed by a barrage of sensation that dried her mouth and electrified every cell in her body.

Only born Scottish Highlanders got away with wearing a skirt, and even they had to call them kilts and jazz them up with pleats and tartans and phallic daggers, not to mention well-cut jackets and snow-white shirts.

Luke did *not* look ridiculous. The moss-green towel contrasting superbly with his coppery hide, he strode towards her, a dark, dangerous male from every woman's most primal dreams, sleek and lethal, grey gaze hooded. The only time he'd kissed her she'd seen electric blue lightning in his eyes, but now they were as burnished and opaque as old silver.

Throat tight, Sorrel surged into speech. 'How long do you think it will take the creek to go down?' she asked, holding his gaze with hers in an attempt to block out the impact of burnished skin over coiled muscles.

'When the tide goes out,' he said evenly. 'Probably

in the early hours of the morning. But if this rain keeps on it might not happen even then. I'll have to stay here.'

Spend the night alone with Luke? A man who looked like something hot-blooded and barbaric from a dim and romantic past? Sorrel's bare toes curled onto the carpet and in the pit of her stomach a forbidden rhythm began to drum, slow and deep and sensual.

'Why on earth was this house built here?' She knew she sounded petulant, but kept doggedly on. 'Between the creek and the estuary, for heaven's sake! Even though your ancestors relied on sea access, surely they must have considered the possibility of the creek flooding.'

His brows rose as he said with infuriating patience, 'Why should they? Scows used to come up the river— which was much deeper then—to the wharf below the house. And they were careful to build on a rise that didn't flood.'

'Just as well,' she said lamely. She fixed her eyes on a point just beyond one bare, broad shoulder, and said brightly, 'I wonder what Baggie's cat food tastes like— is there any here, or do you feed him at Waimanu?'

His mouth curved. 'You won't have to steal from him. When I found out you were coming I organised some staples.'

'Staples?' she echoed, eyelashes flickering as she resisted the urge to retreat. Get a grip, she told herself scornfully; you're behaving like a half-wit! Or a kid who's so deep in a crush she can only think with her hormones.

Laconically he told her, 'Flour, tinned stuff, a few plates and some cutlery, pots and pans—my housekeeper worked out what you might need. It's in the pantry, and there's food in the deep freeze too.'

'Thank you very much.' Stiffening her spine, she turned and walked ahead of him into the kitchen. 'It's very kind of you. You must tell me how much I owe you.'

There was a moment of silence before he drawled, 'It seemed a neighbourly thing to do. I'll send you a bill.'

He was offended? Well, so was she; clearly he thought her too dim-witted to have brought cutlery or crockery, not to mention food, and too thick to think of organising the power and telephone. In the car was a large container of just such staples as he'd mentioned, as well as fresh food in a chilly-bin.

On the other hand, it was she who'd landed them in this ridiculous situation.

She opened the pantry door and stared blindly at an array of tinned and packaged foods, trying to put out of her treacherous mind the image of Luke, big and bronzed and gleaming behind her, clad in nothing but a towel.

Aloud she said, 'On a night like this a casserole would be perfect, but soup will be simpler.' The lights flickered ominously. Ignoring Luke's muttered expletive, she added, 'And faster. I hope the storm doesn't bring down the power lines.'

'Can you make soup?' He didn't try to hide his scepticism.

Sorrel was rather proud of the steady voice in which she said, 'Yes. Is there any firewood in the lean-to? I wish I'd thought to get one of the heaters out of storage, but I was intent on getting home.'

'Home?' he said, without inflection.

'Parenga's always seemed like home.' Sorrel reached for a packet, clutching it as she pretended to study the label. 'I'll put some soup on.'

'I'll see if there's any firewood in the lean-to. Call if you need help,' he said insufferably.

She waited until she heard the door close behind him before letting out an explosive breath.

Call if she needed help? Not bloody likely. She wouldn't give him the satisfaction. And she'd make him literally eat his doubts about her cooking prowess.

Half an hour later, after several other ominous electrical fluctuations, she carried a mug and a bowl of soup into the bookroom—empty of furniture, like the rest of the house. When Cynthia's death had been followed almost immediately by her father's stroke, Sorrel had been forced to store her godmother's furniture and pay an agency to let the house.

It wasn't the forlorn bookroom, shelves empty of books, denuded of everything but heavy drapes and carpet, that stole her breath and set her nerves vibrating.

Luke was leaning forward to dump another couple of logs onto the fire in the hearth. Light gleamed in slabs of copper and rose and gold over his torso, and struck flames from his dark hair. He looked all forbidden male, big and competent and compelling.

And sexy as hell.

A few feet away Baggie sat with tail curled around his paws, surveying both man and fire with benign satisfaction.

Sorrel ventured further into the room, trying to conceal her disturbing response to so much unadulterated masculinity. As well as his potent physical attributes, Luke's tough, hard-edged face was handsome enough to catch any woman's eye, but it was the bone-deep charisma radiating from him, an exciting combination of power and authority and a mesmerising sexual charge, that demolished her carefully built defences.

A long-repressed hunger exploded into life.

Ignoring it, she said chattily, 'I'd forgotten how chilly it could get in a summer storm.' With her heart thudding erratically in her chest, she offered Luke the bowl of soup.

He accepted it, brows lifting cynically when she made sure their fingers didn't touch. 'Smells superb. Here, give me that mug before you sit down.'

'I'll just get the toast.' Putting the mug on the floor, she escaped, to breathe deeply all the way to the kitchen and back.

Once seated in front of the fire, toast-rack between them like a small fence, Sorrel kept her gaze fixed on her mug, hoping Luke didn't realise how conscious she was of his nakedness beneath the towel.

'The soup's excellent,' he said laconically.

As far as eating his words went it didn't go far enough, but it was clearly all she was going to get. She said with dulcet irony, 'It's amazing what you can do with a few tins and some dried herbs.'

Without tasting it she drank some, then hugged the mug with her hands, as forlorn and useless a shield as the toast-rack. 'Tomorrow I'll go into Kerikeri and sort out the furniture.' It cost money she could ill afford to keep in storage.

'If the road's open,' he said negligently.

Sorrel stiffened. 'Is it likely to close?'

'It looked as though it could slip at the top of the hill.'

Of course it was no big deal to him, but if it did the power would inevitably go off. Sorrel brooded over the likelihood of being forced to camp at Parenga until it was restored, but soon thrust the thought away. She couldn't do anything about it now.

The scent of the soup, rich and savoury, mingled with that of the toast, and the eucalyptus logs on the fire. Sorrel drank more of hers before saying lightly, 'Is Baggie still obsessive about hunting eels?'

She smiled at the cat, amused to see him yawn elaborately, tongue flicking over his sharp teeth as though reminiscing about past successes.

Luke gave a quick grin. 'Yes, although he and the eels periodically have a slight difference of opinion over who is catching whom.'

'Cynthia used to hope he'd grow out of it.'

'That's the problem with obsessions—they're not easy to overcome.' His voice altered. 'Where's your husband?'

'*What?*' She looked up to meet coldly metallic eyes. 'Is this some kind of joke? I don't have a husband.'

He watched her steadily. 'When you dropped out of sight a couple of years ago there were hints that you had married.'

'*I dropped out* to look after my father.' After a pause she finished steadily, 'He had a stroke.'

'How is he now?'

She got to her feet and walked across to the window. While she'd been showering the quick New Zealand darkness had fallen, and all she could see now were the pink goblets of a magnolia tossing wildly in the wind and the rain.

'He's dead,' she said bleakly. 'He died a month ago. I've just taken him... He's buried beside my mother.'

'I'm sorry.' Luke's voice was guarded.

Sorrel turned away from the destruction outside to

pin a small, lopsided smile onto her lips. 'Actually it was a relief for him. He spent those two years being lifted from a bed to a wheelchair, and he hated it. He couldn't even speak. We developed a sort of code with eyelash blinks, but after a while he just tried very hard to die.'

Once he'd managed to communicate his bitter regret for everything he'd done and ask her forgiveness he'd given up, unable to bear the burden of what he saw as his betrayal and the subsequent ruin of her life.

'Hell,' Luke said, getting lithely to his feet and coming across to stand in front of her.

To her astonishment he took her cold hands in his lean, calloused ones and held them until they began to warm up. The uncompromising lines of his face had softened, and she read real concern in his dark eyes.

Sorrel blinked back tears. 'Quite literally hell for him. He was desperately unhappy.'

'Did you nurse him?'

Because it was too poignant to stand there with him, she gave a little tug of her captive hands. He released them and stood back to let her sit down again. Crossing her legs, she stared into the fire, mug of soup clutched firmly. 'With help.'

Luke reached out a long arm and snagged another log from the box beside the fire. From beneath lowered eyelids Sorrel watched the towel slide a little way down his flexing hips. Luke turned and caught her, his eyes narrowing into icy grey slivers.

Without any embarrassment he hitched up the towel. 'What made you decide to come back to Parenga?'

'I love it here,' she told him.

'Pull the other leg.' Raindrops hit the windows in a violent blast as he probed silkily, 'What's the real reason?' When she didn't answer, his voice hardened. 'I want the truth, Sorrel.'

Her eyes turned opaque, her gloriously sensuous mouth tightening for less than a second before relaxing into a smile that was a secretive taunt, infinitely alluring, coolly self-possessed.

Dropping her voice a few notes, she said, 'You're an arrogant—' She bit back the first word that came to mind, and with a sweet smile substituted, '*man*, Luke. What makes you think you can demand answers from me?'

His stomach muscles contracted as though she'd hit him in the solar plexus. Much as he'd like to, he couldn't counter her direct challenge by shaking the truth out of her. 'How long will you be here?'

Sorrel's lashes drooped. 'For the next six months, anyway.'

'Doing what?'

'Whatever I want to.' She fixed him with an enigmatic gaze, her lips curving into another of the slow-burning incitements to riot that had scorched out from thousands of photographs—fire beneath ice, control heated by passion's subtle, elemental lure. 'Don't worry, I plan to stick close to home. You won't even know I'm here.'

Going purely on instinct, he said, 'Sell Parenga back to me. Get a couple of land agents to value it; I'll pay a fair price.'

'What would you do with it?'

'I'd find something.'

He was too good a negotiator to watch her closely, but he'd have learned nothing from her guarded expression. She was, of course, a professional at assuming a mask.

'I can't sell it,' she said with composure. 'Cynthia left it to me in a trust.'

'That must have been a shock.' His eyes narrowed when she hesitated and turned her head, her profile etched against to the flames, elegant from the high forehead to the winged brows and short straight nose. *Elegant*, however, was not the term he'd use to describe her sultry mouth—or that surprisingly determined chin.

'Why?' she asked with a delicate flick of astonishment. 'The only thing that saved Waimanu for you was the family trust your father set up.'

Luke's mouth twisted. True. His stepmother hadn't been able to overturn the trust. But she'd spent enough money in the legal battle to almost bleed the station dry.

He said, 'So who was Cynthia protecting Parenga from?'

Another shrug, another cool dismissal from Sorrel's magnificent eyes, wide and challenging as a cat's. 'Nobody. She was a careful woman, I suppose. Or perhaps your experience frightened her.'

The fire hissed, sending up a shaft of blue-green flame that illuminated her flawless ivory skin—skin that attracted touch with its translucence.

Hunger ate into Luke's gut. Cursing it, he told himself he didn't care what she did. In spite of that potent sexual magnetism she meant nothing to him. But something was going on here that he didn't understand. It drove him to ask deliberately, 'She didn't say?'

'No.' But he suspected from her tone that she knew.

For some reason he recalled her car: tough, a workhorse ideally suited for Northland country roads—and about seven years old. An odd vehicle for a successful model.

Sorrel held out her hand to the cat, but Baggie eyed her inscrutably, ignoring the graceful beckoning fingers.

Luke watched her hand fall onto the carpet. Stop this, instinct told him. You don't want to know anything about her—she's dangerous.

But he said curtly, 'Are you hiding?'

'No.'

Her voice was almost amused. If he hadn't seen the momentary tension of her facial muscles he might almost have believed her.

To hide a quick, inconvenient surge of protectiveness, he said curtly, 'You can tell me if you're in trouble.'

She hesitated, her eyes evading his, then laughed, an artificial little sound that reminded him unpleasantly of his stepmother.

'I'm not in any trouble, and I have no ulterior reason for coming to Parenga. I just want to regroup—think things through. Why do you find that so surprising?'

'I'd have thought you'd go back to the world you've made your own.'

Her spine stiffened. 'Two years is a long time, and the fashionable world has a short memory.'

He watched with sardonic interest as her lashes slipped down to hide her wide eyes. She produced another slow smile that lingered enticingly on her soft, full mouth. He'd seen his stepmother do exactly that—use the promise of sex to get what she wanted.

But he'd never before felt anything like this ferocious surge of lust.

Despising himself for his weakness, he reminded himself that although Sorrel had left Waimanu a lovely innocent it hadn't taken her long to collect her first scalp, and there'd been a procession after that.

OK, so much of the gossip was probably fabricated, but if even half of it was false she'd had a lot of men in her life—men she'd discarded without even an attempt at finesse. She'd have made enemies.

He said, 'Are you saying that you've made your pile and now you're ready to enjoy it?'

'I'm saying that at my age I'm not going to find any modelling jobs,' she snapped. 'It's over, done, kaput! I'm twenty-eight, Luke, and that's too old to start again.'

Unwilling to meet his glinting, perceptive gaze, she bent to pick up the empty mug and bowl and toast-rack and wondered what he was thinking.

Nothing good, she decided wearily after a swift glance at his uncompromising features.

He surprised her by standing up in one powerful, fluid movement. When she began to follow suit, he helped her up, his grip casual yet smoothly, effortlessly powerful.

Releasing her, he said, 'The clothes should be dry by now.'

He held open the door, standing back to let her through. The touch of his calloused hands still running like jagged fire through her, she reluctantly obeyed the unspoken order.

As she passed him Sorrel smelt the faint fragrance— a combination of soap and exciting essence of sexy male—that was Luke's alone.

Her step faltered; she was catapulted back in time and memories she'd long repressed sprang new-minted to her mind—memories of that last summer, when she'd been so desperately in love with him.

Sheer terror hollowed out her stomach. She wasn't going through that again.

'Thank you,' she said stonily.

Closing the door behind them both, Luke said, 'It's nothing.' Mockery underpinned the words.

Sorrel turned to find him far too close. Pulses jerking, she took a swift step backwards. For a moment they stared at each other; she saw flames leap up in the grey eyes and thought stupidly, *But there's no fire here in the hall.*

And then the flames died, blanked out by Luke's strong will. He scanned her face with cynical detachment.

Sorrel swivelled away and concentrated on walking steadily into the kitchen. Once there, she deposited the tray on the bench with enough force to set every piece of crockery jumping. Although she couldn't hear him over the rain, she could feel his presence on her skin, right through to her bones.

Breathe slow, breathe easy, she commanded herself as she ignored him to stack the dishes in the sink. The light flickered again while she groped for the plug and turned on the water.

From behind, Luke said dispassionately, 'I meant what I said—if you're in any trouble, I might be able to help.'

Her fingers closed around the handle of the mug. 'I'm not,' she said, giving it a vigorous slosh in the soapy water. Luke's housekeeper was a gem; she'd even remembered detergent. 'Unless you call the imminent loss of power trouble,' she finished flippantly.

This tense conversation—like the thrust and parry of a fencing match—at least stopped her from wondering where they were going to sleep that night.

Aware of Luke's darkening gaze, she spread a clean handkerchief over the draining dishes, grimacing as the wind hurled more rain against the windows.

'When you get back into your clothes,' she said tonelessly, 'you'd better put the towels in after them—we might need them to sleep on. Unless you organised that too, there are no beds, blankets or duvets.'

He said smoothly, 'Fortunately we have a fire and plenty of wood.'

The door closed quietly behind him, and after a silent moment Sorrel heard a low rumble from floor level. 'You,' she said severely as Baggie wove around her ankles, 'are a shameless and opportunistic cat. I don't know why Cynthia loved you so much. Just because I fell for that fake "Save me, I'm going to drown" act of yours I have to spend the night on the floor in front of the fire.'

With Luke.

Fate couldn't have thought up a more unkind trick to play.

Be fair, her rational mind coaxed. If Luke hadn't come along when he did you'd have dashed across the bridge and quite possibly drowned. As it is you're safe, and so is Luke. 'And so are you,' she said to the cause of this inconvenience. 'But then you always would have been!'

Whereas she and Luke were alone until the creek went down.

She'd been so sure that time and distance had exorcised this heated enchantment of the senses. She'd been wrong; even thinking about spending the night with Luke sent her pulse rate soaring, and the dampness in her palms was a straight regression to that painful, ecstatic first love.

It meant nothing, though. Just a kick in the blood, a synthetic addiction to something Luke possessed that no other man appeared to. None she'd met, anyway.

Another shiver of light from the lamp galvanised her into filling the electric kettle and plugging it in. There wasn't any milk, but Luke presumably still drank his coffee black.

A couple of minutes later, carrying a mug of hot coffee, she left the kitchen with Baggie. In the hall, Luke was hanging up the telephone, overwhelmingly sophisticated in a superb Italian cotton shirt and trousers that had been made for him. In fact, she was pretty sure she could give the name of his tailor—an English one.

His years of hard work had definitely paid off. And she was glad of it—he deserved it.

'I thought it was worth a try, but the phone's off, and judging by the fluctuations in the power that'll go soon,' he said briefly. 'Stupidly, I left my mobile in the Land Rover.'

'Is there anyone you need to let know?' Sorrel held her breath.

CHAPTER THREE

'NO ONE.'

Abrupt and emotionless, the word hung without resonance in the damp air. Odd, humiliating relief relaxed Sorrel's tense muscles.

Another blast of wind howled in from the sea and flung itself against the house. The lights flickered and this time, as Luke swore succinctly, they went out, stranding them in thick darkness.

'Stay where you are,' he commanded. 'Don't spill that coffee on yourself.'

He opened the door into the bookroom so that the warm glow of the fire showed her where to go. Carrying the mug carefully, she went in, putting it onto the floor before sitting cross-legged in front of the fire.

After adding another couple of logs to the flames Luke joined her, long legs stretched out on the floor.

'Here,' she said, offering the mug.

He took the mug, but instead of drinking he asked, 'Where's yours?'

'I can't sleep if I drink coffee after dinner,' she told him. 'Goodness, listen to that rain! I hope our cars are all right.'

'Don't worry about them; the creek's never risen above the road.'

The darkness outside was split open by vivid light, gone as swiftly as it came. 'I'd forgotten how heavily it rains here in summer,' she said wryly. She would have liked to close the curtains, but that would make the situation far too intimate.

'It's due to pass over tomorrow. We often get storms from the tropics at this time of year.'

He might have meant to be soothing, but Sorrel thought she discerned a note of impatience beneath his words. Tartly she said, 'I know that.'

'Did you want comforting? Sorry, I don't have much time for spoilt women.' His voice was cool and steady, delivering each word with a crisp lack of compromise that flayed her emotions. 'Or spoilt men, come to that.'

'I'm sure you don't realise how smug and judgmental you sound! My life is my business.'

'If you're going to be living next door to me it may turn out to be my business too,' he said, lifting the mug to his lips.

'It won't be,' she said shortly.

When Luke's eyes drifted to her exposed neck and then back up to her ear lobes, heat scorched her skin. She wished she'd left her hair down, and for once worn a bra.

Too loudly she told him, 'I don't throw wild parties and play loud music all night. I might cross your land to walk on the beach, but that's the only time you're likely to see me. I'll be as good a neighbour as Cynthia.'

Unexpectedly he said, 'I'm sorry I missed her funeral. I was stuck up in the Andes with a government primary industries delegation, and I didn't hear about it until I arrived back in New Zealand.'

Sorrel's teeth clamped onto her bottom lip and she looked away to hide the sheen of tears in her eyes. 'I wasn't there either,' she said in a shaky voice. 'But— she'd have understood.'

Her breath stopped in her throat as strong fingers enclosed hers, once more offering warmth and support. A glance revealed nothing in his expression but distant sympathy, but once again that unsubtle excitement charged through her like a bolt of lightning, burning away everything but her body's involuntary response.

Her brain went into meltdown, just as it had when she'd been a thin, shy teenager, acutely embarrassed by her height and dazzled by his open sexual charisma.

Don't be fooled—this is just chemistry, she told herself sturdily, a matter of pheromones and subliminal signals left over from the distant, primitive past.

She was no longer a shy virgin; this sexual thrill was wonderful, but it wasn't all that important. What mattered in a relationship was respect, and love, and shared interests and values. And she had nothing in common with Luke.

An upward glance revealed him examining her, one side of his mouth tilted in irony as he assessed her response.

Showered by ice, she muttered, 'Thanks,' and tugged her hand free.

Luke let it go, thinking mordantly that it was still there, that blatant, unwanted reaction. Looking into slumbrous green eyes, mysteriously dark in the muted fire-glow, he noticed the soft parting of her mouth.

An innate masculine instinct, honed by a fair amount of experience, told him it wouldn't be difficult to get her into bed. Beneath that restrained, exquisitely composed surface Sorrel was sending off enough signals to organise a naval exercise. Sardonically he wondered whether she was doing it deliberately.

He clamped down on a wild upwelling of hunger,

carnal and potent. Before he took what she was offering, he needed to know why she was offering it.

'I liked her enormously,' he said quietly. 'She was gallant and kind and always bright and entertaining, with a heart big enough to act as the local agony aunt. I miss her.'

Sorrel deliberately relaxed tense muscles. His expression hadn't altered even though he must have felt her pulses leap under his touch. At least the dimness would have hidden her heightened colour. It was plain he didn't feel anything like the overwhelming anticipation licking through her like a forest fire, beautiful and deadly.

But now he knew that she still wanted him.

What he must never discover was that she'd always measured men by his standards—and none of them had made the grade.

Would he laugh if he ever realised he'd stood between her and every other man she'd met?

Probably. But he wouldn't believe it.

So she raised her head and met his unsparing gaze. 'I miss her too.'

'I'm surprised. You hadn't seen much of her since you left,' he said blandly.

'I saw her at least once or twice a year,' she said defensively. 'And we talked often on the phone.'

One dark brow lifted to devastating effect. 'Did you?'

'Yes.' And although they sounded like an excuse she couldn't prevent the next sharp words. 'I don't imagine Cynthia told you everything she did.'

'She certainly didn't mention regular telephone calls,' he returned caustically.

Temper flaring, Sorrel said, 'So because she didn't

mention them you don't believe they happened? You know, you're going to have to work on this habit of judging people.'

'I haven't seen you since the day you left Waimanu to go to New York,' he returned. 'I may not have been here often, but if you'd made regular visits to Cynthia I'd have known.'

Except that whenever she'd come back she'd asked Cynthia for privacy. More thunder rolled around the sky, the rain dropping so heavily that the fire spat and crackled.

Luke said indolently, 'Tell me what it was like being a world-famous model. Did you enjoy it?'

'It had its moments. A lot of it was boring,' she said before she could stop herself. She gave a shocked little laugh and stared into the flames. 'And that's the first time I've admitted that.'

'If you didn't like it, why did you do it?'

Why indeed? 'I went to fabulous places,' she said lightly, 'and met people who were fascinating and stimulating and exciting.'

'I imagine the money would have been hard to resist,' he said sardonically.

'Money is nice. You must agree—you've worked hard enough for yours.'

Luke gave a taut smile. 'Your eyes still glitter green fire when you're angry,' he said, his gaze lingering on her mouth until she felt it softening and heating.

'Don't be patronising,' she retorted.

With forceful precision he said, 'I worked for Waimanu and for the people who earn their living from it.'

'Very noble,' Sorrel said idly.

He looked her over with unhurried deliberation. 'So

modelling didn't entirely fulfil its promise of glamour and high living? I remember a girl who couldn't wait to get away from New Zealand.'

Because he'd just started a hot and heavy affair with Mari O'Neill.

Her smile was as edged as his tone. 'Naturally. What eighteen-year-old girl would turn down an opportunity like that? And what's the difference between a woman—or man—using his or her physical attributes to earn a living, and one who uses her intelligence?'

Luke put the coffee mug down. 'Simply that using intelligence indicates hard work and effort, whereas—'

'Believe me,' she said sardonically, 'a lot of hard— very hard—work goes into maintaining those physical attributes you're so contemptuous of.'

'Contempt doesn't come into it. I'm as affected by beauty as any other person,' he said coolly.

'But you still feel that those with good brains should be applauded for using the assets they were handed in the genetic lottery, whereas those with good bodies shouldn't. I never thought you were a Puritan, Luke.'

She paused, and when he said nothing added with delicate malice, 'Or a hypocrite. Don't try to convince me that your handsome face—' she ran her gaze over it with studied insolence '—and excellent physique haven't made your life easier, even if it's only your love life.'

He astounded her by laughing softly. 'I concede your point. However, it seems a shame to waste an intelligent brain like yours.'

'Ah, but brains don't deteriorate,' she said, irritated because even accusing him of hypocrisy hadn't pricked his temper.

'What have you been doing with yours?'

Two years ago she'd taken a rapid—and very depressing—course in accounting practice, for one thing! 'Using it,' she said curtly, glad when another blast of wind hit the house. She scrambled to her feet. 'I'll pull the curtains.'

She felt Luke's eyes on her as she yanked one of the heavy drapes across the long French windows. Wildly fluttering flakes in the thickening darkness outside caught her eye. 'Oh!'

'What is it?' he asked, instantly on his feet.

'It's all right—it's just the last flowers from the magnolia.'

Torn pink shreds of the glorious chalices were being driven by the merciless wind into drifts and ridges across the brick terrace, and there battered into a mess by the rain. Shivering, Sorrel shut them out.

'Cynthia loved them so much,' she said remotely as she sat down, carefully keeping almost the full width of the fireplace between her and the man who dominated the room.

She should have left the curtains open—now the room was like a cave, disturbingly intimate, the firelight swallowed by empty corners and heavy drapes.

Exhaustion suddenly ached through her, but a rapid glance at her watch revealed that it was far too early to even think of sleeping. Thankful for the glossy mask derived from years spent producing exactly the look each photographer wanted, she gave Luke a slow, glimmering smile. 'What happened to Mari O'Neill?'

'She's taking the corporate world by storm,' he said blandly. 'What happened to that young actor you were linked with a couple of months after you left?'

'No romance—just PR for both of us,' she said with a touch of awkwardness. 'He wanted the publicity and my agent—' and her father '—felt it would be good for my career.'

The unromantic nature of their relationship hadn't stopped the man from trying to seduce her, but he'd given up with good grace when she refused him. He was one of the few friends who'd visited her during her father's illness.

Luke's mouth curled. 'And did it work?'

'I suppose so.' She felt as though she was fighting a duel, using words to deflect a long-repressed pain. A yawn took her by surprise. She covered it with her hand, but of course he saw it.

He frowned. 'Did you fly in today?'

'Yes, from Vancouver.' She made a face. 'Normally I never get jet-lagged, but driving up was a bit exciting.'

'City driver.' But there was a note of amusement in the reply.

Sorrel dragged her eyes away from his darkly arrogant features. A hot urgency exploded in the pit of her stomach. She leaned forward and looped her arms around her knees, staring into the flames. Baggie, curled up a few feet away, opened his eyes and stretched, then began to purr, a pleasant domestic counterpoint to the weather outside and the bewildering turmoil of her thoughts and reactions.

Feeling as though her head was stuffed with cotton wool, Sorrel hid another yawn, but Luke saw it.

'You're worn out,' he said roughly, getting to his feet. 'I'll make up beds while you get ready.'

Sorrel looked up with cool eyes and a tight mouth. 'If I go to sleep now I'll wake up at some ungodly hour of the morning with my body clock still out of kilter.

It's a pity we haven't got a pack of cards—I'd take you on at poker. Or we could take turns to play patience.'

He laughed. 'I don't think it would work,' he said enigmatically.

Sorrel lifted a dismissive shoulder and turned back to rest her chin on her knees again, folding her arms tightly across her shins. The flames danced in front of her—beckoning, dangerous.

Tension warred with her debilitating tiredness. Better give in to the tiredness—yielding to temptation was becoming a seductive option. She said, 'I don't suppose you can produce a toothbrush?'

'No brush, and no toothpaste either,' he said unsparingly.

She sighed. 'There are distinct advantages to civilisation. I noticed salt in the kitchen; I'll use that.'

'I filled the bath in case the power went off, so we have that, but if you want warm water to wash your face you'd better take the jug from the kitchen.'

'I'd forgotten,' she said in a subdued voice.

'No power, no pump, no water.' Her silence must have been eloquent because he gave a soft derisive laugh. 'This is the wilds of New Zealand. You should have gone to the Seychelles or some other expensively exclusive place for your holiday.'

He hadn't *tried* to hurt her, she acknowledged as she got to her feet and made her way out of the room, obeying his injunction to leave the door open behind her. But the casual jibe stung.

Halfway through finger-brushing her teeth, she heard a movement outside the bathroom. 'I'll be out in a minute,' she called.

'I'm going up to bring that box of clothes down.'

She rinsed her mouth. 'The box is too big—just grab as many clothes as you can. I'll come up—'

'Stay where you are. It's damned dark here.'

In the heavy darkness she strained to hear his sure-footed progress. To be home with Luke had once been her sole ambition—the hoped-for, yearned-for haven of the heart. She'd never had it.

But she was over that, thank heavens.

So how did she feel about him now?

Wary, she decided, groping her way back to the bookroom. Very wary. The years had changed him in subtle ways she didn't understand. She sensed a hard authority that hadn't been evident before.

And the swift stab of carnal recognition was simply an involuntary response to his hard masculinity, the aura of fiercely primal sexuality that smoked around him and through him. Exciting, even dangerous, but ultimately meaningless unless it was joined with love.

Instead of easing, the storm had intensified. Thunder growled around the horizon and intermittent flashes of lightning lit up the curtained windows as Luke came back into the room.

'Here,' he said, setting his load down on the floor. 'Choose ones that don't crush.'

'They'll survive,' she told him crisply, kneeling beside the heap.

After a moment he said, 'I'll be back shortly.'

Sorrel spread the clothes out into two piles a suitable distance apart. Taking her place on the smaller heap, she discovered a pleased Baggie in residence and turfed him off before curling up on it. The carpeted floor, perfectly comfortable when she'd been sitting on it, metamorphosed into concrete.

It was going to be a long night. She wriggled around

and pulled a knitted jersey over her knees and feet, then rolled several T-shirts into a make-believe pillow.

Closing her eyes, she wooed sleep with eager desperation, every nerve stretched, each cell in her body tense and expectant.

When Luke come back into the room she watched from slitted eyes as he stoked up the fire, and heard him settle onto the pile of clothes she'd arranged. 'Thank you,' he said formally. 'Goodnight, Sorrel.'

'Goodnight,' she said gruffly.

The old house creaked around them. Sorrel listened to the wind and the rain and imagined the flowers being pounded into slush across the garden; she strained to hear the steady, rhythmic sound of Luke's breathing.

Much later Baggie wandered over and curled up against the back of her knees, and eventually she drifted into a restless sleep, waking whenever Luke put wood on the fire and Baggie shifted his allegiance—and his warmth.

Plagued by dreams, she forced her eyes open from one to find herself shivering.

'What's the matter?' Luke asked quietly from the darkness.

She muttered, 'I'm cold.'

He got up to put another load of wood on the fire. Dusting off his hands, he turned to look down at her. 'The wind's gone around to the south, but at least it's driven away the rain.'

Still hazy with sleep, it took her a moment to remember that in the Southern Hemisphere the south was the cold quarter. 'Is the power back on?'

'Not yet.'

His voice was so much closer that her eyes flew open, to see his shape crouching beside her.

'What—?' she asked as he rested the back of his fingers on her cheek. Heat radiated from him and she had to stop herself from following that fleeting touch. She swallowed and finished huskily, 'What's the matter?'

'You're freezing.'

His curt tone flicked her on the raw. He got up and bent to his own pile; Sorrel lifted herself on one elbow and watched incredulously as he scooped up the clothes she'd put there for him and carried them across to her, swearing mildly under his breath when Baggie skipped out of the way.

'What are you doing?' she asked in a high-pitched voice.

'Warming you up.' He dumped the clothes beside hers, lowered himself onto them, and pulled her into the hard, warm cage made by his arms and body.

Heat surged through her—heat from his body and matching heat from hers—driving up through her skin and turning to fever. Sorrel clenched teeth that threatened to chatter.

'Go back to sleep,' he commanded.

Her pulses thudded so loudly in her ears that she had to go over his words in her mind to understand them. When she did she almost laughed. *Go to sleep!* How on earth could she, with him curved around her, making her so fiercely conscious of him she felt as if her nerves were tipped by razors?

Her heart skipped in her breast as she responded to his heat and the sleek, heavily muscled potency of him. Capturing air between lips that had turned warm and sensitive, she forced her breathing into a slow, deliberate pattern, one she'd used hundreds of times before to summon serenity.

This time it didn't work. Instead of calming her senses and her mind, the exercise honed them. She'd never felt so intensely alive.

'Relax,' Luke said, his voice somehow reverberating through her in a frighteningly intimate closeness. 'You're as tense as a violin string.'

She searched for a flippant answer, but her mind remained obstinately in thrall to sensation. In the pit of her stomach those sensations contracted into a knot of need so powerful it was all she could do to stop herself from turning sinuously in his grasp and pressing against him, offering herself.

As though he sensed her thoughts, his arms flexed around her. He said coolly, 'Stop behaving like a virgin, Sorrel. You must know by now that an erection is a perfectly normal response to a situation like this. It doesn't mean that I'm going to tear your clothes off. Just go to sleep.'

Bitter humiliation chilled her, but it didn't eradicate the aching hunger. So she was just another female body—why should that hurt so much?

She lay rigid in his grip until a bone-deep, irresistible tiredness dragged her under. Slowly the turbulent images faded from her mind, until eventually she sank into a deep sleep.

But she dreamed of the night Luke had kissed her. Even in her dream she responded to that kiss—deep, drugging, terrifyingly pleasurable—and this time he didn't pull away, didn't say in a voice savage with self-contempt, 'No!'

And no cool, guarded apology.

This time one kiss turned to two, and then three, and soon she was lost in a dark enchantment. This time, she thought exultantly, there would be no going back...

CHAPTER FOUR

LUKE said her name. 'Sorrel.'

Just one word, yet it was enough to catapult her into instant awareness.

Her eyes flew open, to be captured by the crystalline glitter of his beneath half-closed lids. Above the fire's quiet hiss and crackle she heard her breath catch in her throat, backed by the fierce tattoo of her heart.

And she drowned in the unguarded hunger in Luke's eyes.

No dream, this! They were lying on the heap of clothes in front of the fire at Parenga, and she was strained against him, her taut, expectant body enfolded by his heat and lean, dynamic strength.

Dazed by sleep and drunk with sensation, she yielded to temptation, lifting her mouth to his. He said something, the word muffled by her lips, and then he kissed her again, a fierce claiming that effectively shut down her mind. Need, primitive and stark, gripped her with claws of iron and velvet. She sighed and her fingers tangled in the springy hair at the nape of his neck, pulling him closer, closer.

He raised his head, but even as she made a little protesting noise his lips found her throat. Pulses jumping wildly, she sighed again at the erotic mastery of his kisses. His hand slid up beneath her jersey, finding the taut, slight mound of one breast.

Fire ran through her. She heard her choked whimper as his fingers stroked over the acutely sensitive skin—

heard too the sudden stop in his breathing. A giddy sense of power rocked through her. For once Luke wasn't completely in control. He held her and touched her like a man forced beyond endurance, almost as though he despised himself for wanting her.

Long fingers pushed up the loose material of shirt and jersey. He bent his head and kissed the pleading centre of her breast, so lightly the warmth of his mouth barely registered, yet she shuddered as unbearable excitement sizzled from her breast to the pit of her stomach.

His big frame hardened, the clear evidence of his passion summoning a feverish need. His scent was delicious to her, the coiled tension of his body infinitely stimulating, and she wanted nothing more than to give in to temptation and find exactly what she'd sought all these years. Her hips jerked in an involuntary summons.

Flames spat in the fireplace, sending a flare of light over Luke's profile, the harshly symmetrical angles and lines barely softened by the curve of his mouth against the pale skin of her breast.

Sorrel whispered his name and her hand curved around his face, fingers delighting in the raw silk of his beard and the arrogant contour of cheek and jaw.

He froze, every muscle in his big body locked in denial. She felt his breath shudder across her skin.

'No,' he rasped, and rolled over, levering himself to his feet in a movement that took him across to the fireplace. He stood with his back to her, light flickering around the dark outline of his big body—light that revealed one fist clenched at his side, the other on the mantel.

Humiliation scored her soul. Curling up in a tight

ball like a wounded animal, she realised it had happened again—she'd submitted mindlessly to the silent promise of his hand cupping her breast, his mouth ravishing her thoughts from her mind, and then he'd flung her surrender back in her face.

Just as he'd done ten years previously.

She jack-knifed into a sitting position and hugged her knees, resting her forehead on them as she fought for sanity. This time she was older, more able to deal with rejection. Well, better able to recover from it, anyway.

'You're right. This is—not wise,' she croaked over the silent scream of outrage from her frustrated body.

'But inevitable.' He paused, and when she neither spoke nor lifted her head from her knees he went on in a coldly judicial tone that effectively doused her aching hunger, 'And now I know that your photographs weren't air-brushed into perfection. And that you still kiss like a siren.'

'And you like a conqueror,' she muttered. 'I was asleep, damn you.'

He said coldly, 'Really? I'm not at my most controlled when I wake with a woman in my arms.'

No, not even the extra years made his rejection easier to cope with. She lifted her head and hissed, 'Are you insinuating that I started it?'

He didn't answer immediately. Instead he stooped and picked up a couple of logs, setting them onto the fire with what seemed exaggerated precision while Sorrel seethed.

'No,' he said eventually. 'I don't know who began, and it doesn't matter. What does matter is that it isn't going anywhere. I know too much about your sort of woman.'

'My sort?' Her voice cracked. 'So I'm tarred with the same brush as your stepmother? Tell me, do you consider all redheaded women to be greedy and amoral and cruel? Or do we have to have long legs as well, to get the full treatment? And don't you realise that she dyed her hair?'

He said tersely, 'Of course I know. It has nothing to do with looks.'

'So you dislike all women?' Made reckless by anger and pain, she added, 'You can get therapy for that, you know.'

'I am *not* a misogynist.'

Oh, she'd touched a nerve there—he spoke with a gritty fury that warned her to go no further.

'Could have fooled me,' she said crisply, scrambling up. 'I'll be back in a minute.' She headed towards the bathroom, raw with a stabbing hunger.

So now she knew that he'd be a magnificent lover. How many women had he kissed, made love to, to acquire that formidable sexual confidence?

Probably too many to count.

With the bathroom door closed behind her, she stood shivering in the dense darkness and vowed that she wasn't ever going to open herself to that again. Luke couldn't have made it more plain that he desired her only in the most basic way, with the impersonal, animal hunger of a man for a pliant woman—for relief, she thought, sickened.

At least he'd had the decency to call a halt. With stark honesty she admitted that she wouldn't have. She'd been completely lost.

And, decent or not, she hated him for being able to.

But why did he categorise her as the same sort of woman as his stepmother? That really hurt.

The thought of meeting those sardonic eyes tore her composure to tatters, but she stiffened her shoulders. Pride forbade that she spend the rest of the night cowering in the bathroom.

Falling back on techniques she'd learned years before, she began to breathe quietly and deeply, submerging her hurt bewilderment in the regular, comforting process.

When she returned he glanced at her before resuming his grim observation of the flames; as far as she could see he hadn't moved. At least he couldn't see the peaked, ultra-sensitive nipples under the fine wool of her jersey.

Setting her jaw, she began to transfer her small pile of clothes to the other side of the fire.

Luke said, 'I'm going to see if the creek's down enough to get across.' When she looked up he said brusquely, 'Stay there. There's no need for you to come and it's chilly out.'

Sorrel sank down onto her meagre bed and watched him leave the room, Baggie following enthusiastically. Both returned a few minutes later, bringing in a gust of rain and wind and fresh vegetation.

'Not yet,' Luke said briefly. 'See if you can get some more sleep.'

She bit her lip, but she knew what she had to do. 'I'm sorry,' she said quietly.

'Forget about it.' His voice was hard.

But when she was once more lying on her side, courting sleep with dogged determination, he asked pleasantly, 'Who were you kissing, Sorrel?'

She pretended not to hear him. He said nothing more, and after a while she realised that he was asleep.

It seemed the ultimate insult. Here she was, unable

to chisel memories from her mind—the touch of his mouth and experienced fingers, the heat and vibrant power of his body against hers—and he thought so little of what had happened that he could sleep!

You should have known, she reminded herself austerely. You found out ten years ago. One night he kissed you stupid, then he gave you a horrified, stunned look and told you he was sorry, that it meant nothing except that you were a very pretty girl and he was fond of you.

And the next night at a beach barbecue he'd met Mari O'Neill.

Acutely conscious of him—and still hopeful that he'd been chivalrous because she was so much younger—Sorrel had seen the glint in Luke's eyes when he'd repeated the newcomer's name in a deep, sexy voice with a note in it she'd never heard before.

Mari, a small blonde with curves and huge dark eyes, had glanced at him through her lashes in a way she'd probably intended to be demure. Luke had smiled down at her, the intent appreciation in his grey eyes barely concealing a purely male speculation.

And Sorrel had accepted with sick finality that the kiss that had fuelled her fantasies the previous night truly had meant nothing to him; her hopes and dreams were doomed to die.

Trying desperately not to let anyone see her misery, she had smiled her way through that evening, inwardly writhing with awareness of the two of them in their own cocoon of mutual attraction.

A couple of days later Mari had come up to her in the main street of the nearest small town, and asked bluntly, 'Is there anything between you and Luke Hardcastle?'

'No,' Sorrel told her, head high.

Mari gave a short, satisfied nod. 'I didn't think there could be, but he was so protective the other night at the barbecue I wondered if there was more to your relationship than the big brother thing.' She shrugged and explained, 'I don't poach, so I wanted to make sure.'

From some hidden reservoir Sorrel dredged up a gritty courage that allowed her to say, 'You're not poaching.' She added with a spark of malice, 'But even if you want to it will be Luke who makes the decision.'

Mari laughed, a sensuous sound that held a wealth of knowledge. 'You haven't got a mother, have you?'

'No.'

'Then think of me as an older sister for a moment and remember this. It's always the woman who chooses.'

Not in Luke's case, Sorrel thought.

Within a week they were a couple. Wounded to the soul, Sorrel gave in to her father's suggestion that she enter a modelling competition, and when, astonishingly, she won it she accepted the contract with an agency in New York and left Luke and Parenga far behind.

Sorrel woke to the sun poking thin shafts of light through the drawn curtains, and the rushing noise of the river streaming by into the estuary. A glance at her watch revealed that it was a couple of hours after sunrise.

Yawning, she stretched, the slow burn of aching muscles reminding her that she'd spent the night on the floor. She was alone, lying in a heap of tumbled clothes. The fire had died down to ashes and Baggie, traitor that he was, had left with Luke.

Oh, God—Luke! She scrambled up and pulled back the curtains, standing in a golden box of sunlight to assess the carnage in the garden. The magnolia had been stripped of its glory of pink and white, but dark blue irises unfurled beneath, and she noted the buds of daylilies, storm-proof and gallant, glowing in the sunlight.

And next year the magnolia would flower again.

So learn that lesson, she commanded herself, turning away. She was every bit as tough as it was.

In the kitchen she found her suitcases on the floor, and a note on the bench.

The creek's down but the power's not on yet because the road's still closed. Come along to the homestead to shower and for breakfast. Baggie's with me.

After a fuming few moments Sorrel decided to accept what was more of a command than an invitation, but only because she desperately needed a shower.

After she'd changed into a cowl-necked jersey of fine caramel wool, and tailored trousers in a darker shade, she pulled leather boots onto her feet and made a mental memo to buy herself a pair of proper gumboots. Garnering up her toiletries and a pair of briefs, she dropped them into a carry-bag and went out into the fresh morning.

Before she left, however, she tried a light switch, pulling a face at its futile click, amending Luke's mocking words to *No power, no water, no shower.*

Although the creek was no longer the voracious monster of the night before it still hurried along, laden with rich red-brown soil. Sorrel picked her way through the layer of silt over the bridge, stretching her legs so that she walked in Luke's footprints.

Striding down the road and breathing in great lungfuls of air heavy with the scent of rain-soaked vegetation and the river and sea, she told herself she had no need to be embarrassed about seeing him again.

OK, so coming back to Parenga was proving to be more—*challenging*—than she'd expected, but she could cope with Luke's obvious distaste for her. Although she'd like to know the reason for it. Surely he didn't really think she was like his stepmother?

She'd disliked Cherie, but then, no one had liked her, and Luke certainly had good reason to despise her.

But to judge Sorrel purely on the basis of their shared hair colour—no, it was ridiculous. He was far too logical to do that.

Who understood what Luke thought beneath that iron reserve? Certainly not her. But, in case he thought she was intent on an affair, she'd make it obvious she hadn't come back to Parenga with any designs on his magnificent body! A quick smile tugged at her lips. Last night had been a mistake, but they had both been asleep...

After all these years she still wanted him. Her smile hardened into irony. She might be safe from him, but how safe was she from herself?

'Perfectly safe,' she said abruptly. 'All you have to remember is the look on his face when he realised who he was making love to. That was a passion-killer if ever I've seen one!'

But deep inside she ached for something she'd never had, never would have.

Movement along the road caught her eye. Baggie,

fur fluffed out, tail held high, paced towards her with sedate complacency.

'Well, hello,' she greeted him, bending to scratch behind his splendid tufted ears. 'You're looking a lot more cheerful this morning!'

He suffered her caress for a few seconds before wriggling away to eye a cheeky fantail in the bottom branches of a huge, ancient camellia tree. 'Don't even think about it,' Sorrel warned. 'Birds are not on your menu.'

But, apart from his obsession with eels, Baggie wasn't a serious hunter. He accompanied her graciously, even stopping further on when she peered between massive old flame trees to the river, smooth and brown and muscular, splitting around the island on its way to spill into the sea.

Her spirits lifting, Sorrel smiled as a tui wooed a mate amongst the spidery orange flowers of a grevillea. Gleaming iridescent blue-green, with a lacy white cape around its shoulders and a bobble of white at its throat, the bird posed and strutted and capered in front of its lady, producing an eccentric collection of whirrs and clicks interspersed with glorious liquid trills like a miniature carillon.

'Stick to the bells,' Sorrel advised him wryly. 'Sweet beats sour every time. Right, Baggie?'

Baggie ignored her to turn his head and gaze behind them.

A second later Sorrel's less acute hearing picked up the subdued clop of hooves. Her heart jumped when Luke rode around the corner, both he and his big bay gelding tiger-striped by the bars of sunlight sifting through the leaves.

He was wearing a thin black crew-necked jersey and

dark trousers, wet to the knees. Relaxed, yet alert, he looked like a warrior from a time out of myth, when battle-hardened barbarians fought for a code of honour as rigid and enduring as their armour.

'Good morning,' Sorrel said, her mouth suddenly dry as she looked up into his bronzed, unyielding face.

The gelding bent its head to nuzzle Baggie, then straightened up to switch a cursory tail over its flanks. Sorrel stepped back; at any other time she'd have enjoyed the familiar earthy smell of horse and leather, but not just now.

'Good morning.' Luke surveyed her in leisurely assessment. 'When I left you looked as though you were ready to sleep for another eight hours.'

Colour heated her skin, but she managed a composed smile. 'What time did you wake?'

He swung down and led the horse towards her, stooping a moment to stroke an importunate Baggie. Straightening up, he said, 'Daybreak. You've got shadows under your eyes. Sleeping on the floor obviously doesn't agree with you. I'll ring the council and tell them to get the road cleared as soon as they can. Once they've done that the power authority can fix the line, and then you'll be able to organise some furniture.'

'Just like that?' she asked sweetly. 'You snap your fingers and the council jumps?'

His broad shoulders lifted and the smile that curled his chiselled mouth was both compelling and ironic. 'If there aren't more important slips to clear. It certainly won't hurt to let them know we're without both communications and power.'

As well as expecting his orders to be obeyed, Luke was a man who took charge. Not, however, of her life. Pronouncing each word with clarity and determination, she said, 'I'll borrow your mobile phone, if that's all right, and ring them myself.'

'Why?' Luke asked casually.

'Because it's my problem,' she told him with more curtness than she'd intended. 'I'll bet you've got a generator for emergencies like this.'

'Of course. The equipment sheds and barns are on this line too, so a generator's a necessity.'

Sorrel tightened her mouth, her gaze direct and unwavering. 'I'll deal with it. I'm grown up now,' she said steadily. 'I don't need a big brother or a mentor.'

Something burned fiercely blue in his eyes. 'I don't feel like either,' he said austerely. 'Perhaps you've been away from New Zealand for so long you've forgotten that neighbours help each other whenever they can.'

She sent him a limpid look. 'You're sounding a bit insular, Luke. Good neighbours exist all around the world.'

When the gelding lowered its head and whickered softly, Luke lifted a lean tanned hand to stroke its nose. 'We'd better get going; he wants his breakfast and you, I imagine, want a shower.' Lightly, easily, he swung up onto the horse, muscles flexing smoothly beneath his cotton shirt. From this position of power he surveyed her. 'Want to get up behind me?'

She shook her head. 'Baggie and I will walk, thank you,' she said coolly.

That was how she'd lost her heart to Luke—when he'd offered her a ride down the hot, dusty road a few days after she'd come back from the modelling course. Until then it had just been the classic schoolgirl crush, almost sexless. But that hot, languorous day she'd been beguiled into first love by the sheer physical pleasure of sitting behind him with her arms around his waist, dreamily listening to his steady heartbeat, her nostrils filled with the fascinating scent of man and horse, dusty road and wild ginger flowers.

Luke remembered too, she could tell. He broke eye contact only when the horse moved restlessly beneath him. Sorrel watched his strong legs clamp its girth as he controlled the big animal.

'I'll see you at the homestead,' she said in a voice that had gone suddenly rough.

He sketched a salute that approached a taunt, clicked his tongue at the gelding, and left her.

Reluctantly Sorrel followed, wondering whether riding like a centaur came naturally or was the result of being tossed onto a horse before you could walk, as Luke had once told her he'd been.

The last time she'd walked along this road he'd been living in an old caravan in a paddock above the river. He could have turned a family out of one of the four farm cottages, but Luke's rigorous conscience wouldn't allow that. The formidable fire that burned beneath his controlled façade, its source the same determination that had driven him to bring Waimanu back to its former glory, meant that he'd been the one to suffer the substandard conditions.

It hadn't taken him long to turn Waimanu around. Over the years Cynthia had faithfully relayed to her his hard work, his successes, and his growing reputation as a businessman with solid ties to the land and innovative ideas about its use.

For Luke, fired by dynamic energy and an inborn love for the land, Waimanu would be the only place to build. The new homestead would be his validation, the final crown, replacing the house he'd been forced to sell and wiping out the last remnants of his step-mother's legacy of mismanagement.

Deep in thought, Sorrel walked out of the tunnel of trees onto a wide sealed area—and stopped.

As a model she'd been photographed in glorious houses all over the world; as a minor celebrity she'd gone to parties and stayed weekends at splendid mansions. But something about this one, settled into gardens that looked as though they'd been there for ever, caught at her heart.

Not that it was a mansion. Modern, designed by an immense talent, the large double-storeyed house fitted like a jewel into the primal setting of garden, river and the fertile hills of Waimanu station. Sorrel swivelled to note a vast garage, connected at right angles to the house, with what seemed to be living quarters above. An island of lush plantings divided the sealed concourse, a more disciplined garden separating the drive and the house.

She let out a long, soft sigh of delighted appreciation—replaced by a surge of adrenalin as Luke strolled around the corner of the garage.

Baggie made a cheerful sound halfway between a purr and meow and set off towards him, tail waving in greeting.

Deliberately relaxing tight muscles, Sorrel composed her face to hide the mixture of apprehension and heady pleasure that warred inside her. Luke took up too much space—in every way.

Yet her eyes lingered on the way the sun bathed him in a shimmering aura. Its warm light should have subdued the uncompromising impact of his silent, graceful stride and the ruthless lines of his face. It didn't. Starkly compelling, he projected a tough maleness that sent a shiver scudding down her spine.

Gesturing at the house, she said, 'Luke, this is *perfect* for Waimanu.'

'Thank you,' he said evenly, a territorial inflection giving the words an edge that made her glance sharply at him. 'The architect did an excellent job. I decided to build it when Cynthia told me she wasn't going to sell Parenga back to me.'

Iron-grey eyes, burnished and unreadable, clashed with hers.

Sorrel turned her head and pretended to examine the façade, following its gracious, welcoming lines. 'That must have annoyed you.'

'A little, but I'm not sentimental,' he said smoothly, watching her with a hard intensity that pulled every tiny hair on her skin upright.

Sorrel looked away. 'I know plants grow fast in Northland, but these seem well established. Surely they're older than the house?'

Luke began to walk towards the garage. 'I had the gardens planted a year or so after you left.'

Something about the way he spoke set alarm bells ringing, but as she set off after him Sorrel couldn't for the life of her work out why. Landscaping a couple of hectares wasn't exactly a deeply significant action.

Another tui set up a musical clamour in the gold-dipped branch of a kowhai. Luke slowed until Sorrel caught him up, then said, 'I took the perishables from your car and put them in the fridge inside. They were still cold, so they should be all right.'

'I seem to be saying thank you all the time.' The scent of flowers and greenery, of Luke—salt and male mixed with the faintest touch of horse—set her senses buzzing as she went with him towards the garage.

He'd parked her middle-aged vehicle inside, thoroughly out of place between a sleekly opulent BMW and the Land Rover.

'Come in,' he invited, and opened the connecting door into the house.

CHAPTER FIVE

'This way,' Luke indicated, mouth quirking at the predatory gleam in Baggie's eyes as the cat paced with dignity towards a container of dry food. 'We'll leave him to enjoy his breakfast—it's the only way we'll get to have ours in peace.'

'Thank you very much for taking care of him,' Sorrel said.

'He's no problem—he's a very self-contained cat except for his over-developed tendency to dramatise,' Luke said drily, and opened another door into the interior of the house.

Sorrel walked past both cat and man into a passage that led towards the front of the house. Even that utilitarian area breathed a subtle, unstudied comfort, but the front hall it led into was magnificent, with a superb flight of stairs soaring up to the next floor.

Luke took her up and opened a door a few metres along a light-filled hall. 'The spare bedroom,' he said laconically, adding with a swift, flashing grin that cut her foolish heart adrift, 'It has an *en suite* bathroom.'

'I am so looking forward to that,' Sorrel said with real gratitude, admiring the decoration in warm vanilla and cream with smoky shades of chocolate and claret for accents. 'I feel grubby and dehydrated and a shower is long overdue.'

'Whereas you look cool and very much in control,' he said evenly. 'The towels are in the bathroom—through that door there. Breakfast in half an hour.'

'Thank you. This is very kind of you—especially as my stupidity cost you an uncomfortable night.'

'Country hospitality,' he said briefly. 'No thanks necessary.'

He didn't actually say, Nothing personal, but he was making sure she understood that. Not that he had to— Sorrel recognised a rejection when it was flung in her face.

Once the door closed behind him she let out a long breath and decamped into the bathroom.

Fifteen minutes later she emerged, rosy from a luxurious wallow, dark hair silky and dry. Sensuously relishing her clean skin and underwear, she pulled on the cowl top and trousers.

For some reason she felt more alert than she had for years, more vital and vigorous. Perhaps it was being back in New Zealand, she thought, wryly aware that, much as she loved her homeland, it wasn't the reason for this singing in her blood.

It took ten minutes to craft a face that looked—well, she'd tried for serenity, but the mirror revealed a soft lick of colour along her high cheekbones and a turbulence in her eyes that no cosmetics could disguise.

'Who cares? He certainly doesn't,' she said aloud, closing her case.

Luke was striding along the hall when she came out of the bedroom. He'd showered and changed too; lean, powerful body supple in a T-shirt and another well-cut pair of trousers, he looked at her with a disturbing glitter of awareness. 'Hungry?'

'Yes.' She wondered why he'd leashed that simmering antagonism. Whatever Luke did, he did for a reason. 'I hope your housekeeper doesn't mind my food in the fridge.'

'Why should she?'

Oops. Lightly she explained, 'Most women get possessive about their workplace. I know people who don't dare go into their own kitchen because their treasured cook might take umbrage.'

'The fridge belongs to me,' he said crisply, 'and so does the food in it—except yours, of course. Penn isn't so foolish as to object. What would you like to eat?'

'Scrambled eggs,' Sorrel told him, 'and I'll cook them. I do really good scrambled eggs.'

Fifteen minutes later Luke said with lazy appreciation, '"Really good" doesn't convey the perfection of those eggs. Where did you learn to cook like that?'

'Cynthia's special technique.' Sorrel smiled, absurdly pleased by the compliment. 'When I was about twelve she was horrified to find out I couldn't do anything more than make toast and heat tinned food. She took me in hand.'

'Do you remember your mother?'

Startled, she looked across the table. Sunlight, scooped into the pleasant living and dining room by wide east-facing windows, burnished his olive skin, emphasising the bold framework that gave his face its strength and power.

He was watching her from beneath lashes that most women would kill for. Yet, long and black and thickly curling though they were, they didn't soften his face any more than the classical perfection of his mouth did. Luke looked exactly what he was—part buccaneer, part tycoon, and all hard, uncompromising male.

'Just snatches,' she said, pouring herself a cup of coffee. The homely little task gave her something to do with hands that itched to trace the outline of his mouth. 'I was four when she died, but I can remember her singing to me, and laughing with my father. And how empty our house was afterwards. Dad did his best, but nothing was ever the same again. He told me once he'd never met another woman he could love like he loved my mother.'

'Cynthia said he wasn't able to settle after that,' Luke said in a non-committal tone.

'He was always restless, always moving on,' she said defensively, wondering now if it had been gambling debts that had driven him away from each place. 'I think he got worse after my mother died.'

'So you lived a nomadic life.'

'Well—yes. But he did his best for me. I was cared for, and I knew he loved me. Do you remember your mother?'

'Very well.' Luke got to his feet and walked across the room to open the French windows onto a terrace overlooking the garden. Looking out over his domain, he said levelly, 'I was eight when she escaped from Waimanu.'

Sorrel bit her lip. 'I didn't know,' she murmured.

He gave her a swift, unreadable glance over his shoulder. 'That she left my father?' he drawled. 'I'm surprised local gossip didn't fill you in on the juicy details. She married a rich Australian who didn't expect her to live at the back of beyond. She's still with him, as far as I know.'

'As far as you know?' she asked, wondering what he meant.

'I've only seen her a few times since she left Waimanu.'

Shocked, Sorrel stared at him. 'Did your father refuse to let you go overseas?'

Luke shrugged. 'She didn't want to see me,' he said coolly.

What sort of woman would leave her child behind? 'I didn't know,' she said again, tentatively.

'It didn't make much difference; I was a proper little savage, out on the station with Dad whenever I could be.'

And what sort of answer was that?

The only one she was going to get.

Luke suddenly stooped to pick up a tennis ball, hurling it with speed and deadly accuracy at a hawk swooping low across the lawn towards helpless prey—a duck anxiously shepherding her brood up from the riverbank.

The ball landed exactly where he'd aimed it, close by the duck, and bounced high, scaring off the hawk. It soared into the air again and flew above the river towards the other side.

'Well done,' Sorrel applauded from the table, hoping he wouldn't note the false note in her voice. The swift, explosive power of his reaction had released a flood of hot response in her, something so raw and unexpected she shook with it.

She'd become a connoisseur of men's bodies after working with male models who spent hours each day in the gym, buffing and shaping their muscles set by set until they reached a peak of physical perfection. Luke had probably never set foot in a gym. Broad-shouldered, narrow-hipped and long of leg, his body had been shaped by years of punishingly hard work in the sun and rain.

And she wanted him so badly she could feel the need splintering through her—this man, only this man.

Only *ever* Luke.

Over the years she'd met nice men, sexy men,

charming men, rich men, even a few dangerously attractive men; not one had roused anything more than her mild interest. She'd even thought she'd loved a couple of them, yet making love had always been a disappointment.

But Luke—a man she didn't even like much—could make her stomach turn over with a glance and melt her bones every time he touched her.

Wide-eyed and stunned, she stared at him as he turned back towards the room. The sun gilded his tanned skin and black hair, warming those grey eyes with their rare, fugitive flash of blue. Beneath his sculpted face and the physical perfection of that big body there glowed a dark fire, an inborn sexual expertise instantly recognised by any woman who set eyes on him.

Her breath came fast through trembling lips. Sorrel lifted her coffee cup and drank. Was she so shallow that sex meant more to her than all the other things she valued in a man—love, respect, kindness, intelligence…?

No. But what made Luke different from any other man?

'I have to admire the hawk—it's nothing if not persistent,' he said, strolling inside to sit down again. 'And the ducklings make it so easy—they're imprinted to follow their mother in a single file. The hawk would take every duckling if someone didn't intervene; as it is, between it and the eels not many survive, but I do try to redress the balance.'

She tried hard for light irony, relieved when her voice came out a little stiff but without a quaver. 'It's charming to see you display your nurturing side.'

He shot her a keen look and her brain made a connection, homing in on that elusive difference.

Luke's face and bearing, the tone of his deep voice and his choice of words, every action—even the way he wore his clothes with such casual confidence—signalled a man who could be trusted to deliver on any promise he made. He didn't have to proclaim his competence—it was simply there, like his formidable intelligence and rock-solid integrity.

Perhaps she was like those ducklings, Sorrel thought with a desperation that came close to panic. Perhaps she'd been imprinted at such an early age that no man would ever measure up to Luke.

A bleak grief shivered through her. No, that was ridiculous; she was exaggerating her normal reaction to a very sexy man she'd met at an impressionable stage of her life. Every woman remembered her first love.

All she had to do was remember that, although she might be obsessed by the past, he'd moved on.

And so would she.

'Something wrong with the coffee?' Luke asked blandly.

Sorrel blinked. 'Sorry?'

His smile didn't reach the metallic grey eyes. 'You've been holding the cup in mid-air since I came back in.'

'It's delicious.' Hastily she took a sip, before putting the cup down to improvise, 'I hope it won't take too long for them to clear the slip on the road.'

'Don't worry about it.'

'Easy enough for you to say, with your thumping great generator!' she retorted crisply. 'Lovely though this house is, I want to go home to Parenga.'

He held her gaze for two of the longest seconds of

her life, before he glanced at his watch. 'I'll give Forbes a ring now.'

Sorrel said evenly, 'I'll do—'

He got to his feet, deliberately towering over her. 'Sorrel, just drink the rest of that coffee, all right? I have to contact my farm manager—make sure that everyone in the cottages is all right, that sort of thing. It's going to take me all of two minutes to ring the council after that.'

She said between her teeth, 'Stop interrupting me. It's rude, it's a form of bullying, and I won't put up with it.'

Much to her indignation he nodded. 'OK, it's a bad habit. Blame it on being an only child.'

When Sorrel snorted, he laughed softly and flicked a careless finger along her cheekbone as he went by her chair.

Which was just as well, because he didn't see the havoc that light, insulting touch made of her composure. Heat flooded up through her skin and her hand shook so much she almost spilt the coffee.

She gulped down the rest and got to her feet to pace across the room with swift, silent steps. Surely the power line would be repaired soon? Duelling with Luke was perilously exhilarating, but every minute she stayed in his house was another hole punched in her defences.

Restlessly she walked out onto the terrace, staring over the bright lawn to the red-brown gleam of the river through a screen of shrubs and trees. Bees hummed amongst flowers, the hawk flew high in the blue sky, and the cold patch in her stomach expanded.

Perhaps she should turn her back on Luke and Parenga—just walk away and leave before she got in too deep. From the wreckage of her affairs she'd saved enough money to survive for a very frugal six months; fewer if she had to find another place to live. She could manage that. And although she probably wouldn't be able to resurrect her career, she might find a job in fashion somewhere.

Except that she didn't want to go back to that world, and if she left Parenga she'd be letting Cynthia down; for some reason it had been important to her godmother that she spend six months here.

Her head came up unconsciously and her lips firmed. For Cynthia she would do it, Luke or no.

When he was near she might flutter like a moth snared by the fatal fascination of a candle, but she was safe enough; he didn't want her.

She went back inside and began to clear the table. When he returned she'd just lifted the marmalade pot in one hand, the jug of orange juice in the other.

'Hardcastle Road is well down the list,' he said aloofly. 'They didn't know you were back, of course, but even so other roads have more people living on them. And until McLeod's Hill is cleared the power board can't get in.'

Frowning, she elbowed open the door between the family room and kitchen. 'How long will that take?'

'Probably not until tomorrow morning.'

She spluttered, 'That's outrageous!'

'You're in the north of New Zealand,' he said, a whiplash of contempt slicing into her. 'The world doesn't revolve around you. Yesterday's storm was a bad one, and coming after a long, dry spell it's created mayhem. It doesn't matter anyway—you can stay here until the power's restored.'

Cynically Luke waited for her to protest; she didn't

disappoint him. Her eyes narrowed, the black lashes concentrating their pale clarity into green-gold crystals. Her chin lifted, and the luscious mouth that had fuelled millions of feverish male fantasies tightened.

Her voice, however, was patient. 'Thank you for the invitation, but that won't be necessary. I can manage.'

'How?' he demanded, clamping down on a hot spurt of anger. 'In a house with no furniture, no blankets, nothing to keep you warm except a fireplace?' He paused before adding deliberately, 'And that's not counting the lack of water and sewage.'

Luke's eyes narrowed as she sauntered into the kitchen, hips swaying in the seductive movement that still figured in his dreams. Silently he cursed the involuntary tightening of every muscle in his body. He began to collect the utensils.

From the other side of the door she said quietly, 'It's not your problem, Luke.'

He strode through into the kitchen. 'If it were Cynthia, would you expect me to leave her there?' He waited for the next objection, wondering why he bothered. Why not just let her go back to Parenga, muddle uncomfortably around until the road opened and she could get Cynthia's furniture out of storage? She was nothing to him.

Nothing but trouble.

He despised himself for wanting her, even in this uncomplicated, purely sexual way. He shouldn't have held her sleek, fragrant body in his arms last night, calling up old memories, an old hunger...

Yet he couldn't just let her go.

'That's different,' she parried. 'Cynthia was old. No one would expect her to sleep on the floor!' She changed tack. 'It's very kind of you, but—'

'I'm not kind,' he told her, the words echoing in her mind.

Steadying her voice, she said, 'Listen to me, Luke! I can't just dump myself on you.'

'Unless you camp in the car or go back and sleep on the floor at Parenga, you can't do anything else,' he said curtly, dumping the utensils onto the granite counter. 'And either of those would be cutting off your nose to spite your face.'

He was right, damn him. Grabbing at her self-possession, she said formally, 'If I could just borrow a mattress—'

'I have no spares.'

Furious, she expostulated, 'This house must have at least four bedrooms.'

'Five.' His eyes mocked her.

Sorrel said jerkily, 'Then surely I can borrow a mattress?'

'No,' he said, his voice coldly final. 'Apart from mine, the only other room that's furnished is the one you showered in. Stop it, Sorrel. You're going to have to come along here for meals and to wash, so you might as well sleep here too.'

Sorrel seethed. One glance at his face told her he wasn't going to yield. Luke was a hard man, but he had an inbuilt protectiveness she had no answer to.

'As dictatorial as ever,' she said stiffly. 'I'm not a mother duck, Luke, nor one of those helpless fluffy ducklings.'

He divined the cause of her reluctance and disposed of it with rapid ruthlessness. 'But you see me as a predator, like the hawk. Surely last night showed you that you're quite safe with me?' His mouth curled in contempt. 'I won't demand any payment if you accept the offer of a bed here.'

His cold gaze and flinty features told her exactly how little impact she had on him. Well, she was immune to him—except for that brutally physical response, and she wasn't going to surrender to it. She wanted much more from a man than emotionless sex, however magnificent it might be.

Controlling the chaotic mix of emotions that rampaged through her, she said coolly, 'I certainly don't expect you to demand that I sleep with you in return for the loan of a bed.'

Beyond a compression of his wide, arrogantly outlined mouth he didn't show any surprise at her frankness. 'Then you have no reason to go back to Parenga until you've got furniture and utilities.'

Her eyes clashed with his uncompromising gaze. Sorrel raised hers heavenwards, but accepted as gracefully as she could. 'Thank you.' Then spoilt it all by adding, 'You're as stubborn as a pig.'

'So I've been told,' he said blandly. 'That's settled, then.'

Trying—and failing—to tap into the core of serenity she'd worked so long to acquire, Sorrel opened the door under the sink and peered into the interior of the cupboard.

'Leave those,' he commanded when he saw her pull out the detergent.

'Why?' She straightened up and sent him a belligerent stare.

'Most of them go into the dishwasher, and those that don't the housekeeper will do.'

Sorrel squirted liquid into the sink. 'You stack the

dishwasher and I'll do these,' she said crisply. 'How will your housekeeper get here? By balloon?'

'She lives over the garage, so she'll just walk down some stairs and in the back door.' He glanced at his watch. 'In fact she'll be here shortly.'

It was too intimate, doing this. Sorrel remembered other occasions, nights when Cynthia had asked him along for dinner and fussed a little over him—fussing he'd endured with a smile because, as Cynthia had once observed to Sorrel, 'He knows it makes me feel better about buying the homestead from him!'

He'd been so young to assume the burden of responsibility for Waimanu, but he'd never asked for sympathy. And he'd been astute and unsentimental enough to make hard decisions like selling Parenga so he could use the money to drag his inheritance out of its mire of mismanagement.

The sound of the door opening made Sorrel turn; a woman in her mid-forties came into the room. The smile on her face froze when she saw Sorrel, but only for a second—she replaced it with an enquiring glance at Luke, who was carrying butter and honey across to the refrigerator.

He said, 'Sorrel, this is Penn Turner, who keeps the place running. She is Parenga's owner, Penn, but Sorrel will be staying here until the power comes back on.'

Sorrel and Penn exchanged greetings, and then the housekeeper, a pretty, dark-haired woman with wide blue eyes and a ready smile, bustled into the kitchen and said, 'I'll do that!'

'It's all right,' Sorrel said automatically.

Smiling with polite determination, Penn made shooing motions. 'Guests at Waimanu do not do the dishes!'

She looked at the pile on the bench and said, 'Or stack the dishwasher! Off you go!'

Sorrel stepped back, surrendering with an inward smile at the smaller woman. 'Of course,' she said lightly, and walked out of the kitchen through the door that Luke held open.

He followed her silently, but when they turned a corner in the hall he asked, 'What's the problem?'

He'd always been able to read her mind. 'It's not *my* problem.' She lowered her voice, mimicking his. ' "Sorrel will be staying." A classic male statement—on a par with, *Darling, I've just brought ten friends home for dinner!* No query about whether the food will stretch far enough.'

'I pay Penn to deal with that.' His smile was edged. 'And I'm sure no famous model worries about cooking dinner when her lover of the moment wanders in with a guest. Surely that's what restaurants are for?'

'You have a restaurant close by?' she asked sarcastically.

'We always have plenty of food in store.' His shrug indicated that this was completely unimportant to him. 'What would you like to do today?'

'I'm going to start cleaning Parenga.'

His brows met together across the blade of his nose. 'What?'

'You heard. The house needs cleaning.'

'It also needs painting and a fair few minor repairs—repairs that should have been done over the past two years—and the garden needs a considerable amount of attention,' he pointed out relentlessly. 'Are you planning to do all that too?'

Clearly he thought she had the strength and stamina—not to mention the brains—of a jellyfish. Sorrel said crisply, 'Some of it. I certainly don't plan to sit around and paint my toenails. Now, if you show me where the sheets are kept I'll make my bed in the spare bedroom.'

'Do you remember how?' he drawled.

She looked him directly in the eye. 'Why are you being offensive?' she said without a tremor. 'Of course I remember—I make my own bed every morning! Do you?'

'Yes.' He glanced at his watch. 'I've got a phone call due, but if you'll give me five minutes I'll see that the sheets get to you.'

She started up the stairs, suddenly so angry that she couldn't stay with him. Halfway up she stopped and turned, leaning over the banister. He was watching her, his face dark and closed. In a syrupy voice she said, 'It's time you realised I'm all grown up and that I know what I'm doing.'

'You've always known that,' he said indifferently, adding with a glance that pierced her composure like a sword-blade, 'Most women seem to be born knowing it.'

'Now that,' she said, straightening up, 'sounds very close to misogyny.'

'I don't hate women.'

'But you don't trust them.'

With the kind of smile a lion probably bestowed before opening its jaws on its prey, he said, 'I trust anyone who's earned it.'

An icy chill ran down her spine as he swung on his heel and disappeared into a room along the hall.

Five minutes later she'd stripped the covers from the bed, and was setting out the contents of her sponge bag in the bathroom when she heard a knock on the outside door.

It was Luke, armed with a pile of linen. He ignored her outstretched hands and dumped the sheets and pillowcases on the elegant bench at the foot of the bed.

Footsteps along the hall, accompanied by the calling of his name, summoned him. 'Telephone!' Penn announced. 'It's Mr Sutherland—you said he was important.'

He stood for a moment, face expressionless, before turning. 'I'll be right down.'

As the door closed behind him Sorrel hastily sorted through the sheets and made the bed. She was smoothing out the claret coverlet when there was another knock at the door.

'Come in,' she called, expecting Penn.

It wasn't the housekeeper; Luke stood in the doorway, brows drawn together.

'What's the matter?' she asked quickly.

The frown deepened. 'Nothing,' he said. 'I'm going to Auckland.'

'How?'

'Chopper,' he said succinctly. 'Do you want to come?'

'No, thank you,' she said in her most precise voice. 'I'll be fine.'

'I won't be back tonight, but Penn will look after you.'

'I don't need looking after,' Sorrel said, a hint of frost in her tone, adding with a wry smile, 'But I have to admit I'd rather sleep in this lovely bed than on the floor at Parenga.'

He gave a tight smile. 'So would I,' he said, in a voice that made her look up sharply.

For a moment memories of the night before flooded Sorrel's brain; colour ran like fire through her skin, but she lifted her chin aggressively. Luke's gaze moved to her mouth and then back up to clash with hers.

'Have a good trip,' she said harshly.

Without a word he went out, closing the door behind him.

Heart racing, Sorrel sat down on the edge of the bed, her long fingers caressing the richly coloured silk. Last night in Luke's arms had been heaven, and it meant far too much; if she let her busy mind dwell on it she could recall everything.

And that she couldn't afford to do.

Another knock on the door brought her across the room. This room, she decided as she flung open the door, was getting more like O'Hare Airport every minute!

But it was Penn. 'Oh,' she said in a startled voice, 'you've made the bed! I was just coming in to do it.'

'I don't want to give you any extra work.' Sorrel wished she could rid herself of this feeling that the other woman had taken an instant dislike to her.

'Well, that's my job.' Penn smiled tolerantly. 'I'll come back and do the bathroom when you're out.'

'I can do that too,' Sorrel told her.

The older woman's smile set. 'I don't think Luke would appreciate his guests doing the housework,' she said with a light little laugh. 'It's all right—I don't pry.'

'I didn't—I'm sure you don't.' Round two, Sorrel thought dourly, to the housekeeper. Closing the door, she shrugged. Eventually Penn would realise that she wasn't fighting. In the meantime she was going back to Parenga. She needed time out.

Setting her jaw, she set off down the stairs. She'd

almost reached the bottom when she heard a slight sound and saw a door open along the hall. Luke strode through, stopping when he saw her. He stood in shadow, but she sensed his intent, focused attention, and in spite of everything she was fiercely glad she'd learned to walk with such casual grace.

And that was another dangerous reaction...

'I'm off,' she said, directing a restrained smile in his direction without quite meeting his eyes.

Abruptly Luke said, 'Penn seems to think you've accused her of prying.'

'I'm sorry if she thought that.' Sorrel frowned, trying to recall exactly what she'd said. 'I told her that I'd do the bathroom because I don't want to make any extra work for her, not because I don't trust her.'

'That's her job,' Luke pointed out, adding deliberately, 'You surprise me.'

'Because I'm capable of cleaning a bathroom?' she returned, her voice rising slightly. 'I've stayed in the occasional house that has servants, and in hotels, of course, but in New York I had my own apartment, and although there was a house-cleaning service I did quite a lot of it myself when I was there.' She lifted a brow and finished acidly, not caring that she'd let her irritation get the better of her, 'Have a great time in Auckland.'

Steadily, body poised and relaxed, she took the final step, irritated because it destroyed her temporary advantage of superior height, and walked past him with her back so erect she thought she heard her spine complain.

She felt his eyes boring into the sensitive part between her shoulderblades until she disappeared around the corner.

Why did Penn want to make trouble?

CHAPTER SIX

IN THE midst of scrutinising the main bedroom at Parenga, Sorrel heard the *whump, whump, whump* of helicopter rotors turning. She blinked as the engine noise increased to a shriek, and ran across to the windows, pushing them open to the sunny air to crane out.

She couldn't see the chopper take off, but she heard it rising high to clear the hills. What had called Luke to Auckland?

'None of your business,' she said aloud, and stooped to stroke Baggie.

Almost immediately she straightened up and looked around the room again. She had work to do.

'I'd better make a list,' she said to the cat, who'd taken up residence in a patch of sunlight.

He bestowed her a narrow, long-suffering look, and after an elaborate stretch and a wide yawn that displayed his splendid teeth subsided back into sleep. Smiling, Sorrel ran down the stairs to unearth her handheld computer, a relic from the days when she'd needed all the help she could to keep up with appointments.

Two hours later a cold, unpleasant ball of worry consolidated beneath her ribs as she scrolled down the screen. She hadn't bargained on having to make so many repairs to Parenga. And those were only the visible ones; there were bound to be more she hadn't noticed.

How much would it cost?

'Cleaning first,' she told Baggie, then frowned. 'I

wish the road was open—I need stuff. Oh, well, I'll see if I can borrow a bucket and some detergent from Luke's rather obstructive housekeeper so I can start after lunch.' She glanced at her watch. 'Which I'd better get back to!'

The meal was scheduled for midday, so she just had time to walk along to Waimanu.

At Luke's house she paused inside the back door and listened. Silence and stillness enveloped her, isolating her from warmth and life, telling her in some uncanny, subliminal way that he wasn't there.

Scolding herself for being foolishly fanciful, Sorrel sketched a shrug and headed for the kitchen. 'Hello,' she said cheerfully, opening the door.

Penn dumped a casserole dish onto the bench before swivelling around, one hand pressed to her heart.

'Oh!' she exclaimed, then let out a huff of breath and smiled. 'Sorry, I get a bit jumpy when I'm alone. Lunch is ready—I've set it out buffet-style on the table in the family room, if that's all right with you. It's through here.' She bustled towards the hall.

'Great,' Sorrel said, following her and deducing that from now on she'd better knock whenever she arrived at Waimanu. 'How long has Luke being flying helicopters?'

'Oh, it must be four or five years—ever since he bought one.' The other woman pushed open a door and stood back to let Sorrel go first into the pleasant room in which she and Luke had eaten their breakfast. 'He wouldn't be able to manage without it. Running a big agricultural company means a lot of travelling, and of course he has a busy social life too.' She added with a guileless smile, 'He's going to some big film premiere tonight with his—his friend, Miss O'Neill.'

In spite of the sliver of dark emotion that stabbed Sorrel to the heart, she kept the mask of polite interest in place. 'Sounds fun,' she said noncommittally.

'I suppose you used to go to lots of them when you were modelling.'

'Quite a few.'

Another wide, ingenuous smile from the house-keeper. 'It must have been so exciting to have cameras flash at you and everybody watching you go in!'

'You get used to it. One of the good things about being a model,' Sorrel told her cheerfully, 'is that because you're there as decoration nobody expects you to have enough intelligence to string more than a couple of words together, so at least they don't ambush you with microphones.'

Penn looked startled. 'Well, yes, there's that, I suppose. By the way, Luke asked me to reassure you that you're welcome to stay here as long as you like, and of course if there's anything I can do to help you, you must let me know.'

'How very kind,' Sorrel murmured. 'As it happens, there is...'

An hour later she strode back to Parenga, carrying a bucket of cloths, scrubbers and various bottles of detergents. The housekeeper had handed them over with a polite smirk that indicated she didn't believe her unwelcome guest knew anything at all about housework.

'So I will show her,' Sorrel said between her teeth. 'And anyone else who thinks I'm just a useless ornament!'

Not that her afternoon of ferocious cleaning was really to show anyone that she wasn't a useless ornament; instead, she used the hard work to block out the violent jealousy that had needled her since the housekeeper told her why Luke had gone to Auckland. Scrubbing and mopping the kitchen and bathrooms kept her busy enough not to dwell obsessively on mental pictures of him with Mari O'Neill. In fact, she sometimes went for ten minutes without more than an occasional thought of them making love.

By the time she arrived back at Waimanu that evening she was grubby and hot, longing only to wash and then eat. Cleanliness came first, and when she finally came down the staircase after a long, luxurious bath, Penn was waiting at the foot of the stairs.

'Why don't you go into the sitting room?' the housekeeper suggested. 'I'll pour you a drink and serve dinner when you're ready. You must be exhausted.' She marched down to a door and opened it.

'I'm a little tired,' Sorrel admitted, curbing the impulse to point out that, although she wouldn't have been able to spend a day wielding a crowbar, she was neither fragile nor useless. Just inside the sitting room she stopped and said, 'I'm sure you're busy enough without having to bother about me. It seems a waste of your time to prepare meals when I can do it myself.'

'Luke wouldn't like that,' Penn stated, as though Luke's wishes were edicts engraved in stone. She met Sorrel's eyes with a movement of her lips that was less a smile than a challenge.

Why, if Mari O'Neill was still an important part of Luke's life, did Penn see Sorrel as a threat?

Possibly because a woman climbing the corporate ladder in Auckland didn't interfere with her position at Waimanu. More likely because the housekeeper liked Mari. That wouldn't be surprising; most people did.

Hell, even with her adolescent heart breaking, *Sorrel* had liked her!

'What would you care to drink?' the housekeeper asked in a tone verging on the proprietorial.

'Nothing, thank you,' Sorrel said collectedly, refusing to be irritated by the attempts to patronise her. 'I'll have dinner on a tray and then go up to my room.'

Penn looked taken aback. 'Oh, but—'

'Thank you,' Sorrel said firmly.

'If you're sure that's what you want?' the housekeeper said doubtfully.

'Certain.' Sorrel waited until the woman had left before looking around the opulent sitting room with its view of the river across a long terrace. Gracious and relaxing though it was, it didn't soothe her at all.

And neither did meditation later that evening. Years before, Sorrel had discovered meditation as a tool for serenity, but this time it failed her. After a frustrating twenty minutes spent visualising Luke with Mari in full Technicolor, she opened her eyes.

Loneliness punched her in the heart, driving her to her feet and across to the windows. Her best friend lived only an hour's drive away, but Emma and her husband, Kane Talbot, were in Canada with their delectable four-year-old daughter—Sorrel's goddaughter Cressy—and not due home for another three weeks. It would be great to live so near them...

She'd flown up to Vancouver to see them before she'd come on to New Zealand. It had been a bittersweet occasion; Emma was so happy with her gorgeous husband that Sorrel had to try hard not to envy her.

As for Cressy...

Sorrel leaned out and breathed in the cool, faintly saline air. An unknown scent—almost overpoweringly sweet—rose strongly from the garden below. It had been a real wrench to leave Cressy behind. Still, she'd see her again soon.

Sorrel bit her lip. Little Cressy was a darling, but she wanted her own children, she realised with something close to shock. OK, cuddling her goddaughter had probably set her biological clock ticking, but why did her childless state suddenly seem so poignant?

What was Luke doing right this moment?

'Oh, for heaven's sake!' she muttered, trying hard to banish Mari's voluptuous figure and her lovely, vital face from her brain.

Had Luke thought it was Mari he was kissing last night, until he'd woken sufficiently to realise who was in his arms?

Humiliation drained the colour from her skin.

Perhaps that was how it had begun, she reassured herself, but he'd known who she was when he'd touched her breast. And somehow she couldn't see Luke as a betrayer.

So whatever relationship he had with Mari had to be less than an affair. Or was she merely thinking wishfully, endowing him with virtues he didn't have?

She didn't know enough about Luke to be sure.

Her brooding gaze swept the garden below, taking in a froth of white along one border, a glimmer of silver through the trees where starlight was reflected from the water. A quick knock was a welcome interruption to her tormented thoughts.

'Sitting in the dark?' the housekeeper enquired brightly when Sorrel opened the door to her.

'Enjoying the view from the window.'

'It's beautiful, isn't it? Now, I've finished for the night,' Penn said, 'but before I go I thought I'd better tell you that the house has security all through it, so if you need anything from outside your room you should get it now, before I turn the alarms on.'

'I don't need anything,' Sorrel said quietly. 'Goodnight.' She closed the door with a sharp click.

Talk about a heavy-handed hint not to go wandering around!

Fuming, she went back to the window. If she leaned out a bit she could just see the roof of Parenga through the trees, dim in the gathering darkness.

Yesterday she'd arrived with such high hopes, expecting to build a new life here, only to find her plans crashing around her ears within the first twenty-four hours. She'd been confident Luke meant nothing to her; instead she'd taken one look at him and responded to his potent masculinity with the same shaken, helpless intensity as she had ten years ago.

Spending the first night in his arms had been a particularly nasty twist of fate. She'd burned with a forgotten, familiar need, her common sense driven like ashes before the wind in a firestorm of hungry sensation.

Just thinking about it fuelled an elemental longing so urgent she had to grit her teeth and clench her hands on the windowsill to stop them from shaking.

'Degrading,' she muttered. She drew back and turned around to look at the beautiful room. Something that had been teasing her popped into the forefront of her brain. Why hadn't Luke furnished any other bedrooms but his own and this one?

Perhaps because he was waiting for Mari to do it?

'Oh, stop it,' she muttered, heading into the bathroom. If twenty-four hours at Parenga had done this to her, how was she going to last out six months?

'Because you have to,' she said clearly, turning on the taps over the basin. 'And because Cynthia wanted you to.'

This obsession with Luke was just a hangover from adolescence, something she didn't want and couldn't afford—but something she could overcome with doses of common sense and will-power. She'd find salvation in cleaning and painting Parenga's shabby walls and woodwork; surely it wouldn't be too expensive, or difficult. Sorrel wasn't afraid of hard work, and nowadays—if television ads were to be believed—paint flowed onto walls by itself.

But what about exposing her heart in the process?

A chill of foreboding shivered through her.

Automatically going through her nightly routine, she wondered fretfully why Luke seemed to have taken up permanent residence in her—well, not in her heart, that was certain. She didn't love him, but oh, what he did to her hormones! It was unfair and unnerving and dangerous.

Other women smiled a little sentimentally when talking about their first love, then tied the memories in pastel scented ribbons and tucked them away for ever. Why hadn't it happened that way for her? She'd never managed to struggle free from the memory of one kiss.

One kiss! Hardly enough to build a lifetime of memories on. Yet her recollection glowed, still bright and unfaded, as though she'd never grown older than the girl of eighteen who'd loved Luke from afar. If she closed her eyes she could see the way he'd bent down to her, the glitter of blue in his grey eyes, his dark, suddenly taut face. She'd held her breath, waiting to be rejected...

Instead, his lips had touched her mouth so gently she'd barely felt it, yet she'd shuddered with delight.

'You're so lovely,' he said in a deep, gentle tone without lifting his head.

Entranced by the feel of his words against her sensitive skin, it took her a moment to register a kind of regret in his voice. He was going to stop.

No! Her height and the constant moves from school to school meant that this was Sorrel's first kiss; she had no idea what to do next, but she remembered films she had seen and shyly opened her lips, put one hand lightly, tentatively on his chest.

He froze, but beneath the heel of her hand his heartbeat ricocheted into a hard, pounding beat. Exultant, her hold on reality slipping fast, Sorrel wasn't expecting what followed. Luke made an odd raw noise in his throat and his mouth hardened on hers as his arms tightened around her, bringing her against a taut, almost aggressive body, lean and so big she was swamped by his assertive male strength.

But she melted against him, enchanted by new and thrilling sensations. He possessed himself of her mouth in a kiss that laid claim to everything female about her, and she yielded, submissive yet demanding her own surrender, her own power…

'Oh, yes, it was magnificent—soul-shattering, mind-bending, earth-shaking—but don't forget what happened next,' she reminded herself now, staring belligerently into the mirror. 'Let's see. He pulled away, just as he did last night, and he apologised—very abruptly, as though he hated you—and then said he'd never do it again.'

But it was the remembered note of self-contempt in his deep voice that haunted the gold-green eyes gazing back at her. He'd kissed her with a starving intensity that still sent shivers down her spine, yet he'd despised himself for it—just as he had last night.

She stiffened her jaw and turned away to dry her face.

Despise himself or not, however, he wanted her. So why not indulge in a wild affair and finally douse that consuming desire that had smouldered in her for so long? The realities of an affair—sex without commitment—would certainly strip those pretty ribbons from her memories and replace them with workaday string. No man could live up to the expectations she'd built of Luke.

The idea was seductively attractive, but even as her heart beat faster and colour scorched her skin she discarded it. An age-old feminine instinct warned her that taking Luke for a lover was *not* the way to root out the hold he had on her emotions. It would change her for ever.

Besides, the previous night had reinforced with cruel force that he felt nothing more for her than a crude, sexual hunger. She deserved better than that.

Yes, she had a life to make for herself, and Parenga was the first step. She'd find the strength to resist Luke's effect on her.

Probably she should be grateful that if he knew about it he'd wholeheartedly support her decision!

The morning after Luke flew out the road was cleared and the power switched back on, so Sorrel collected her provisions from the fridge at Waimanu, thanked Penn, and drove back to Parenga.

That afternoon she went into Kerikeri to replace the cleaning equipment she'd borrowed and liberate

Cynthia's furniture from the storage unit. The carriers piled it carefully in the garage. She hated to see it like that, a life reduced to a heap, but at least she was now saving the weekly rental. She needed that money.

Days passed in a blur. Sorrel scoured the inside of the house, then chose paint colours and bought the paint, working so hard that every night she fell into bed and slept dreamlessly without stirring.

The difficult part was actually getting to sleep; each night she lay for hours with memories of Luke's kisses burning through her with erotic intensity.

Now, more than a week after he'd left, Sorrel walked back in the dusk from a jaunt along the beach, realising with angry irritation that she'd spent every one of those days listening for the unmistakable sound of the helicopter.

'Get over him!' she commanded on a caustic note, bending to sniff the sweet, musky scent of the first gardenia bloom. Summer was rapidly ousting spring, bringing with it other flowers—brilliant vireya rhododendrons from the tropics and the first frilly, saturated scarlet hibiscus to blend with the bright buds of lilies and the bold blue of agapanthus.

Wincing at an ache in her back, she straightened up and surveyed her domain. She'd told the gardener she no longer needed him, and had resurrected Cynthia's elderly mower for the lawns, but the flowerbeds were still showing a lack of care.

'I'll get to you as soon as the house is in shape,' she promised.

Next week would be devoted to painting and polishing and a painful, judicious weeding out of the furniture her godmother had collected over a lifetime. Cynthia's magpie instincts had crowded every room in the house, and selling some of her treasures would bring in money to help pay for a replacement length of guttering and, if she was lucky, a few of the minor repairs needed.

'In the meantime,' Sorrel told Baggie as she put out his food and opened the back door a fraction so he could head out for his nightly inspection of the property, 'I'm going to have a bath and soak for at least half an hour.'

Ten minutes later she lowered herself gratefully into the bath, almost purring as the water, silky with a few drops of oil, lapped around her.

'Bliss,' she groaned, and leaned her head back, stretching out her arms along the cool sides of the old-fashioned tub and wallowing in the immeasurable comfort of scented water.

I'd better get out, she thought the second time she had to force her eyelids up.

She woke with a jolt to the sound of her name, shouted in a furious masculine voice. 'Sorrel! Sorrel, where the hell are you?'

'Here,' she croaked before she had time to think, blinking and reaching for her towel in the darkness.

'Where?'

Her mouth dried and she sat up. *Luke!* Her bones weighed her down so that when she tried to stand her legs refused to accept her weight. A startled cry broke from her lips as she slipped, falling back into the water with a splash.

'What—?'

Light blinded her.

He strode in, absorbed in one comprehensive glance the sight of her cowering in the bath with the wet towel held against her like a shield, and bent to pull out the plug. 'For God's sake, Sorrel, don't tell me you were idiotic enough to go to sleep in the bath!'

'I—yes,' she muttered, horrified by her foolishness.

'You could have drowned yourself!' Grim grey eyes took in her feeble attempts to hide behind the towel.

'Luke, go away, please.' She shivered and looked numbly down at her long bare legs revealed by the gurgling water.

'Get up.' When she didn't move he said tersely, 'You can't, can you?'

In one powerful, economical movement he leaned over, picked her up and set her on her feet on the bath-mat. Once more her treacherous legs collapsed, but as Luke's arms clamped around her something feverish stirred in the pit of her stomach, a primitive response, needle-sharp yet melting and honey-sweet.

She said, 'I'm making you wet—'

'Of all the stupid, reckless, carelessly irresponsible things to do,' he snarled. 'Damn it, Sorrel—'

He lifted her off her feet and strode out into the hall, with her positioned like a child—or a lover—in his arms.

Trembling with shock, she stiffened and fought the weakness that relished the heat from his body and its solid, feral strength.

'Put me down,' she said in a jerky voice, her heart beating crazily in her breast.

'You can't even stand up; what makes you think you'll be able to walk?'

He was right. Changing tack, she said, 'Not up-stairs—I'm sleeping in the maid's room at the back.'

After a second's hesitation, he moved steadily and surely through the darkened house. 'How long were you in that bath?' he demanded.

'I don't know—since dusk.'

'Over an hour.' His voice hardened even further. 'You need a keeper.'

'It won't happen again.' Thank heavens for the friendly night; he wouldn't be able to see anything more of her naked body than a pale blob in his arms.

His icy, ferocious anger engulfed her. 'It had better bloody not. Why are you sleeping downstairs?'

'It's more convenient.'

He elbowed the door open, switched on the light and took a couple of steps into the small room, swearing under his breath when he kicked the end of the double bed that took up most of it. A moment later she was on her feet, white-lipped and swaying.

Lean hands fastened onto her shoulders; ignoring her protest, he turned her to him, dark face closed against her as he began to rub her dry.

'I can do that,' she said thickly, clutching the towel around her.

'At the moment I feel more like shaking common sense into you than flinging you onto the bed and making wild, passionate love, believe me,' he said with satirical emphasis.

Gritting her teeth, she said, 'I can dry myself.'

'All right, show me.'

Her muscles were as floppy as jelly, and she was still paralysed with horror at what might have happened if Luke hadn't come in. Nevertheless, she wasn't going to let him dry her. She said raggedly, 'Get out, Luke!'

Baggie, who'd appeared from nowhere, wound himself around Luke's ankles. Ignoring the cat, Luke asked in a voice that sent frigid shivers scudding down her spine, 'Can you manage?'

'Of course I can,' she muttered, and began to dry her shivering skin.

'I'll make some tea,' he said curtly. 'Yell if you need help.'

Without looking at her he strode across the room and disappeared silently down the hall towards the kitchen.

Sorrel watched him go, then collapsed onto the side of the bed and finished drying herself.

When that was done, she looked at the jeans she'd been planning to wear and knew she wasn't going to be able to get into them. She had all the strength of a cooked noodle.

Forced into action by the thought of Luke coming for her, she got to her feet and staggered to the wardrobe, where she chose a long wrap-around skirt and a shell top, thankful that she didn't need to worry about a bra.

Even so it was a struggle, but she was decently covered and combing her hair when Lucas appeared in the doorway.

He scanned her face with a frigid, thin-lipped lack of compromise. 'How are you feeling?'

'Much better, thanks.' Sorrel's glance slipped past the wet patch across his shirt where he'd held her.

Avoiding his intent stare, she got up and walked with deliberate care towards him, encouraged by a spurt of adrenalin-induced energy. 'Perfectly normal, as you can see.'

He watched her narrowly, reluctantly appreciating her stubborn determination not to give in. She was steady enough on her feet, but he'd stay close by to make sure she didn't fall.

He stood back to let her through the door and caught a light fragrance—sweet, yet with a sultry undernote—

that stripped the years away as though they'd never happened. Cynthia had given her that perfume for her eighteenth birthday; perhaps, he thought, calling on cynicism to rescue him from a humiliating enslavement of the senses, she was wearing it because she knew of perfume's ability to lodge in the memory.

Face bare of cosmetics, hair pulled back in an untidy knot, shadows beneath her eyes, she looked heart-shakingly beautiful—even more beautiful than in that photograph of her naked in another man's arms, her lovely face lifted to his, her smile a slow, wondering invitation.

Savagely angry, Luke followed her down the hall, ready to catch her if she fell. She didn't, but she stumbled occasionally, once putting out a hand to brace herself against the wall.

In the kitchen she sat down at the table in the breakfast area, more colour in her face. 'I'm sorry,' she said unexpectedly.

'For almost killing yourself?' he asked, tamping down on his anger.

She nodded, her gold-green eyes avoiding his. 'Well, for being stupid. From now on I'll shower, or set an alarm.'

'I suppose it's no use asking you to come and stay at the homestead?'

'No.' She gave a swift little shudder. 'Believe me, falling asleep like that scared me. I won't do it again.'

She looked so fragile he wanted to drag her back to Waimanu and chain her to his wrist. He'd never forget the sight of her in the bath, unable to stand, unable even to think. If he'd been even a few minutes later she might well have drowned.

Frustrated, because he knew there was no way he

could make a direct order stick, he poured two mugs of tea and brought them to the table. 'You always were as obstinate as a chunk of granite,' he said bluntly as he sat down opposite her.

Sorrel laughed and picked up the mug he pushed across to her. 'It takes one chunk of granite to know another,' she said. Without looking at him she drank, managing not to wrinkle her nose at the overdose of sugar in the hot liquid.

'Finish it,' he said, judging her reaction too well. 'Why were you so tired? What have you been doing?'

Sorrel turned her head away from him, presenting her elegant profile. 'Sanding down the woodwork in the main bathroom.'

She was acutely conscious of that steady iron-grey gaze as he drank some of his own tea, watching her above the rim of the mug. It was an oddly intimate moment, made more so by the dark patch on his shirt. Shivery excitement replaced Sorrel's exhaustion. She said reluctantly, 'Do you want to put your shirt in the drier?'

'No, it's almost dry,' he said indifferently. 'What's going on? Penn tells me you borrowed cleaning things from her, and that you've been working solidly ever since I left. Trying to prove something, Sorrel?'

She examined the bottom of her cup. 'Why should I do that?'

'I don't know,' he said with cool calculation, burnished gaze fixed on her face. 'What exactly are your plans?'

She glanced away. 'If I decide to stay I'm seriously thinking of turning Parenga into a very upscale bed and breakfast.'

His eyes narrowed into slivers of molten metal. 'The

hell you are,' he said softly. He leaned back in his chair and surveyed her with chilling intensity. 'You'll need council permission.'

'I contacted them today,' she said levelly. 'The man I spoke to said he didn't anticipate any problems unless my neighbours object. Are you going to object, Luke?'

CHAPTER SEVEN

'I'LL need more information before I make a decision,'
Luke said drily. 'Drink your tea, and then come and
have dinner with me at Waimanu. You can tell me
about it there.'

It wasn't a threat—he even smiled faintly at her as
he made the invitation—but Sorrel detected a note in
his words that sent prickles of unease down her spine.
He might not be able to prevent her from setting up
Parenga as a bed and breakfast, but he wielded a lot of
power in the North; he could delay the process and
make it much more expensive.

So she agreed with a certain amount of reserve. 'All
right. I'll just get changed.'

His brows lifted as he surveyed her. 'You look fine.'
And after a pause, in a harder voice, 'Exquisite.'

Did he think she planned to seduce him into accepting her plan? Resentment pulsed through her, burnish-
ing her skin and restoring her strength. 'Thank you,'
she said with composure. 'Did you enjoy the film premiere?'

The shutters slammed down, leaving his handsome
face expressionless. 'Very much. Mari sent her regards,
by the way.'

'That's kind of her.' It sounded so stiff that she drank
more tea, striving to come up with some light—but
sophisticated—remark. Her brain remaining obstinately
blank, she finished the repulsively sweet tea and
stood up.

112

'How do you feel?' Luke asked, rising with her.

'Slightly odd,' she admitted. 'A bit floaty, but that might be because it's a couple of hours after my usual dinnertime. Better than I deserve to feel.'

'Indeed.' The crisp intonation told her he was still angry. 'Next time lock the door to the house. I walked straight in.'

An undercurrent in his voice sent her heartbeat soaring, reminding her of the moments when he'd held her naked in his arms.

And not shown the slightest interest in her beyond a surprising unleashed fury at her stupidity. 'Baggie likes to go for an evening prowl after his night meal,' she said, striving for an objective tone instead of infuriating defensiveness. 'Besides, if I hadn't left it open you wouldn't have been able to come in.' And she might have drowned.

Luke paused, hiding his thoughts behind that impassive face and those hooded eyes. 'Your car's there, so I knew you were home. If you hadn't answered I'd have hammered on the door until you did. Next time you go into town buy a cat door. It's not safe, even here, to leave doors unlocked. I've lost cattle to rustlers, and there have been farm burglaries in the district.'

She said sombrely, 'So there's no safe place any more?'

'Nowhere in this world,' he said, adding with brutal realism, 'But then, there never has been.'

Sorrel was more afraid of the heady combination of arousal and anticipation in her blood than she was of any criminal. Near Luke she came alive, as though she'd spent her previous life sleepwalking.

Stay cool, she told herself. He doesn't want to want

you, and you aren't going to scratch his itch just for the excitement of it.

He's more than you can handle.

In the big sitting room at Waimanu he waited until she was sitting down before measuring her with a glance as sharp as a scalpel, a glance that clashed with his smooth tone. 'Wine? There's a rather nice *sauvignon blanc* here from Marlborough.'

'I'd love some, thank you.'

He brought across a glass of pale golden liquid that hinted at summer, before pouring himself a short whisky with water. With it untasted in his hand, he sat down in the largest armchair opposite her. 'Now, tell me why you've decided to set up in the hospitality business.'

She lifted the fragile barrier of the glass against him and sipped, letting the chilled liquid slide down her throat. 'I have to do something. I like entertaining and I'm a good cook.'

'It's a huge change from the high life.'

'The high life as in nursing my father?' She didn't try to hide the satirical inflection in her words.

Thick dark lashes drooped over gunmetal eyes. 'You were a very dutiful daughter,' he observed neutrally.

She shrugged. 'He needed me.'

'I admire you for taking care of him, but I still can't see why you want to set up as a glorified motel-keeper. Why don't you go back to modelling?'

'Once you drop out it's pretty hard to get back in,' she said lightly, 'especially at my age. There are lots of gorgeous sixteen- and seventeen-year-old girls out there, who don't need much in the way of airbrushing to look perfect.' She smiled with cynical understanding. 'And they're much cheaper.'

A harsh scream from outside startled her. 'What—? Oh, a pukeko,' she said on an uneven little laugh. 'Until I came back I'd forgotten what a noise they can make, and they still startle me.' The blue swamp hens with their scarlet legs and Roman beaks were a common sight on the riverbank.

'So you've given it all away,' Luke said reflectively, although his regard was keen and perceptive. 'It must have been difficult to turn your back on success.'

She swallowed some more wine, fragrant and delicious. Half a glass, she decided later, wasn't enough to explain her decision to say, 'My father wasn't getting anywhere in hospital. As long as I was there I could bully him into therapy, but if I left him he refused to do anything. Besides, it was no great sacrifice. Modelling wasn't really my choice as a career.'

He lifted black brows in a movement both ironic and disbelieving. 'So you said before. Why do it if you disliked it?'

Of course *he* wouldn't have. Luke made his own decisions and followed them through no matter how much it cost him. She got to her feet and walked across to the window. The outside lights had been left on and in their gentle glow the garden assumed a beauty and mystery that caught at her heart.

Although it had been a cloudy, humid day, the sky had cleared to reveal the curl of a new moon, a sliver of pearl in a sky of velvet, its light softly polishing the waters of the river.

She said, 'When I was thirteen I started to grow. In six months I shot up from being small and thin and redheaded to being tall and thin and redheaded, far more than head and shoulders above everyone else in the classroom. I was teased unmercifully until I took that modelling course and won the competition. And then suddenly it was a wonderful thing to be tall, to have red hair; I was photographed and flattered and sought-after, welcomed everywhere I went.'

'You were welcomed here,' he said crisply.

'As an appendage to Cynthia, yes.' She leaned forward to watch a pukeko strut across the lawn, arrogantly striding out of the pool of light into darkness.

Choosing her words carefully, she continued, 'It was intoxicating stuff, and I'd be lying if I said I didn't enjoy it, but I soon found that modelling itself wasn't satisfying. I liked parts of it—working with intensely creative people enriched me enormously—but most of it I just…endured.'

Not like her father, who'd loved the stimulation, the fascinating, larger-than-life people inhabiting that world, the full-on intensity of it.

Yet even that hadn't been enough for him; he'd craved more.

'But the money was too good to turn down?' Luke said levelly.

She flicked a sideways glance at him. 'Yes,' she said in a muted voice. 'That too.'

Burnished eyes scanned her with cool appraisal. 'You're looking a bit fragile. Come and sit down again.'

Sorrel obeyed, gazing into the fragrant depths of her glass and wondering what had driven her to confide in him.

Certainly not the hope that he'd understand!

He said, 'So you've always seen yourself as an outsider?'

Her head came up swiftly. Startled at his perception, she shook her hair across her face and hid behind it as she sipped some of the wine. 'I suppose so, although I hadn't actually put it in words. Every other kid had a mother, to start off with. We moved around a lot, so I was always the new pupil at school. Then I grew into the freak who towered over her classmates.'

'And finally the unattainable trophy woman smiling from the pages of expensive magazines,' he finished blandly.

She nodded. 'Don't think I'm wallowing in self-pity, because I'm not. I've had more luck than most women my age, and I don't regret any of it.'

'But?'

Lips tilting wryly, she said, 'I suppose I feel that I don't know who I am, where I belong.'

'So you've come back to find yourself?'

The mocking question set her temper alight. 'Don't put words in my mouth. And it's easy to scoff when you've always known who you were—as the heir to Waimanu, with the prestige of being a Hardcastle, your position has always been secure.'

'We do share some experiences,' he said, his eyes hard as they measured her face. 'Mothers who abandoned us—'

She made an instinctive sound of rejection but he went on ruthlessly, 'To a child, death is abandonment. And we both had fathers who were—unsatisfactory.'

'What do you mean?'

'My father was a fool over women. Yours had itchy feet and couldn't—or wouldn't—provide you with any sense of stability, of belonging.'

'He did his best for me,' she flared, refusing to accept his dispassionate summation.

'When it didn't clash with his aspirations,' Luke said inflexibly. 'My father submerged himself to please his wives, but they left him anyway.'

She said, 'So you don't trust women.'

'That's too easy and pat.' His jaw tightened. 'Do you believe that if you love someone they'll abandon you?'

'Of course I don't,' she said, shrugging to hide an uncomfortable shiver. If he didn't trust his father's taste in women, then he didn't trust her. Sorrel shared fine bones and height and a coppery mass of hair with the woman the district called The Wicked Stepmother— always pronounced in capitals. Cherie Hardcastle had been about four inches shorter, but the superficial resemblance had been startling.

He stood up. 'Dinner must be ready—bring your wine, you can finish it at the table.'

Over an excellent meal they discussed books and music and television programmes. Slow-burning excitement lent brilliance to Sorrel's eyes, sharpened her wits and lifted her spirits.

Halfway through the main course a knock on the door surprised them both. Frowning, Luke looked across the room. 'Come in.'

The housekeeper said, 'Sorry, Luke, but Miss O'Neill's on the phone. She says it's important.'

'Thank you,' Luke said. He waited until Penn had closed the door before asking with cool courtesy, 'Do you mind if I take this call?'

'Of course not.'

Sorrel watched him go before forcing herself to eat a mouthful of beans, followed in due course by a small amount of sesame steak—tender and delicious before, tasteless now.

Just as well Mari had rung, because Sorrel had fallen

into a trap she'd set herself. Stimulated by Luke's incisive intelligence and his wide knowledge, she'd forgotten about the woman who was clearly still very much a part of his life.

He was like a drug, fascinating yet addictive—so dangerous that once in the bloodstream it could never be exorcised.

Panic clawed her as she realised for the first time how like her father she was, how close she was to losing everything he'd lost—self-respect, integrity, peace of mind—in a reckless, risk-filled fixation on something she'd never be able to reach.

No, she thought desperately. Unlike her father, she knew when to pull away.

Right now.

No more dinners, no more matching wits with Luke, no more lazy surrender to a need she didn't dare appease.

He wasn't away long, and although his expression remained inscrutable some subliminal part of Sorrel recognised a buried anger behind his detachment.

'Sorry,' he said calmly.

'Not to worry.' Sorrel cut off another slice of steak and chewed it with dogged perseverance. Did Mari ring him every night?

And this slash of dark emotion was *not* jealousy. Jealousy implied some prior rights, and she had none.

She began to talk about a magazine article she'd read.

Eventually dinner ended; she drank a cup of tea before producing a yawn. 'Time for me to go, I think,' she said with her most charming smile. 'I know we haven't discussed my plans yet, but I'm suddenly very tired.'

Luke stood immediately, keen eyes scrutinising her face for an intent moment. 'Yes, you look as though you could do with an early night,' he said crisply.

Outside the crescent moon had long set. Once in Luke's car Sorrel sat in silence, watching the competent movements of his hands on the wheel.

Just over the bridge he stopped the vehicle. 'Did you feel that?'

'A slight shudder? Something wrong with the car, do you think?'

After grabbing a torch he opened the door and got out. 'It's probably nothing.'

Sorrel emerged from her side. 'If it's not the car, what would it be?'

'That's what I want to find out.' Luke directed a hard-edged beam of light towards the bridge.

The warm night was heavy with the scents of early summer—the tang of the sea, sensuous perfume from Cynthia's climbing roses, the green lushness of growth and fecundity. A poignant, aching hunger twined its way through Sorrel, feeding on repressed emotions, deliberately forgotten memories.

Straightening defiantly, she walked around to join him as he played the torch across the wooden bridge decking. 'Is it the bridge?'

Say no, she pleaded silently. Tell me the bridge is fine…

'I can't see anything,' he said, turning back. 'It may just have been a stone lying the wrong way.'

She nodded, hoping sickly that he was right. Bridge repairs had to mean serious money—money she didn't have.

Luke said, 'I'll look at it tomorrow morning.'

Be firm she told herself. You've made your decision; carry through on it. 'You don't need to—I can.'

'Do you know anything about bridges?' He sounded amused.

'I could probably tell whether there was something wrong with it,' she parried, climbing back into the car.

He joined her and tossed the torch into the back seat. 'Independence is a fine thing, but it won't take me long to check it out.'

While he put the car into gear Sorrel chewed her lip and gazed up the drive. Of course he was right; what did she know about the structure of bridges?

Allowing a neighbourly act on his part wouldn't feed her addiction.

Outside the house, wrapped by the perfume of a thousand flowers on the mock orange, Luke said, 'Is the back door locked?'

'Yes, I made sure before we left.' When he held out his hand for the key she said lightly, 'I can open my own door.'

He stepped back with an ironic inclination of his head, and she inserted the key and pushed the door open, switching on the inside light before she turned to face him.

'Thank you for a lovely evening,' she said inanely, trying to sound formal and fully in control as she stared at his throat. She'd probably have coped if she hadn't glanced up.

The light revealed a face dark and drawn, intent and angular. 'No,' Sorrel whispered, but she didn't move. She couldn't.

'Why not?' A jagged edge of raw desire in his voice unmasked a hunger that called to the wildness in her. Yet he didn't touch her.

Her lips shaped his name and he reached out and traced it with a long forefinger on her mouth. Need flowered, violently insistent, sweet as comb honey, ruthless as a flooded river.

Then he cupped her chin, tilting her face so that she was exposed to his devouring gaze. She almost cried out at the blaze of his eyes, the heated, merciless sensuality that prowled their pewter depths.

Words thick and impeded, she said, 'I don't poach.' Just as Mari had said all those years ago.

'I've made no commitment to anyone.' He spoke as though it wasn't important, as though he could think of nothing but the hunger that linked them both with unbreakable bonds. 'And there's no one for you.' It wasn't a question.

'No.' There never had been. Not like this.

He kissed the word away, and with it fled all the shoddy conjuring tricks she'd played on her mind to convince herself she didn't love him.

Because this wasn't some obsession, an addiction she could fight.

She had learned to love Luke when she'd been too young to know what love was, and before she'd understood the daunting force of sexual passion.

When he'd kissed her she'd discovered that desire hit like an earthquake, ferocious in its force, mindless and inevitable, changing everything. Now, mouth crushed beneath his and the heated fumes of carnal longing shutting down reason and logic, she realised with a stripped, stark flash of insight that, like her father, she would only ever love once.

Here, in Luke's arms, was her true home.

He lifted his head and said harshly, 'Tell me now if you still feel weak.'

'No.'

Her doubts, her fears, the reasons she'd refused to accept this hopeless love, still echoed around her brain. But although she knew she was courting heartache she craved her moment of glory.

Luke picked her up and walked through the door, kicking it closed behind them. Safe against him as he navigated the dark house with sure confidence, Sorrel turned her face into his throat, inhaling the faint, potent scent that was his alone.

His heart slammed into her side, gaining speed when she kissed his throat and then delicately licked the skin. He tasted of Luke—warm, sexual, all male. All hers. Exulting, she murmured his name in a voice she didn't recognise, slow and husky and sensuous, letting her lips linger against his skin.

Old fantasies flared in her mind, to be swamped by the reality of this—the quiet house, the heat from Luke's body, the careless, casual strength that supported her and surrounded her.

In the pit of her stomach, racing through her veins, exploding from cell to cell, the wildness inside her began to build, singing a song as ancient as Eve. Fingertips tingling, she traced the strong framework of his face, the lines of each brow and the sweep of an autocratic cheekbone. She touched him in the small, intimate ways of a lover, testing the smooth skin of his forehead, the roughened silk of his shaved cheek, the heat of his mouth.

Without faltering he bent his head and kissed her fiercely, then swung her down onto the bed.

The bedside lamp bloomed, casting a gentle pool of light over the bed. Pulses pounding, Sorrel lifted weighted eyelids and looked through her lashes into the hard, leashed danger of Luke's face.

For a moment her heart failed her, but caution was vaporised by the turbulent blue-grey depths of his eyes. He wanted her as no other man had, she realised with fierce delight. His unchained, elemental desire melted every defence. Lifting her hand, she followed the outline of his lips, and smiled.

Sultry, beckoning, that smile sent Luke's blood pressure through the ceiling. The night she'd spent sleeping in his arms had cracked his defences, sensitising him to the satin feel of her, the graceful warmth of limbs and breasts and hips.

Since then he'd caught himself listening for her laugh and the throaty, sensuous catch in her voice, watching the rich fall of red-brown hair, the sheen of ivory skin, the slow, radiant promise of her smile. Her sheer physical perfection had lodged in his brain until hunger had driven every logical thought before it, like clouds streaming ahead of a cyclone.

Why Sorrel? He'd enjoyed other beautiful women—and not just in bed. Most of his lovers were still friends. He could never be friendly with Sorrel, he thought grimly as he watched her on the bed, lovely face turned up to him in tantalising surrender. Perhaps he was a true son of his father—a fool about this woman.

But he had enough control not to surrender everything. Although she knew how her fine-boned, delicately sexy body affected men, making them wonder if they'd be the lucky one to coax her cool beauty into flames, she'd never learn that she was the only woman who could shatter his control.

He bitterly resented—even feared—her power; he'd

despised himself for not being able to ignore it and until a few minutes ago he'd been certain he could resist her.

But now to hell with restraint and self-sufficiency and everything else he'd lived his life by. He wanted Sorrel like he wanted to breathe. No—more than he wanted to breathe.

And this time nothing, not even his own defeat, was going to stop him.

'What are you thinking?' she asked huskily.

His mouth compressed, then relaxed into a sardonic smile. 'That I should have known this was inevitable.'

The abrasive cadence in his voice quickened a primal need. Shivering, she whispered, 'For both of us?'

'Yes.'

Her mouth softened. 'You are so beautiful,' she said on a sigh.

He laughed and came down beside her, sliding an arm beneath her head and turning her face towards his. 'Those are my words,' he said ambiguously. 'Beautiful beyond bearing. Beautiful enough to fog a man's mind, to drive his dreams at night and haunt him by day. More beautiful than any fantasy could be…'

For a long, taut second he looked into her eyes. Her stomach clenched. He was demanding complete capitulation, yet she couldn't read anything except desire in the iron-grey glitter of his eyes.

It didn't matter. *It didn't matter.* She loved him whatever he felt for her. When his name sighed out through her lips she heard her surrender in it, mingled with the longing that had been building for half her life.

And then he kissed her, and again Sorrel discovered what real passion felt like.

It was fire in her fingertips as she curved her hands around his face, fire in the masculine mouth that took hers and made it his, fire in the way he slipped the little shell top over her shoulders and bent his head to her breast.

She arched into his mouth, into the lean hand that cupped the slight mound, into his body, fierce and hot and urgent against her. That perilous, primitive fire leapt from her to him and back again, arrowing from the budding aureole of her breast to the sensitive inner passage that clamoured for him.

She pulled at the buttons on his shirt, wrenching them free so that she could feel the slow flex and play of his long muscles beneath his sleek skin, the sheer male strength of him calling to everything that was female in her.

Luke laughed under his breath. 'What do you want?'

'This.' Again she curved into his hard body, shuddering as she felt his involuntary response.

'Is that all?' He kissed her again until she was mad for the embrace his deep, deep kisses imitated.

Arms tight around his back, Sorrel curved once more into him, an unspoken plea catching in the back of her throat. 'I want you,' she said when she could speak.

'Everything?'

She bit his earlobe. 'Everything.' It was a vow.

'Just as well,' he said, thrusting against her. 'Because that's what I want from you—everything. All you can give me. All that you are.'

Held against his big, taut body, Sorrel gazed up, mouth drying when she realised the iron-grey irises of his eyes had been swallowed by smouldering blue.

There would, she knew, be no going back. Once she made love with Luke, no other man would do.

She smiled and kissed the hard perfection of his lips. Who cared? She'd never want any other man.

'All that I can give you,' she said into his mouth. 'All that I am.'

His arms contracted, and for the first time she felt the full force of his strength. They relaxed immediately. 'I'm sorry,' he said harshly. 'I won't hurt you.'

'I know.'

He kissed her with a heart-shaking blend of tenderness and desire, but the layers of fabric between them had become intolerable. She groaned into his mouth, and he found the fastening of her skirt as she found his trousers.

'Not yet,' he said, his voice deliberate yet raw. 'Let me.'

He stripped the skirt and shell top and the fragile pair of briefs from her, and began to kiss her slender, naked body, taking his time, dazzling her with his expertise and his knowledge of all the pleasure points in a woman's body. She'd had no idea that a man's mouth and hands could be so ruthlessly tender, or that each caress, each kiss, could pierce her body with a hungry rapture.

'I don't break,' he said quietly.

Sorrel blinked. 'I didn't—' she said in a dazed voice.

He knew, of course. He knew that she had never experienced anything like this deliberate, purposeful seduction.

And he must have guessed that she'd never responded like this before, with an untamed sensuousness that would have shocked her only a few weeks ago.

She turned her head into his chest and kissed the hot swell of muscle there, let her hands roam wherever they wanted to, skin against skin in a world that had narrowed down to this room, this bed, this man.

Still Luke continued his erotic voyage of discovery,

using skills she'd never heard of to summon pleasure, until eventually her whole body screamed for satisfaction. She said his name again, almost unable to hear her own voice above the jarring crash of her heartbeat in her ears.

Then, moving with silent speed and grace, he removed the rest of his clothes. He stood a moment by the bed, feasting his eyes on her.

Aching with keen-edged need, Sorrel leaned back against the pillows, committing to memory the powerful bone structure, the muscles earned by years of brutal physical work, the sleek, richly tanned skin...

Words trembled on her lips, but she bit them back. He didn't want to know that she loved him. So she leaned over and kissed the arrogant jut of one hip, letting her mouth linger until he said, 'Sorrel,' and came down beside her, pulling her down into his arms.

For a few precious seconds just lying half beneath him was enough, but soon she wanted more than this pressure from shoulder to thighs, the heat of his loins hard against hers.

'Please,' she whispered.

Luke lifted himself slightly, but Sorrel slid her arms around his shoulders to pull him back. 'Wait,' he said curtly, and she waited while he dealt with the condom he'd put on the table.

That done, he kissed her again, and this time he pushed slowly into her.

Sorrel's breath locked in her chest; she stared up into eyes as blue as exploding stars. He was uncomfortably big so she widened her legs, and when she'd opened herself to him he pushed home in a single, forceful movement.

He froze at her choked cry and began to withdraw,

but she clamped tight interior muscles and refused to allow it, claiming him as he had claimed her.

'God!' he said harshly, and kissed her deeply, holding her captive with his mouth until she relaxed. He withdrew and found her again, setting up a rhythm of discovery that echoed the patterns of her life.

Her hands slid lower, past his waist, to the flexing muscles of his buttocks, holding him against her. Sensation shuddered through her, wild and sweet and hot. She adjusted to his possession, carried further and further into a realm she'd only ever heard of before.

Higher and higher he took her, until the swirling waves of sensation coalesced into ecstasy and she came apart in his arms, pitched into a universe where the only thing that registered was a rapture beyond bearing.

He followed her there, face dark with intolerable ecstasy, his big body rigid as he poured himself into her.

Still in thrall to the aftershocks of her overpowering orgasm, she realised eventually that she was crying. Horrified, she tried to stop the silent tears, but they kept coming.

'Sorrel,' Luke rasped, turning onto his side with her still in his arms, 'did I hurt you?'

'No.' She wept harder.

He held her against his wide, bare shoulder. 'So what's going on?' His voice rumbled against her cheek.

'I don't know,' she whispered, wiping the tears away with the heel of her hand. She couldn't tell him that she'd never experienced anything like that before. Somehow he'd ripped her soul from her body and made it his.

'You're tired,' he said, smoothing the tumbled silk of her hair back from her face. 'Go to sleep.'

She wanted to stay awake, but almost instantly she sank into slumber. And Luke lay there with her lax, slender body draped across him and stared bleakly into the darkness.

CHAPTER EIGHT

SORREL woke to morning light pouring across her face and an importunate Baggie calling crossly from the doorway.

'OK, OK, give me time!' She stretched sensuously, wondering idly where her incredible sense of well-being came from.

And then she turned over and opened her eyes. There, on the pillow beside her, was the indentation made by Luke's head.

'Oh no,' she whispered, chilled to her bones. 'You crazy woman—how *could* you?'

Last night she'd decided to protect herself against Luke—then immediately surrendered with insulting, humiliating speed to his kisses, not even making a pretence at resistance.

Idiot! Fool! Ever since she'd come back she and Luke had fought a tense emotional duel; falling in love with him in adolescence had probably been inevitable, but making love with him at twenty-eight was an act of madness.

Groaning, she rolled over and buried her face in her pillow. She hated her weakness, the susceptibility that drowned out the sensible promptings of her brain in a flood of mindless fire. Was this how her father had felt when faced with the urge to gamble?

'Oh, Dad,' she whispered, 'I wish I'd realised how easy it is to give in.'

Unfortunately she couldn't hide in bed for the rest

of the day, however much she wanted to. She sat up and stared around the room, averting her eyes from the clothes she'd discarded so swiftly and thoughtlessly the previous night. Her mouth trembled. She'd never sleep in this bed again, come into this room again, without remembering her passionate, unrestrained response to Luke; his dominating presence would always haunt her.

Gripped by a cowardly impulse to run as far and as fast as she could, she eased herself out of the bed and shrugged into her robe.

No, she wasn't going to decamp, however tempting the idea. That had been her father's response; if she followed his example she might never be able to overcome this sensual enslavement. Facing it, dealing with it, was the only way she'd conquer it.

Besides, Cynthia had wanted her to stay in the house for six months, and she'd do that for her godmother, whatever the cost. Last night she'd reneged on her vow; all the more reason to stick to this decision.

'All right,' she said grimly, to a still yowling Baggie, 'what's done is done. Now I have to learn to live with my own stupidity and make sure I never repeat it.'

Having changed the linen on the bed and set the washing machine going, she was sanding down the skirting boards in the main bedroom when she heard Luke's car turn into the drive. It stopped on the other side of the bridge.

She bit her lip, her heart thudding with a kind of terrified excitement, and continued working. About ten minutes later he knocked on the front door.

Sorrel took a deep, shaking breath and went down to meet him.

He didn't look any different. Tall, dark, inflexible, his mouth a thin line, he said abruptly, 'It looks as though the last flood loosened the decking on the bridge.'

For a moment she couldn't think of what to say. 'I see.'

He said, 'I'll call a firm in Whangarei to fix it.'

'No—I'll do it.' At least while she was worrying about this she wasn't thinking about those maddened hours in his arms—well, not much.

'Sorrel, I know you're perfectly capable of doing it,' he said between his teeth, 'but I know this man. He's built a couple of bridges for me and repaired others. If I contact him he will give your job priority. And you need it done quickly—it's dangerous as it is. You'll also need to put a sign at the entrance to make sure no one else drives across it.'

She said quietly, 'Before I make any decisions I need a rough idea of how much it will cost.'

'Is that a problem?' He scrutinised her face with narrowed, intent eyes.

Her mouth folded into an obstinate line. 'I'm not stupid; I won't give a firm freedom to do what they like without an estimate first.'

Silence hummed between them—taut, filled with unspoken words. Sorrel sensed the swift, ruthless working of Luke's mind, and thought wearily that she should have shut up. But he couldn't have possibly heard anything about her father—she'd worked hard to prevent any gossip.

'Surely,' he said, in a voice that slashed her skin like a whip, 'you haven't let the entire, obscene amount of money you earned parading that glorious body slip through your fingers?'

She gasped. Mind completely blank, she looked into

eyes as cold and pitiless as granite. Inside she began to shake.

'Has it all gone, Sorrel?' he asked with merciless determination.

'It's vulgar to talk about money,' she parried, 'especially other people's. Have you any idea how much repairs might cost?'

He paused, then gave her a figure.

The hollowness in her stomach expanded, but she braced herself to meet his unsparing gaze with a limpid one of her own. 'I see,' she said.

Something in the way she said it—perhaps a note of panic—solidified Luke's barely formed suspicion into certainty. Knowing he was jumping to conclusions, he asked evenly, 'What did you spend it on, Sorrel? Cocaine? I believe it's the drug of choice amongst models nowadays.'

Disgust darkened her eyes as she returned with icy precision, 'You've been reading too many tabloids. I don't do drugs—never have.'

'So what did it go on?'

She stared straight at him, the fine-boned allure of her beautiful face replaced by open challenge. 'Bad investments.'

Luke was a man who followed his hunches, and so far they'd never let him down. She was lying.

He seized her chin between thumb and forefinger and tilted it, forcing her to meet his gaze. Deliberately, she lifted her lashes to uncover golden-green eyes, eyes that could turn overnight from smouldering passion to cool dismissal…

Flesh still hot with the remembered taste of her sultry mouth, he knew that beneath that beautiful, sexy mask, within the body that had given him ecstasy, hid a lying heart.

Did she, like his stepmother, see the owner of Waimanu as a source of ready cash? Had she come back to Parenga to see if that old, violent enchantment still had any life in it?

Fighting down a black rage, he forced himself to think dispassionately. It made sense. If she'd lost her money and been unable to take up her career again after the years spent looking after her father, then why not look around for some way of replacing that enviable lifestyle? A rich man...

And if she'd faked that passion last night it was just as well he'd found out immediately, before any damage was done.

He dropped her chin as though the silky skin burned his fingers and surveyed her with eyes as cold and keen as the blade of a sword. 'Gambling, Sorrel?'

'Go to hell,' she said with cool composure, but he saw the shock in her face, in her voice.

Yes, she'd wondered whether raking through old embers would start another fire, one big enough to keep her warm and secure for the rest of her life.

His mouth hardened into a smile as frigid as the polar wind. 'You gambled on the wrong man,' he told her. 'I learnt the lessons my father never did—look carefully at beautiful women when they offer themselves to you. Usually it's because they want something, and the something is usually money.'

For some reason she almost looked relieved, but the fleeting expression was instantly replaced by scepticism. 'You can't possibly believe that your only appeal to women is your money!'

He said contemptuously, 'Looks are important in

lovers and playthings, but they count for nothing when it comes to the serious business of lining pockets. My stepmother would have married my father if he'd been the ugliest man on earth.'

'How do you know?' Sorrel demanded, suddenly angry. 'An onlooker never understands the truth in a marriage.'

His eyes were cold, so cold she shivered. 'I understand that within six months of their marriage she tried to seduce me.'

Horrified, Sorrel stared at him. She read the truth in his relentless expression, heard it in his flat voice.

'Yes,' he said. 'I know what greed looks like in a woman—and desperation. Tell me, why did you sleep with me last night?'

'Not to line my pockets,' she retorted, ashamed and humiliated. 'And not because I was desperate either, believe me.'

'So why?'

Hands clenched at her sides, she took a step closer. 'To scratch an itch,' she hurled at him, hiding the pain that tore her apart with assumed hauteur. 'A ten-year-old itch. And now that I've dealt with it, that's an end to it.'

His eyes blazed. 'It's never that simple,' he said in a low, savage voice, and kissed her, imprisoning her against him as he plundered her mouth, stamping a claim on her that had nothing to do with desire and everything to do with angry possession.

Sorrel tried to fight him off, but the fire that roared through her overwhelmed any sensible decisions, all the promises she'd made for the future, and she kissed him back.

And somehow, even though she knew Luke intended

that kiss to be an assault, it changed. They kissed like lovers parting for a long time—like lovers who knew they would never meet again...

Tears sprang into her eyes, ached through her heart, because they were saying goodbye.

Slowly he released her, slowly straightened. She saw thin streaks of colour across his high cheekbones and knew that he was furious with himself for succumbing to temptation.

Anguish clamped her in a shroud of darkness. It took every last shred of strength to jut her chin in quick arrogance and step back. 'Goodbye, Luke,' she said with as much finality as she could manage. 'I'd be grateful if you'd drop the name of that bridge firm into the letterbox.'

He swung on his heel and walked out. She stood shaking, her hands clenched at her sides, fighting the need to run after him and tell him that he was wrong, that she loved him, that the intervening years hadn't been enough to break the link between them.

But he wouldn't believe her. And although it hurt that he should believe her to be tarred by the same brush as his stepmother, she thought now that she could see why. A young boy, unsure of himself and loving his father, having to fight off his father's new wife— oh, she thought viciously, there was enough trauma in that to mark him for life.

The sound of her car engine brought her out of her trance. She raced across to the window and saw it heading down the drive. Of course—she'd left the keys in it. She pressed her knuckles to her mouth, stifling the cry that longed to escape, and watched with hot, dry eyes as Luke drove slowly across the bridge and parked on the verge just inside the entrance.

He didn't look back. She saw him toss the keys into the letterbox, swing into his Land Rover and drive away.

'Go and get the keys,' she told herself brutally. 'You can cry later. You've got work to do and decisions to make.'

The bridge seemed firm when she walked over it, so presumably it was safe enough for pedestrians. But if she was going to open a bed and breakfast she'd have to find the money for repairs. Guests wouldn't want to carry their suitcases in from the road.

She went up to the main bedroom and began on the skirting boards again, finding some relief in the monotonous rhythm.

It was late when she forced herself into bed, and she was exhausted, but for hours she lay staring bleakly into the warm summer night while vivid images played and replayed through her treacherous mind.

In a morning heavy with the scent of sun and rain and growing greenery, she walked over Luke's land to the beach and tried to forget everything in a brisk run along the sand to the mouth of the river. It didn't work—but then years of pretence hadn't worked either.

'It seems Dad bequeathed me his addictive personality,' she told Baggie bleakly. 'No, idiot cat, don't go near the river—it's too clear for eels, and if you fall in there you'll get washed out to sea!'

For once the cat obeyed her and they turned for home. At the entrance Sorrel looked in the letterbox and found an envelope with her name on it in Luke's strong handwriting.

Heart skipping a beat, she ripped it open and read the name and telephone number of the bridge-builder. She wasn't surprised later, when she rang and the woman who answered the telephone told her she'd already pencilled in a date for a check and an estimate.

Just like a dentist, Sorrel thought wearily. And Luke had made the appointment.

The engineer turned up a couple days later, after a night when Sorrel had at last managed to snatch a few hours' sleep and so was feeling marginally human. Young, redheaded and confident, he was all business, although she recognised the admiring appraisal in his eyes.

After poking around the bridge for an hour or so, he knocked on the door of the house.

'How did it go?' Sorrel asked, hiding her concern with a smile.

'Not good, I'm afraid. Come on down and have a look—I can explain it better if I show you.'

Luke was right—the flood had managed to loosen the decking from the beams.

'Mind you,' the engineer said cheerfully, 'it needed replacing anyway.' He kicked a loose board. 'See? That's pretty close to disintegration.'

'What about the beams?' she asked, bending to survey the steel underpinning to the deck.

'No problems there.' He grinned at her.

'That's a relief. Can you give me a rough estimate of the cost?'

He warned, 'It'll be very rough. I'll send you a more accurate one when I've had a chance to crunch the numbers,' and stated an amount a little less than Luke's guess, but not by so much she could feel anything but despair.

She was wondering how on earth she was going to convince a bank manager to lend her enough to cover it when the engineer looked past her and nodded. 'Hello, Luke,' he said. 'Didn't hear you coming.'

Sorrel froze at Luke's deep-voiced answer. Colour abandoned her skin in a chilly tide, but she managed to fix a smile on her lips before she turned.

In the swift glance she allowed herself she noted that he looked grim and a little tired. And the dark, good-looking face was still closed against her.

'Good morning, Sorrel,' he said after he'd greeted the engineer.

Unable to trust her voice, she smiled uncomfortably.

He looked back to the man beside her. 'Job done?'

The engineer glanced from one to the other. 'Yep,' he said. 'I'll send Ms Maitland a proper estimate immediately. How's the new bridge on your place, Luke?'

'Bearing up well,' Luke said drily. 'I'll see you to your car.'

Sorrel held out her hand to the engineer. 'Thanks very much,' she said with another smile, much more open this time.

After they'd shaken hands she went back to Parenga, feeling so cold inside she wondered whether the sun would ever be able to warm her again.

I can't do this, she cried soundlessly to an indifferent universe.

But she gritted her teeth and set her jaw and went up the stairs. She had to cope, even though loving Luke was a life sentence. It was no use wailing to the sun and the moon and the stars for help, because Luke would never trust a beautiful woman. And how could you prove love?

Only by a lifetime of commitment—and that was a choice she'd never be given.

The stepladder she'd found at the back of the garage

was rickety, but it was the only one high enough. Nevertheless she regretted being halfway up it when someone knocked on the door below—a knock followed by Luke's deep voice calling, 'Sorrel!'

She jumped, almost dropping the tray of paint. Beneath her the ladder rocked wildly, then steadied down. 'I'm up here.'

He came silently up the stairs to fill the doorway, frowning when he saw her. 'What the hell are you doing on that wreck of a thing?'

'Painting,' she told him crisply, climbing higher until she could reach the ceiling.

She heard a muttered oath as he strode across the covered carpet and gripped the legs of the ladder.

He said harshly, 'Get off before you fall off.'

'It's all right,' she told him, glancing down to see his eyes narrow, as though he could read every defiant thought surging through her brain. She applied a swathe of white to the ceiling.

'Don't be an idiot. How much painting do you plan to do?'

Sorrel hadn't been conscious of tension knotting her stomach, a knot that intensified when she looked down and saw his lean, strong hands on the ladder only inches from her legs. Stiffly she said, 'The rest of this room and the bathroom next door, to start off with.'

He eyed her with frowning consideration. 'That's a lot of work.'

'So?' she said, applying another swathe of paint.

'So what's giving you circles under your eyes?'

'Paint fumes.' She dipped the roller back in the paint tray, adjusting her weight swiftly as the ladder lurched sideways.

He stilled it and said, 'I'll lend you a decent ladder.'

'How kind of you,' she purred, producing the smile that had lit up thousands of photographs. It was armour, that smile, hiding her thoughts and emotions behind its seductive aloofness. 'But you really don't need to—this ladder might seem rocky, but it's strong. And it's high enough for me to reach the ceiling. I've spent quite a lot of time on it and we understand each other now.'

She was quite proud of her voice; it sounded so normal she decided to push her luck a little further. 'Did you call in for a reason?' she asked, making another sweep across the ceiling.

'To make sure you were all right,' he said shortly.

Absurd to feel a warm glow in the region of her heart. She swallowed. 'I'm fine, thank you. How are you?'

His eyes gleamed as he caught her around the hips and, without breathing any more heavily, lifted her down.

'What the hell—?' she spluttered, clinging to the tray so that no paint landed on the carpet cover.

Luke took the tray and the roller from her hands, dumped them onto a step on the ladder, and as she opened her mouth to protest closed it with a fierce kiss that scrambled her insides and filled her head with the smoke and fumes of desire. Reckless hunger drowned out everything except a mindless clamour for satisfaction.

And then he let her go and stepped back.

Stunned, her heart leaping, Sorrel stared up into eyes that had darkened from threatening grey to dangerous storm clouds. There was nothing soft about the angles and planes of his face, nothing that met or matched the love she'd so reluctantly accepted in herself.

Heart contracting in her breast, she rubbed the back of her hand across her mouth. 'What was that for?'

He watched her as though she was an enemy, his scrutiny as flinty as his voice. 'Punishment, perhaps,' he said, drawling the words with lazy derision.

Sorrel's head came up. Eyes smouldering, she stated, 'There's a word for men who get their kicks hurting women.'

'I know it.' His voice was coldly precise. 'I was punishing myself for being so stupid as to think there might be more to you than a lovely face and a great body.'

Emotion raked her, anger and fear and a humiliating anticipation. 'That,' she said flippantly, 'is all you can expect from a one-night stand.'

'It doesn't have to be a one-night stand.' He spoke with cool control, unyielding eyes in an unyielding face. 'I want you—I've wanted you since you turned eighteen.'

'So you started an affair with Mari O'Neill.' She hid the pain with a scoffing smile.

He said quietly, 'You were just a green kid. I was twenty-five. The last thing you needed was an affair that would end in tears. Mari didn't make the mistake of putting her heart on the line and she was a welcome distraction.'

'How very noble of you,' Sorrel said politely.

He shrugged. 'Nobility didn't come into it—it was self-preservation. Virginal schoolgirls tend to fall pregnant, and their hearts break easily. At that time I couldn't afford to support a child, and I didn't want to hurt you any more than I already had.'

Anger smouldered inside her, but with it a kind of relief that he had wanted her. Ever pragmatic, he'd chosen the simplest way to get them both out of a situation she hadn't been able to deal with.

'But you're not eighteen now,' he said, voice no longer cool. 'And I doubt very much that an affair between us would break your heart. Even if it did, perhaps that would be good for you—you've broken so many in your time.' He startled her by looping his fingers around her wrist, letting his thumb rest over the small throbbing vein there. 'And you still want me, Sorrel.'

She was tempted beyond endurance. More than anything in the world she wanted to forget everything but the fever spinning its rapid heat through her body.

But Luke was offering false coin, counterfeit love, and she didn't dare accept it. He hadn't wanted to kiss her, and when he had she'd sensed resistance as much as passion.

Having an affair with Lucas would be the stupidest thing she could do. He desired the surface glamour of skin and hair and lips and body, whereas she needed so much more.

But most of all, she thought with brittle determination, she needed him out of her system, not embedded even more deeply than he already was.

Get out of here—now! instinct screamed silently, but her brain had seized.

Unconsciously she licked her lips. Luke's eyes narrowed further until all she could see were gleaming splinters of grey, and his hand slid from her wrist to her elbow, turning her and easing her towards him.

With her last shred of will-power Sorrel said, 'No!' and pulled back, jerking free.

'Why not?' he asked, his voice harsh and abrupt.

'Because I don't *do* meaningless affairs,' she said angrily.

'Meaningless?' he said in a neutral voice, but a raw undertone pulled every tiny hair on her skin upright.

She nodded vigorously. 'Meaningless,' she repeated, swallowing because her mouth and throat were suddenly dry. She felt as though she'd stepped up to the edge of a precipice. 'I don't want an affair or a relationship or anything else. Old embers, and all that sort of thing. I'm rather insulted that you think I might be...interested in taking up where we left off just because I'm conveniently right next door. The last thing I need is complications in my life—I want to finish redecorating Parenga.'

She swept a desperate hand around the room, trying to distract herself and him from that dangerous bit of brinkmanship they'd just indulged in.

'Convenient is probably the last word I'd use to describe you,' he said thoughtfully, a blue glint of satirical amusement lighting his eyes.

'I'm not available either,' she told him, trying to sound convincing in spite of her erotic little internal shivers.

One raised brow indicated what he thought of that defiant statement, but he didn't take her up on it.

She met his hooded gaze with her chin angled at him and lips tense, but he'd have to be totally inexperienced not to read the signs her treacherous body was sending out. And he certainly wasn't inexperienced.

'Point taken,' he drawled, the ironic smile hardening his chiselled mouth in savage contrast to his glittering eyes. 'Don't get on that ladder—I'll send someone up with a decent one.' He swung on his heels and left her dazed, the touch of his mouth on hers still tangible. She looked down at her wrist, almost expecting to see his fingerprints on the delicate skin.

'Oh, don't be so bloody stupid!' she snarled, and climbed back up the shaky ladder.

What exactly had he intended?

A raging affair, no strings attached? Which was, presumably, what he had with Mari.

Feverish elation thrummed feverishly through every cell, but beneath it she felt nauseated. 'Damn!' she whispered. 'Damn, damn, damn!'

Baggie uncurled in his patch of sun, pink mouth and white teeth gleaming as he yawned mightily.

'It's all very well for you,' Sorrel said on a half-laugh that sounded suspiciously like a sob. 'You're neutered—sex is no big deal for you! As for love— well, everyone knows that cats are totally self-centred!'

The ladder Luke had promised didn't arrive, which was unlike him. Sorrel, however, had no intention of chasing it up. Painting doggedly, she tried to banish him from her mind by working out where to find the money to fix the bridge.

She'd promised herself this life, this future, and what sort of person would she be if she gave up so easily?

After mulling the possibilities over, she finally made a decision. 'I'll use the money I planned to live on to fix the bridge, and then I'll get a job,' she told the sleeping Baggie. 'I'll contact an agency in Auckland and see if they've got something they can use me for— that would probably be the most lucrative. If they don't want me there are tourists galore around here, so I must be able to find some sort of job that will keep me until I get Parenga up and running.'

A knock on the front door broke into her reverie. 'Coming,' she shouted. The ladder rocked, and she tripped, clutched at air, and fell backwards into pain, and then nothingness.

CHAPTER NINE

'SORREL! Sorrel, can you hear me?'

A man's voice, urgent and filled with concern, was forcing its way past the pounding of her head. Carefully forming the word, she whispered, 'Luke?'

'Yes. Open your eyes for me.'

She winced as she forced her eyelids up. His hard, intent face swam into view, wavering at first. She blinked a couple of times and it steadied. Wonderingly she surveyed tanned skin tautly stretched over a strong foundation, narrowed, piercing eyes and a sinfully beautiful mouth.

'Good,' he said, his deep voice laced with relief. 'Now squeeze my hand.'

Her lashes drifted down. His hand? Oh, he was holding hers. Concentrating, she folded her fingers around his long ones.

'Let it go.' He waited until her hand relaxed. 'Is there any part of you that's really painful?'

She croaked, 'Apart from my head?'

'Yes.'

'My hip,' she muttered. 'My shoulder.'

Quickly and deftly he probed her hip and shoulder. 'I don't think you've broken anything,' he told her when he'd finished. 'You landed on that side so they'll be bruised. Now, I'm going downstairs to get a pillow. Stay still.'

By the time he got back the pounding in her head had decreased a fraction, but the light still hurt her eyes.

Gently Luke lifted her head and slid a pillow under it. 'Did that hurt your neck?'

'No.'

'OK, I'll put a compress on your forehead. Can you hold it there?'

He must have grabbed ice cubes from the fridge and wrapped them in a towel. The icy chill felt wonderful against her aching head. 'Mmm, that's good,' she murmured.

'I'll ring the medical centre.'

He barked into the mobile phone in a way that made Sorrel vaguely sorry for the person on the other end.

'She knocked herself out,' he finished, 'so she should see the doctor... OK, I'll bring her straight in.'

Sorrel lifted her lashes to see him keying in another number. 'Penn, bring the car up to Parenga,' he said without preamble, dark eyes fixed on Sorrel. 'Stack several pillows in it. And a bucket.'

Penn must have said something because he cut her short in a voice so cold it bored through the fog in Sorrel's head, jolting her into awareness. 'Just get here as soon as possible.'

Sorrel closed her eyes against his grim face and said, 'I'm sorry. I don't remember what happened.'

'You fell off that bloody ladder and gave yourself concussion.' His voice came closer. 'Could you get up if I helped you?'

She thought about it for a moment. 'Yes.'

He was wonderfully gentle, and once she was standing he picked her up and carried her down the stairs. Still holding the ice pack against her head, she felt dreamily contented, safe in his arms.

'The car will be here soon,' he told her, the words

rumbling against her, 'and then I'll drive you in to the doctor.'

'I'm being an awful nuisance. Making you sleep on the floor, and then almost drowning myself in the bath, and now this.' She gave a ghostly little laugh. 'I don't suppose you'll believe that until I came back I hadn't had a single accident in ten years?'

'I believe you,' he said. 'How's your head?'

'It's easing off a bit,' Sorrel said, adding, 'You're a good neighbour, Luke.'

'Not good enough,' he said obliquely, shouldering open the front door and setting off down the drive.

Of course she'd forgotten that the bridge was a no-go zone. Eyes clamped shut, she frowned against the bright sunlight. 'I think I can walk now.'

'Not all the way to the road,' he said curtly, 'and not with your eyes closed. Don't worry—you're not very heavy.'

Penn was waiting for them, her face concerned as she opened the back door of the car for Sorrel. 'I've put a couple of pillows in,' she said, 'and the bucket.'

'Thank you,' Sorrel said, trying to smile. 'I won't be sick—I feel much better now.'

Luke eased her gently into the back seat against the pillows, reaching across her to do up her seat belt. 'All right?'

'I'm fine,' she said. But the movement had started her head throbbing again; hastily she closed her eyes and clutched the cold compress to her forehead.

'Do you want me to come in with you?' Penn asked Luke quietly.

'No. She looks like a piece of paper, but she'll be all right. Thank you,' he said, and slid behind the wheel.

The doctor did some poking and prodding in various places of her anatomy, shone a light into her eyes, prescribed a cream for the bruises, and sent her on her way with instructions to rest for twenty-four hours under observation.

'No driving and no sport, of course,' he said to Luke outside the surgery, after detailing a list of symptoms to watch for during that time. He smiled at Sorrel. 'But she looks a pretty tough character to me. Just keep an eye on her.'

In the car Sorrel said with some of her usual crispness, 'Thank you for everything you've done, but you don't need to worry. I feel almost human again.'

'If you're trying to tell me that you don't want to come home to Waimanu with me, forget it,' Luke ordered, backing skilfully out of the car park. 'Why didn't you use the ladder I sent up?'

'What ladder?'

'Sorrel—'

Her spurt of energy evaporating, she leaned back against the pillows as he set the car in motion. Wearily she told him, 'If you'd sent up a ladder I'd have used it.'

The dark, tangible force of his anger surged through the car, but he didn't say anything more than, 'Anyway, you've only got one bed at Parenga.'

'So?' Her astonishment made two syllables of the word.

'You heard the doctor—you should be under observation for twenty-four hours. If I stay the night at Parenga I'll have to share your bed, because I am not sleeping on the floor or in one of those chairs.'

Beneath the teasing note in his voice she heard determination. 'Oh, all right. I'm not feeling strong enough to fight with you,' she yielded on a sigh. 'Waimanu it'll be.'

'Now I am alarmed,' he said. 'Such meek acquiescence!'

She could tell that he was smiling. Her heart twisted, but she retorted, 'Enjoy it while it lasts.'

At Waimanu she refused to let him carry her, saying stubbornly, 'I can walk. The headache's easing off now, and my legs work fine.'

'It didn't last long,' Luke said, deadpan. He watched her take a couple of tentative steps. 'You're still a bit shaky.'

His arm around her shoulders supported her up the stairs and into the spare bedroom, with Penn in close attendance. Sorrel told herself sternly that this care and concern wasn't personal—a man who protected ducklings on his lawn would do his best for anyone who'd been hurt.

'I brought along some of your clothes and toiletries from Parenga,' the housekeeper said. 'I hope you don't mind me going through your things...'

Perched on the side of the bed, Sorrel gave a resigned smile. 'Of course not. Anyway, I bet Luke told you to.'

'I did,' Luke said calmly. 'Penn will stay until you're in bed. If you need anything, ring the bell.' He indicated the bedside table, where a small bronze bell waited. 'I'll go to Parenga and clear up the mess the paint made when you dropped the tray.'

The housekeeper said quickly, 'That's been done.'

'Good.' Dark eyes cool and objective, Luke examined Sorrel closely, then, apparently satisfied, said, 'If you feel up to it later you can come down for dinner.'

Sorrel watched him walk out of the room before turning to the housekeeper, who asked hastily, 'Do you want a shower?'

'I'd love one, but, whatever Luke says, I really don't need you in attendance. Apart from the remains of the headache and a few aches and pains I feel pretty good, and you must have other things to do.'

Penn gave her a constrained smile. 'Around here we're used to doing what the man says. I'll wait until you're in bed.'

Later, dressed in a loose, comfortable T-shirt and a pair of knickers, Sorrel lay in bed and sighed.

The headache had retreated to a dull, barely noticeable throb, but it didn't seem a good idea to read or watch television. Although Penn had delivered a large jug of delicious lime juice and some tempting little cakes, Sorrel wasn't hungry and there was only so much liquid she could drink.

She tried very hard to nap, but every cell in her body was alert, excited by the nearness of the man she loved. Useless to tell herself that this was merely a truce; her foolish heart was a fifth columnist, working at her downfall from within.

She watched clouds creep by in a blue, blue sky; without a sea breeze the air was so still that more clouds built over the land, and by dusk thunder was rumbling gently around the hills.

A slight tap at the door brought her upright in the bed. Head swimming slightly, she called, 'Come in.'

It was Luke, filling the room with his powerful presence. 'How do you feel?'

Men with his unforced, prowling sexuality—a sexuality backed by his innate authority and total competence—ought to be locked up. They did too much damage to impressionable feminine hearts.

'Bored,' Sorrel told him frankly, fighting back a singing joy.

His keen steel-grey gaze lanced across her face. 'Do you want dinner up here or downstairs?'

'Downstairs,' she declared with fervour. 'I love this room, but I already know it too well.'

His smile showed strong white teeth. 'How's your head?'

'The headache's almost gone.'

'I'll wait outside until you're ready.'

Penn had brought down elegantly tailored trousers, left over from Sorrel's modelling days, and a silk shirt in a clear soft honey-yellow that turned her eyes into golden jewels. After combing her hair cautiously, to avoid the bump on the back of her head, she emerged.

Luke turned away from the large abstract oil painting hung in the hall and checked her over again. 'All right?'

'Fine,' she told him. 'The bump is developing nicely, but it doesn't hurt unless I touch it. I'm a fraud.'

He didn't answer that, merely offered his arm. Chilled, Sorrel rested her fingertips on it and let herself be escorted down.

Penn served them a superb meal; it was a pity Sorrel's appetite had disappeared with Luke's arrival. However, with a mixture of persuasion and gentle bullying he saw to it that she ate more than she'd thought she wanted.

And while he was doing this he led the conversation smoothly, so that before long she found herself indulging in an animated and absorbing discussion of a book they'd both recently read.

'Would you like something to drink?' he asked later.

'Alcohol isn't appropriate, but I'm sure Penn can find something more interesting than that water for you.'

'Water's perfectly all right; if you want wine feel free to have it.' She ate an asparagus tip, delicate and succulent, silkily enrobed in butter.

'Water's fine for me too,' he said, and glanced at her plate. 'Ten years ago you had a much better appetite.'

His words hung on the air, deliberate and flat.

Sorrel kept her gaze down for several seconds. 'Ten years ago I hadn't finished growing up.'

'You mean you hadn't yet learned to starve yourself.'

'Normally I eat very well,' she said. 'Don't believe everything you read about starving models. Only women with our particular set of genetic traits make it in the business. Sure, some go to dangerous lengths to diet, but most eat normally.'

'So your lack of appetite tonight is a result of your fall?'

She put down her knife and fork. 'Probably,' she evaded.

Luke leaned back in his chair, long fingers loosely clasping his water glass, his eyes uncompromising and hard as they scanned her face. 'No sign of nausea?' he asked. 'No double vision?'

'None whatsoever. I got off lightly.' She set her jaw and ploughed on with the apology she'd been rehearsing since she arrived at Waimanu. 'I'm sorry I used that wretched ladder. I seem to have done nothing but stupid things ever since I came back, and unfortunately you've had to pick up the pieces. When you said that my life might impinge on yours, I scoffed, but you were right. From now on I'll be more careful.'

'If it's time for apologies, I've got one too. I told someone to take a decent ladder up to you, but didn't think to check that it had arrived.' His tone and eyes as hard as quartz promised retribution for whoever had been negligent.

'Luke, that's not your fault,' she said, shocked that he should think so. Of course it was typical of the man; over the years so many people had depended on him that he automatically assumed responsibility.

'If I'd made sure it got there, you wouldn't have fallen.'

'It wasn't your fault,' she repeated. 'Please don't think that—I'd hate to feel that what I've been thinking is nice New Zealand neighbourliness is just guilt. I don't associate you with guilt!'

Luke laughed, and for a moment a fragile camaraderie warmed her. 'Oh, I've done things I'm guilty about,' he said drily. 'Anyway, your ladder is now reposing in a heap of splinters on the bonfire.'

Sorrel's mouth opened. She met gleaming grey eyes, and said with rigid courtesy, 'I'm so grateful you saved me from having to carry it there myself.'

He grinned. 'It was nothing. See if you can eat some more of that chicken before Penn brings in pudding.'

It was more of a command than a suggestion, but delivered in a voice like a caress. Flushing, she applied herself to another couple of mouthfuls, and by the time she'd finished she'd regained her composure.

She did refuse the delicious dessert Penn brought in, and coffee afterwards. The apologies had cleared the air, and, while she was still very aware of the effect Luke's intense masculinity had on her, she felt that they'd achieved a more durable truce. It was probably her brittle state too; Luke treated her with an exquisite courtesy tinged with subtle, low-key flirtation. Relaxing, she dropped her guard enough to talk on until she startled herself with a huge yawn.

'Bed,' Luke said abruptly, and got up.

Sorrel followed suit, only to find the room swirling around her. She grabbed the edge of the table and closed her eyes.

'Sorrel!'

He came around the table in a silent lunge, pulling her against his chest, arms catching her around the waist and holding her upright.

'It's all right—I just stood up too fast.' Cautiously she opened her eyes, relieved when the room stopped dipping and swaying.

Luke said, 'Are you sure?'

It was too easy to lie against him and accept the support he offered. Straightening her backbone, she said firmly, 'Certain.'

True, her breasts were heavy and tender under the silk shirt, her body warm and lax and intensely responsive, but such an alarming sensitivity had nothing to do with her head.

He turned her in his arms, measured her with narrowed, perceptive eyes, and startled her by picking her up and carrying her across to the door.

'This is getting to be a habit,' she said in a tight, small voice, all of that lovely ease and relaxation fled. Held so close to him, she flinched as the heat of his body enfolded her and stripped the strength from her bones.

'You don't look capable of walking,' he told her roughly.

'Of course I can...' Her breathless words so shocked her she bit off the rest of the sentence.

He said nothing, but his arms tightened as he negotiated the doorway into the hall.

Sorrel drew a ragged breath into painfully compressed lungs and gazed stiffly ahead until slowly, with excruciating care, he lowered her onto the bed. She looked up, and sizzled in hot blue flames.

He's going to kiss me, she thought, half-horrified, half-exultant, as she closed her eyes and fought a bitter battle with herself.

And I'm going to kiss him back...

Resist it though she might, she wanted the touch of Luke's mouth rather more than she wanted to breathe.

And she couldn't deny him, just as she'd never been able to deny him before. The dark enchantment of the senses still held. Only Luke, she thought. Only ever Luke...

'I'll take off your shoes,' he said, and crouched to unbuckle her sandals.

She nodded, watching the pulse in his tanned throat. When he slid the leather strap free his cool hands brushed her ankle, sending electricity stabbing through her. She was fascinated by the blue sparks in his eyes—compelling, almost hypnotic against the grey iris. Electricity coalesced into heat and fire in the pit of her stomach.

He leaned forward a little and began to massage her feet, running his thumbs over the fine bones of her ankles and the high arches.

His touch, and the sight of his black head so close to her, summoned a wild, painful expectancy.

'There you are,' he said and looked up to catch her watching him. He froze, and then he touched her cheek, and her mouth, slowly, almost tenderly. The fiery blue lights in his eyes danced recklessly. 'Sorrel, tell me to stop.'

Above the soft murmur of the river his voice was thick and uneven. Sorrel fell into the molten depths of his eyes; she leaned forward and groaned softly as his mouth met hers.

This kiss was different—more tender, deeper, more gentle than any other. When it was over she found herself lying against him on the bed, listening to the rapid sound of his heart with a bemused smile.

And then he said in a low, self-derisory voice, 'I'm certain this isn't what the doctor meant when he said to keep you under observation.'

'No,' she said dazedly, aware of a dull thud behind her eye.

He eased her back onto the pillow. 'I'm sorry,' he said abruptly. 'I didn't intend that to happen. How's your head?'

'Letting me know it's there,' she sighed.

He said something under his breath while he stroked her cheek and forehead in slow sweeps. 'You're exhausted, and no wonder. I'll go now—try to get a good night's sleep. I'll come in during the night just to make sure you're all right, so don't be scared if you hear me moving around. Goodnight, Sorrel.'

'Goodnight, Luke.' She bit her lip because the words sounded bereft. 'And thank you for everything.'

Sleep refused to submerge her in the oblivion she craved. For a long time she stared out at the silent glory of the stars and listened to the river sweep by. Luke came in several times and stood beside the bed in silence, and each time she pretended to sleep, until eventually she did.

*   *   *

Over the dinner table the next evening Sorrel announced that she was going home the following day.

'All right,' Luke said, as though he had the right to grant permission, 'but I'll come up a couple of times a day to see how you're getting on.'

He'd worked out his tactics the preceding night, when he'd stood by her bed listening to her breathe. She could have hurt herself much more severely. Even now he felt sick at the memory of her graceful body crumpled on the floor.

Sorrel eyed him with irritation. 'My head's fine,' she said spiritedly.

'What about the bruises?' Although her face wasn't the paper-white that had shocked him so much yesterday she still looked delicate.

She pulled a face. 'They're going to be dramatic, but the cream helps.'

'Don't do any more painting or sanding—anything that requires effort on your part.'

When she didn't answer he said with silky menace, 'Sorrel?'

'You have no right to set conditions,' she returned, her lush mouth obstinate.

His smile was lethal. 'If you don't promise me that you won't do anything more than a little gentle housework I'll tie you to that bed upstairs.' It wasn't like him to make wild threats, but he'd do whatever it took to stop her doing anything that might put her recovery back.

She measured glances with him. 'I know you mean well, but—' she began.

'It probably took ten years off my life to see you on the floor. If I'd made sure the ladder had got up to Parenga, it wouldn't have happened.'

Yes, that was the way to play it. The smouldering brilliance of her big eyes was transformed into instant comprehension, and her mouth gentled. He remembered the feel of it beneath his and his body hardened unbearably.

'Luke, please don't blame yourself,' she said swiftly.

He shrugged. 'I do. Penn will prepare your dinner each night until the doctor clears you.'

Ignoring her half-eaten meal, she leaned forward and glared at him. 'Do you ever give up?'

'No,' he said calmly.

Temper lent a glow to her exquisite ivory skin and a glitter in the gold-green eyes. Heat and hunger hit him like the fierce blast from a bushfire. His fingers curled on his knife. It took him a second to relax them enough to let it drop onto the tablecloth.

She clearly wasn't up to par, because she satisfied herself with another mutinous look before saying levelly, 'I hadn't planned to do any work until the doctor said it was all right.'

The following morning she sat beside him in the car and thanked him, sounding absurdly stilted. 'I didn't have to climb that wretched ladder, you know,' she finished.

Luke gave a slanting smile that released a slow flood of sweet fire through her. 'Just take care from now on.'

So she did.

He came up two or three times each day, careful not to touch her or do anything that might lead to another kiss. Sorrel knew that this cool detachment was sensible, but as the bruises faded it grew more difficult to cope with the need that gnawed her every time she saw him—or even thought of him.

'I can't come tomorrow,' he said one afternoon as

they met on the road, he in his car, she striding towards the beach with Baggie.

Sorrel resented the disappointment that ached through her. 'That's all right,' she said airily, smiling at him with a determination that made her cheeks ache. 'You really don't need to be so religious about checking on me—I'm fine now.'

He got out of the car, overpowering and lethal and more than a little predatory. 'I've got a round of meetings in Whangarei, and at least one of them will run late. I might have to stay there.'

'Have fun,' she said flippantly, and, to show him that she didn't really care whether he came to see her or not, she raised her hand and casually patted his cheek. His hand came up to hold hers there, and he turned his face into the palm and kissed it, his lips lingering with erotic intensity against her skin.

Sharp, delicious needles of sensation pierced her.

'Then again,' he said softly against her mouth, 'I might not.'

He released her and she stepped back, pink-cheeked and breathless.

That kiss stayed with her all night and into the next day, a teasing, tormenting promise.

At lunchtime she put down her paintbrush and went down to make a sandwich. She'd just finished eating it when she heard a knock at the front door. Frowning slightly, she went to open it.

Small, blonde and voluptuous, the woman who waited for her said, 'Hello, Sorrel. It's been a long time.'

'Mari.' Sorrel swallowed. 'Come in.'

'Thanks.' Mari O'Neill looked around with composure. 'I see you're redecorating.'

At a disadvantage in her paint-spotted T-shirt and elderly shorts, Sorrel said, 'Yes. Would you like a cup of coffee? Some lunch?'

The other woman gave a wry smile. 'No, thanks. I need to talk to you.'

Her shock expanding into an icy void, Sorrel led the way into the room Cynthia had always called the small parlour. The two chairs and a table looked out over a brick patio scented with gardenias and roses, her godmother's favourite flowers.

They sat down. Mari examined her expensive Italian shoes and said, 'Did you know that Luke and I have been lovers for years?'

CHAPTER TEN

NOT trusting herself to speak, Sorrel nodded.

'I assumed that eventually we'd get married,' Mari said quietly. 'Oh, it was never spoken of; we are—were—good friends, and Luke made it quite clear that he was happy with the status quo. And most of the time I was happy too—I've got a demanding job, and, well...' she made an aimless gesture before letting her hands drop back into her lap '...it worked.'

'I don't think—'

'Bear with me, please.'

But Mari paused so long before she began again that Sorrel gave her an anxious look. She saw nothing beyond a skilfully made-up face, calm and serene.

Mari said slowly, 'The thing is, of course, I fell in love with him. It's very easy to do.' Her smile was tinged with wry sympathy when she looked across at Sorrel. 'As you found out. Apart from being magnificent in bed, he's got a brilliant brain and he really listens to what you have to say—so many men don't.'

Sorrel bit her lip.

'But he didn't fall in love with me,' the clear, remorseless voice went on. 'Because of his bitch of a mother and that appalling stepmother I don't think he'll ever trust a woman enough to love her. When he marries—and he will, because he's a Hardcastle and he wants a son to inherit Waimanu—he'll choose a wife with just as much care and just as cold-bloodedly as he breeds his pedigree stock.' She looked up at Sorrel, her

163

eyes magnified by tears. 'It's not going to be me, and it won't be you, either. You're everything he distrusts—beautiful, sophisticated, sexually active.'

Sorrel made a small, shocked sound.

Mari shrugged. 'He's not a hypocrite, but he dislikes promiscuity. So he despises himself because he's never been able to get you out of his system. Of course it didn't help to have your face splashed over massive billboards and in every magazine and newspaper for years.'

'How do you know all this?' Sorrel's voice was low and tightly controlled. She had no intention of refuting Mari's hint at her supposed promiscuity; two men, she thought fiercely, did not make for a wildly abandoned love life, but the gossip columnists tarred all models with the same brush.

'I know him very well,' Mari said, her mouth tightening. 'I liked you all those years ago, and that's why I've come. To warn you. He'll be a magnificent lover, but don't let him keep you dangling like he did me. Believe me—' her voice broke but she caught herself up and finished evenly '—the game isn't worth the candle.'

She got to her feet with a pale smile. 'At least you've acted as a catalyst,' she said without emotion. 'I might have gone on wasting my time if you hadn't come back. Remember once I told you that the woman always chooses—and you said that Luke would do his own choosing? I wish I'd listened to you. Goodbye—and good luck.'

Sorrel watched her walk down the drive and over the bridge, listened to the sound of her car until it faded away.

Mute agony scythed through her, holding her prisoner until she forced herself back to work. Mari's words had only reinforced a truth she'd refused to face: Luke's distrust of women went so deep that he'd probably never be able to overcome it.

What was she going to do? Accept him as he was, or pull up the drawbridge and refuse him?

Each choice offered unending pain. She realised she'd been staring at the wall without doing anything for some minutes, her brain desperately seeking ways out of the impasse. Moving slowly, she climbed down from the ladder, automatically tipping paint back into the can before washing the roller.

'Come on, Baggie,' she said in a voice flat with repressed despair, 'let's go for a walk on the beach.'

She walked too long beneath the blazing sun before seeking refuge under the sheltering limbs of a pohutukawa. Thoughts tossing endlessly around her tired brain, she stared blindly out across the glittering sea, deaf to the whisper of waves on the white-hot sand and the ugly screams of a pack of gulls fighting over something on the tideline.

I'm not going to run away, she thought, picking up a handful of sand, mercifully cool in the deep shade of the tree, and letting it sift through her fingers. I have to stick this out.

So either she became Luke's new mistress, to be abandoned in her turn when he found a suitable candidate for his planned, bloodless marriage, or she cut off all communication between them except the most impersonal.

She looped her arms around her knees and rested her head on them, listening to the uneven beat of her heart. Pride chose the latter course, but what if loving him without conditions, without hope and without limit could restore his lost trust?

Stupid, she scoffed. Rescued by the love of a good woman? It hadn't worked for Mari, and it wouldn't work for her.

One night at Parenga might have taught her that she loved Luke, but she wasn't going to sacrifice years of her life in a useless, heartbreaking attempt to persuade him that she was loyal and trustworthy.

'Like a dog,' she said bitterly, scrambling up and brushing the sand off her legs. 'Time to go home, Baggie.'

Tomorrow she'd ring a contact in Auckland, seeking work; it would keep her away from the house, but surely if she made Parenga her base that would fulfil the conditions in Cynthia's will. Then she'd sell, and make a new life somewhere else.

Her hand stole up to clench over her heart, as though she could stop its bleak anguish with sheer will-power. In time she'd get over Luke, because this time she'd decided to leave.

Tonight, when he came back, she'd tell him she didn't want to take their relationship—if you could call it that—any further. Unless she was misreading that final kiss that morning...

No. There had been too much significance in his smile, in that fleeting caress. He wanted her, and he meant to have her, presumably to get her out of his system.

She was staring at her uneaten dinner when the telephone went—Luke on his mobile.

'Hi,' she said, her heart jittering crazily in her breast. 'How did your day go?'

'Good,' he said. 'I should be at Parenga in half an hour.'

'I—OK. Fine. See you then.'

It was an oddly formal conversation—no, she thought bleakly, not formal. Impersonal.

Perhaps she hadn't had to make that painful choice on the beach. Perhaps he'd already made it for her.

A mixture of shock and agitation drove her into the garden. Baggie prowling at her heels, she paced through the scented evening until she saw a movement down by the bridge.

Trembling, she stopped under the magnolia tree and rested her hand on its cool bark. The setting sun, a golden ball in a dramatic scarlet sky, caught Luke's black head, turning it into sable fire. He'd left his car down by the road and was walking across the bridge with a confidence that bordered on arrogance.

Baggie strolled down to meet him; two imperious males, Sorrel thought, trying to banish the chill seeping through her.

She'd changed out of her paint-spotted jeans into long sleek trousers, and topped them with a loose smock the same pale gold as her eyes, tying her hair up onto the top of her head in a ponytail. Clothes seemed very fragile armour, but they were all she had.

'You look intriguingly artistic,' Luke observed as he came up the drive, hard grey eyes surveying her with an assessing glint.

She gave him her most remote smile. 'And you look for all the world like a tycoon. How did your meetings go?'

He wore tailored trousers that reinforced the power of his long legs, and a shirt subtly cut to reveal the blatant width of his shoulders. Sexual confidence and energy radiated from him in a sensual aura that targeted her every nerve.

'Well enough,' he said. 'Ask me in.'

Sorrel observed him through her lashes. He looked tired and grim, his expression set in lines of controlled detachment. Pain squeezed her heart. 'Is there something powerfully symbolic about inviting you into Parenga?'

'Stop fencing with me, Sorrel. I need to talk to you.'

'All right,' she said stiffly, almost flinching at his final words, exactly the same as Mari's. 'Come in.'

Once in the parlour, she didn't offer him a drink. She did sit down, but he stood at the window looking out over the garden.

Tension spiked through the room, tightening her skin in the age-old response to danger. When she couldn't bear it any longer she asked abruptly, 'What's happened?'

'For starters,' he said with forbidding detachment, turning to face her so that all she could see of him was his outline against the crimson sky outside, 'what did Mari say to you this afternoon?'

Shock held her speechless.

'Mari has apparently made a confidante of Penn.' His voice gave nothing away. 'Penn told her when your box arrived, and when Mari left here today she went down to Waimanu to see Penn. Who rang me when she'd left.'

'So that's why—?'

'Yes, that's why Penn's been distant. It's also why she didn't pass on my message about the ladder. I told her to tell one of the farmhands to bring it up. She didn't.' His face hardened into ruthless lines. 'For which she's very sorry—and not just because she almost lost her job. She didn't intend any harm to you.'

'I'm sure she didn't.'

He said remotely, 'It won't happen again.' He looked around the room as though he'd never seen it before. 'What did Mari say?'

'Nothing I didn't already know,' Sorrel returned with spirit.

Luke's half-closed eyes gleamed. 'Tell me,' he said in a gentle tone that sent shudders scudding the length of her spine.

'Are you still seeing her?'

His head came up. She could read nothing in his expression, nothing in his voice when he said, 'No,' but the soft, deadly syllable shook her as shouting and fury would never have.

Nevertheless she said levelly, 'And you're not seeing me, so you have no right to hear details of a conversation between two people who mean nothing to you.'

He stared at her, eyes molten, mouth compressed into a white line. 'What the hell do you mean—I'm not seeing you?'

Sorrel took a deep, painful breath and forced the words past a painful constriction in her throat. 'If you want the same arrangement that you had with Mari, I'm afraid I'm not good mistress material.'

He pinned her with a cruelly speculative scrutiny that brought stinging colour to her skin. 'Oh, I'm sure you're just being modest,' he drawled silkily, coming towards her with purposeful strides.

She braced herself. She couldn't bear it if he kissed her in anger, in lust and contempt.

Of course he saw it; he stopped a stride away, his

face grim. 'What's the matter? You know I won't hurt you.'

'Luke, please don't do this.' She dragged in a shivering breath and he closed his eyes a second before transfixing her with a glittering gaze.

His voice cold and unsparing, he asked, 'Tell me, how do you plan to pay for the bridge?'

'I'll manage,' she said remotely.

'No doubt. Would it make things simpler if I offered you a loan—on very easy terms, of course?' He looked at her with a disturbing mixture of anger and desire. 'Perhaps with enough extra so that you can afford to hire renovators for the house? What price do you put on yourself?'

Without volition her hand swung at his face. He didn't move, not even when the imprint of her fingers was branded red on his cheek.

Her hot colour drained away, leaving her pale and cold. 'I am not a prostitute,' she whispered, sick with humiliated anger.

'You're certainly no shrinking, virginal violet.' He surveyed her as though she disgusted him, as though disgusted with himself for wanting her. 'Perhaps I've been too blunt. Let's call it security I'm offering. It means the same thing but it sounds better. The sex was fantastic—how much do you think it would be worth on a regular basis?'

'Nothing without love,' she said angrily.

He laughed.

How many times had she read about breaking hearts and thought it a tired, worn-out cliché? But she felt hers shatter, split from top to bottom to splinter into fragments, each one a sliver of agony. It hurt so much she could only survive by summoning anger to temporarily ease the pain of grief.

'So you're just like all the others,' she said savagely.

'Others?' he asked. And when she shook her head and turned her face away, he demanded, 'What others are you talking about?'

'There are plenty of men out there like you, Luke, prepared to pay for the kudos of having a minor celebrity share their bed. Is that what you want?' she asked, goading him because if she didn't she'd shame herself by breaking down and howling. 'A mistress just along the road? Fantastic sex whenever you decide to take it?'

He was right—love entailed disillusion and pain; she should have settled for casual sex. It would have been so much easier to live for the moment and keep her heart locked away from pain. If she'd done that she wouldn't be longing for anything other than what Luke could give—honest commerce.

He said nothing, just held her with a narrowed stare that summoned stinging colour up through her skin. High in the maple tree outside a tui sang his evening aria, his heart throbbing through the glorious song. A soft breeze billowed the curtains inward, bringing a gust of gardenia-scented air.

Finally Luke said, 'I want you.'

Stark, simple and true; she couldn't doubt his honesty. Or his determination; it smouldered in his eyes, roughened his voice, radiated from him. So Mari had been right.

In spite of everything his words fanned passionate desire deep inside Sorrel, summoned flames and a scorching sexuality. But his admission wasn't enough.

She knew she didn't have the stamina to love him and receive only lust in return.

Unable to think, almost unaware of what she was saying, she demanded in a raw voice, 'Is this the arrangement you had with Mari? Sex in return for money?'

'No.' He looked down at her with a closed, hard face. 'I was going to marry Mari.'

Sorrel flung out a hand to grasp the back of the nearest chair, clinging to it with white knuckles until she could draw a breath that didn't stab her. With dilated eyes she searched Luke's dark, unyielding face. 'Why didn't you?'

'Because you sent a box to Parenga,' he told her evenly. 'And I discovered that I'd been marking time, waiting for you to come back. Once I realised that, I also realised I couldn't marry another woman with you still lodged under my skin.'

Oh, Mari did know him very well. Sorrel said thinly, 'Why do you hate me so much?'

His head came up. 'I don't hate you,' he said curtly.

'You think I'm like your stepmother.'

'No. She would never have given up a high-flying career to care for a man like your father, paralysed and unable to talk.' He paused, dark eyes surveying her face, then went on deliberately, 'Especially not if he'd lost every cent she earned playing roulette and backing horses.'

Sorrel's jaw dropped. For a moment she couldn't breathe, but she rallied to ask in a shaken voice, 'How did you find out?'

'It's easy enough if you know where to look,' he said dismissively. 'When you dropped so dramatically out of sight there were rumours—of marriage, drug addiction, bankruptcy. Cynthia confided once that your father was a gambler—it worried her. So when I realised you had no money I made enquiries. The results came through last night.'

Sorrel turned abruptly away. 'You had no right to pry,' she said, pronouncing each word carefully.

Luke's merciless voice went on, 'You wouldn't have told me.' It wasn't a question.

'Of course not.' She looked down at hands twisting together in the classical gesture of helplessness. Stopping them, forcing them to hang limply at her sides, gave her something to concentrate on. 'Why should I? You wouldn't have believed me. And if you had,' she said with a spurt of malice, 'you'd have assumed that I'd come back to seduce money from you.'

'Why didn't you take on another perfume campaign?' he asked with silky contempt. 'I can vouch that your body is still as beautiful and provocative as it was when you did the last one.'

The skin on the back of her neck prickled. Stiffening her shoulders, she said dully, 'I—needed the money.'

'I hope they paid you well. It certainly caused controversy, so I suppose it did what it was supposed to do.' He didn't have to say what he thought about the campaign. The edge of contempt in his tone said it for him.

'Luke,' she said, shaken and exhausted but still valiant, 'please go. This isn't getting us anywhere, and I'm tired.'

After a silent tense moment, he swivelled on his heel and left without a word.

Sorrel waited until the front door closed before collapsing into a chair and beginning to weep—painful, difficult tears that wrenched through her and brought her no relief.

Eventually she got up and went to wash her face, knowing now that staying at Parenga was out of the question.

She was dragging her way to bed when the knocker on the front door sounded in several sharp, staccato knocks. 'No,' she whispered. 'Oh, please no.'

It didn't stop, so she opened the door.

'You'd better get a peephole put into this,' Luke said curtly, walking in.

He sounded normal, but she sensed a dark rage in him that had her falling back.

Leading the way into the bookroom she enquired dully, 'What do you want?'

'You asked me that before. I want you.' In a voice rigid with some strong emotion he said, 'I've spent the past ten years waiting for you to come back. I didn't furnish the other rooms at Waimanu because I wanted you to do them. I don't know anything about love, but I know about wanting.' He stopped, big hands clenching at his sides. Then he added starkly, 'And needing.'

Afraid to move, to speak, she stared at him with huge, dilating eyes.

He said, 'Sorrel, have I spoiled everything so much that it's beyond repair? Can you forgive me? I've been mad since you came back, fighting this...this desperation. I thought making love to you might sate it, but although it was a miracle it simply made me want you more.'

'It's not enough,' she said heavily. 'I couldn't live with distrust. And you don't trust me.'

'I want to care for you, protect you from anything that might hurt you or worry you or upset you.' He spoke dispassionately, his tone at odds with the words. When she stayed silent he finished, 'I want to come home at night and know you're there for me. I want you to bear my children. You mean more to me than anyone I've ever known. Surely that indicates some degree of trust?'

She should have been ecstatic.

Yet it wasn't enough.

'I've heard a lot about what *you* want,' she said. 'You've never asked me what I want.'

She read anger in his eyes, and a coldness that shook her, and then he turned away with a swift, slicing gesture. Harshly, as though each word was painful, he said, 'So tell me.'

'I want you,' she said simply, knowing she couldn't go back now, gambling with her life and his for higher stakes. 'Because I love you, Luke. I can't remember a time when I didn't. But I'm not going to be a partner in an uneven relationship—as your father was.'

Luke went white. He stared at her for several seconds before swinging on his heel and striding across to the window. Cynthia's roses glimmered in the darkness, and from beyond came the hush of the sea—eternal, sad, inexorable.

He said uncompromisingly, 'Love made him into a weak, whimpering fool, and I vowed I'd have nothing to do with it.'

Sorrel's mouth dried. She heard her heart beating wildly as she waited.

He turned his head and looked at her, eyes hooded and hard. 'But it seems I don't get a choice. Love isn't something you can organise or control; it chooses its own way, and its own time.'

'I think we do get a choice,' she said, speaking

slowly because this was hugely important to both of them. 'Sex—no. That's physical. But love—I love you because as well as being the most exciting man I've ever met you're honourable and hard-working and kind and intelligent and I—you're a man I respect.' Tears ached at the back of her eyes as she chanced everything on this final throw. 'But respect must be a two-way thing.'

'I admire you more than I can ever tell you,' he said quietly. 'You looked after your father when he'd betrayed you, you came here ready to work on Parenga, you're bright and gentle and nobody's fool, you were prepared to risk your life to save a blasted con artist of a cat—and you're so beautiful you stop my heart.'

'I won't always be beautiful,' she said, a tiny frown pleating her brow. She shot a fleeting glance his way, but could make out nothing in his face; his formidable self-control rebuffed all attempts to discover his real feelings.

'You will always be beautiful to me,' he said with such simple conviction that she at last had the proof she needed so badly. 'The moment I saw you again I knew I was in trouble. And when I found you unconscious I had to accept that something had taken me over, and I couldn't control either it or myself.'

He looked at her with something very like bitterness. He still hadn't admitted that he loved her, but this was what she'd longed for without realising it until she came back—Luke's trust, freely offered, willingly given.

Shaking, she repeated his words as though making a vow. 'Luke, I want to care for you, protect you from anything that might hurt you or worry you or upset you. I want to come home at night and know you're there for me. I want you to be the father of my children. And I will love you all my life.'

He covered the floor separating them in two long strides and caught her up against him, holding her so close she couldn't breathe.

When she began to struggle he loosed her; she lifted her face to meet his, and they kissed.

This time their loving was long and sweet and tender—so tender that when it was over and she was lying in his arms, her head on his shoulder, her hand smoothing over the sleek, taut skin of his hip, Sorrel was certain that nothing in her life could ever match this.

'Why did Mari come here?' he asked, stroking the damp fall of chestnut hair back from her cheek.

The other woman's name intruded into her cocoon of joy. 'To warn me that you'd be perfectly happy with a relationship provided I didn't want anything more than sex and companionship.'

He called Mari something that made Sorrel wince. 'After you left Parenga we became lovers for six months or so,' he said flatly. 'We only got back together again about a year ago; I liked her, I respected her, and so I decided she'd make a good wife. I knew she wouldn't refuse me, because she's level-headed and sensible. Then you sent that box back and all my cold-blooded, pragmatic plans crashed in disarray around me. I think I must have been crazy with—oh, fear, I suppose.'

'Fear?'

He said harshly, 'The night my stepmother came into my bedroom clad in a nightgown and nothing else I promised myself that I'd never be like my father, never let a woman get under my skin so that I lost not only autonomy, but every scrap of integrity.' His arms tightened around him and in his voice she could hear the echoes of that long ago betrayal. 'He loved me, but although he knew what Cherie was—that she'd bleed Waimanu of every cent—it didn't stop him from doing his best to disinherit me.'

'You're not like that,' she said fiercely.

'Perhaps not, but when your box arrived I thought, She's coming back! And my life suddenly turned from workaday grey to a rainbow of colours. That was when I realised I was too much like him to be safe.' He kissed the satiny skin of her throat. 'Yet I couldn't marry Mari, so I broke it off with her as gently as I could. I don't blame her for wanting revenge.'

Sorrel recalled the woman's face and knew that Mari loved him and had fought for him in the only way she knew how. Wisely, she said nothing.

Sombrely Luke went on, 'I'm not proud of myself for hurting her, and even less proud of blaming you for my own weakness and behaving like an arrogant bastard when you arrived back.'

Showing her teeth in something a little less friendly than a smile, Sorrel pushed herself up and examined his angular face, so beloved, so uncompromising.

'Why did you?' she asked. 'I can understand why you were afraid to love—your father's problems would have put anyone off!' She poked a long forefinger into his chest. 'But you *knew* me—I'd more or less shadowed you for years, and we'd always got on quite well. You'd been a kind, aloof big-brother figure for years, yet you acted as though my modelling course had come with a character transplant!'

Luke looked at her with narrowed, burning eyes and said with brutal self-contempt, 'I'd just got rid of

Cherie, who'd done her best to destroy my father and me, and then you arrived—beautiful, forbidden and a powerful threat to my self-image. About a nano-second after I saw you I realised that somehow, over those big-brother years, you'd stolen away an essential part of me. I started manufacturing anger and resentment to hide a terrified self-disgust.'

'You? I don't believe it!' She stared at him, read the truth of his statement in his eyes, and her heart sang, because he was no longer hiding himself behind the handsome mask of his face.

'Believe it,' he said briefly, and pulled her down to lie on top of him. 'I can be as screwed up as the next man.'

Wriggling, Sorrel relaxed onto his sleek, hot body, shivering as the powerful and resilient length hardened beneath her. Her breath came fast through her lips, but although loving was wonderful, this quiet conversation was vital.

'Stop that,' he said, eyes possessive and hungry. 'I need to tell you this.'

She gave him a teasing, tender smile. 'All right. I think we'd got to the stage where you were going to explain why you behaved like a case history from a handbook for tyrants and despots that last summer at Parenga. Before you kissed me, that is.'

'Because even if I hadn't had a hang-up as big as Mt Cook I couldn't have asked a kid of eighteen to marry me, or even wait for me. Apart from the fact that you deserved a life of your own, all I had to offer was a run-down station that was going to take years of hard work to get back into any sort of shape. So I had to keep my distance.'

'Why did you kiss me?'

He gave her a grim smile. 'Because I couldn't help myself. You smiled up at me, and I gave up.'

'So you found a way to warn me off,' she said sadly, wishing she'd known all this then. It would have saved her so much heartache.

'Mari was a godsend; she gave me an excuse to pull back, to regroup, to convince myself that I was fine, it was only a temporary madness, one I'd soon get over.'

'I thought that too,' she said soberly. 'In fact, I was certain of it. Yet I kept you like a talisman at the back of my mind; I measured other men by you, and they all failed the test.'

'Idiots, both of us,' he said sombrely, turning his face into the warm curve of her throat. 'If I hadn't been so sure that loving you would make me humiliatingly dependent, we might have been able to work something out.'

'I was too young.'

'I know. And I was too angry with my father, too disgusted by Cherie to make any sort of commitment.' He kissed the beating hollow at the base of her throat, smiling at her response. Easing her sideways, he ran his hand across the slight curves of her breasts, cupping one to tease the nipple with his thumb.

Sorrel's pulse-rate soared. More than anything she wanted to forget everything in the honeyed fire of oblivion, but this was too important to rush through. She contented herself with nipping the rounded swell of a shoulder muscle, then sucked delicately on the smooth, hot skin.

His voice turned rough. 'I dreamed about you during those years. That final ad campaign haunted me—I wondered if you and the model were lovers, and I hated feeling vulnerable.'

'Luke—'

He interrupted with abrupt aloofness. 'No, let me get this out. I'm not going to ask about your lovers; it's none of my business.'

'And I have no intention of asking you how many lovers you've had,' she told him with a steely note in her voice.

'Probably fewer than you think.'

She looked him straight in the eyes. 'Likewise!'

His smile was twisted. 'By the time you came back I'd finished with Mari and accepted that I was going to have to deal with the way you affected me. I was in a filthy temper before you got here, but the reality of you, and the feel of you in my arms that first night at Parenga, sent me straight to hell. When Mari rang to ask if I was still taking her to that bloody premiere I ran like a coward; she sounded sensible and normal and I was torn by desires and needs I'd renounced years ago.'

He slid his fingers into her hair, letting it ripple through them in a fiery flood of red-brown silk. 'And it got worse. I started to wake every morning feeling that the only thing that validated each day was your presence. I was getting closer and closer to the abject adoration I despised in my father.'

Sorrel rested her cheek on his shoulder. 'But you don't feel like that now?' She held her breath.

He shook his head. 'It simply doesn't matter any more,' he said with calm conviction. 'I need you as much as I need to breathe. As for distrusting you—the first thing you did was risk your life for a cat. That was when I realised I was in real danger, so I tried to re-inforce all my defences by taking another leaf out of that handbook for tyrants and despots.' He gave an un-amused laugh. 'For all the good it did me!'

'It doesn't matter,' she murmured. 'It's the past, and the past is over; we own the future now.'

His fingers tightened in her hair; very gently he turned her head and tilted her face so that he could see it. 'When do you want to get married?' he asked casually, but his gaze was keen and intent.

'Are you sure?' she asked, searching his eyes.

'Absolutely.' He stretched like a great cat, tawny skin rippling, then kissed her. 'And the sooner the better,' he said against her lips in a voice velvet with pleasure.

'Can you still get married in three days here?'

He laughed. 'Yes, but you know, I think I'd like to marry you with all the pomp and ceremony I can manage. How about in a month's time?'

EPILOGUE

THEY were married in the garden at Parenga, beneath the magnolia. The bride wore ivory silk satin in a slender classical style with a small train, the South Sea pearls Luke had given her the night before, and the lace veil her mother had worn at her own wedding.

Her matron of honour was her best friend, Emma Talbot, whose amber dress hid the slight evidence of her second pregnancy. Kane, her tall, harsh-featured husband, gave the bride away.

Sorrel's goddaughter Cressy made a delicious little flower girl; once her father surrendered the bride to Luke, she curled up in his lap and watched the rest of the service with wide, dark eyes.

The guests were mainly local, although a couple of slender, gorgeous creatures with exotic accents had winged in from overseas to cut a swathe through the male guests. One incredibly handsome man was recognised as the model who'd starred with the bride in her final campaign; there was flutter of regret amongst the women when they realised his partner was another equally handsome male.

Sorrel's radiant face brought lumps to many throats, as did Luke's tenderness. The reception, a very cheerful affair, was held at Waimanu, and as they left for their honeymoon they were showered with rose petals.

They spent the first night at Luke's beach house on an offshore island. As they walked along the deserted beach, with the sunset filling the sky with a glory of gold and rose and orange, Sorrel said drily, 'I hope seeing Jason and Raoul together convinced you not to worry about those perfume ads. They're a very committed couple.'

'Nice guys,' he said, adding with an amused smile, 'I'm sure they suspected you were marrying some bone-headed hick, if their relief when they saw Waimanu was anything to go by. Last night they gave me a gentle grilling about my financial and emotional status—a follow-up to the one Kane put me through.'

He waited for her delighted gurgle of laughter, and when it was over finished smoothly, 'I think I managed to convince them all that I could keep you in silk and good food, and that I was reasonably good husband material.'

'The best,' she said immediately, smiling up at him.

Luke stopped and pulled her into his arms. 'I love you,' he said fiercely into her hair. 'But you know that now, don't you?'

She kissed his throat. 'I have a pretty good idea,' she murmured, heart swelling with joy.

He lifted her hand and gently bit the mound of Venus under her thumb. As little rills of pleasure ran through her, he said, 'I will always love you, and I know you're nothing like either my mother or Cherie—I don't know how I managed to persuade myself you might be.'

His mother had attended the wedding with her husband. A thin, brittle socialite, she'd watched her son with something like despairing hunger. Sorrel felt sorry for her, and intended to keep in touch.

But now was not the time to make plans. 'Nobody likes to feel they're a slave to their emotions.'

Luke tilted her face up and said quietly, 'Control's

always been important for me. Then you came along, and it shattered into a million pieces.'

He looked at her with naked longing, the strong framework of his face prominent beneath taut tanned skin. 'I didn't want to be like my father, caught in a relationship where I was the importunate one, the one who needed. But I didn't realise what I was asking from you—when you said you wouldn't accept an unequal relationship I realised that I was like Cherie, demanding all and giving nothing.'

'You are not like Cherie,' Sorrel said fiercely, trying to shake him and unable to move him at all. 'It's not like that for us—we're equals in everything.' She summoned a smile. 'Except in physical strength.'

'I love you, and you love me,' he said intensely. 'That's all that matters.'

He kissed her forehead, the tips of her eyebrows and the lobes of her ears; secure at last, she relaxed into him.

'I wonder how Cynthia knew,' Sorrel murmured, pushing aside his collar to punctuate the sentence with a little nip between each word.

When their engagement had been announced, the trustees for Parenga had sent her papers for dissolving the trust, with a letter from Cynthia. In her message Cynthia had said that she'd insisted on the six months' residency because she was sure that Sorrel and Luke were made for each other.

'She was a wise old bird,' Luke said, his voice thickening as her eager mouth moved slowly across his chest. 'What will you do with Parenga?'

She lifted her head to say, 'I think it would be a wonderful place for people to stay when they've been ill—families with sick children, perhaps.'

'My darling, kind-hearted Sorrel,' he said, his voice deep and tender. 'We'll work it out together later. At the moment I want you so much…'

'And I want you,' she said in a smoky, sensuous voice. 'Let's go up to the house.'

Together at last, safe in their love, they walked through the glory of the sunset into their future.

HIS ONE-NIGHT MISTRESS

by

Sandra Field

Although born in England, **Sandra Field** has lived most of her life in Canada; she says the silence and emptiness of the north speaks to her particularly. While she enjoys travelling, and passing on her sense of a new place, she often chooses to write about the city which is now her home. Sandra says, 'I write out of my experience; I have learned that love with its joys and its pains is all-important. I hope this knowledge enriches my writing, and touches a chord in you, the reader.'

CHAPTER ONE

GLITTERING. Dazzling. *Magnifique!*

Lia d'Angeli edged toward the wall in the vast foyer of the hotel, whose floor-to-ceiling, gilt-scrolled mirrors reflected what could have been a scene from one of Louis XIV's revels. Her fingers tightened around her invitation with its elegant gold script, an invitation given her just yesterday by her Parisian friend Mathieu. "A masked ball," he'd said with his charming, lop-sided grin. "I can't go, *malheureusement.* Take some handsome young man, Lia, eat, drink and dance your heart out." His grin took on a satyr's edge. "You could try ending up in his bed——you're far too beautiful to have the reputation of a nun, *chérie.*"

Mathieu's endearment Lia took with a grain of salt; he was known for romantic dalliance in every district of Paris. But his advice——at least some of it—she fully intended to take. Eat, drink and dance. Yes, she'd do all three with pleasure. But she had come to the ball alone, and she intended to leave it alone.

Alone and anonymous, she thought with a sigh of pure pleasure. Her fame was new, and not altogether pleasant. But this evening she wasn't Lia d'Angeli, the brilliant young violinist who'd burst on the international scene by winning two prestigious competitions within six months of each other. No, she thought, glancing sideways at herself in the nearest mirror and feeling her lips curve in a smile. She was a butterfly instead, flirtatious and enigmatic, fluttering from partner to partner with no intention of being pinned down by any one of them.

Her costume consisted of a shiny turquoise bodysuit that faithfully outlined her breasts, hips, gently incurving waist and long, slender legs. Jeweled turquoise sandals were on her feet. Flaring between arm and thigh were her wings, folds of delicate chiffon, turquoise and green. But it was her mask that made the costume. Like a helmet, it covered her high cheekbones, revealing only the darkness of her eyes, and hiding her tumble of black hair in a glimmer of sequins and exquisite peacock feathers. She'd carefully smoothed turquoise makeup over her cheeks, her chin and her throat; her lips were a luminous gold.

An outrageous costume, she thought with great satisfaction. A costume that freed her to be anyone she wanted to be.

No one here knew her. She planned to take full advantage of that, dance her heart out and leave by midnight. Just like Cinderella.

Her eyes ranged the crowd. Marie Antoinette, the Hunchback of Notre-Dame, a cardinal worthy of an El Greco portrait, a sexy dancer from the Moulin Rouge. All masked. All strangers to each other. And perhaps to themselves, she thought with a tiny shiver of her nerves.

She shook off her sudden unease, making her way to the doorman and presenting her numbered invitation. A uniformed official was whispering something in his ear; the doorman waved her into the ballroom impatiently, scarcely glancing at the calligraphy on the card as he added it to the stack beside him. Lia slipped past him quickly; she'd worried a little that there might be some objection to her having Mathieu's invitation rather than one in her own name. A good omen, she thought lightheartedly, and tucked herself around the corner out of his sight.

The ballroom was alive with the lilt of an old-fashioned waltz, although by the look of the sound equipment the music wouldn't be that sedate all evening. More mirrors adorned the sapphire-blue walls, while sparkling gold chandeliers were suspended from a ceiling painted with more chubby cherubs than there were springtime lovers in Paris. Against the far wall long tables with immaculate white cloths held a feast that even King Louis wouldn't have scorned. White-jacketed waiters circulated among the crowd, holding aloft silver trays of wine and champagne.

And then she saw him.

Like herself, the man was standing with his back to the wall, surveying the crowd. A highwayman, cloaked and booted, a black mask making slits of his eyes, a black hat with a sweeping brim shadowing his features.

No costume in the world could have hidden his height, the breadth of his shoulders or his aura of power, of command, of complete and utter self-control. An aura he clearly took for granted.

A man who took what he wanted. A highwayman, indeed.

He, like her, was alone.

As another of those chills traced the length of Lia's spine, his gaze came to rest on her. Even across the width of the huge ballroom, she felt his sudden, searing focus; his body stilled, like a bandit's when he sights his victim.

She couldn't have moved to save her soul.

The butterfly pinned to the wall, she thought crazily, her heart racing against her rib cage. She'd been frightened many times in her life; it was part of the striving for excellence that had driven her for as long as she could remember. But pre-concert nerves, for all their terrors, were at least backed by the sure knowledge of her own technical accomplishments, and by the inner certainty that, once again, she could over-come those nerves.

This terror was different. She felt stripped, laid bare, ex-posed. All because a stranger had chanced to look at her. A man she'd never seen before——of that she was sure——and need never see again.

Ridiculous, she thought, gathering every vestige of her courage to fight an assault unlike any she'd ever known.

Assault? The man hadn't even touched her.

In a flare of defiance Lia gestured to the nearest waiter, took a glass of red wine from his tray and, with a mocking salute to the man across the room, raised the glass in a toast

He swept off his hat, revealing a crop of untidy, sun-streaked blond hair, and bowed to her from the waist, a courtly gesture that brought an involuntary smile to her lips. Then he straightened and started toward her across the wide expanse of floor.

In total panic she heard a male voice say in clumsily ac-cented French, *"Voulez-vous danser avec moi, madame?"*

A British soldier from the Napoleonic wars had inserted himself between her and the highwayman. Quickly Lia put her wine down on the nearest table and said, in English, "Thank you, yes."

"Cool—you speak English," the soldier said, put his arm around her and with a certain flair eased her among the other dancers. He waltzed with a competence for which she was grateful, and didn't seem to require much from her in the way of conversation, for which she was more than grateful. From the corner of her eye, she watched the highwayman be ac-costed by a group of curvaceous chorus girls, then extract him-self with a remark that left them all giggling. She said breathlessly, "I'd love to get a closer look at the orchestra—can we go that way?"

The soldier obediently whisked her to the opposite end of

the room. The waltz ended, followed by a rhumba. A clown with a garish red slash of mouth cut in; automatically Lia followed the rhythm, her diaphanous wings fluttering as she raised and lowered her arms. The clown was superseded by a dignified gentleman who could have emerged from the pages of a Jane Austen novel.

As the two-step came to its predictable close, another partner loomed behind the elderly gentleman. The highwayman, his black cloak swirling. Lia's nerves tightened to an almost intolerable pitch, even though from the first moment she'd seen him she'd known this meeting was inevitable. "My turn, I believe," he said pleasantly, yet with an edge of steel underlying a voice as smooth as brandy.

Lia smiled at her partner, thanked him and turned to face her opponent. For opponent he was; of that she was in no doubt.

She could have refused to speak to him. But pride had always been one of her besetting sins, and besides, weren't challenges meant to be met?

Before she could even open her mouth, he said with that same steel edge, "You've had your fun. Now it's my turn."

She'd see about that. Raising her chin, Lia said with rather overdone politeness, "It's very warm in here, isn't it? I'd love a glass of champagne."

"What's your name?"

"Subtlety certainly isn't yours."

"I don't believe in wasting time."

"Mine or yours?" she demanded.

"Mine."

"Then perhaps you should find yourself another partner."

"Oh, I don't think so," he said.

"So tell me *your* name," she said, fully expecting him to refuse.

"Seth Talbot. From Manhattan. You're American as well."

Her home base was a tiny apartment in Greenwich Village.

She said coolly, "I was born in Switzerland, Mr. Talbot," and with equal aplomb gestured to the nearest waiter, who presented her with a crystal flute of champagne. She raised it to her lips, feeling the bubbles tickle her nostrils.

"So you take what you want," Seth Talbot said softly.

"Is there any other way?"

"Not in my world. I'm glad we understand each other."

"You can't possibly understand me—because you don't know what I want," she retorted.

"From the first moment we caught sight of each other, we've wanted the same thing."

Back off, Lia. Be sensible. End this before it begins. "Since I'm no mind reader," she snapped, "why don't you tell me what that is?"

He wrapped fingers as unyielding as handcuffs around her wrist. Long, lean fingers, she saw, ringless, with well-kept nails and a dusting of blond hair where his shirt ended in a tight cuff. She said evenly, "Let go."

With almost insulting abruptness he dropped her wrist. The music had started again. "We're in the way," he said, draped an arm around Lia's shoulders and drew her off the dance floor.

His cloak had enveloped her in its dark folds; his arm was heavy, its weight as intimate as a caress. She could have protested. Screamed, even. In a room full of people there was no way he could do anything to her without her consent.

Had she ever felt like this in her life? It was as though he'd mesmerized her. Her heart was beating in slow heavy strokes, and the warmth from his arm had spread throughout her limbs. From a long way away, Lia watched him toss his hat on a table. He took her free hand in his and raised it to his lips, caressing her knuckles. Then he turned her hand over and kissed her palm with lingering sensuality.

His hair was thick and silky clean. All she wanted to do

was drop her champagne glass on the floor and drag her fingers through those untidy, gold-tipped waves, exploring the tautness of his scalp, cupping her hand to his nape. With a physical effort that felt enormous, Lia gripped the stem of her glass, holding onto it as if it were all that was keeping her sane.

His mouth was still drifting over her palm. Her eyes closed as sensation swept through her in waves of pleasure. Deep inside her, desire sprang to life in a tumultuous, imperative ache; for a few moments that were outside of time Lia gave herself over to it, her body as boneless as a butterfly's. She was spreading her wings to the sun, she thought dizzily. Drawing in its heat, laved by its golden rays. Fully alive, as surely she was meant to be.

Come off it, Lia. Say it like it is. You're allowing yourself to be seduced by a man who lives in the same city as you.

She snatched her hand back, champagne sloshing over her dainty shoes, and said raggedly, "You've got to stop!"

He lifted his head, although he was still clasping her fingers. "You don't want me to stop—tell the truth."

"I don't know the first thing about you, yet you're—"

"We've skipped the preliminaries, that's all," he said hoarsely. "Gone for the essentials."

With a jolt of her heart she heard that roughness in his voice, and saw how the pulse at the base of his throat was pounding against his skin. "You feel it, too," she whispered.

"I felt it the first moment I saw you across the room."

Hadn't she known that? Wasn't that why she'd run for the dance floor with the nearest available man, and stayed there as long as she could? She said faintly, "A highwayman's a thief, Mr. Talbot."

"A butterfly's sole purpose is to mate."

Her breath hissed between her teeth. "A thief takes what he wants regardless of the consequences."

"If you're willing to be taken, I can scarcely be called a thief."

"Oh, stop it," Lia said peevishly, "you're turning me around in circles."

"Good," he said, and suddenly smiled at her.

It was a smile that crackled with pure male energy. Steeling herself against it, Lia clipped off her words with cold precision. "I'm not looking for a mate. A costume's just that——a costume. Not a statement about my character."

He looked her up and down, taking his time, his gaze scorching her flesh almost as though she was naked. "Yet you look highly provocative."

Two could play that game, Lia thought in a flare of temper. She glanced downward. His soft leather boots clung to his calves and were cuffed at the knees; his thighs were black-clad, strongly muscled against the taut fabric. Her eyes traveled upward, past his elegant white shirt with its laced neckline over a slash of tanned skin, to the wide shoulders under his cloak. A wave of primitive hunger attacked her, shocking her with its intensity. Had she ever felt this way in her life?

No, she hadn't. Ever. She said with admirable coolness, "Let's face it, you didn't choose to dress up as a clown with ears like jugs and white paint all over your face—like the one I danced with a few minutes ago. Your costume's sexy, too. So what?"

"You're finally admitting you find me sexy——we're making progress."

"Don't be coy," she said, exasperated. "I've got eyes in my head and any woman worthy of the name would find you sexy."

His voice roughened. "This is all very amusing and it's nowhere near the truth. There's something going on between us that's never happened to me before——not like this. Not once in my life have I seen a woman across a crowded room and known in my blood and my bones that I had to have her. You've got to trust me on that—I swear it's true."

The crazy thing was that she believed him instantly. "This kind of thing's never happened to me, either," she said shakily.

With a gentleness that disarmed her, he stroked her cheek with one finger. "Thanks——for being so honest."

Longing simply to rest her forehead against his shoulder and be held by him, Lia said as steadily as she could, "Then let me continue to be honest. I don't make a habit of getting into bed with strangers."

"Neither do I. So why don't we begin with you telling me your name?"

She'd come here to be anonymous; and from some deep instinct, she intended to remain so. Tossing her head, she said, "I can give you a false name. Or no name at all. Your choice."

He took her glass from her hand and thunked it on the table beside his hat. "Why are you being so mysterious?"

"It suits my purposes."

His eyes narrowed. "Are you someone I should know?"

He didn't look the type of man to sit in a concert hall listening to Beethoven; he'd be more at home in a smoky jazz bar. "I doubt it," she said.

"If we go to bed tonight——and that's what we're talking about——I have to know who you are."

He was right, she thought in horror, she *was* considering going to bed with him. Was she clean out of her mind? "If you insist on knowing my name," she said, "then it's no dice."

"Are you in trouble with the law?"

"No!"

"If you're neither famous nor on the lam, you could have given me a false name and I'd never know the difference."

"I dislike lying."

"You like winning."

She laughed, a warm throaty chuckle. "Well, of course. Is there anything wrong with that?"

"I like winning, too."

"Then——as far as my name's concerned——it'll be good for you to have a new experience. We should all expand our horizons occasionally, Mr. Talbot."

"The name's Seth," he said tersely. "And even though you may disbelieve this, I've had more than enough experience of losing in my life."

Her smile faded; once again she believed him instantly and wholeheartedly. "For that, I'm sorry," she said.

"You are, aren't you?" he said in an odd voice. "You're beginning to intrigue me——is this about more than lust?"

Again panic flared in her chest. She said obliquely, "If a highwayman even noticed anything as ephemeral as a butterfly, he'd crush it underfoot."

"How about my version? He sees it as something so beautiful that he simply wants to enjoy it."

"But then he has to let it fly away," Lia said, and heard in her own voice something of the steel she'd earlier heard in his.

For a moment he was silent, his eyes trained on her face. Then, with a suddenness that startled her, he ripped his mask off and flung it on the floor. His eyes were deep set, a startlingly deep green, flecked with amber. His cheekbones were imperative, and for the first time she saw the full strength of a face that was both too rugged to be truly handsome, and too strongly carved to be anything but formidable. She swallowed hard and said the first thing that came into her head. "I must be mad to be even contemplating going anywhere near a bed with you…and I'm stone cold sober, so I can't blame it on the champagne."

"It's nothing to do with champagne," he said softly. "Take off your mask."

"No," she said. "If we go to bed together, you have to promise not to touch my mask. You'll never know who I am——that's the way I want it and that's the way it's going to play. If you don't agree to my conditions, then I'm walking out of here right now, and if you try to stop me I'll scream the place down."

"So the battle lines are drawn…I could change your mind, you know."

"But you won't try. Not if you respect me as you should."

Incredibly he began to laugh, throwing his head back so the muscles in his throat stood out like cords. Then he looked straight at her. "I have the feeling my life's been entirely too dull and predictable for the last many years. Both in bed and out. I'll tell you one thing——you're not dull, and not the slightest bit predictable."

Wasn't that one of the things the critics always said of her? Lia d'Angeli never plays it safe. Never takes the well-worn path. Risks everything to find the heart and soul of the music.

Nine times out of ten, the risks paid off. But would that be true of tonight? With this man? Or would tonight be the tenth concert, the one the critics pounced on with glee?

She had no way of knowing.

CHAPTER TWO

THE band had struck up a tango, a dance that was a battle of the sexes. Meeting Seth's eyes full on, Lia said, "You don't look like someone who'd live a dull life."

With an underlying bitterness Seth said, "Appearances can be deceptive, pretty butterfly."

So he had indeed known unhappiness, this tall stranger in the black cloak. Somehow that strengthened a decision that was already made. Standing tall, Lia said, "Do you agree to my conditions, Seth Talbot? I don't tell you my name, and my mask stays in place."

He stepped closer, took her face between his palms and bent his head to kiss her. It was all there in that one kiss: the compulsion toward each other, the fierce hunger, the dissolving of all her boundaries. His mouth was sure, the slide of his tongue engulfing her in need; his teeth grazed her lips like the flick of fire. Without hesitation Lia met him thrust for thrust, depth to depth, flame wrapped around flame.

Very slowly, he drew back. The green of his eyes had darkened, like a forest falling under the shadows of sundown. His heightened breathing wafted her cheeks as he said unsteadily, "I'd agree to anything to get you in my bed. I don't like your conditions—I don't like them at all. But I agree to them, and I promise I won't go against them."

She let out her pent-up breath in a tiny sigh. With the faintest of smiles she said, "Well. We can stay here, dance, eat, drink and make small talk. Or we can do what we both want to do——go somewhere where we can be alone."

"I like your style," Seth said.

"Life's short," Lia replied, feeling her heart racket in her chest, "and I believe in living on the edge." She gave a sudden rich chuckle. "A cocoon would never be my choice."

He said abruptly, "I'm booked into a suite in this hotel. We'll go there."

Her lashes flickered. A suite here would cost more than she earned in a month. So he was rich, this man from Manhattan. She said lightly, "I've often wondered what it would be like to stay here. Now I'm going to find out."

"So you're not one of the rich socialites who hangs around Paris at this time of year, waiting until she can open her villa on the Riviera?"

The image amused her. "I work exceedingly hard for my money," she said incautiously, "and hanging around wouldn't suit me at all."

"Just how do you earn this money?" he flashed.

She lifted one finger, tracing the sensuous line of his lower lip, and with a tiny flare of power felt his jaw tighten. "I don't think we're really interested in a discussion of our respective occupations," she said. "I earn my living legally, I'm ferociously ambitious, and I guarantee in ten years' time you will have heard of me. And that's all you're getting out of me. Unless——" she smiled at him artlessly "——you've changed your mind about seducing me?"

"I very rarely meet my match," Seth said. "Most particularly in a woman. No, I haven't changed my mind." With ruthless speed he plunged to find her lips, searing them in a kiss as incendiary as it was brief. Raising his head, he said with a calmness belied by the sparks of fire in his eyes, "Shall we go?"

As he offered his arm, Lia rested her hand on it, the frail colors of one wing dulled by the dense black of his cloak. Another frisson of terror flicked along her nerves. Keeping her head up, she stayed close to him as he threaded his way through the masked revelers; and knew in her heart that this was the biggest risk she'd ever taken. The violin was her home territory, known, loved with a passion and, at times, hated with equal passion. But in affairs of the heart, she was a novice.

Unlike, she was sure, Seth Talbot.

They walked past the doorman, who was absorbed in sorting the piles of invitations. The elevator was made of such highly polished brass that she could see her outline in the walls, a shimmer of turquoise. The scarlet-uniformed attendant pushed the button without Seth saying a word: so he was well-known here, she thought, her nerves tightening another notch.

The elevator took them to the top floor. The brass doors smoothly closed behind them. Clasping her by the hand, Seth led the way along a high-ceilinged hallway to a pair of tall cream-colored doors scrolled in gilt, and swung them open, gesturing for her to enter. But her limbs refused to obey her. Frozen to the spot, she croaked, "I don't know the first thing about you."

"You know what's between us——what more do you want?"

Her nostrils flared. "You're six inches taller than I am, you probably weigh seventy pounds more, and if you're not a black-belt in karate, it wouldn't take much for you to become one."

He let out his breath in a small sigh. "I've never in my life crushed a butterfly, and I'm not about to start with you."

"I'm supposed to believe you? Just like that?"

"I don't know what the hell's going on between us," he rasped, "but it sure isn't casual, that much I do know. We're going to strip each other naked, little butterfly, in more ways than the obvious one. So this is about trust as much as it's about seduction—I thought you'd already figured that out."

"I hadn't," she said, her eyes smoldering behind her mask. "Trust's a very big word."

He added edgily, "I don't force myself on women, that's not to my taste. Plus there's at least one telephone in every room, and all you have to do is pick up the nearest one for an immediate connection to the front desk. You're safer here than you'd be anywhere else in Paris, believe me."

She was damned if she was going to apologize for her attack of nerves. Walk onto the stage, Lia, she thought wildly, and stalked past him into his suite.

It took her breath away. Her eyes ranged from one end of the room to the other, tarrying on the delicate gold chandeliers, the luxurious embroidered brocades and tasseled velvets. The spacious parquet floor was spread with antique handwoven carpets. "There's even a balcony," she breathed.

"With a wonderful view of the Eiffel Tower," Seth said solemnly. "Would you like to see it?"

All her doubts dropped away. She turned to face him. "Later. Maybe." Then she stood on tiptoes and kissed him with an ardor all the more touching for its lack of expertise.

His eyes narrowed. Taking her face in his hands, he said with careful restraint, "Tell me one thing—you're not a virgin, are you?"

Her head reared back; it never occurred to her to lie. "No, of course not. But I've only been with one man, and that was three years ago. It wasn't about lust on my part, it was about curiosity—and perhaps that's why it didn't move me, body or soul. Serves me right, I suppose."

"I see," said Seth. "Then we'll have to make up for lost time, won't we?" He bent his head, finding her mouth and teasing it open, his tongue dancing along her lips.

She gave a tiny purr of pleasure, molding her body to his, giving herself over to the unknown and the new with the daring that was so characteristic of her. As she thrust her hands beneath his cloak, wrapping them around the taut curves of his rib cage, he dragged her closer; her breasts were crushed to his chest, his arousal so fierce and imperative that she felt a thrill of sheer, feminine power.

His kiss deepened, demanding all she could give. With another thrill of power, Lia knew she wanted to give him everything that was in her, all the passionate hunger for life that had driven her for as long as she could remember. His tongue was hot and slick, his body hard and utterly masculine; reveling in a host of sensations, she dug her fingers in his scalp, pulling his head lower, her knees buckling as wave after wave of desire surged through her belly and throbbed between her thighs.

He muttered between kisses that imprinted her cheeks, her chin, her throat, "We should go slow…it's been a long time for you and I want to give you—"

Her answer was to pull at his shirt, loosening it from his trousers. "Don't fight what's between us," she begged. "I want you now, Seth. Now."

Swiftly he threw his cloak to the floor and hauled his shirt over his head. Lia's breath caught in her throat. "You're so beautiful," she choked, and briefly laid her cheek against his chest. His heart was pounding. His skin smelled cleanly of soap and of the essence of this man who was both a stranger and yet utterly known to her.

He said with that thread of laughter already so familiar to her, "How do I get you out of your costume? You could be sewn into it for all I know."

She turned deliberately in his arms. "There's a zipper down the back," she said, and bowed her head.

His mouth traced the softness of her nape, savoring every inch, sending shudders of longing through her frame. Then he caught the zipper and with a single tug bared the long line of her spine. She turned again, her eyes glittering, eased her arms from the tight sleeves and let her costume fall to her waist.

"God, you're lovely," he breathed, his heated gaze causing her nipples to harden involuntarily. He cupped her breasts, stroking the ivory curves of flesh, then dropped his head to suckle her.

She cried out in instinctive response, her body arching toward him, her eyes closed in ecstasy; and all the while his hands, those wonderfully sensitive hands, were tracing the taut curve of her belly and the delicate arc of her ribs. Her breathing quickened, the heat between her thighs mounting to an unbearable pitch. As though he knew, he touched her there, just once, and she rocketed into a climax that made her cry out his name in shocked abandon.

Boneless, she collapsed against him. "I never—that didn't…"

"There's more," he said fiercely and swept her into his arms, carrying her the length of the room into a vast bedroom. He laid her on her back on the king-size bed, covering her with his body, kissing her breasts, her shoulders, her mouth, giving her no mercy where none was needed. Then he reached down and ripped her suit from her hips.

After kicking off her shoes, Lia tugged the turquoise fabric from her legs and feet, only wanting to be naked for him; within her, something never touched before rose and broke at the wonder in his face as he took in the length of her slender body. She said unsteadily, "It's only me."

"You're so beautiful. So generous and brave."

The look on his face made her want to cry. This was about lust, she thought frantically. Only lust. "Seth," she said forcefully, "you've got too many clothes on."

His green eyes blazed at her. "Take your mask off," he said. "Please."

She bit her lip, feeling herself weaken at this passionate pleading from a man, she'd be willing to bet, who rarely begged for anything. "I've shown you too much already," she cried. "We have one night, Seth, just one night. But one night can be a lifetime, you understand that as well as I do."

She couldn't tell him who she was. Because Seth Talbot, she knew this in her bones, had the power to change her life.

From the time she was five, when her first violin had been put in her arms, she'd worked single-mindedly toward one goal: to be one of the best in the world. She wasn't there yet. With the humility of the true artist, she knew she had a long way to go. She'd also discovered in the last hour or so that a man called Seth Talbot could totally derail her. Distract her from her ambitions, from all she'd studied and practiced and longed for.

She couldn't afford to have that happen. No one was going to do that to her.

"I'll give you anything you ask but my identity," she said in a low voice.

He stood up in a surge of raw energy, pulling off his leather boots and dark trousers. "Anything?" he snarled. "Are you sure of that?"

"Yes," she said, refusing to back down. "I'm sure."

His body entranced her with its hard planes and flow of muscle. She rose to her knees, the light from the open windows catching on the sequins of her mask. Leaning forward, she very delicately tongued his nipple, hearing his harsh gasp of pleasure over the thrumming of blood in her ears. Then she clasped him by the hips, burying his arousal in the soft valley between her breasts. He threw back his head, thrusting into her, then suddenly pushing her back to fall on top of her on the bed.

"I can't think of anything but wanting you," he gasped, laving her breasts and belly with hands and tongue, then moving lower to push her thighs open. She was all too ready for him, wet, hot and slick.

"I can't believe I—" she began, then forgot everything as

again he overpowered her, sending her, sobbing his name, to topple over the edge. But even then he didn't let up. From a long way away, she felt him ease between her legs, felt that first hard push and enveloped him as if he'd been made for her, and her alone.

His silken thrusts, her own heated welcome…she writhed beneath him, out of control, beyond herself, in a joining that she couldn't have resisted to save her soul. Possessiveness, primitive and furious, drove her upward until his elemental rhythms were her own.

She heard him cry out sharply, saw his face convulse, and felt deep within her the strength and surrender of his release. Her own followed inexorably, throwing her against him as waves dash themselves against the cliffs.

Utterly spent, Lia drew him down to lie over her. His forehead dug her mask into her cheek even as his breath cooled her throat. When she could find her voice, she whispered, "I've never in my life felt anything like that."

"Neither have I."

Part of her wanted to toss off a joke, to make light of a mating that had thrown all her preconceptions of herself into disarray. But she knew she'd regret it if she did; for this mating was not to be defused so easily. "So for you it was different, too?"

"Couldn't you tell?"

"I'm not exactly experienced."

"My second name is control," he said tightly, raising his head to look straight through the slits in her mask into her eyes. "But I lost it. Totally. With you."

What was she supposed to say to that? For she believed him without a sliver of doubt. Trust, indeed, Lia thought with a quiver of panic. How could she trust a man she'd only met an hour ago? Trust was the word on which friendships were based. Not one-night stands. "So did I," she mumbled. "Lose it, I mean."

"I noticed," he said dryly.

She gave him the faintest of smiles. "Perhaps we could go a little slower next time?"

"Your guess is as good as mine," he said harshly. "If there's one thing I've learned in the last hour, it's not to anticipate as far as you're concerned. A useless exercise."

Suddenly intensely curious, Lia said, "You must have had a lot of women…I don't see how I'm so different."

"I've never gone from woman to woman, that's not the way I operate. Nor do I ever allow a woman to get too close. You're different because I had no choice."

His expression was inimical. With a shiver along her spine, she said, "That's what's so frightening—neither did I."

"Right now, I want you again," he said with passionate intensity. "I want to take my time, explore every inch of your body and learn what pleases you—I want to put my seal on you so you'll never forget me."

"Seth," she said quietly, "I'll never forget you."

Lines of frustration scoring his cheeks, he said, "But you won't tell me who you are."

"You know more about me than anyone else in the world!" she said with explosive truth. "You've got to be content with that."

"We'll see," he said, and ran his hand down her hip. "Your skin's so silky, so smooth…like the inside of a shell." He took the tip of her breast between his fingers, gently tugging on it. "You like that, don't you?"

"Yes," she breathed, seeking his mouth with hers, "I like that."

He carried her with him, caress by caress, and each one, she would have sworn, was imbued with tenderness and the simple wish to give her pleasure. With an answering tenderness she traced collarbone, rib and hipbone, kissed muscle and flank, then finally encircled his arousal, watching his eyes darken and hearing his breath quicken. "Not so fast," he gasped, lifting her to straddle him, his hands spanning her waist as the light of a Parisian moon fell white on her skin.

She slipped over him like a glove, her eyes closed as he entered her more and more fully, until she was filled with him. Then he drew her body down in a lissome curve until her breast was in his mouth. Sheer delight transfixing her, Lia buried her fingers in the tangle of blond hair on his chest and threw back her head. This time her climax came as slowly as the heat of a summer day rises with the dawn; her heart began to race against his palm. Not until then did Seth start moving deep within her, long, slow strokes that drove her closer and closer to the edge.

With exquisite timing he waited for his own release until the sharp cries of completion were breaking from her lips. As she rode him, her own excitement like a goad, he rose to meet her and fell with her into that abyss that was both a presage of death and the joy of rebirth.

This time it was Lia who fell on top of Seth, her mask digging into his chest. Part of her wanted to rip it off just because it was uncomfortable; part of her longed to rid herself of it so that he could see her eyes, stunned and slumberous with fulfillment.

But she mustn't. She couldn't. She had a life outside this room. She'd lose any ability to focus on that life if she allowed Seth Talbot to become part of it; she wouldn't even be able to pick up her violin, let alone tune it.

She couldn't toss away something that had been her sole purpose for seventeen years just because of one man. Just because his green eyes with their darts of gold fire had cast a spell over her.

"Are you all right?" Seth said gently, his arm tightening around her in a way she could only interpret as possessive.

She strove to find her voice. To move back from a place

where she'd turned into a stranger, a woman whose existence she'd never suspected. "Yes. No. You sure ask complicated questions."

He chuckled, a deep reverberation in his chest. "You flatter me."

"Believe me, this has nothing to do with flattery."

"So you like making love with me."

"There's no need to fish for compliments, Seth Talbot. *Like* nowhere near approximates how you make me feel. But do you know what?"

"I couldn't possibly guess."

"I didn't have any supper, because I was going to eat at the ball. I'm hungry."

"For food? When you've got me?"

"Yep," she chuckled. "Sorry about that."

He sat up, pulling her with him. "There's a wonderful invention called room service. What would you like?"

His smile had warmed those remarkable green eyes. Was she mad to think tenderness was the emotion behind that warmth? A tenderness that curled gentle fingers around her heart. She said hastily, "Seafood crêpes and surprise me with dessert."

"Done," he said. He reached for the phone, spoke rapidly into it in impeccable French, and replaced the receiver. Standing up, he stretched with lazy sensuality. "I feel great."

"You look better than great," she said primly, "and shouldn't you put something on before you answer the door?"

"Wouldn't want to shock the management." He disappeared in the direction of the bathroom. Moments later he came back with two white robes, monogrammed in gold on the pockets with the insignia of the hotel. "One for you," he said, tossing it in her lap. His voice deepened. "I don't want anyone but me seeing your beauty."

I want to put my seal on you...wasn't that what he'd said?

She couldn't handle such possessiveness; yet didn't the mere thought of him with another woman spur her with a hot jab of jealousy?

Explain that, Lia, she thought; and knew she couldn't.

CHAPTER THREE

LIA lifted the soft white folds of the robe to her face so that her breasts—which she'd always thought were rather too full—were hidden from Seth. "Beauty?" she repeated. "My body's okay. But it's not—"

"You're exquisite," he said shortly.

"Oh," said Lia, knowing she was blushing under her mask and makeup. "Not much point in arguing with that tone of voice."

"None whatsoever. I get the feeling you haven't had many compliments in your life."

Her parents, wrapped up in their own careers, had each had extraordinarily high standards. They'd dispensed advice when they'd thought of it, but little in the way of praise. Lionel, with whom she'd had that short-lived affair, had been too self-absorbed to bother with compliments. As for her music, it was only lately that the critics had started noticing her. A few had doled out cautious doses of praise; and how she'd hungered for that, she thought with uncomfortable truth.

"You've gone a long way away," Seth said.

With a tiny jolt Lia came back to the present. To a man who demanded the truth from her, just as the violin did. She said irritably, tracing the gold monogram with one finger, "You shake me up…and I don't just mean sexually."

Because her head was downbent, she didn't see how his eyes sharpened, nor how intently they were studying her. "Good," he said. "Ah, there's the door. I'll be right back."

She heard the murmur of voices from the other room, then Seth wheeled a mahogany trolley covered with starched white linen into the bedroom. He whipped off the coverings with a flourish, and within moments she was sitting beside him in bed, balancing a Limoges plate on a tray. The crêpes looked and smelled delicious. *"Bon appétit,"* she said, and tucked in with gusto.

Seth poured her a glass of chilled Chardonnay from one of the most famous of French châteaux; again she was unaware of how watchful his eyes were as she ate and drank, enjoying each mouthful. After she'd wiped the last drop of the luscious, velvety sauce from her plate with a piece of crunchy baguette, he removed the silver cover from a platter of French pastries.

Lia's eyes widened. "They're works of art. Oh look, perfect little swans filled with whipped cream…I'll have one of those."

She let her teeth sink into the delicately crunchy puff pastry; the cream was flavored with Grand Marnier. "I've died and gone to heaven," she pronounced.

"So I have a rival already."

She laughed, dabbed some cream on his chin and leaned over to lick it off with deliberate seductiveness. "Can't I have the swans as well as you?"

He passed her a glazed strawberry embedded in *crème anglaise* and the lightest of pastry. "You have an appetite for life, little butterfly."

Lia licked more cream from her fingers. "Life is meant to be lived," she said grandly.

"You're what—twenty? Twenty-one? And only one bed partner until tonight? That's not what I'd call living life to the full."

"I'm twenty-two years old and I'm interested in things other than sex," she retorted. "Don't let's argue, Seth, I'm having too much fun."

"What things? What do you do with yourself when you're not going to masked balls?"

Subconsciously, hadn't she been expecting his curiosity to surface? Her chin defiantly tilted, she said, "I'm not asking you what you do for your living, and I don't want you asking me—you promised you wouldn't pry."

"I own and run Talbot Holdings. Ever heard of them?"

Her hands had stilled. "Tal-Air?" she said. He nodded. "I often fly with your company. The planes are on time, the seats are comfortable and the staff friendly."

"We try," Seth said, adding easily, "so you fly a lot?"

She'd been stupid to have volunteered that scrap of personal information. "Not a lot," Lia said coolly. "Do you own Tal-Oil as well?"

He nodded. "Along with a line of tankers and cruise ships."

"This suite makes more sense," she said, and took the last mouthful of her pastry. "As do the swans. You're a very rich man." On purpose she made this sound, subtly, like an insult.

Seth bit into a chocolate éclair. "Belgian chocolate," he said amiably. "Want some?"

His change of subject threw her. As he'd probably intended. "Is Paris for lovers?" she rejoined, and rested her hand on his as she bit into the smooth, rich chocolate.

"So are we making love or war?" he asked with deliberate provocation.

"You tell me."

He lifted the tray from her lap, swung his feet down and pulled her to her feet. "Come with me—I want to show you the balcony."

His hand was tugging her along, the hand that had explored her body with such devastating intimacy. In her bare feet Lia padded across what felt like an acre of carpet. Seth swung open the doors and she stepped outside into massed potted flowers, the cool of night and the magic of this most magical of cities. Behind them sighed the unending traffic from Rue de Rivoli; past Jardin des Tuileries lay the river Seine; the lights of the Latin quarter and Les Invalides spangled the sky. Lia gave a sigh of pure happiness. "Glorious," she whispered.

"Glorious," he agreed, turned her hard in his arms and jammed her against the wall. Her robe slipped from her shoulder as his own fell open. Then they were kissing each other as though they'd never mated so passionately in the bed indoors. Skin to skin, heat to heat, desire igniting desire, until Seth lifted her bodily as though she weighed no more than a butterfly. Lia wrapped her thighs tight around him, panting with need, pushing her hips into his first hard thrust. As her climax ripped through her, Seth groaned deep in his chest, throbbing deep within her, emptying himself.

Slowly Lia returned to reality. The stone wall was digging into her back. Her feet were cold. "Even in Paris, we could be arrested for that," she croaked.

"Then we'd better go inside," he said, and carried her through the doors into the green and silver luxury of the bedroom.

"I need to lie down," she mumbled, her face buried in his chest. Would she ever forget the scent of his skin? Her own skin was suffused with it. He had indeed put his seal on her, she thought in a flash of terror.

When he reached the bed, he put her down with a gentleness that made her eyes sting with tears. If she'd been honest, she'd have told him it was love they'd been making all night, not war. But she didn't want to go near the word *love*. Not with Seth. "Hold onto me," she said raggedly, scarcely knowing what she was asking for.

Swiftly he lay down beside her, gathering her into his arms

and drawing her into the warmth of his long body. She melted into him, knowing with complete certainty that she wanted to make love to him again…in a minute, when she'd caught her breath.

With the suddenness of a very small child, Lia fell asleep.

She woke to night and the instant remembrance of where she was. Someone, Seth she could only presume, had drawn the heavy damask curtains over the windows; a soft glow from a nightlight in the bathroom was the room's only illumination.

Seth. Who'd ravished her, body and soul.

He was curled into her back, his breath wafting her bare shoulder. He was, she could tell, deeply asleep. She twisted in his arms, her eyes adjusting to the darkness. His face, in sleep, was both full of strength and yet undeniably vulnerable in a way that touched her to the heart. She looked away and knew with every fiber of her being that she had to get out of here. Away from him.

While there was still time.

Moving as carefully as she could, she eased his arm off her ribs and shifted toward the edge of the bed. Her bodysuit was draped over a Louis XVII chair, her shoes neatly aligned on the carpet nearby. She'd dropped all three of them on the floor all those hours ago. So Seth hadn't fallen asleep as quickly as she.

Had perhaps watched her as she slept.

Taking her clothes, Lia crept into the bathroom. Her makeup was smeared, her body a flow of pale curves in the long mirrors. She dragged on the bodysuit, struggling with the zipper, the wings drooping forlornly from the sleeves. The costume no longer looked outrageous: merely silly. Picking up her shoes, she tiptoed across the expanse of parquet toward the big double doors that led to safety.

Seth's cloak had been thrown carelessly over a delicate an

tique table by the door. She grabbed the cloak with deep relief and swathed herself in its dark folds. Then, her pulse racketing in her ears, Lia slid the door open, slipped through and closed it as quietly as she could.

Quickly she traveled the length of the hallway toward the red Exit sign. After jamming her feet into her pretty sandals, she ran down several flights of stairs, emerging in the front lobby. The concierge had his back to her. The doorman opened the glass door with impeccable courtesy, asking if she'd like a taxi.

"Non, merci," she said with a distracted smile, and walked down the street as though she made a habit of leaving luxurious hotels in the dark hours before dawn.

No coach, she thought wildly. No pumpkin, either.

Cinderella had only danced with the prince. Not made impassioned love to him...how many times had it been?

Early roses were blooming in the gardens, their fragrance languorously sweet. The half-moon had sunk in the sky. A taxi whipped past, and a scooter. Lia turned a corner, then doubled back on herself, knowing at some subliminal level that it was essential she cover her tracks.

The cloak had a hood. She drew it over her head and hurried along the deserted streets, taking the most circuitous of routes to Mathieu's flat in the 8th *arrondissement.* Mathieu had left for a concert tour. His key was in the tiny pocket in her bodysuit; its small metal outline felt immensely comforting against her thigh.

Thirty minutes later Lia was inside the flat, her heart racing from climbing the five flights of wooden stairs. Once inside, she looked around with the air of a woman who wasn't entirely sure where she was.

Or whether she wanted to be here.

Mathieu believed in minimalism. White walls, black leather chairs, three black and white photographs over his expensive stereo equipment: as different from Seth's luxuriously decorated suite as a space could be.

Seth. She mustn't think about Seth. She couldn't afford to. She had a rehearsal in Stockholm at four this afternoon, a concert tonight. Her flight left from Orly early this morning.

In the bathroom, it took Lia several minutes to take off her mask, which she'd anchored with glue just over each ear. But finally she was free of it. She then scrubbed the last of her makeup from her face and unpinned her hair so it tumbled to her shoulders. Taking off her bodysuit, she packed it, along with the mask and shoes, in the box the rental shop had given her. In a move that she was now hugely grateful for, she'd affixed the correct postage yesterday evening before she'd left for the ball. She could mail the box on her way to the airport.

Because she'd been so hungry for anonymity, she'd given a false name at the rental shop. They could keep the deposit, she thought. It was a cheap price to pay to preserve her privacy.

To keep her safe from Seth, when he came after her? He would, wouldn't he? He hadn't become the head of a vast international network of planes, ships and oil companies by sitting back and letting the world come to him.

She was thinking about him again. She'd sworn she wasn't going to do that. Knowing she should hurry, Lia walked, naked, back into the bathroom. The mirror was a sleek rectangle, edged with cold, unforgiving chrome. In it she saw a woman she no longer knew. Her features were the same, the lustrous black hair and dark brown eyes, legacy of her Italian father; her high cheekbones and winged brows, her long, slim body, all gifts of her Norwegian mother.

It was everything else that had changed.

As though she couldn't help herself, Lia lifted her palm to her nostrils, and caught, elusively, the scent of Seth's skin. As pain washed over her, she closed her eyes, conjuring him up remembering with frightening clarity all the gifts of his body, the turbulence in his green eyes as he came to climax.

He'd entered her. Physically, of course. But more than that, he'd invaded her soul.

Biting her lip, she turned on the shower and stepped inside, grabbing the soap and lathering herself. Surely if she washed Seth from her skin, she could as easily wash him from her memory.

He was a man. Just a man. She'd never see him again.

Hadn't she taken every precaution she could to ensure that was true?

Not yet fully awake, Seth reached across the bed for his butterfly lover. He'd fallen asleep with his arms wrapped around her, knowing that what he wanted most in the world was to wake up with her beside him. In the daylight, he'd find out who she was. She'd understand as clearly as he did that they couldn't simply go their separate ways...

Where was she?

His eyes flew open. Morning light gleamed through chinks in the curtains. Other than himself, the bed was empty.

Her bodysuit was gone from the chair.

Seth shoved himself up on one elbow, ears straining for the slightest sound; and heard only the distant roar of traffic far below. He surged out of bed. Her shoes were gone, too.

Naked as the day he was born, his heart like a cold lump in his chest, he strode into the bathroom. Blankly, his own face stared back at him from the mirror. He turned away from it. The vast living room was deserted. His cloak was gone from the table by the door.

Far beyond pride, he searched every surface in the suite for a note, and found nothing.

She'd gone. Without a trace.

Like a man stunned, Seth walked back into the bedroom

and sank down on the bed. The trolley was still there, the left-over pastries looking nowhere near as appetizing as they had the night before. He remembered with aching clarity how she'd sunk her teeth into them, then licked cream from his chin, her lips a voluptuous curve… With an inarticulate groan, Seth lowered his head into his hands. How could he have been so stupid as to fall asleep? To let her escape?

He didn't know the first thing about her. Not her name, or her occupation, not even what she looked like under that glamorous, all-concealing mask.

The mask she'd refused to remove.

He could scarcely fault her. She'd done exactly what she'd said she'd do—make love to him for one night and then vanish.

As though he'd meant nothing to her.

He dug his fingers into his forehead, forcing himself to recognize the single, dangerous mistake he'd made, out of pride and overweening arrogance. All evening and far into the night, he'd been convinced that he could change her mind. That sooner or later, she'd rip off her mask and tell him her name.

She hadn't done either one. Instead she'd waited until he was asleep, then fled.

How dare she have left him as though what had happened between them was of no more consequence than a game of cards or a few drinks at a bar?

He got up, marched over to the windows and ripped back the curtains. Sunlight streamed through the panes, making him wince. Far on the horizon, the Eiffel Tower gleamed like a needle in the light.

It should have been raining. A sky dark with thunderclouds, wind scudding through the wet streets.

Sure, he thought, and with the smallest glimmer of humor knew he was being ridiculous. So she'd gone. So what? She was a woman. Just a woman. The world was full of them, and he'd never had the slightest trouble finding one to warm his bed.

But not one of them had ever touched him in the places he'd been touched last night. In his heart. His soul.

He'd never allowed them to. Never wanted them to. But from the moment he'd seen the woman in the turquoise body-suit, he'd had no choice. In a way he didn't understand—and bitterly resented—she'd pierced every one of his defenses.

And now she'd run away. Leaving him more alone than he'd ever been in his life.

CHAPTER FOUR

SETH hit his palm hard against the window frame, the sudden pain bringing him to his senses. He was going to shower and get dressed. Then he'd get on the phone and have her traced, his mysterious lover in the feathered mask.

She'd have left a trail. Everyone did.

He'd find her. Sooner or later, and he had the money to pay for sooner. Then he'd tell her exactly what he thought of her for sneaking off under cover of darkness, like a common thief.

His eyes suddenly widened, his hand gripping the window frame with vicious strength. Godalmighty, he thought. Protection. I didn't use any. I never even thought of it.

He'd broken one of his cardinal rules.

How many times had they made love? Three? And not once had it occurred to him to get out the foil packets he kept in his suitcase.

She hadn't mentioned protection, either. In a surge of relief he realized she must have been on the Pill. Most modern women were. Took it for granted.

But she hadn't had a lover in three years. Why would she be on the Pill?

She was an intelligent woman, far too intelligent to get into a stranger's bed without taking precautions against pregnancy.

He considered himself of more than average intelligence.

But last night he'd been thinking with his hormones, not his brains. Why should she be any different?

Again he pounded his fist against the window, trying to stop the desperate seesawing of his thoughts. He'd just have to pray that she wasn't pregnant. From the time he'd been old enough to think about it, he'd never had any intention of causing a child of his to enter the world. His parents had rid him of that particular desire many years before.

Along with so much else.

He wasn't going to think about his parents. Not at—he glanced at the bedside clock—seven in the morning, when he'd had no more than four hours sleep. Decisively Seth marched into the bathroom, showered the last traces of the night from his body, and dressed in a pinstriped suit with a custom-made blue shirt and a silk tie. His Italian leather shoes, thanks to the hotel staff, gleamed like polished glass.

He was no longer in the garb of a highwayman. Although he still felt like one. Picking up the phone, Seth got to work.

Twenty minutes later, he'd covered all the angles. He'd talked to the concierge, the doorman and the manager, none of whom had been of the slightest use. He'd then contacted a professional investigator, ordering him to alert taxis, buses and the Métro; to phone every last place in the city that rented costumes; and to advertise very discreetly for anyone who'd seen a woman on the streets of Paris after 3:00 a.m. wearing a long black cloak over a turquoise butterfly costume.

Seth could have contacted all these sources himself. But he was too well known, and the last thing he wanted was the press getting hold of this. It was too private. Too personal. Too close to the bone.

He might be desperate to find her. But he couldn't splash her image over every newspaper in Europe.

Putting down the phone, he scowled at the ormolu clock

sitting sedately on the carved marble mantel. Now all he could do was wait. Wait and hope.

He left the suite and ran downstairs to the waiting limo. He was going to focus on the job at hand, he told himself forcefully as he hurried outside into the spring sunshine. Business as usual.

Some high-powered negotiations, followed by a meeting with his Paris staff, took up the whole day. Seth finally left the office at seven-thirty and walked to his favorite café on the Champs-Elysées, loosening his tie as he went. Snagging a table on the sidewalk, he ordered coquelet and crème brûlée, two of the house specialties. Then he took out his cell phone and punched in the investigator's number.

Five minutes later, his face set, he put down the phone and took a big gulp of an excellent merlot. The investigator had located the shop that had rented the turquoise costume; but the woman who'd chosen it had been wearing dark glasses and an all-concealing floppy hat, and had given a false name and address.

This dead end had been accompanied by many others. No one, it seemed, had seen anyone in a long black cloak on foot, in a taxi, on a bus, on the Métro, at an airport or in a hotel. In terms of concrete information Seth had gained exactly nothing. *Rien.* Zero. Zilch.

His butterfly had disappeared from the face of the earth.

No, he thought slowly. He'd learned a little more than nothing. She'd disguised herself and given a false name when she'd rented the costume, which was well before she'd met Seth. Why had she done that?

She must in some way be famous. Her name so well known, at least locally, that she didn't want her actions traced.

That really narrowed the field, Seth thought sarcastically. Now all he had to look for was a famous young woman who loved to eat French pastries at midnight and whose naked body he could have described in embarrassing detail.

Nothing to it.

One thing was sure. She wasn't after his money.

Which differentiated her from most of the people he met.

A plate of thinly sliced rare meat decorated with julienned carrots and *haricots* was put in front of him, and his wineglass topped up. Blindly Seth stared at the food. His appetite had deserted him; a chunk of ice had congealed in his gut and his hands were as cold as if this were winter, not a warm spring evening.

What if he never saw her again?

Three weeks later, striding along Broad Street on his way to his broker, Seth suddenly stopped dead in his tracks. Two men cannoned into him; he muttered an apology and stepped to one side of the pavement.

That was her—wasn't it?

A leggy blonde in a chocolate-brown Chanel suit had stepped out from between two of the massive Corinthian columns of the New York Stock Exchange. Something in the confidence with which she was looking up and down the street was irresistibly familiar. Then, as if she sensed him staring at her, she turned around.

Too tall. Too thin. The angle of her jaw all wrong.

She gave Seth the once-over with a calculation she didn't bother to hide, and said with a smile that masterfully combined interest with hauteur, "Can I help you?"

"Thanks, no—I thought you were someone else," Seth said.

"Have we met before?"

Oh, yeah, he thought, underneath that patrician glaze you're definitely interested. "No. My apologies for bothering you," he said, smiled at her with no particular sincerity and walked away.

He'd made a fool of himself. Again. How many times in the last twenty-one days had he seen a woman whom he'd been convinced was his butterfly lover? Who'd left his heart pounding in his chest and his body irradiated with hope?

The only place it hadn't happened had been on a recent trip to the slums of Rio de Janeiro. He'd gone there as the new president, treasurer and, so far, sole member of the philanthropic foundation he was setting up, as a way of figuring out how best he could give away some of his money. He'd been too devastated by what he'd seen in Rio to be on the lookout for a woman of any age or shape.

Back home, the story was different: he'd been unable to forget that single, tumultuous night in Paris.

In the course of those few impassioned hours, had he fallen in love? Surely not! If, as a much younger man, he'd sworn off having children, he'd even more strongly vowed to avoid such romantic claptrap. Falling in love was for teenagers. Not for a man like himself with a family fortune and the driving ambition to quadruple that fortune.

To show his mother and father that he didn't need their money? Or their love?

Allan, his ineffectual, unhappy father, and Eleonore, his mother, with her cold will of steel: Seth felt equally distant from both of them.

Eleonore wanted Seth married to a woman of her choice, someone who would present no threat to her authority. His butterfly lover wouldn't do, for sure. Too beautiful, too sexy, too intelligent and much too strong-willed.

Not that Seth wanted to get married. He never had.

He wasn't in love. He was in lust. A very different thing. Instead of mooning after the unattainable, he should start dating again. Find himself a sophisticated blonde who'd demand nothing more of him than he was willing to give.

Like the woman by the stock exchange?

She was the last woman he wanted.

Fuming inwardly, Seth took the granite steps of his broker's building two at a time and for the next hour and a half focused his mind on the risks of commodities and the vagaries of currency exchanges. Then he went home to his brownstone near Central Park, and stripped off his work clothes. He hauled on shorts and a tank top, lacing his sneakers with vicious strength.

Enough, he thought, as he stepped on his treadmill and adjusted the slope. He wasn't going to let a snip of a woman ruin his life. So she'd vanished. Good riddance to her. If she'd gotten under his skin this much in one night, imagine what she'd have done if he'd continued seeing her. He was well rid of her.

He was going to get his life back on track and forget about her. If by any chance he ever saw her again, he'd run like hell in the opposite direction.

Not that he would see her. She'd made sure of that.

Holding fast to his anger, because he liked it a whole lot better than the agonies of regret he'd been suffering ever since that night in a Paris hotel, Seth turned up the speed on the treadmill and started to jog. He was indeed back on track, he thought with a grim smile.

With the past where it belonged. In the past.

And the woman of mystery where she belonged. Out of his life.

Locking her fingers in her lap to control their trembling, Lia stared at the thin blue line. It was the second time in as many days that she'd used the pregnancy test, and it was the second time it had turned out positive.

The first time, she'd convinced herself it was a false positive. She couldn't be pregnant. She just couldn't be.

But this evening she could no longer muster such certitude. The evidence was staring her in the face.

She was carrying Seth's baby.

Suddenly and unexpectedly, joy flooded her. She would

bear the child of a man who'd brought her felicity beyond her imagining, and who'd aroused in her a passion she hadn't known she possessed. Hugging her belly in instinctive protection, she grinned at the opposite wall, her dark eyes luminous with happiness.

She was going to be a mother.

Then, with a jolt, the hard voice of reason asserted itself. Lia's smile vanished. She was seven weeks pregnant by a man she'd vowed never to see again.

Unable to sit still any longer, Lia walked over to one of the two small windows in her bachelor flat. This one looked out on the iron balconies of the neighboring apartment block; the afternoon sun shone hot on the bricks. She was pregnant with Seth Talbot's child. Seth, who ran a host of international companies from his headquarters a mere thirty blocks from here, and who was listed in Fortune magazine as one of the richest men in America.

Well done, Lia.

In two days she was flying to New Zealand to take part in a festival of young musicians. In a wave of panic Lia felt the tidy rows of bricks blur in front of her eyes. How could she fit a baby into her life? She couldn't. It was impossible. She had concerts booked as far ahead as three years from now; and her career was taking off in a way that both exhilarated and challenged her. She couldn't abandon it for motherhood.

Abortion?

Everything in her cried out in repudiation. Seth's child? She'd never be able to live with herself. Besides, she was responsible for this baby's existence: Seth hadn't forced himself on her. She'd gone willingly to his bed and now was paying the consequences.

Seth was also responsible.

So what was she supposed to do? Phone him up at work

and say, "Remember me? The woman you had torrid sex with in Paris? Guess what, I'm pregnant."

She couldn't imagine doing that. Wouldn't he assume she was trying to trick him into marriage? He was a very rich man, and it was one of the oldest gambits in the book.

Oh God, she thought in despair, what was she going to do?

Go to the doctor. Find out for sure she was pregnant. Then she'd have the long flight to Auckland to sit quietly and consider her options.

She'd been right to worry, when she'd first met Seth, that he could derail her life.

He had. By making her pregnant.

Two weeks later, Lia sealed two identical letters, one addressed to Seth at his Manhattan headquarters, the other to an address in the Hamptons that she'd found on the Internet. The Hamptons boasted beachside homes for the extremely rich; she could only assume it was his retreat from the city. She was almost sure he must have a Manhattan address; but he would, of course, guard it from general knowledge. She, of all people, understood the value of personal privacy.

The decision she'd come to over the last few days was that she owed Seth the truth about her pregnancy: for pregnant she was, the doctor having merely confirmed something she'd already known.

Yet she dreaded him getting the letters. She couldn't bear to tarnish that magical night in Paris with accusations that she'd neglected to warn him she was unprotected against pregnancy; or, worse, with suspicions that she'd planned the whole thing to entrap him into marriage.

Whatever his reaction would be, she was sure of two things: it would be forceful and it would be disruptive. The owner of a company as far-reaching as Talbot Holdings hadn't gotten there by being nice. Lia got up from her desk, carrying the letters, took the stairwell to street level and pushed open the door. The July heat hit her like a blow, and for a moment she wavered, attacked by the dizziness that so far was her only symptom; she had, to her enormous relief, avoided morning sickness.

With a sense of putting herself in the hands of fate, Lia pushed away from the wall, walked two blocks and thrust the letters through the slot in the mailbox. There. She'd done it. The rest was up to Seth.

CHAPTER FIVE

LIA lay back on the chaise longue. Over her head, palm trees rattled their fronds in the warm Caribbean tradewinds, while a torrent of bougainvillea spangled her with shadows. On the blindingly white beach only a few feet from her private cottage, waves splashed gently up and down. Another kind of music, she thought idly. One she didn't have to work for.

Heaven. Utter heaven. How often did she lie back and do absolutely nothing?

Never was the short answer.

She'd get up soon and shower, put on her jazzy new sundress and wander to the least formal of the three restaurants that the resort boasted. Tomorrow afternoon, after a morning snorkeling on the reef, she had an appointment at the spa.

So what if the few days she was spending here were straining her budget to the breaking point? She'd gotten off-season rates, and only once a year did she treat herself to time spent entirely on her own.

She'd been here just over seven hours, and already she felt like a new woman. Just wait until tomorrow, she thought. A massage, a pineapple scrub and a dip in the thalassotherapy pool. Whatever that was.

She was quite willing to find out.

Lazily she got up from her chair and wandered toward her charming, air-conditioned cottage, which was nestled in a miniature botanical garden where brightly hued butterflies lit on the blooms, opening and closing their wings as they feasted on nectar. Lia stood on the stone walk, watching them for a moment. So careless, so hungry for the world's sweetness... once she'd been like that. But she'd changed in the last eight years.

How could she not have?

Ruefully she smiled at the iridescent turquoise patches on the wings of the nearest butterfly. After that night in Paris, it had been years before she could bring herself to wear turquoise again. But now she did. In fact, her new swimsuit was also iridescent turquoise, and fit her like a glove.

She looked very good in it, she thought smugly, and went indoors to change.

She was going to have a wonderful time here. All on her own.

Seth scowled at his reflection in the mirror of his cottage. He looked godawful. He certainly looked like he could do with a good dose of R&R. What better place to get it than at the White Cay Resort?

He picked up his razor, running it over his face. The wound that furrowed his ribs was healing, although too slowly for his liking. It itched like crazy under the tape. If he could rid himself of the nightmares that all too often plagued his sleep, he'd be more or less okay.

Dinner, he thought. He wasn't in the mood for formality. The Tradewind Room would do fine for tonight. Nor was he in the mood for conviviality, so hopefully he wouldn't know anyone here. If he kept to himself for a couple of days, he could go back to the rat race refreshed.

He ran a comb through his thick blond hair and left the cottage, glancing with pleasure at the long stretch of pale sand

and the impossibly blue sea. But as he entered the foyer of the restaurant, his heart sank.

"Seth," Conway Fleming said cheerfully. "Wouldn't have expected to find you here—not enough action."

"I came here to get away from it," Seth said, not very tactfully.

Conway laughed heartily. "Don't we all! Do you know Pete Sonyard? Sonyard Yachts...and his wife Jeannine."

Seth dredged up what he knew about the builder of the world's fastest yachts, and discovered Jeannine was an authority on the history of the Caribbean islands. As for Conway, Seth had known him, off and on, for years; he was well regarded on Wall Street, and known as a serious patron of the arts. As the conversation gathered momentum, Seth started mentally rehearsing how he was going to get a table to himself.

Then he saw the woman.

She'd just pushed open the door to the foyer. She had on a brief red dress, her hair a silky fall of raven-black. Her legs were bare and slender, her feet in ridiculously high-heeled red sandals. Her skin seemed to glow in the warm rays of the setting sun.

She was incredibly beautiful.

She glanced behind her, then held the door wider for a mother and two little children to enter. The boy had black hair like hers. He looked up, asking her something; she crouched to answer him, taking off her dark glasses, the dress drawn tight across her thighs. The boy tugged at her hair. She said something that made him laugh, and glanced up at his mother, the line of her throat making Seth's heart thud in his chest.

How long since he'd felt such instant and imperative lust?

Too long. Much too long.

She and the two children made a delightful tableau, he thought painfully, and across the room heard her laugh. Husky. Undeniably sexy. As she stood up, smoothing her dress, his blood pressure jolted up another notch. The dress was sexy, too, all the more so for being so sophisticated. It was sleeveless, the neckline and armholes square-cut; just above the hem, small squares had been cut out of the fabric, hinting at the skin beneath.

With one final remark to the little family, the black-haired woman turned and headed for the Tradewind Room. She hadn't even glanced his way. Infuriated that the intensity of his gaze hadn't caused her to as much as turn her head, Seth heard Conway say, "Gorgeous, isn't she?"

"You know her?"

"Who doesn't?"

"I don't," Seth said. Her face and body were unforgettable, let alone her air of confidence and poise, along with the genuine warmth she'd shown the little boy. She was stunning, he thought, and knew he wanted to meet her very badly.

Maybe, finally, he'd gotten over that debacle of eight years ago.

"I'm surprised you've never run into her, Seth," Conway remarked. "You have an interest in classical music, don't you?"

Seth did. A fledgling, but very genuine passion for something he'd connected with only a couple of years ago, through his old friend Julian in Berlin. He frowned. "What's that got to do with it?"

"That's Lia d'Angeli," Conway replied. "Darling of audiences and critics alike—not to mention the press and the makers of CDs. I'll introduce you." Raising his voice, he called, "Lia?"

She looked over, saw Conway and smiled spontaneously. Her eyes were dark, Seth saw, almost as dark as her hair. Both her lips and her nails were a fire-engine red. It was a very generous and voluptuous mouth, he thought, his own dry. She said warmly, "Conway! How lovely to see you."

Lia had known Conway for nearly six years; his foundation in support of the arts had permitted her, four years ago, to purchase a Stradivarius violin, which had enriched her playing immeasurably. For Conway, she'd even give up her precious solitude. For one evening, anyway.

He leaned over and kissed her European fashion on both cheeks. "Let me introduce you to some friends of mine."

She glanced over at them, prepared to like them as much for Conway's sake as for their own, and heard him say, "Pete and Jeannine Sonyard, from Maine. And Seth Talbot, who's based in New York. Lia d'Angeli, the violinist."

Seth Talbot was standing there. Right in front of her. The late sun was gilding his blond hair, while his green eyes were fastened on her. The shock hit Lia with the force of a tidal wave. As the color drained from her face, the polished mahogany floor swayed and dipped under her feet. Seth, she thought frantically. It can't be. Oh God, get me out of here.

With all her strength she fought for control, willing the floor to stay firmly under her feet where it belonged. But to see him again, after so many years...briefly she closed her eyes, praying that she'd wake up and find this was nothing but a bad dream.

"Are you all right, Lia?" Conway asked in quick concern, taking her elbow in his hand.

"Yes...sorry. Too much sun today, I guess." With a huge effort she produced a smile for the Sonyards. "I flew from Helsinki to Toronto yesterday. A lot of dirty wet snow in Helsinki, and a downpour in Toronto—I don't recommend visiting either place in April. Do you blame me for lying out in the sun the minute I got here? But I must have overdone it."

She was babbling, she thought. Normally she rarely talked about the weather, there were too many other more interesting things to discuss. Jeannine laughed, making a commonplace remark about Maine's climate. Lia's eyes skidded sideways, met Seth's and winced away again.

He said with a pleasure that sounded entirely genuine, "I'm delighted to meet you, Signora d'Angeli. I have all seven of your CDs, and I've played them many times."

Shock and dismay were usurped by a torrent of rage that almost incapacitated Lia. How dare he act as though they'd never met before? As though she'd never written him two letters eight long years ago telling him about his impending fatherhood? "I'm flattered," she said with icy precision, and watched his jaw tighten at her rudeness. Deliberately allowing her voice to warm, she asked, "Conway, how long are you staying?"

Conway was looking understandably puzzled; he knew her well enough to have witnessed her unfailing courtesy to those who were interested in her playing. "Until tomorrow afternoon," he said. "You'll join us for dinner this evening?"

"I'd like that very much," Seth interposed.

You would, would you, Lia thought vengefully. Too bad. Not for one hundred Strads would she sit at the same table as Seth Talbot, whether they made small talk about the weather or discussed her *legato*. Because, of course, he'd now repudiated her twice. Eight years ago and right now. Just as if the two of them had never spent the night in each other's arms, and just as though she hadn't gotten pregnant as a result. She stretched her mouth in a smile that felt utterly false. "I'm afraid I must decline. I'm dining in the Reef Room tonight, I only came in here to look around."

Seth was looking at her quizzically. "We've never met, have we, Signora d'Angeli? I can't imagine how I've offended you."

She should have known he wouldn't take her bad manners lying down. Not the internationally known Seth Talbot, who in the last eight years had made more money than an entire orchestra earned in its lifetime. It was on the tip of her tongue to say sweetly, *But Mr. Talbot, have you forgotten how we made love on the balcony of a hotel in Paris? Or the two letters I sent you afterward, mentioning the minor problem of my pregnancy?*

Although it would have given her great satisfaction to have said all this, Lia bit the words back. If Seth Talbot wanted, once again, to deny her existence, she should let him do so. That way she'd keep him out of her life. Preserve her privacy, as she'd done so strenuously for so long.

She said mendaciously, "I don't think we've ever met before, Mr. Talbot. But you remind me very strongly of someone I'd much prefer to forget...please forgive my lack of good manners." There. She'd given an excuse for her rudeness without publicly embarrassing him by telling the truth. Turning to Conway, she added, "I'd love to meet you tomorrow for breakfast, if you have the time."

Conway bowed gallantly. "I always have time for you, Lia. Eight-thirty here in the foyer?"

"Wonderful," she said and smiled at the Sonyards. "Please excuse me." Then she made the mistake of glancing at Seth. He was staring at her, his brows knit, a look of such genuine puzzlement on his face that she could have slapped him. The man should have been an actor, not the head of a giant corporation.

Calling on all her self-control, she said lightly, "I'm going to be late for my reservation, I must go. Enjoy your evening."

"Until we meet again," Seth said in a clipped voice.

That'll be never if I have my way, thought Lia, turning on her heel and leaving the foyer as though she had nothing more important than dinner on her mind.

She didn't have a reservation in the Reef Room; she only hoped they'd have room for her. Not that she was the slightest bit hungry.

Another wave of anger surged through her. Her heels tapping sharply on the stone path, she walked between banks of plumbago, frangipani and hibiscus. Until Seth Talbot had crossed her path, she'd been looking forward to her solitary meal in the Tradewind Room. How dare he act as though he'd never laid eyes on her before? How dare he? And then to have the gall to ask how he'd offended her. The bastard. The cold-hearted, irresponsible bastard.

Her steps faltered. It was her own child who was the bastard. Her beloved Marise.

Whose eyes were the green of a summer meadow. Just like Seth's.

Once Lia had realized, eight years ago, that Seth had no intention of answering her letters, she'd made it a policy never to speak about her personal life to the media; so Marise's existence, although generally known, only rarely emerged in print. She'd been fortunate in that she'd put on very little weight during her pregnancy, and had had a dressmaker who'd expertly masked the gentle bulge of Lia's belly with Empire waistlines and concealing panels of stiff fabric. She'd had to miss two concerts. That was all.

As her due date had approached, Lia had cashed in half the bonds her parents had left her and, using them as security, had bought a small, but very lovely old farm in the country eighty miles from Manhattan. The bank had come up with the mortgage and a local carpenter had done the renovations. Her daughter had been born in the little hospital five miles down the road.

She'd hired a nanny. She'd bought a car. She'd made a life for herself and her child. The farm had become home, giving mother and daughter a very necessary stability.

Despite his betrayal, she hadn't allowed Seth to derail her life. But neither had she been able to forget him. For one thing, every time she looked into her daughter's eyes, Lia saw him. For another, she'd never replaced him. Not once, in eight years, had she felt pulled toward a man the way she had been toward Seth. So her bed had remained empty, and her heart untouched.

Passion, once experienced in all its overwhelming power,

couldn't easily be duplicated. That had been one of the lessons Seth had taught her. That, along with the disillusion and wariness of the deeply wounded.

What was she going to do? She could leave the island tomorrow morning on the resort's helicopter, pleading a family emergency. Nancy, Lia's nanny, wouldn't be happy with her; it was vivacious, dependable Nancy who insisted Lia have a few days a year all to herself.

If she left, she wouldn't have to face Seth again. Breakfast with Conway, and then she'd be gone.

Seth was going to seek her out. He'd said as much, and he wasn't a man for idle words. How long would they be together before he spoke about the past? More important, how long could she keep her fury to herself?

Her fiery temper had gotten her into trouble more than once in the past. She couldn't risk it here, not with Seth. There was too much at stake. Because she wasn't going to let him near her daughter, not for anything. He'd done nothing to earn such a gift, and everything to desecrate it.

But if she ran for the farm with her tail between her legs, she'd be the loser. She needed this holiday desperately, for she was returning to a killer schedule of concerts and recording sessions. Why should she leave here just because Seth Talbot had turned up out of the blue?

He didn't want anything to do with her. If he had, he could have contacted her at any time in the last eight years.

Standing in the warmth of a Caribbean sunset, Lia snapped off a single bloom of hibiscus and defiantly tucked it behind her ear. She was going to march into the Reef Room as though she owned the place, and eat her way down the menu. Then she'd go to her cottage and read one of the books that had been sitting on her bedside table for the last six months.

Seth Talbot wasn't going to ruin her holiday.

But neither was he ever going to meet Marise.

CHAPTER SIX

A BIRD was screeching in the bushes next to the cottage. Seth turned over in bed and stared blearily at the clock radio. In bright red numerals it said 0545: numerals that were just as red as Lia d'Angeli's dress. Ouch, he thought, and buried his head under the pillows. The first bird had been joined by a second; it sounded like full-blown domestic warfare was being waged two feet from his open window.

He'd stake his brand new red Porsche that Lia had been planning on eating in the Tradewind Room until she'd seen him. Then she'd changed her mind *prestissimo*. He tried to block out the image of her crouched by the door, making a little boy laugh. Or the way her long black hair waved to her shoulders, gleaming like satin. Her skin was like satin, too, he thought, and felt his groin harden in instinctive response.

Trouble. That's what she spelled with her lustrous dark eyes and sensuous, red-painted mouth. Big trouble.

He didn't need that kind of trouble in his life. Why couldn't she have gone somewhere else for her holidays? Somewhere a long way from here.

Knowing sleep was out of the question, Seth turned on the bedside light and reached for the novel he'd started a couple of days ago. But he couldn't concentrate on the plot, and kept having to flick back through the pages to see who was who.

Impatiently he put the book down. It hadn't been the birds that had woken him; it had been a nightmare, one that seemed totally out of place in this luxurious setting.

The images were still fluttering at the edge of his vision: miserable shanties, burned villages, refugees displaced with only what they could carry on their backs. He'd seen it all only a few days ago in a rebel-torn area near Africa's equator. It was the children who had gotten to him. Orphaned children, weeping. Starving children beyond tears. A newly dead little boy, his mother wailing her sorrow…what were his troubles compared to that?

As always, he'd done his best to see that the money his foundation was channeling into the area went straight to those who needed it; in the course of which he'd run foul of a gun-happy rebel and a bullet had plowed across his ribcage. He was just lucky the guy's aim had been off.

No matter what he did, one thing was obvious. Single-handed or with the help of his admirable staff, he couldn't stop the war or stamp out the root causes of the poverty…those went far beyond the reach of one man, no matter how rich or how well-meaning.

Oddly enough, among Seth's primary emotions as he'd flown home had been a searing realization of the aridity of his own life. Sure, he had friends, good ones, scattered all over the globe. But otherwise, he was detached. Uninvolved. He could tell himself he was the inevitable product of the disas-trous marriage between his mother and father. Blame his need to be a loner on them. But wasn't he, when all was said and done, poorer than any of those close-knit families he'd seen struggling to survive under a tropical sun? They at least had each other.

Who did he have?

No one. With a disgusted grunt, Seth heaved himself out of bed. Despite his sore ribs, he was going swimming. Afterward, so he wouldn't bump into Conway and Lia d'Angeli, he'd order room service: a calorie-laden breakfast of all the things that were bad for him, like bacon and hash browns. He needed this holiday and he was darn well going to enjoy it.

While the swim woke Seth up, breakfast made him drowsy, so he slept for nearly an hour in his lounge chair on the shaded, breezy deck of his cottage. Waking midmorning, he decided he had just enough time to join the boat that should be heading out to the reef for some snorkeling. Grabbing his gear, shoving his dark glasses on his nose, Seth set out for the dock.

The boat was ready to leave. Its sole occupant, other than the guide, was Lia d'Angeli, wearing a dazzlingly white cover-up over her swimsuit, her hair bundled under a wide-brimmed sunhat. Because she was chatting with the guide, she hadn't seen him.

He could change his mind. Hightail it back down the dock and bury his nose in his book. Peacefully, all by himself.

He didn't like backing down from anyone, least of all a woman.

Then his mind was made up for him. "Mornin', Mr. Talbot, sir," said the guide, a grin splitting his face. "You comin' with us this fine day?"

"Good morning," Seth said. "Yeah, thought I would."

In utter dismay Lia swiveled to face him. Seth Talbot was the last man she wanted to see this morning. He had cost her a very expensive dinner last night in the Reef Room, and he'd haunted her sleep. When Conway had brought his name up over breakfast, she'd changed the subject with a singular lack of grace. And now Seth was sauntering down the dock at the last minute to join an expedition she'd been very much looking forward to. Why couldn't he just leave her alone?

She said sarcastically, "What an unexpected pleasure."

"For both of us," he replied, mockery sparking his green eyes. "Surely you exaggerate."

The guide said amiably, "If you're both ready, we'll get going."

Although Lia could have jumped out of the boat and run for her life up the dock, a healthy dose of stubbornness was one of the attributes that had brought her success in a highly competitive field. "Hurry up, Seth," she said tightly, and watched him step into the dinghy, settling himself beside her on the thwart.

He was wearing a thin white T-shirt over lightweight shorts that doubled as swim trunks. His forearms were strongly muscled, his hands resting easily on his thighs...had she ever forgotten those long, lean fingers, the way they'd played her body as sensitively as any musician's? Like a lightning bolt, desire slammed through her and unconsciously Lia's body swayed toward him. Betraying her, just as he'd betrayed her so long ago.

No, she thought frantically. Not again.

Appalled, she straightened on the seat, holding herself rigid as the boat chugged away from the dock. The bow slapped the waves, the foam an effervescent white shot through with blue. Beautiful, she thought, trying with all her might to focus on anything other than the man sitting so close to her.

The small outboard motor was noisy, so at least she didn't have to talk to him.

All too soon, they reached the reef. The guide cut the motor. "Anyplace around here is good. We ask you not to touch the corals, it damages them, and some of them are poisonous." He gave another big grin. "I'll just sit here and wait for you...we got all the time in the world."

Lia bent to fasten her fins. Then, feeling absurdly self-conscious, she took off her white top. Her turquoise maillot, sleek-fitting, was low-cut front and back, and high-cut over her hips. She should be wearing a nun's habit, she thought irritably, not a swimsuit that exposed far more of her than it covered.

In spite of herself, she glanced over at Seth. His eyes were riveted on her, such raw hunger in them that she flinched away from him. So he felt it, too. After eight long years of silence, he still wanted her.

Her. Not her child.

Her temper flared to life, gloriously reviving. She'd been his victim years ago, when he hadn't answered her letters. But she didn't have to be anyone's victim right this minute. She was going to make him suffer. Unwise of her, no doubt, but understandable under the circumstances. She tossed her shirt across the forward thwart and leaned across him to get her mask, thereby giving him an unobstructed view of her cleavage. As she picked up the mask, she deliberately let her thigh brush his.

With a bland smile she watched him jolt on the seat, his jaw tightening, desire smoldering in those incredibly green eyes that Marise had inherited. Too bad, Seth Talbot, she thought meanly. There's not a hope in hell that I'll ever let you touch me again.

She said lightly, "Enjoy." After tucking her sunhat under her shirt on the thwart, Lia swung her legs over the edge of the dinghy and slipped into the sea. She rinsed her mask with water, fitted it over her face and swam away from the boat. Facedown, she was instantly transported to another world, where tiny fish flashed yellow, purple and black through a lacy network of indolently swaying coral.

Her heartbeat slowly settled back to normal, her anger subsiding. She shouldn't have thrust herself so blatantly at Seth when she had no intention of coming across. It had been crude of her. Crude and potentially dangerous.

But, she thought with a small smile, very satisfying.

Then she did her level best to put him out of her mind. He wasn't worth it. Nor was she going to allow him to ruin her precious and hard-earned holiday.

Seth had waited a couple of minutes before leaving the dinghy. He kept his T-shirt on, mostly because he couldn't stand advertising the wide strip of white plaster over his ribs. Bad enough to have stepped in the way of a stray bullet, without having to talk about it. Especially to the likes of Lia d'Angeli.

Who'd read his flare of lust like an open book and thrust her breasts practically in his face.

With an entirely predictable response on his part, he thought savagely, not sure whether he was angrier with her for arousing him or with himself for responding like a hormone-ridden adolescent. Calling on all his self-control, he made light conversation with the guide, whose name was John, while he adjusted his fins and rinsed his mask over the gunwale. Only then did he lower himself into the sea.

He let himself sink, as always struck by the myriad, sun-shot hues of the sea. Favoring his ribs, he began to swim, the silky warmth of the water laving his body.

He needed a woman. That's what he needed. Just as long as her name wasn't Lia.

As he surfaced to breathe, he caught sight of her snorkel not that far ahead of him. He should head in the opposite direction, he thought, and knew he wasn't going to. Smoothly he took off in pursuit. When he was a few feet behind her, he sank again, watching her through the wavering currents of the tide. She was swimming steadily along the reef, her body lissome as a mermaid in her turquoise suit, her masked face giving her an alluring aura of mystery.

A turquoise suit. A mask.

Seth's eyes widened behind his own mask. His jaw dropped so that he inadvertently swallowed a mouthful of salt water. He surged to the surface, coughing and spluttering. He had to be wrong. His imagination was working overtime.

Lia d'Angeli his mysterious butterfly lover? Lia as the

woman at the ball in her shimmering turquoise bodysuit and her all-concealing mask?

He was out of his mind to even think it. Get a life, Seth. So you've never really forgotten her. So, subliminally, you know she ruined you for any other woman. So what?

You're letting a turquoise maillot and a snorkeling mask play tricks on you. Because you never really let her go.

He'd never admitted this to himself before. Seth cursed out loud. Which did he hate more, the fierce stab of hope that he'd found her again, or the swirling terror that he was wrong? He took a deep breath, filling his lungs, and again sank below the surface. The slow, graceful finning of her legs, the long arc of hip, waist and breast…had he ever forgotten them? Her face he'd never seen. But her body was unmistakable.

He should have recognized her the first moment he'd laid eyes on her in the foyer of the restaurant last night.

Again Seth rose to the surface, and this time conviction rose with him, hope replaced by certainty. The woman in Paris and the woman he'd met last night at the resort were one and the same. He'd found her. After eight years, he'd found her; and her name was Lia d'Angeli.

His first reaction was joy. Joy of a depth and intensity that was extraordinarily rare in his life.

But then, belatedly, Seth's brain started to work. Lia hadn't wanted to be found. She'd known his name from the beginning, and could have tracked him down anytime in the intervening years. Meeting him last night hadn't been her choice, he was sure of that. She'd been, to put it mildly, horrified and antagonistic. Not to mention enraged.

Why? What had he done? She was the one who'd disappeared. And he was damn well going to find out why.

He swam away from her, his movements choppy and uncoordinated. He felt as though he'd banged his head hard on the reef; or as though the bullet had hit a vital organ. But through the confusion of emotion in his chest he did know one thing. He wasn't going to have a shouting match with her while he was treading water within earshot of John the guide. No, the confrontation would keep. After eight years, another hour meant nothing.

Forty minutes later, Seth saw Lia heading for the dinghy. He got there first, trying to disguise how much it hurt to lever himself over the gunwales. When she reached the side of the boat, he held out his hand. "Let me help you," he said.

She yanked off her mask, throwing it over the gunwale, refusing to meet his eyes. The sunlight on her jaw...why had he taken so long to recognize her? It was all there. The slender line of her throat, the delicacy of her bones: he'd been an idiot not to have known who she was yesterday evening.

The instant he'd seen her, he'd lusted after her. That, too, had been a clue he'd ignored.

She said in a clipped voice, "I can manage."

"I'm sure you can. Grab my hand."

She could make a scene. Or she could do as he asked. With bad grace Lia took his hand, the strength in his fingers making her shiver with a mixture of panic and passionate longing. He lifted her as if she were weightless. When she'd gotten her footing in the boat, she tugged her hand free. "Thanks," she said grudgingly.

"No problem."

Scowling, she jammed her sunhat on her wet hair and threw the white shirt over her shoulders. She was going to need every one of the spa's ministrations to get rid of the tension that right now was tightening her muscles and seething along her nerves. Trying to gather her wits, she gave John the smile she hadn't given Seth, and said warmly, "That was wonderful, thanks so much for bringing us out here."

"You're welcome, ma'am."

He pulled the cord and the boat swirled in a circle to head

back to shore. The scene was like a picture postcard, from the tall palms to the white sand ruffled by waves. Her shirt flattened to her body, Lia gripped the thwart and knew that the minute the boat docked she was going to run for her cottage, go inside and lock the door.

As the dinghy nudged the dock, Seth uncoiled a rope and tied it to the bollard. Picking up his gear, he stepped out. Lia followed suit, clutching her fins to her chest like a shield as she said goodbye to John. She then started marching down the dock, the wood hot under her bare feet. Seth seized her by the elbow. "Slow down…we have to talk."

She whirled, trying to pull free. "We don't have to do anything—go away and leave me alone. Or I'll complain to the management."

He said flatly, "We're not going to have a fight in full view of the resort. You've got two choices. You can walk to your cottage and we'll talk there. Or I can pick you up and carry you."

"That kind of behavior went out with the Neanderthals… you're kind of slow to get the message."

His answer was to swing her up into his arms and stride off the dock straight for her cottage. He grated, "You have a reputation for privacy. So, as it happens, do I. Let's hope no one's watching us right now."

Years ago he'd picked her up and carried her out on a balcony where the lights of Paris had twinkled and shone. Fighting against memories whose potency had never really subsided, as well as the all-too-present potency of steel-strong arms and a taut, warm shoulder, Lia struck out at him with her elbow.

A flash of pure agony crossed his face. "Don't! I've got sore ribs."

"If you can't take the heat, don't go out in the sun," she snapped. She sure wasn't going to apologize; even though he was white about the mouth.

What had happened to his ribs?

What did she care?

He was marching toward her cottage, with its thick screen of bougainvillea and hibiscus. Too much privacy, Lia thought frantically. Privacy plus Seth Talbot equaled danger. "Put me down," she seethed, wriggling in his arms.

His hold tightened. "Where's your key?"

"If you think I'm letting you inside my cottage, you've got the wrong woman."

"No, I haven't." On impulse—because where in that skin-tight swimsuit could she possibly have hidden a key?—Seth tried her door, finding it unlocked. He shoved it open and plunked her down on the smoothly polished floor. "If it'll make you feel better, we'll leave the door wide-open. Okay, Lia d'Angeli, let's cut to the chase. I know who you are. You're the woman I went to bed with in Paris eight years ago—I've finally figured it out."

Rage almost choked her. "You've known all along who I was!"

"What the hell do you mean? You never gave me your name and you sneaked out in the middle of the night while I was asleep. For the better part of two weeks I had investigators turning over every cobblestone in Paris. Not a trace. You even used a false name when you rented your costume, for Pete's sake. You didn't want to be found—and now you accuse me of knowing who you were? Don't make me laugh."

He looked as far from laughter as a man could. "I used a false name because I wanted to be anonymous," she blazed. "I'd just won the two top European prizes, and the press was falling all over me—I wasn't just talented, I was also beautiful, sexy, voluptuous, you name it. They were having a field day and all I wanted to do was get away for a few hours. So, yes, I covered my tracks that night and I did leave in the middle of the night. But—"

"You could have gotten in touch with me later—or did that night mean so little to you?" He took her by the shoulders, his fingers digging into her flesh. "Forgettable sex—that's all it was for you?"

"I did!"

"Did what?" he snarled.

"I wrote you two letters," she said, biting off each word. "And now you dare pretend that you didn't get them?"

"When?"

Briefly she hesitated. His anger was so convincing, so powerful. What if there was a one in a million chance both letters had gone astray? What then? If she said two months later, wouldn't he twig to her pregnancy? Overriding all her other concerns was the certainty that she had to keep her beloved Marise out of the picture. "Not that long afterward," she said evasively and saw his eyes darken with suspicion.

"You're lying."

"I am not! I sent one to your headquarters in Manhattan, and the other to the Hamptons—I got the address off your Web site."

"That's my parents' place," Seth said, thinking furiously. "If you did write to me—and I'm far from convinced—what were the letters about?"

She said steadily, looking right at him, "I just wanted to stay in touch. That's all. But you never bothered answering. As we both know."

"It's pretty hard to answer a letter you never got," Seth said sarcastically.

"Why do you think I was so rude to you last night in the lobby? *Delighted to meet you,* you said. Then you had the gall to add, *I can't imagine how I've offended you.* As though we'd never made mad, passionate love for hours at a time in that ritzy hotel. It isn't me who's forgotten all that sex, it's you."

He pounced. "So you haven't forgotten?"

She bit her lip. As usual when she was in a temper, her

tongue was running away with her. "When you didn't do me the common courtesy of acknowledging my letters, I forgot about you in a hurry," she said, with absolutely no regard for the truth.

He said furiously, "One letter going astray I could understand. But two?"

"That's why I know you got them. Or, at the very least, one of them."

"So now you're accusing *me* of lying?"

"You're such a smart man," she said mockingly.

He thrust her away from him, prowling around the room. A yellow sweater was thrown over one of the bamboo chairs. A closed laptop computer rested on the teak table, while a music stand had been set up by the window with its magnificent view of the ocean. "How long are you staying?" he demanded.

Her nerves had tightened to an unbearable pitch. She'd left her bedroom door ajar; on the bureau was her favorite photo of Marise. Her daughter, and his. "I could ask you the same question."

"I leave in three days. What about you?"

"It's none of your business," she said coldly, keeping to herself the fact that she'd have only a day left of her holiday after he'd gone. "We have nothing to say to each other. You think I'm a liar, and I know you're one. Yes, we shared something many years ago. But it's over and done with and we've both moved on."

"Speak for yourself," he said softly, taking two swift steps toward her.

"Do you honestly think I could ever trust you again?" she cried. "I took the risk of getting in touch with you, and you chose to ignore me. Now you're paying the consequences. Grow up, Seth."

"Once I get home, I'm going to find out what happened to those two letters. Assuming you wrote them."

"It's too late to check your wastebasket."

His green eyes blazing with anger, Seth put his arms hard around her and dropped his mouth to hers in a kiss that was an impressive mix of rage and lust. Lia dug her fingers into his nape and kissed him back.

Fiercely she welcomed the first thrust of his tongue, greedy for more. Her hat tumbled to the floor. Her hands probed his damp hair, the taut line of his throat, the bump and curve of bone under his wet T-shirt, memory flooding her and casting aside caution.

Her response shot through Seth's body. He dragged the shirt from her shoulders, flinging it to the floor, then tugging the straps of her swimsuit down her arms. His mouth plummeted to find the sweet, bare curve of her breast. Her skin tasted of salt and sunlight, her nipple tight as coral. She gasped his name, throwing her head back, her heartbeat racing beneath his cheek.

He'd never wanted a woman as he wanted this one. And now he'd found her again.

She was yanking at the hem of his shirt, pressing her belly to his, her hips writhing. His arousal had been instant, fierce and imperative. He put one hand to her buttocks, jamming her against it, and kissed her again, tasting her, laving the slick heat of her mouth. Knowing he couldn't wait much longer, he lifted his head long enough to say hoarsely, "Let's go to the bedroom."

The bedroom…her photo of Marise.

She couldn't possibly allow Seth in her bedroom.

CHAPTER SEVEN

LIA went rigid in Seth's arms; he might as well have thrown a bucket of cold water in her face. "What's wrong with me?" she cried. "I'd have done it all over again—gone to bed with you and not a thought for—" She'd been about to say *the consequences*. In sheer panic she bit back the words. "Not a thought for tomorrow," she stumbled. "We don't know each other, we don't trust each other and yet we'd fall into bed?"

"You're the truest thing that's ever happened to me," Seth said harshly, and heard the words echo in his head. "Come to bed with me, Lia. Let me make love to you again. And this time I'll be able to see your face and call you by name…"

The intensity in his green eyes made her belly ache with longing. But she wasn't going to surrender to it. Or to him. How could she tell him about Marise when she couldn't condone his long silence? She said jaggedly, "Why didn't you answer my letters? Did you have another lover by then? Tell me, Seth. Tell me the truth! I swear I'll do my best to understand."

"Lia, I never got them," he said forcibly. "Do you think I wouldn't have answered? It took me nearly two years to replace you in my bed, and—hell, what am I saying? I've never been able to replace you, and that's the God's truth."

A truth he'd never intended sharing with anyone.

Lia gazed up at him. He was lying. He had to be. Two letters couldn't just disappear off the face of the earth. If only the stakes weren't so high, so impossibly weighted by the simple fact of Marise's existence. "Then what happened to them?" she demanded.

Ever since Lia had told him she'd sent one to the Hamptons, Seth had had his suspicions. But they were only suspicions, and a huge part of him dreaded for them to be proved true. He said flatly, "As soon as I get back to Manhattan, I'm going to find out. But I have to do it face-to-face."

"You're saying someone might have interfered with your personal mail? Someone at work? Or one of your parents? I can't believe that!"

His jaw an inflexible line, Seth said, "I don't want to talk about it until I have the facts."

"Well, I'm not going go to bed with you until I know. The letters are too important. Too basic."

He let out his breath in a frustrated sigh, moving away from her to pace up and down the room again. Like a caged tiger, she thought. She'd always hated zoos. Then he turned to face her. "You don't trust me."

"Of course I don't! Why should I?" His wet hair curled around his ears, his green eyes pinioning her like the butterfly she'd been. Stabbed with need, her whole body aching, Lia hugged her arms around her chest. "I'm cold," she said in a low voice. "You'd better go, Seth."

"So are we going to avoid each other for the next three days? Pretend we've never met?"

"If we're smart, that's exactly what we'll do."

Her head was downbent, and there were goosebumps on her bare arms. Stabbed with compunction—or that's what he chose to call it—Seth said impulsively, "Have dinner with me tonight, Lia. Just dinner." He added with a crooked smile, "We could call it a date. Seth meets Lia, they're attracted to each other, and he asks her out. You'll be quite safe—we won't make love on the floor of the Reef Room."

"I wouldn't bet on it, and the answer's no."

Seth came closer, deliberately running a finger down her cheek and watching her tiny shiver of response. "Eight o'clock in the Reef Room. In the meantime, have a hot shower… Lia, I'm sorry about the letters, more sorry than I can say. It must have hurt you when I didn't answer—typical guy, he has a one-night stand, gets what he wants and crosses you off the list. It was never that way, and I swear I'll find out who interfered with my mail."

Torn between the sincerity in his voice, and her own knowledge of just what it was she'd said in those letters, Lia struggled to find her bearings. Either he'd received at least one of her letters, in which case his sincerity was nothing but a ruthless ploy to get her in his bed again; or someone had destroyed both of them: a scenario she couldn't begin to encompass.

"I won't have dinner with you, Seth, it's playing with fire," she said evenly. "I don't trust a word you're saying—that's objection number one, and it's huge. There's more, though. Today was like a repeat of that masked ball—when I get within ten feet of you, I want to rip the clothes off your body and jump your bones. But I'm eight years older now, and I've learned a thing or two. No more one-night stands, for starters."

He opened his mouth to protest, and shut it again. Having found her for the second time, he'd been overwhelmed by his compulsive need to take her to bed again. But what then? He hadn't even thought about the consequences. If he went to bed with Lia in the warmth of a tropical island, could he walk away from her? Drop her, as sooner or later he dropped all his women?

Marriage was out, and he'd never wanted children. What did he have to offer but an affair? A six-week stand, he thought with a grimace.

She deserved better than that.

What was he going to do?

He said curtly, "Tomorrow then. Let's meet for breakfast. No risks attached."

"Your middle name is risk."

"So you've turned into a coward in the last eight years?"

"I'm being sensible," Lia cried. Wanting nothing more than to put her head down on the nearest pillow and weep her eyes out, she added, hearing the thread of desperation in her voice, "Please go."

"Nine o'clock tomorrow," Seth said in a steel voice. "The Reef Room. They do dynamite scrambled eggs."

"I hope you enjoy them. All by yourself."

"You'll turn up. I know you will. Because I've heard you play, and that woman doesn't know the meaning of coward-ice or caution."

Two days ago, she would have agreed with him. Lia walked toward the door and pushed it wide, her fingers gripping the cool wood. The first thing she was going to do once he'd gone was hide the photo of Marise in the depths of her suitcase. She said with icy emphasis, "Stay away from me, Seth."

He brushed his lips against her cold cheek and heard himself say, "No…I'm too happy to have found you."

What did that have to do with a six-week stand?

For the second night in a row, Seth scarcely slept. This time, it wasn't nightmares that kept him awake. It was Lia.

Or rather, Lia's absence.

He hadn't laid eyes on her yesterday after he'd left her cottage. The knowledge that she was within a few hundred feet of him every minute of the day was a constant and powerful irritant. Unable to settle to anything, he went to bed at eleven, planning to make up for his lack of sleep the night before. But at 4:00 a.m. he was wide-awake and staring up into the darkness. It wasn't her absence that was the problem, no matter how empty his bed felt without her. It was her presence.

She wanted nothing to do with him. According to her, in those weeks after Paris she'd sent him two letters that he'd never bothered answering. A cold-blooded philanderer, that's how she saw him.

Had she really sent the letters?

If she hadn't, why would she bother constructing such an elaborate system of lies? And why would she be so angry with him?

Even if he left the letters out of the equation, this reunion was still horribly fraught. He had nothing to offer her. He'd never marry her; no amount of hot, glorious sex could change that.

But a one-night stand—or its equivalent—was also out. Lia d'Angeli wasn't like the women he always dated: emotionally cool, malleable, as rational in their way as he was in his. Lia was hot-tempered, strong-willed, intense and generous. All he had to do was think back eight years to know just how generous.

He couldn't mess around with her. One of her strengths as a musician was that she took risks, opening herself to the music and making herself vulnerable. She'd do the same in bed with him, he knew it. He couldn't abuse that vulnerability, any more than he could take advantage of her generosity.

Several months ago, a friend in Berlin had introduced him to one of her CDs. He'd never forget how her playing had penetrated every one of his defenses; it was as though she knew him intimately, and was addressing only himself: the lonely little boy he'd been, the guarded man he'd become.

After that, he'd bought every one of her recordings. But he'd never gone to a live recital. He'd known it would be too much for him; he loathed exposing his emotions in public.

So he'd never seen her in the flesh. He always steered away from reading reviews of music, preferring to make up his own mind, and the society pages weren't part of his reading matter; he also, therefore, knew very little about her. But there was one more reason he hadn't recognized her in the lobby of the Tradewind Room. Her CDs all had reproductions of famous paintings on the cover; her own photo, if there at all, was tucked somewhere in the liner notes, her face merged with those of the players in the orchestra. Presumably it had been against her principles to use her beauty as a sales pitch.

Hadn't she refused to have dinner with him last night because of her principles? She didn't trust him, and therefore was refusing point blank to spend time with him. Odds were he'd be eating breakfast alone.

If that's what happened, he'd track her down afterward and tell her calmly and logically that she was right, they shouldn't see each other again; it was out of the question that he have either a brief fling with her, or commit to any kind of long-standing relationship. He'd keep the whole thing low-key and under control.

Game over. Before it had begun.

As for himself, there'd be no risk that, once again, she'd touch him in that indefinable place called the soul. It had taken too long to get over her the last time. He didn't want a repeat.

His decision made, Seth should have found it easy to fall asleep. The numbers on the clock jumped from one digit to the next; the night sky slowly lightened, and the birds began warming up outside his window in a medley of chortles, whistles and screams.

It didn't matter what his decision was, Seth thought in near despair. He still wanted Lia. If she were here with him now, her slender warm body pressed to his, he'd be kissing her until he couldn't breathe, tasting her skin, exploring its every secret...dammit, why couldn't the birds shut up?

At six Seth got out of bed, dragged a T-shirt over his head

and went outside. He had three hours before he met Lia for breakfast. He lay down in the hammock strung between two tall trees, wedging a pillow under his head. The sky was a gentle eggshell blue, washed with streaks of pale pink and gold. Listening to the soft shushing of waves on the sand, he closed his eyes. He wouldn't sleep. But at least it would be better than being caged up indoors…

In the dream, it was blinding sunlight. Mud huts, an army jeep, a mute array of helpless villagers. The soldiers were dragging a mother away from her little boy. The boy was screaming. As one of the soldiers took out his machete, Seth gave a hoarse shout of horror and ran toward him. But his feet were as heavy as lead and he couldn't cover the ground quick enough. The machete was descending and again he shouted…

"Seth! Wake up, please wake up!"

He was tangled in ropes, his whole body bathed in sweat. Seth's eyes flew open. Lia was bending over him, shaking him by the shoulder, her dark eyes appalled. The sun made a brilliant aureole behind her head.

He wasn't in Africa. He was at the White Cay Resort. Tangled up in a hammock. The machete still inscribing its deadly arc in his mind, Seth rasped, "What the hell are you doing here?"

"I was walking back to breakfast when I heard you yell— I thought someone was murdering you."

His humiliation that she'd heard him screeching like a banshee translated itself into rage. Seth yanked his fingers free from the weave of the hammock and swung his feet to the ground. "Just what were you going to do if someone was?"

"I don't know—I hadn't got that far. Were you having a nightmare?"

He stood up, swaying momentarily. As she grabbed for his arm, he shook her hand off, his face a rictus of fury. "Why don't you get lost?"

"I asked you a question."

"Which I'm choosing not to answer."

Her lashes flickered. "You're ashamed of yourself," she said pithily. "Embarrassed. Because I've seen a part of you that's private."

"Whadda ya know," he snarled, "you're not just gorgeous, you've got brains as well. Vamoose, Lia."

It would have been all too easy to have snarled back. Lia had had very little sleep, and what she'd managed to get had been riddled with dreams so sexually explicit that she'd been more than embarrassed. The object of those dreams was now glaring at her, all six feet three of him. But when she'd woken Seth a couple of minutes ago, the sick horror in his eyes had struck her to the heart. Horror, pain and helplessness…they'd all been there. Reining in her errant temper, she said tightly, "Let me tell you something about myself. My father was Italian, a very famous baritone—"

"Arturo d'Angeli," Seth interrupted impatiently. "I'm not a total ignoramus." His voice gentled. "I read somewhere that he and your mother were both killed in a car crash several years ago."

"When I was eighteen. I still miss them." Grimacing, Lia picked up her train of thought. "My father was passionate and romantic, all his emotions as volatile as an erupting volcano— including his rages, which were legendary. My mother was Norwegian, though. A harpsichordist of world renown, who was cool, rational and controlled."

"Gudrun Halvardson."

"Right now I'm trying very hard not to act like my father. To be my mother instead. Calm and moderate." Lia's voice rose. "Even though I'd like to bang your head on the nearest tree."

Despite himself, a smile tugged at Seth's lips. A reluctant smile, maybe. But still a smile. "I hate to tell you—Arturo's winning."

"Why wouldn't he? You're so goldarn stubborn! Stubborn,

strong and silent. A bad combo—in my books, that adds up to dull. Deadly dull. So why don't you tell me what you were dreaming about?"

Her hair, black as a raven's wing, had the same blue glint of raven feathers in the sun. She was wearing a dress he hadn't seen before, the fabric a dizzying swirl of red, black and white. Her earrings were huge red hoops, while clunky red and white enamel bracelets circled her wrists. "You won't get lost in a crowd," he said.

"If that's supposed to be a compliment, I'm underwhelmed."

Before he could lose his nerve, Seth said rapidly, "I was in central Africa last week. Saw more than I wanted to of a local insurrection—that's what I was dreaming about. If you'll give me five minutes, I'll shower and take you to breakfast."

Her face softened. She said quietly, "I was part of a benefit concert to raise money for AIDS's relief in Africa last year. I made myself look at a lot of news footage…I had awful dreams for weeks afterward. I can't imagine what it would be like to actually see that kind of stuff."

He ran his fingers through his hair. "It's the kids that get to me. I can't get them out of my mind."

"Why were you there? On business?"

He could have lied; he rarely talked about this side of his personality. "I started a charitable foundation several years ago…it's grown over the years, perhaps you've heard of it."

She shook her head. "After you didn't answer my letters, I avoided any mention of you in the press."

He labored on. "I take a personal interest in it—visit all the places to see the money goes to make people as independent as possible."

Her brow wrinkled. "Not just handouts, you mean."

"Right."

Lia gazed at him thoughtfully. There was a lot he wasn't saying, but she was quite capable of filling in the gaps. He was involved. He cared. And in the process, he put his life on the line. "Yesterday, when you kissed me in my cottage, I noticed there was a bandage around your ribs."

He winced. "Bullets were flying. I didn't duck fast enough."

Lia picked a leaf from the nearest shrub, absently rubbing it between her fingers. He was a man of integrity, that's what she'd learned in the last few minutes. How could she square that with the man who hadn't answered her letters? *It's the kids that get to me*, that's what he'd just said. So would he have disregarded any responsibility toward his own child?

As if this would give her the answers she sought, she stepped forward, looped her arms around his waist and reached up to kiss him, her breasts pressed to the hardness of his chest.

Seth went utterly still. Then he pulled his head back. "Don't, Lia," he said.

She quivered as though he'd struck her. "Why not?"

"I figured something out in the night—I was going to tell you at breakfast."

"You'd better tell me now."

She'd moved back from him, her dark eyes wary. Get it over with, Seth, he thought. The quicker the better. "For reasons of my own, I'm not into marriage and I don't want children. You're not the kind of woman I can have a casual affair with—on one day, off the next. That didn't work eight years ago, and I see no reason why it would work now." He gave her a faint smile. "I should have listened to you yesterday when you told me to leave you alone—because you were right."

I don't want children... Clenching her fists, she pushed the words away and said sharply, "You're not in love with me?"

"Of course not. Nor was I eight years ago. But whatever happened between us meant something to me."

"Why are you so opposed to marriage and having a family? They're normal enough needs."

His face closed against her. "It's a long story, and not one I'm about to tell."

Her brain made another lightning-swift leap. "I sent one of my letters to your parents' house—if I can believe you when you say you didn't get them, then it's possible they're the ones who intercepted the letters. Do they hate you? Is that what the problem is?"

"Lay off," he said in an ugly voice.

"Don't tell me what to do! Was it your parents who scared you off commitment? How, Seth?"

He said with vicious emphasis, "Thick-skinned doesn't begin to describe you—you've got a hide like a rhinoceros."

"It'd take a rhinoceros to make any impression on you." Or a rebel bullet, she thought sickly. "I hate this conversation," she muttered. "Surely we don't have to stand here trading insults like a couple of kids."

He said brusquely, "I'll leave here a day early, and in the meantime I'll make sure our paths don't cross."

"So you can be hostage to your parents for the rest of your life?" she cried, and wondered if, deep down, she wasn't fighting for Marise as much as for herself.

"You have no right to ask questions like that."

She had every right. Because Marise, particularly since she'd started school and met other children, all of whom had fathers, had on occasion expressed the wish that her own father appear on the scene. A wish that Lia had been quite unable to fulfill.

Marise's father was standing right in front of her. Adamant, hostile and immovable. She said, not bothering to mask the bitterness in her voice, "Very well. I'll eat in the Tradewind Room and I'll do my best to stay out of your way. Goodbye, Seth. Have a comfortable life."

He made no move to stop her as she turned on her heel and left the clearing behind his cottage. His face had been like a mask, she thought. Hard and empty, blank-eyed.

She'd totally lost her appetite. Lia hurried back to her cottage and went inside. It looked exactly as it had when she'd left. It was herself who'd changed.

The only man she'd slept with in eight years wouldn't so much as kiss her. Wouldn't marry her, or have an affair with her. Certainly would never act as a father to their child.

And how that hurt.

When Marise had first asked about her father, Lia had said carefully, "We only met once, Marise. He wasn't able to marry me, and we've never been in touch."

"Was he nice?" four-year-old Marise had asked, big-eyed.

"Very nice."

"Can we go for ice cream now?"

So the two of them had walked down the lane from the old farmhouse to the little village, where they'd eaten banana splits in the shadows of the tall elms…

So long ago, Lia thought with a sigh. She'd have to keep this meeting with Seth a secret. How could she possibly tell Marise that the man who'd fathered her didn't want to have children?

Tension was knotting her shoulders again, just as if she hadn't spent a wad of money yesterday at the spa. She could do with a massage right now, Lia thought, opening her laptop to check her e-mails. There was one from Nancy, with a digital photo of Marise grinning at the camera in her long white nightgown, her brown hair tumbling down her back. In a surge of love and protectiveness Lia gazed at the image, into eyes the green of summer meadows. The farm that was their home was called, appropriately, Meadowland.

Should she tell Seth he was a father? When she'd mailed the two letters, that had been her decision: he had the right to know. Maybe, just maybe, he hadn't gotten those letters. But did that change anything? Marise wasn't an unborn baby anymore; she was seven years old, trusting and vulnerable.

In all this mess, one thing was clear. Marise mustn't get hurt.

Added to that, Seth didn't want any further involvement with Lia herself: he'd made that clear a few minutes ago. Not that he'd ever really been involved with her. So why did she feel like bawling her head off? Just like Marise when she fell down, or when one of her friends was mean to her.

Damned if she was going to cry her eyes out over a man who was all over her one day and then the next wouldn't even kiss her. Lia peeled and ate a mango, scarcely tasting the juicy yellow flesh, then changed into her swimsuit. However, a very vigorous swim in the sea didn't help at all. She was tired, she was hungry, and her brain was in a state of total confusion. Moral dilemmas were just that: dilemmas. Difficult to solve, and without any assurance that the choice made was the right one. Should she or shouldn't she tell Seth about Marise?

Sooner or later, he'd read something about her daughter. Although Lia did her best to keep Marise safe from any publicity, the media had a long reach and an even longer memory. Wouldn't it be better to tell him herself rather than have him find out by accident?

She didn't know. She simply didn't know. Maybe telling him was no big deal: if he didn't want children, he'd pay no more attention to Marise now than he had since her conception.

Lia gritted her teeth. She'd despise Seth if he neglected her daughter that way.

After showering the salt from her hair and skin, Lia dressed in shorts and a brief top, and took her precious Stradivarius violin from its case. The truths of music had always sustained her in times of trouble; perhaps they'd help her now. She tuned the violin and began to play, standing by the window of her bedroom with its view of jade-green sea and gently swaying palm trees.

She should practice the Brahms she'd be playing in Vienna next week. Instead she let her mind wander, drifting from melody to melody, pouring into the music all her confusion and pain.

How could one man have so much power over her?

CHAPTER EIGHT

SETH had gone to the Reef Room for breakfast, burying his nose in the newspaper and eating the food as if it was so much sawdust. He'd done the right thing by ousting Lia from his life. So why did he feel like a number-one louse?

He rattled the papers irritably, trying to concentrate on the latest uprising in the Philippines. But Lia's face kept intruding itself between him and the newsprint. She'd fought, but she hadn't begged. She'd been hurt, but she hadn't cried.

He wanted her as he'd wanted no other woman in his life.

Was she right? Was he still in thrall to his parents? One thing he knew: when he got home, he was driving straight to the huge stone mansion where he'd grown up and confronting his mother about the letters. His father would never have tampered with Seth's mail; but Eleonore could have, Seth thought, sickened. She'd have seen Lia as a penniless musician after the Talbot money; but did that mean she'd behaved so underhandedly? So maliciously?

He wanted answers from her, and he was going to get them.

Were the kids he got so involved with through the foundation his surrogate children? Had a woman ever shaken him up as Lia could?

With a low growl of frustration Seth folded the paper and

left the restaurant. He was going to bury himself in work today and forget about Lia d'Angeli.

But as he sat down in front of his computer, through the open window drifted, faintly, the notes of a violin. She was playing, he thought. Three cottages away, the wind carrying the music toward him. Slowly he got up, the melody tugging him like a magnet.

He threaded his way through the lush gardens behind the cottages, the sun hot on his shoulders. When he got to Lia's cottage, he walked around to the front and stood still for a few minutes on the steps, listening intently, feeling all her unhappiness and uncertainty as his own. But as each perfect note took possession of him, the last of Seth's doubts vanished. Lia had written the letters: her music searched too profoundly for truth for him to doubt her word.

His mind shied away from the mechanics of their disappearance. Later, he thought. Later.

That she'd written to him must mean she'd longed to reconnect with him. No wonder she'd been so hurt and angry when they'd met again, here on the island.

He had to tell her he believed her.

The front door was unlocked. Seth pushed it open and walked in. Her laptop was on the table, open, the screensaver shifting brightly colored musical notes from top to bottom and side to side. She must be in the bedroom; she'd shifted from Tchaikovsky's lyricism to a modernistic lament, full of dissonance and a wild, unappeasable grief. Struck to the heart, his feet anchored to the floor, Seth forgot this wasn't his cottage or his computer; with his mind on automatic pilot, his fingers briefly hit the space bar.

An image flashed onto the screen, distracting him from the music. A little girl wearing a white nightgown was smiling right at him. A very pretty little girl with brown curly hair and green eyes.

Green like his.

Seth sank down into the nearest chair, his gaze riveted to the screen. The little girl's chin was tilted, just as Lia sometimes tilted hers. Lia's child, he thought numbly. She looked to be about seven.

His child?

He'd used no protection that night in the hotel in Paris. It could be his child. Was that why Lia had written him two letters, two so that he'd get the news even if one of them by chance went astray?

How often did he see eyes of a true, deep green? It had to be his child.

He, Seth, was the father of a daughter.

His heart was thudding in his chest as though he'd run from one end of the island to the other. His hands were ice-cold. For over seven years he'd been a father, and hadn't known it. Seven long years...

As he pushed back the chair, it scraped on the floor. The music stopped with startling abruptness. From the bedroom Lia called, "Is someone there?"

His voice was stuck somewhere in his throat. He heard her footsteps pad across the polished wood floor and from a long way away watched her walk into the living room. She was still holding her bow and violin. When she saw him, she stopped dead in her tracks.

Seth, Lia thought. In her cottage. In front of her laptop with its photo of Marise. He was white-faced, his eyes blank with shock. She took a deep breath and said, trying hard to be calm and instead sounding heartless, "She's your child, Seth."

He cleared his throat. "I'd already figured that out."

"That's why I wrote to you, two months after we met. To tell you I was pregnant. But you say you didn't get my letters."

"I didn't—although I do believe you wrote them. Whoever

intercepted them has a lot to answer for," he said, his voice as clipped as a robot's. "What's her name?"

"Marise. She's seven."

"Does she know about me?"

"Not really…when she first asked about you, I told her I'd known you only very briefly, and that you couldn't marry me. She's never asked your name."

He said with painful truth, "You were left alone to bear my child. I've never seen her, written to her, given you any money for her support—"

"I didn't write to you because I wanted money!"

"I never said you did." He asked another crucial question. "Why didn't you tell me about her yesterday?"

"How could I, when I still don't know what to believe about the letters? For someone to have intercepted them—intervened in your life and mine so callously—it's monstrous."

"Yes," Seth said quietly, "it was monstrous."

"Plus you were so intent on informing me you didn't want children. Never had and, I presumed, never would. What was I supposed to do?"

"Were you planning to tell me at some time in the future?"

"I don't know." She put the violin and bow down on the table, running her fingers through the silky darkness of her hair. "That's why I was playing. To try to figure out what I was going to do."

Some of his anger escaped in spite of himself. "You should have told me the minute we met!"

"When I was introduced to you in the lobby? *Oh hi, Seth, nice to see you again—what's it been? Eight years? By the way, I left your daughter home this trip.* Give me a break."

"You've been acting ever since we met. Lying to me, in effect." Wasn't that what really hurt?

"It's not that simple," she fumed. "I won't risk hurting my daughter, Seth. Not if you're going to pull another vanishing act because children aren't in your life plan. A child wasn't in mine eight years ago, believe me. But I had to make the best of it and—"

The words were torn from him. "Didn't you consider having an abortion?"

"No. Not even for a minute." She added in distress, for he looked like a man in torment, "Seth, what's wrong?"

"Nothing," he rapped, struggling to subdue all the demons of the past. "Abortion would have been a logical step. You were alone, your career was taking off…"

"I did my best to combine the two—motherhood and career." She smiled wryly. "Several critics wrote how my music deepened and grew richer in my mid-twenties. Little did they know."

Seth said, through the tightness in his chest, "You're a good woman, Lia."

Unexpectedly tears swam in her eyes. "Thank you," she gulped.

"I have to meet Marise."

"You're going too fast for me."

"Seven years, Lia! That's what I've been cheated out of. And now you say I'm going too fast?"

"Cheated? But you don't want children."

"I've got one. Whether I want one or not."

She said with careful precision, "I love Marise more than anyone else in the world. I won't let you, or anyone else, hurt her. Not if I can help it."

"What kind of man do you think I am?"

"How can I answer that? I scarcely know you."

"That's not true," he retorted. "We spent most of one night together—you can find out a lot about someone when you share a bed."

"I've changed since then, and so, I'm sure, have you. I won't gamble Marise's happiness, Seth."

His eyes like gimlets, he said, "Who's with her now?"

"Nancy. My full-time nanny, tutor and good friend. Marise adores her. Nancy insists that for a few days every year I go away somewhere to relax. No child, no concerts, and she'd really prefer I leave my violin at home, too. That's why I'm here. Not that I've had much in the way of relaxation."

"So does Marise stay home when you're on tour?"

"Is this an inquisition to see if I'm a fit mother?"

He stepped closer, tracing the angry lift of her chin with one finger. "No. I'm sorry, I'm not thinking straight. I can't imagine you being anything but the best of mothers."

She rested her forehead on his shoulder, more touched than she wanted him to know. "It's hard sometimes. The tours are exhausting. If I'm going to be away for a while, she and Nancy travel with me for part of the time. But otherwise, Marise stays home—I've tried my best to give her as normal a life as I can. But I couldn't give up my music!"

"Of course you couldn't." He put his arm around her waist, drawing her closer. "She looks like a very happy little girl," he said huskily.

Lia glanced up, mischief glinting in her dark eyes. "She inherited my temper."

He laughed. "Is she musical?"

"Can't play a note. But she loves books, and she's already written about ten stories of her own."

Seth said painfully, "My father's a great reader. He ran a publishing house until he retired, and he's been working on a novel for years."

One more strand tying them together. "Oh, Seth, what will we do?"

"I'm going home and finding out what happened to those letters. You're going home and telling Marise about me. Then she and I will meet."

"You make it sound much too easy. No marriage, no children, that's what you said. I don't want marriage, either, so that's no problem. But you have a child, a real live flesh-and-blood child. Fatherhood requires commitment—it sounds to me like you're commitment-phobic."

He was. Always had been. "I can't ignore Marise, as though she doesn't exist. I've been landed with a commitment, like it or not. Just as you were left pregnant, like it or not." He scowled at her. "What have you got against marriage?"

She scowled right back, pulling free from the circle of his arm. "I don't have the time for it."

"You're too busy being a musician and a single mother."

"Exactly."

"If you were married, you wouldn't be a single mother."

"If you're so clever, will you kindly explain to me how we're going to handle this?" she exploded. "What about us? We just have to look at each other and our hormones spike way off the chart. Marise is trusting and innocent. I won't carry on an affair right under her nose."

"That's right, you won't. I'll visit her when you're not there."

Trying desperately to conceal how his casual dismissal had hurt her, Lia said, "Don't you get it? We'll be tied together for years."

"We'll both be free to live our own lives."

She gripped the edge of the table. "We first saw each other, masked and costumed, across a crowded ballroom. But we recognized each other right away. We're playing with fire here, Seth."

"Marise exists. I have to see her."

Feeling utterly exhausted, Lia leaned back on the table. If Seth were to meet Marise, it would be at Meadowland. Which was Lia's sanctuary, her home, the place where love bloomed, unforced and peaceful as the wildflowers of the meadows. How could she bear for Seth to invade it?

He said inflexibly, "Let's set a date right now—have you

got your datebook handy?" Because he'd been working, his Palm Pilot was in his pocket. He took it out. "How about one day next week?"

She said in a hostile voice, "I'm playing in Vienna with Ivor Rosnikov a week from today."

Rosnikov was a wildly popular Russian pianist with a well-earned reputation as a womanizer. The words were out before Seth could censor them. "Is he your current lover?"

"If he is, that's none of your business. Didn't you just say I was free to live my own life?"

He had. Not one of his smarter pronouncements. "He's bedded half the women in Europe."

"He's also a marvelous musician," she snapped.

There was a red smudge under her chin where her violin had rested. Seth stared at it, willing himself to stay where he was. But a split second later, he was crushing her to his chest, kissing her as though she was the only woman in the world. All the curves of her body, the sweetness of her mouth, were so achingly familiar, so passionately desired...

Lia clung to him, her lips parted to the dance of his tongue, her hips tight to the surge of his arousal; and knew she'd come home. Home? she thought in confusion. Meadowland is home. Not Seth. Seth's too dangerous, too unpredictable.

Then he thrust her away, his breathing harsh in his ears. "You can kiss me like that, and tell me in the same breath you're Rosnikov's lover?"

"I never said I was!"

Sunlight was flickering through her hair like tiny electric sparks. Seth said implacably, "Tell me when I can meet Marise."

"I'll decide whether you can or not after you've found out about the letters. After you've had time to think very hard about what fatherhood implies. Marise has done just fine without a father for seven years. I won't allow you to wander in and out of her life as your busy schedule permits—I won't have her hurt, Seth."

"I'm damned if you'll deprive her of her father!"

"I'll give you my phone numbers, including my cell. You can get in touch with me after Vienna. Assuming you can offer me concrete proof about the letters, we'll talk then."

He said, keeping any trace of emotion from his voice, "I know you sent them. I believe you, in other words. I trust you. Why can't you do the same for me?"

"Try seeing it from my point of view," she flared. "Eight years ago I was convinced you'd abandoned me, betraying our lovemaking in Paris by ignoring its consequences. The hurt went deep. Much too deep for me to now say blithely, *sure, we'll sleep together, Seth, and of course you can see my daughter any time that's convenient for you.*"

"It wasn't my fault that you were abandoned. Nor will I be kept from Marise."

"But you'd have to make a genuine commitment to her— I'm not sure you're capable of that."

She looked as fierce as a mother bear defending her cub. Deep within him, respect stirred, mixed with unwilling admiration. He spoke the simple truth. "The commitment's already made. The moment I saw Marise's green eyes, I had no choice."

Lia let out her breath in a long sigh. "I play again with Ivor in Hamburg two days after Vienna. Then I fly home." She did some quick calculations. "The fifteenth. You can call me then."

He already knew he wasn't going to wait that long: a piece of information he kept to himself. If Lia d'Angeli thought she was going to call all the shots, she'd very soon find out she was wrong. "Fine," Seth said.

She'd expected him to argue. Conscious of a huge sense of anticlimax, Lia said, "When are you leaving the island?"

"Tomorrow morning."

"I'll get room service the rest of the day."

I'll stay out of your way—that's what she meant. And wasn't that what he wanted, too? He took a scrap of paper from his pocket and wrote down the number for his personal cell phone, along with his e-mail address. "Will you forward me that photo of Marise?"

Briefly she closed her eyes. "Yes."

"Thanks." What else was there to say? Or do? He sure wasn't going to kiss her again.

There were faint blue shadows under her eyes and a tired droop to her mouth. He said roughly, "Take care of yourself, Lia," and let himself out the door.

His personal jet couldn't get here until tomorrow. Otherwise he'd be leaving right now. Getting as far away from Lia as he could.

Lia d'Angeli, the mother of his child.

Dawn was normally Lia's favorite time of the day: everything fresh, the illusion of a new beginning, the flourish of hope as the sun broke the horizon.

On this, Seth's last morning on the island, she merely felt miserably unhappy. After he'd left her cottage yesterday, she'd practiced her heart out, until she was more confident of the Brahms *cadenza*. She'd eaten outside on the patio, trying to convince herself she was getting the solitude and peace she craved. She'd even slept, off and on.

There was no reason to feel so jangled and off-center. She'd kept in control of the situation yesterday, insisting Seth meet her terms. Well, almost in control. That kiss didn't exactly qualify; and was no doubt the reason she'd woken so early this morning.

When she got up, Lia had decided a swim might settle her nerves. Now she lay back in the saltwater, trying to empty her mind of anything but the beauty of her surroundings. On the waves, pearl-pink flecks reflected the dawn sky; a white tropic bird winged overhead, its long streamers flashing in the light. The sand was newly washed, the tulip tree near her cottage blazoned with huge orange blooms, each a miniature sunrise.

She'd feel a lot better once she knew Seth had left.

Hold that thought, Lia.

She was trying to as, fifteen minutes later, she wandered up the beach toward her cottage, tugging off her swimcap and shaking out her long black hair. On the boardwalk, she used the little tap to rinse the sand from her feet, absently admiring the iridescent polish on her toenails. Frosted Mocha. She must buy it again.

In the bushes, a bird gave a loud squawk of alarm. Lia glanced up, every nerve on alert. Her pulse skipped a beat. Seth had just emerged onto the beach, wearing skintight navy trunks, a towel slung over his shoulder. He hadn't seen her.

Then, as though he sensed her watching him, he looked right at her. The sun was in his eyes. He raised one hand, shading his face, and started walking toward her.

Her heart was pounding in her rib cage; her feet were glued to the boardwalk. As he came closer, she saw that he'd removed the tape that had circled his chest. The scar, a livid, angry red, traversed his ribs from front to back.

He could have been killed, she thought. If the bullet had gone a mere two inches to the left, she would never have seen him again. Did anything matter beside the immensity of that fact? Calmly, as though it was what she'd intended all along, Lia walked to meet him.

To Seth, she looked like a goddess from the sea in her wet turquoise suit, the sunlight glinting on the droplets of water on her skin. Her level gaze was confident of its power, her gait so graceful it hurt him somewhere deep inside, a place he only rarely allowed to be touched. He swallowed hard, knowing he should run in the opposite direction, knowing equally strongly he was going to do nothing of the sort.

She was his fate.

He didn't believe in fate.

Then she reached him. With that same confidence she looped her arms around his neck, stood on tiptoes and kissed him full on the mouth.

Desire slammed through him, hot and powerful. The kiss deepened, until Seth was aware of nothing but a fury of need. Her breasts, pressed to his bare chest, were hard-tipped, her nipples like tiny shells; grasping her by the hips, he ground her body to his, swamped by wave after wave of desire.

Not here, he thought, desperately reaching for some restraint, you can't make love to Lia on the beach. He took her by the hand, rubbing his cheek against the silky fragrance of her hair, and tried to slow his breathing. "Let's go to my cottage," he said huskily, and watched her smile her assent.

Hand in hand, they walked the length of the boardwalk toward his cottage. Ushering her in, Seth kicked the door shut behind him and led her to his bedroom. He hadn't made the bed, Lia noticed; the tumbled sheets where he'd spent the night seemed incredibly intimate to her. Turning to face him, she said urgently, "I want to make love to you again, Seth. I want to stand naked in front of you."

As she strained upward, his head dropped to find her mouth; her lips were salty, soft and warm and passionately hungry. She drew his hips to hers, her fingers probing his taut buttocks. He said hoarsely, "You drive me crazy, Lia. But this time we mustn't forget—"

Quickly he opened the drawer on the bedside table, and took out a small foil envelope. She said in an odd voice, "Would I have thought of that?"

"Just as long as one of us remembers." His voice deepened. "I want you so much…"

"You can have me. All of me. Now."

Reaching up, he dragged the turquoise straps off her shoulders. Her breasts were fuller than he remembered, their tips a rosy-pink in the dawn light. He slid the wet fabric down her hips, kneeling to pull the suit all the way to her slender, high-arched feet. Then he buried his face in her belly, moving lower, his hands clasping her thighs.

She opened to him, burying her fingers in his thick blond hair, throwing back her head in ecstasy as he parted the petals of her flesh and unerringly found her center. Like wildfire, the climax ripped through her, so powerful that she cried out in mingled shock and satiation.

Slowly Seth rose to his feet, his mouth traveling all the curves of her body until he was standing upright. She said, trying to catch her breath, "Do you know what? I want more—how can I? It's disgraceful!"

"We've scarcely begun," he said, his eyes trained on her face as she pulled back from him, her smile infinitely seductive. She was tugging at his chest hair, sliding her fingers over the rippled muscles of his belly, then edging his swimsuit free of his erection. The brush of her fingers against his taut flesh nearly drove him over the brink. As he kicked the suit to the floor, she said, "Your body's so beautiful…kiss me, Seth—now. Drive me out of my mind."

It was all he needed to hear. Devouring the delectable softness of her lips, his teeth grazing her tongue, he drank deep of all the sweetness that was Lia. She was so willing, so eager, so incredibly generous that within moments he lost the last shred of his control. Flinging her back on the bed, he cupped her breast and took her nipple into his mouth, suckling her as she whimpered his name. Briefly he raised his head, drinking in the stunned pleasure on her face; her rib cage was a long arch, her eyes dark pools in which he could lose himself. You're mine, he thought. All mine.

Her hands were everywhere, teasing and enticing until they encircled him in a paradoxical mixture of passion and gentleness. Wasn't that the essence of Lia, Seth thought in sudden insight; and then stopped thinking altogether. "I can't wait," he gasped, shoving himself up on his elbows and reaching for the envelope. He dealt with it swiftly, even as her legs widened to gather him in.

As he plunged deep, her face convulsed, her breath rasping in her throat. Like a great surge of the sea, he was lifted until he could no longer withstand her fierce inner throbbing; they fused and fell together in a tumble of dazzling whiteness.

Joined, Seth rolled on his side, pulling her with him. He dropped his face to her shoulder, dimly aware that his forehead was filmed with sweat. Salty, he thought. Like the sea.

Her heart was thrumming, her body limp. He muttered, "Lia, are you okay?"

His voice seemed to come from miles away. Slowly Lia came back to herself, to the weight of Seth's arm over her ribcage and the hammerbeat of his heart so close it echoed in her ears. So close it could have been her own.

But it wasn't her own. It was Seth's. Seth, with whom she'd just made love.

It had happened again. Just like in Paris.

What had she said to him yesterday? *I won't have an affair with you.*

This high-minded stance had lasted less than twenty-four hours. The basic truth was that she couldn't keep her hands off him. Not here on a tropical island. Not, in all likelihood, at Meadowland, were he to go there. Meadowland, where Marise lived.

"Are you all right, Lia?" Seth repeated patiently.

"No."

She'd burrowed her head deeper into the pillow, hiding

from him. Seth pulled free of her, went to the bathroom, then marched back into the bedroom; she was lying in exactly the same pose.

His heart now felt cold in his chest. Making love to Lia definitely hadn't been in his plans. Or in hers, he'd be willing to bet. In spite of himself, he glanced over at the clock. His plane was due to take off in less than two hours.

He knelt on the bed and tugged on the silken fall of her hair. "Look at me."

She reared up, her dark eyes hostile. "We're like a couple of alley cats—we can't keep doing this!"

"It's only the second time in eight years."

"We've only seen each other twice in eight years," she flashed with impeccable logic. "You can't meet Marise—I won't allow it. I won't have her hurt because you and I behave like sex maniacs."

"Listen to me, Lia," Seth said forcefully, and wondered who he was trying to convince, himself or her. "All the trappings of romance were in place this morning—tropical beach at dawn, you in that goddamned swimsuit, wet from the sea—what did you expect? Your farm won't be like that—it's domesticated, a family setting, you even have a nanny, for Pete's sake. I've steered clear of stuff like that for years. A total turnoff."

"If you're going to have anything to do with Marise, you're going to tell me why the mere thought of a nanny makes you go into orbit."

"I'll tell you what I choose to tell you, and no more."

She hated it when his eyes went as hard and sharp-edged as emeralds. "I call the shots as far as Marise is concerned," she announced with matching adamancy, and in a flurry of bare limbs rolled off the bed and grabbed for her swimsuit. It was cold and damp, gritty with sand. She yanked it up her body, wishing with all her heart she'd gone to any other island than this one for her yearly vacation.

Seth stood up, seizing her by the elbow. "I'll be in touch after your concerts and we'll make the arrangements then."

"No, Seth," she said softly, "first you'll find out what happened to my letters and you'll tell me about it. The how and the why."

"Twenty minutes of scorching sex sure hasn't affected your brain."

"I'm fighting for two—not just for myself."

With no idea where the words came from, Seth said, "What if I'm fighting for three?"

"You're not. So don't kid yourself."

She was right. He wasn't. "I've always dated malleable women who never raise their voices," he said caustically. "No danger of that with you."

"None whatsoever."

"Say it, Lia. Before you're the one who goes into orbit."

"A nice faraway orbit sounds like a fabulous idea. You can get in touch with me once I'm home from my concerts and I wish to heaven you'd put some clothes on."

Her eyes were dark pools of fury. He stepped closer. "We could shower together before you leave—that way we save water."

"Conservation's a very fine cause, but it's not my top priority right now."

"What is your top priority, darling Lia?"

If his eyes had been jewel-hard a few moments ago, they now held all the shifting greens of a tropical sea. "Darling Seth," she retorted, "it's to get out of here so I don't spend the rest of the day ravaging your body."

He lowered his head and kissed her with lazy sensuality. Then, taking his time, he nibbled his way along her lower lip, seeing with considerable satisfaction how her eyes were now blurred with desire. For once, he wasn't going to yield to that desire. He'd show her—and himself—that he could resist her.

"We both have to get out of here," he said agreeably. "I have a business to run and you have to practice. I'll see you in a week or so." Then he stepped back, hoping she couldn't hear the pounding of blood in his veins.

She was gaping at him, looking totally at a loss. He added kindly, "Shut your mouth, sweetheart, you look like a stranded fish. Enjoy the rest of your stay, won't you?"

She snapped, "I will. Without you. Dearest."

Then she whirled and stalked out the door, slamming it hard behind her. Seth winced at the noise and sank down on the bed. The empty bed. Which was rumpled, and smelled sweetly of Lia.

He should have canceled his jet. What was the use of being the boss if he couldn't do as he pleased?

He wasn't the boss where Lia was concerned. His glands were. Brute testosterone. Him and Australopithecus.

He loved the way she never gave an inch.

Loved it? What kind of language was that?

CHAPTER NINE

SETH marched up the steps, ignoring the stone lions at their base. The whole house—or, more accurately, the whole mansion—was made of stone. Like his mother's heart, he thought grimly, and let himself in with his key. He'd phoned Eleonore to let her know he was coming; he hadn't seen either of his parents for several months.

The entrance hall with its marble floor and enormous arched windows was intended to intimidate; the architecture as well as the rigidly formal gardens were, in his opinion, totally mismatched to their surroundings of ocean and woods. Surroundings that had allowed him the escape he'd needed as a little boy.

He took the wide oak stairs two at a time, loosening his tie as he went. He hadn't planned what he was going to say. He scarcely needed to.

Tapping on the door of his mother's private sitting room, he walked in without waiting for her to answer. Heavy velvet drapes and carved mahogany furniture fought against the light coming through the tall windows. Fought and won, Seth thought. "Hello, Mother," he said.

He dropped a dutiful kiss on her cheek. Every one of her iron-gray hairs was in place, her black Valentino suit was elegant without ostentation, and diamonds sparkled on her fingers. She said coolly, "Your tie's a disgrace."

He hauled it over his head and threw off his jacket; Eleonore always kept the room too warm for his taste. "I just flew in from the Caribbean."

"Would you like tea? A drink?"

"No. This isn't a social call." He paused for a moment, wishing, as he'd always wished, that he could see even a sliver of warmth in her cold blue eyes.

"Then why don't you come to the point?" she said.

"Eight years ago, in Paris, I had a brief affair with a woman whose name I never knew," Seth said bluntly. "She wrote to me two months later, to tell me she was pregnant. She sent one letter to my office, the other to this address. I never got either one. Did you by any chance intercept them?"

"Of course I did."

"Of course?" he repeated tersely.

"Some little nobody who plays the fiddle and gets herself pregnant with your child? You think I'd let her anywhere near the Talbot fortune?"

So his suspicions had been well-founded; Eleonore had cold-bloodedly destroyed two letters and thereby deprived him of any knowledge that he was about to become a father. He said at random, because he could scarcely take in her perfidy, "Lia's far from a nobody—she has an international reputation as a violinist."

"Then why didn't you know her name?" Eleonore flashed.

"She wanted to be anonymous—her fame was new to her then. I did my best to trace her, without success…if one thing's clear in all this mess, it's that Lia wasn't then, and isn't now, after my money."

"You're far too naïve! I opened the letter that came here, and went straight to your office to destroy the second one; fortunately, she'd mentioned she'd sent two."

"The child she was carrying—that was my child," Seth said harshly.

"I'm quite sure she had an abortion once she knew she wasn't getting a penny out of us."

"She didn't. My daughter—your granddaughter—is now seven years old. Her name is Marise."

"So when are you getting married, Seth, and making the child legitimate?"

Eleonore had always had the ability to get under his skin. "I'm not," Seth said, his voice rising. "You and father put me off marriage permanently. But I've been cheated out of seven years of my daughter's life because you destroyed those letters. How could you have done that?"

"Easily," Eleonore shrugged, "and I'd do it again."

"You would, wouldn't you? Luckily Lia didn't choose to emulate you and have an abortion."

Eleonore's voice was like a whiplash. "Just what do you mean by that?"

"That fight you and Father had when I was eight—I overheard it. I heard you tell him how you'd aborted his second child. A girl, you said. She would have been my sister."

"You were in bed asleep."

"I was hiding in the library, where I'd gone looking for a book. You destroyed a life because it would have inconvenienced you."

"I'd already produced an heir to the Talbot name—it was my duty to do so. But there was no need for a second child."

"Why do you think I've never married? Never wanted a child of my own? Could it possibly have anything to do with overhearing my own mother discuss how she'd cold-bloodedly rid herself of a child she considered nothing but a nuisance?"

"Don't blame me for your shortcomings!"

"Who else is there to blame?"

"Eavesdroppers get what they deserve."

"Isn't that the truth," Seth retorted, and took a deep breath. A shouting match hadn't been in his plans. He said evenly, "I want a signed confession from you, saying that you destroyed those two letters."

"Why should I do that?"

"Because if you don't, I'll make sure the information goes public."

Eleonore's breath hissed between her teeth. "You wouldn't."

"Try me."

"What will you do with it should I sign such a ridiculous document?"

"Show it to Lia. So she knows why I left her totally alone to deal with her pregnancy and our daughter."

"She's blackmailing you!"

"That's the last thing she'd ever do—Lia has ethics. Unlike you. Sign it, Mother, or I'll make sure every one of your high-class acquaintances finds out exactly what you did eight years ago. Tampering with the mail is a federal offence, by the way."

"Go to the desk and bring me my leather folder."

Seth did so, then sat like a stone as Eleonore wrote a single brief sentence on her elegant letterhead. She signed the crisp vellum, and passed it to him. "I hope that satisfies you," she said bitterly.

He read it, folded it and tucked it in his jacket pocket. "You're not even remotely sorry for what you did, are you?"

"I've already told you I'm not. Now that you've gotten what you came for, I'd suggest you leave."

"Did you ever love me?" Seth said very quietly.

Her eyes a glacial blue, she snapped, "I did my duty by you, Seth. What more do you want?"

What, indeed? Seth got to his feet, picking up his jacket and tie. "I'll let myself out," he said.

He strode out of the sitting room, closing the door with exaggerated gentleness behind him. But as he crossed the hallway, his father came out of the adjoining room. Allan Talbot was the last person Seth wanted to see right now. "Father," he said, dredging up his good manners with conventional politeness, "how are you?"

Allan had Seth's green eyes, coupled with auburn hair thickly threaded with gray; although he was nearly Seth's height, his shoulders had a perpetual stoop and his face was prematurely wrinkled. If Eleonore had seized control in their marriage, Allan had abdicated it in a way Seth had found difficult to respect; and all too often in Seth's youth, Allan had found solace in the most expensive of wines. Now Allan said with unusual forcefulness, "I need to talk to you."

"I'm in a—"

"Please, Seth."

Stifling a sigh, Seth followed Allan further down the wide hallway to the library where Allan spent most of his time. Allan closed the door behind him, shutting them in with the long-remembered odors of leather upholstery, old books and beeswax polish. "I overheard what you just told your mother," he said unevenly. "I'd seen your car outside, so I was looking for you. I never realized you knew what happened all those years ago—about the abortion, I mean. That was a terrible burden for a small boy to carry."

"It's a long time ago, Father."

"If I'd only known you'd heard every word your mother and I said...right here in this room." An old pain scored Allan's face. "That was the worst night of my life—and to find out that you witnessed it is almost more than I can bear."

"I survived," Seth said dryly. "As you see."

"I'd always wanted another child, Eleonore knew that. Once she'd told me what she'd done, I couldn't bring myself to get close to her again. To reach out to her in any way." He dashed a hand to his eyes, adding with scathing self-criticism, "I reached for the bottle instead."

"You're scarcely to be blamed."

"I wish I could agree. I couldn't bring myself to divorce her, either—what kind of man does that make me?"

"How about loyal?" Seth ventured, feeling his heart ache with unaccustomed sympathy. Had he ever really allowed himself to see his father's pain before?

"Gutless is a better word."

"You're being too harsh. The past is done with, over. Beating up on yourself doesn't accomplish anything."

"I'm not sure the past is ever over."

He, Seth, had certainly been living his life as though the past rode him like a millstone. He said awkwardly, "Why don't we change gears here, Father? You have a granddaughter now. A little girl called Marise who's seven years old and who inherited the Talbot green eyes."

Allan's eyes filmed with tears. "Have you seen her?"

"Not yet. Lia's being very protective of her, understandably so. For eight years she thought I'd abandoned any responsibility for that night in Paris and its outcome...until we met again by sheer chance a few days ago at White Cay, and it all came out in the open. But sooner or later I'm going to see Marise. I have to."

"I'd love to meet her," Allan said wistfully.

Seth took one more step into new territory. "Perhaps that can be arranged. Given time."

Clumsily Allan put an arm around his son's shoulders. "Marise," he whispered. "Such a pretty name."

"Her mother is the most beautiful woman in the world," Seth said hoarsely.

"You're in love with her."

"No, I'm not—I don't seem to have that ability. But I admire and respect her. And," Seth's smile was wry, "lust after her. That hasn't changed over the last eight years."

"Respect and passion aren't a bad basis for marriage."

"Lia doesn't want to get married."

"Then you'll have to change her mind, won't you? That shouldn't be any problem for the man who runs Talbot Holdings. Iron fist in the velvet glove, and all that."

"Lia's fists aren't what you'd call velvet and she doesn't bother with gloves," Seth said with a grin.

"She must be quite a woman."

"That's one way of describing her."

"I look forward to meeting her," Allan said. "Will you send me a photo of Marise, Seth? Of Lia, too, if you have one."

He didn't. "I'll send them to your private postbox," Seth said tautly. "Otherwise Mother'll tear them to shreds."

"What she did was unconscionable—you have every right to be angry."

"So do you."

Allan sighed. "The hard truth is, I still love her. Don't ask me why. But I do. Who knows, perhaps little Marise will cause some sort of miracle."

"I won't bring Marise into this house!"

Allan rubbed his forehead. "I'm so sorry, for so much," he said. "But you mustn't let my failings and Eleonore's keep you from your own happiness, Seth. That only compounds the tragedy."

Seth felt his throat tighten. He said roughly, "You know what? This is the nearest we've ever come to a real conversation."

Allan suddenly smiled, a smile that made him look years younger. "Good," he said. "Keep in touch, son. I'll travel anywhere at any time to meet my granddaughter."

The two men exchanged another unaccustomed hug, then Seth ran downstairs and let himself out. It was already growing dark and he had a long drive ahead of him. But plenty to think about on that drive, he realized, checking that he had the single piece of paper his mother had signed.

He was going to make sure Lia saw that piece of paper. Nor was he going to wait ten days for it to happen.

Quickly Seth punched in the numbers. The connection was made and the phone began to ring. The receiver was picked up and a woman's voice said crisply, "Lia d'Angeli."

His mouth dry, Seth said easily, "I'll meet you in half an hour at the Klimt Coffee House. It's right across from your hotel."

There was an instant of dead silence. "Seth, is this your idea of a joke?"

"We won't jump each other at the Klimt. I promise."

Lia scowled at the opposite wall of her hotel room and said the obvious. "You're in Vienna."

"Yep. Did you really think I'd wait until you came back?"

"Actually I did. Silly me. I can't meet you, I've got a rehearsal this afternoon and a concert tonight."

He kept his voice light with a huge effort. "So are you shacked up with Rosnikov?"

She made a very rude noise down the receiver. "Are you traveling with a malleable woman who never raises her voice?"

"I've discovered they bore me," he said meekly.

"And I don't?"

"Not so far."

"You have such a winning way with words."

"Spend half an hour with me and I'll see if I can improve," he said. "You can leave in lots of time for your rehearsal."

"I—dammit," she exploded, and slammed down the phone. The portrait on the opposite wall was of a plumply naked Renaissance woman with artless blue eyes and loopy blond curls; Lia glared at her and yanked open the doors of the immense baroque wardrobe in which her few clothes hung like orphans. Seth was here. In Vienna.

She didn't have to meet him.

If she didn't turn up, she wouldn't put it past him to storm the hotel.

She couldn't allow him to come to her room. It had a bed in it.

She snagged her jersey pants and tunic from the hanger; they were a rich shade of aubergine. Quickly she dressed, making up her face with care and leaving her hair loose. Then she flung a glittering silver-embroidered scarf over her shoulders and jammed silver hoops into her earlobes. The supple leather boots she'd bought in Paris were the final touch.

She looked very classy. No way was she going to let Seth Talbot know she was a mass of pre-concert nerves.

He'd be a useful distraction, she thought. Anything to make the hours pass until tonight.

Pulling a rude face at the portrait, Lia left the room. Her hotel was in the Belvedere district, near the monumental Musikverein, where she would be performing tonight. Trying to breathe slowly and deeply, as her coach had taught her, Lia walked to Karlsplatz, mentally saluting the two carved angels at the entrance to the magnificent Karlskirche. Then she stopped to smooth the curves of the Henry Moore sculptures by the pond.

The spring sunshine was warm on her face; the ducks were in an amatory mood. Why had she thought about Seth entirely too much in the past few days?

Maybe when she saw him again, she'd find some answers.

The Klimt Coffee House was one of her favorites, not the least for its fine quality reproductions of the artist's fiercely beautiful portraits of women. She could add to that the high ceilings and elegantly arched windows, the civilized murmur of conversation and the delicious odor of Turkish coffee. Her eyes flicked around the room.

Seth was seated beneath a huge reproduction of *The Kiss,* that unabashedly erotic blend of golds and reds depicting a man and a woman so entwined as to be almost indistinguishable. Her heels clicking on the marble floor, she walked toward Seth. He got up to meet her, kissing her on both cheeks.

"What's up?" he said abruptly. "You'll do fine tonight."

Scowling at him, she replied, "Is it so pitifully obvious that I'm a mass of nerves?"

"To me it is—although I've never been known for empathy."

She raised her brows. "Well," she remarked, "I should've realized we wouldn't waste time with small talk...I'll have a Turkish coffee and a big slice of Sachertorte."

"Chocolate cake layered with apricot jam?" Seth said, amused. "You're in a bad way."

She was rhythmically tapping the tabletop with her fingernails; he'd never found her to be a jittery woman. "It's always this way before a concert," she said. "I'll be fine once I start to play."

"So there's a cost to being the best."

"Right now I'm not convinced it's worth it."

Seth dropped his hand over hers, stilling her restless movements. "I wish I could help."

Very briefly her fingers curled into his palm. A wicked glint in her eye, she said, "You're distracting me. That helps."

He raised her hand to his lips, kissing her fingers one by one. "A man's gotta do what a man's gotta do."

Her cheeks, which had been too pale, were now patched with hectic color. Flustered, she said, "You gotta order my cake, that's what you gotta do."

"Lia, you disappoint me—you'd choose Sachertorte over seduction?" Seth said, grinning as he signaled the waiter. After he'd given their order, he drew a plain white envelope from his jacket pocket, his smile fading. "This is for you."

She took the envelope from him as warily as if it were a

poisonous snake. Then, with sudden decisiveness, she tore it open and read the words on the single sheet of embossed notepaper. "Your mother destroyed both of my letters," she said blankly.

"Yes. I wish to God she hadn't."

Lia's own mother, for all her enormous professionalism and high standards, had always loved her only child and wished the best for her. "How could your mother have done that? Intervened so cruelly—altered the course of three lives, one of them her own son's?"

"I don't know, Lia—I don't have the answer."

"It was a vicious thing to do," Lia said faintly. "All those weeks I waited for you to get in touch with me, and tried so hard not to hate you…then feeling utterly alone when Marise was born…"

Her eyes were shining with tears. "I'd have been there for you, had I known," Seth said hoarsely. "I swear it, Lia."

"But you didn't know, because your mother destroyed my letters. Why, Seth? Why?"

He'd realized this question would arise; realized, too, that to attempt an answer would be to reveal things about himself he'd always kept private. Stumbling a little at first, Seth began to describe the stone mansion, Eleonore's coldness, Allan's subservience and his own escape as a boy to the woods and the shore. The waiter brought their order, and still he talked, encouraged by Lia's complete and unforced attention. Then he looked up, knowing he was making a momentous decision. "Do you remember I asked you, when I found out about Marise, if you'd considered having an abortion?"

"Yes. You looked…overwhelmed when I told you I hadn't."

He forced himself to keep going. "When I was eight my mother had one…I think it broke my father's heart when he found out. I overheard them the night she told him."

This time Lia covered his hand with hers. "Seth, I'm so sorry," she whispered.

"I can't ever thank you enough for having Marise," he said in a raw voice, "just as I'll always regret I wasn't there for you."

A tear dropped from her dark lashes to the back of his hand. He gazed at it, seeing how the light from the chandelier had refracted into a tiny rainbow in its midst. Why had he told her something he'd kept secret for years? And why did a single tear feel like the most precious of gifts? "This is the last thing we should be talking about when you've got a concert to-night," he muttered.

"Is it? Why, Seth?"

"Because I've upset you."

"You trusted me enough to share what must have been a huge trauma for a little boy," she said in a low voice.

"Telling you hasn't changed anything."

"Change happens, whether you want it to or not," she said implacably. "Do you have a ticket for the concert?"

"No. I prefer CDs. Music at a distance."

"I'll see there's a ticket at the door for you."

His eyes narrowed; if she could throw down a gauntlet, so could he. "When do I get to meet Marise?"

"I haven't told her about you yet."

A knife seemed to have lodged in his gut. "You haven't? Why not?"

She said defensively, "I wanted to hear about the letters first."

"Is that the only reason?"

Her lashes dropped to hide her eyes. "When I got back from the Caribbean, it was all too new—I had to deal with my own feelings first."

He purposely didn't ask what those feelings were. "But you won't keep me from her?"

"I don't know." Fury smoldered in her eyes. "Am I sup-posed to ignore what your mother did?"

"I'm not responsible for my mother's actions," Seth said tightly.

"She's part of your family. Her, and your father."

"He wants to meet Marise, too."

Lia was rapping her nails on the table again. Was she in danger of blaming Seth for his mother's crimes? "I can't deal with this right now."

"I shouldn't have shown you my mother's confession. The timing's lousy."

"I'm the one who demanded proof. I can scarcely complain when I get it."

"You can complain all you like," Seth said. "For seven years you were a single mother as a direct result of my mother's actions. How the hell do you think that makes me feel?"

"I have no idea," Lia said tautly. "You're far too adept at keeping your feelings hidden."

With no idea where the words came from, Seth said, "I'll go to the concert."

Letting out her breath in a tiny sigh, Lia angled the last mouthful of luscious chocolate icing onto her fork. She'd learned a great deal about Seth in the last few minutes: information that only served to bind him closer to her, in ways that both intrigued and terrified her. Frowning, she said, "Why do men have to be so complicated?"

"To keep women guessing. Want another piece of cake?"

"I wouldn't get into my dress if I did. It's a very slinky dress, and you can come to the reception after the concert if you want to."

"Providing we leave it together."

She raised her brows. "Autocratic, aren't you?"

"When it suits me."

"So you want a commitment from me."

"Only about the reception."

"You've made it all too clear you won't commit yourself

to me in any other way. But if I let you anywhere near Marise, you can't operate like that with her."

"I won't," he said harshly. "That's a promise."

Could she believe him? Was she in Karlsplatz, Vienna, sitting across the table from the man who'd been haunting her dreams? "Suppose I allow you to see Marise," she said. "Suppose you and she develop a relationship, and in the course of that, you and I end up having an affair. What happens when you get tired of me, Seth?"

"We'll deal with it when it happens."

"I won't be dumped like so much garbage."

"I won't dump you like you're garbage!"

"Well, that got a reaction," Lia said.

He ran his fingers around his collar. "I'd like to be in bed with you right now."

"One of my professors at Juilliard said in class one day, peering at us over the rims of his glasses, *No sex before a concert. It drains the music of its passion.* Too bad, Seth."

"So by abstaining, I'm doing my bit for Brahms?"

"We all have to sacrifice for art."

"You can always make me laugh," Seth said in a voice of discovery. "Sex and laughter—that's quite a combo."

"Almost as good as Turkish coffee and chocolate cake." Lia pushed back her chair. "I've got to go. The rehearsal's in a couple of hours and I do breathing exercises beforehand."

"A concert brings you face to face with yourself," he ventured.

Surprised and pleased that he'd understood, she said, "That's right—what do I have to give to the music? Will it find me wanting?" Her mouth quirked. "Minor little questions like that."

Seth got to his feet, and, ignoring the other customers, kissed her full on the mouth. "You couldn't possibly disappoint yourself, the audience or the music," he said. Reaching in his pocket, he took out a small box. "This is for you," he added, not meeting her eyes. "To bring you luck tonight."

She was staring at the box, making no move to take it. "Seth, I can't take a gift from you."

"Why not? Do you think I'm trying to bribe you?"

"Of course not." She looked right at him. "You're as different from your mother as you can be."

He pushed the box toward her, more affected by her simple endorsement than he cared to show. "Open it, Lia...it's nothing much."

She took the box and flipped the lid up. Earrings, each a single, multifaceted diamond, flashed colored fire in a bed of black velvet. "They're gorgeous," she exclaimed. "But—"

"They reminded me of you." His crooked smile made her, inexplicably, want to weep. "When you feel passionately about something, even your hair seems to spark."

She blurted, "I should have believed you about the letters without having to have proof—I'm truly sorry I didn't."

"You're forgiven," he said lightly.

Lia took a deep breath. "The earrings are lovely, Seth, I'll be happy to wear them tonight...thank you."

He kissed her again. "Too many sexy paintings in this room—you'd better go. I'll stay here for a while and read the paper. *Auf Wiedersehen,* beautiful Lia."

Her cheeks were bright scarlet, clashing with her outfit. She made a sound that would have translated in any language as *humph,* and walked out of the coffeehouse with perfect aplomb.

A foolish smile plastered on his face, Seth sat down again. He'd given a woman diamonds, revealed a lifelong secret and agreed to go to a concert. None of these behaviors was typical of him.

And he was going to leave the reception with Lia.

The professor hadn't said she couldn't have sex after the concert.

CHAPTER TEN

AFTER the intermission, the orchestra tuned their instruments, then silence fell over the house. Seth sat still in his box seat, his eyes glued to the stage, which was crowded with tuxedoed musicians. He felt as nervous as if it were he who was about to play.

All this time Lia had been waiting backstage. How did she stand it?

In a tap of high heels Lia walked out onto the stage, followed by Ivor Rosnikov and the conductor. She was wearing a smoky purple satin dress with inserts in the full-length skirt that were filled with tiny pleats; they kicked out as she moved. Her bare arms were as pale as ivory, her hair drawn back severely from her face. The diamond earrings he'd given her sparkled in her lobes.

The conductor adjusted the score, Rosnikov settled himself at his cello, and after a quick glance at his two soloists, the conductor raised his baton. The orchestra played the first somber, flowing notes. Seth sat very still, waiting. Lia, also waiting, looked indrawn and remote.

Why would she need him, Seth, when she had her music? She'd never fall in love with him; at least he was safe from that complication.

As the orchestra fell silent, Rosnikov began to play a rich, sonorous melody. Lia raised her bow and joined him, the two instruments separating only to blend, blending only to separate. She and Ivor, Seth saw in an uprush of heated and primitive emotion, were also completely in tune with each other, making frequent eye contact in a way that seemed to him immensely intimate.

He, Seth, could never share such intimacy with Lia; he was, in comparison with Ivor Rosnikov, a musical ignoramus.

The cellist was, subtly, both more handsome and younger-looking in the flesh than in his publicity photos. The emotion that was surging through Seth was jealousy.

He'd never in his life been jealous of another man. For a very simple reason: he'd never cared enough about a woman to feel jealous.

Lia was different. Hadn't he known that from the first moment he'd laid eyes on her?

The wonderfully lyrical second movement swept to its conclusion, followed by a joyful finale that brought a smile to Lia's face; it was achingly obvious that she was doing exactly what she'd been born to do. The final triumphant chords filled the magnificent hall; there was an instant of total and respectful silence before the audience erupted into a storm of applause.

Lia and Ivor had linked hands; the conductor stepped down from the podium, kissing Lia on the cheek. Ivor then leaned over and kissed her full on the mouth, his hands clasping her waist. Seth's fingers dug into his palms. How dare he?

Not that Lia looked as though she was objecting to this public display of—what? Affection? Mutual achievement? Or just plain sex? Rosnikov's dark locks and romantically pale face had women flocking to him the length of Europe. Why should Lia be immune?

The last thing Seth wanted to do was stand around at a stuffy reception watching Ivor Rosnikov drape himself all over Lia; and simultaneously having to subdue the urge to throttle, publicly, a world-famous cellist. Would Lia even miss him if he didn't go? He very much doubted that she would.

He, Seth, was superfluous to her world. That was what he'd learned tonight by attending her concert. But was running away from that world an option?

He'd never been one to back down from a challenge. Seth went to the reception, where he downed a glass of inferior champagne and disdained to join the crowd that eddied around Lia and Ivor, and that included members of the media whose flashlights went off with monotonous regularity. The whole time, the cellist's arm lay over Lia's bare shoulders. Throttling Rosnikov began to seem entirely too merciful. For the sake of his sanity, Seth wandered over to a group of acquaintances on the far side of the room, stood with his back to Lia and talked about the economy as though his life depended on it.

Gradually the crowd thinned. Then, behind him, Seth heard the click of heels on the marble floor. As he turned, Lia said, "Ivor, I'd like you to meet my friend, Seth Talbot...as I mentioned, Seth and I are going out together after the reception. Seth, Ivor Rosnikov."

Seth had to admire her gall. He smiled at the cellist and produced some conventional words of congratulation about the concert. "How is it you know Lia?" Ivor asked in his heavily accented English.

"We met some time ago," Seth said casually. "Though we've seen nothing of each other for years."

"Yet you take her out tonight?"

"Yes," said Seth, "I'm taking her out tonight."

"Then I am—how do you say?—the loser," Ivor said, and with elaborate gallantry raised Lia's hand to his lips. "I will see you in Hamburg the day after tomorrow, *liebchen*," he said, smiling deep into her eyes. Baring his teeth at Seth, he added, "You will look after her. Late hours are not good."

"I'm sure Lia is quite capable of deciding how late she'll stay out," Seth said amicably. Punching the guy on the nose instead of throttling him wouldn't do, either. Bad publicity for all concerned.

Ten minutes later, he and Lia were walking into the cool of a spring night outside the imposing terra-cotta and cream façade of Musikverein. She glanced around to check that they were alone. "Where are we going?"

"Do you want highbrow, lowbrow or somewhere in between?"

"Middle. With grub and a dance floor."

"Okay. Want to walk?"

"Providing it's not halfway across Vienna, yes." Falling into step beside him, yet preserving a careful distance between them, Lia added, "What did you think of the concert?"

"You played extraordinarily well," he said truthfully.

"I missed a note in the 54th bar of the third movement."

"I didn't notice," he said dryly.

"You didn't like Ivor."

"Any more than Ivor liked me."

"You looked like a couple of roosters about to square off."

She looked as belligerent as a rooster herself. "How long were you his lover?" Seth asked. "Or are you still?"

"What are you—the lawyer for the prosecution?"

"You sure weren't objecting to being kissed by him in full view of two thousand people."

It had been a very long day. "What was I supposed to do?" Lia retorted. "Whack him with my violin?"

"Is he a good lover?"

"I wouldn't know—since I've never been his lover. Apart from anything else, his ego's so big there'd be no room for me."

"You and I are in perfect agreement on that point," Seth growled, and smothered a relief strong enough for ten men.

Lia stopped on the sidewalk, her dark eyes level. "You congratulated Ivor for his playing. But I had to ask before you'd tell me what you thought about mine."

He'd hurt her; that was what she was saying. "You think I was going to bare my soul in front of that Paganini lookalike?"

"So bare it now."

"Dammit, Lia, I felt the way I always feel when you play—only more so because you were right there in front of me. The club we're going to is just down here."

She planted her feet. "Keep talking—how do you always feel?"

"As though you know me through and through. As though all my defenses are useless and my soul an open book. Is that what you want to know?" he said furiously.

She bit her lip. "Don't hate me for it."

"Why don't you give me a list of your various lovers in the last eight years—in case I meet up with any of them at one of these fancy receptions."

She drew her lacy white shawl closer around her shoulders. "No list. No lovers."

"Oh, sure."

She said irritably, "I need to sit down, take off my shoes, have at least two lagers and a big plate of *rindsgulasch* with extra dumplings. Are you or are you not taking me to this club?"

He seized her by the elbow. "You must have had a lover—it was eight years, Lia!"

"I know how long it was. I was a single mother most of that time, remember?"

"There were lots of times when you were on the opposite side of the Atlantic from your daughter. Free to bed whom you pleased."

The music she'd played was still coursing through her veins. Lia said flatly, "I discovered passion with you and I wasn't about to settle for less."

He felt as though she'd just hit him hard in the chest with a double bass. "Is that true?"

"I try not to tell lies. Lager and dumplings, Seth."

Reeling, Seth tucked her arm through his and walked the last two blocks in silence. The club was crowded and noisy. Skillfully Seth threaded through the patrons to an empty table near the dance floor, got the waiter's attention and placed their order. "Shoes off yet?" he said economically.

"You bet. Do you believe me?"

"About the lovers? Yes."

"Good."

He'd have hated hearing the names of her lovers; equally, he'd hated being told there'd been none. Because it scared the pants off him to find out she'd been faithful to him for eight long years?

He was a yellow-bellied coward, Seth thought scathingly, watching as the waiter brought two tankards of beer and set them on the table, the froth overflowing. Lia raised hers and drank deep, the muscles moving in her throat as she swallowed.

Her exquisite, ivory-smooth throat.

She said edgily, "Is something wrong?"

"Did you fall in love with me in Paris?"

"No," she said. "But it was as far from casual as it could be. And not just because of Marise."

Wasn't the same true for him? But he'd gotten his life back on track, finally, and there it had remained ever since. Until he'd seen her in her turquoise suit swimming as gracefully as a dolphin in the sea.

Seth took a big slug of beer. "Have you ever fallen in love?"

"No," Lia said, her fingers tightening around the tankard. She wasn't going to start now by falling in love with Seth, either. She'd be out of her mind to do that. The man was as barricaded as a fortress.

"You've got your music—no room for a mere man alongside that."

"That's not true," she said sharply. "I love Marise with all my heart...why should a man be any different?"

Was he now going to be jealous of a seven-year-old child? With a sigh of exasperation Seth took another gulp of beer. "Let's change the subject."

"Better still, let's dance."

Discovering he craved action, too, Seth led her out onto the crowded floor, where to the raunchy blast of disco and the flash of strobes, they gyrated and swung. Her hair began to slip from its pins; her body, in the clinging satin of her gown, was unbearably sexy. He was going to end the evening in her bed, thought Seth. But this time, it would be a controlled decision with no postmortems.

He leaned closer to Lia, raising his voice. "Our food's arrived."

She gave him a brilliant smile, twirled and fell back into his arms. "Lead me to it."

Yeah, he thought. In bed, that's where we belong.

At their table, Lia tucked into her stew and dumplings, washing it down with liberal quantities of lager. "Luscious," she said, licking her fork. "I want dessert now. *Apfelstrudel.* Warm with whipped cream on top and a big glass of Riesling to go with it."

"A woman of immoderate appetites."

She leaned over and kissed him with sensuous pleasure. "Dumplings, lager and you."

"In that order?"

"Tonight."

"Is this how you always relax after a concert?"

She laughed. "I usually go back to my hotel room and pace the floor, agonizing over all the mistakes I made. This is much more fun."

Pink Floyd throbbed through the smoky air. "It ain't exactly Brahms."

"We could dance again."

Seth ordered dessert and a bottle of Riesling, and this time took Lia in his arms on the dance floor. They were the only couple in formal clothes in the entire club and he, too, was having fun.

Not a word his parents had understood.

The level of Riesling sank in the bottle, Lia drinking most of it. The wine loosened her tongue. She talked about the ups and downs of her career and the costs to her personal life; she described some of the hilarious contretemps of working with autocratic conductors and temperamental pianists; noticeably, she didn't talk about Marise. She also flagged the waiter and ordered a double crème de menthe, a choice that made Seth shudder. He, by now, was drinking coffee. One of them ought to stay sober, he thought, amused that she simply became wittier as her words began, very slightly, to slur. "Lia," he said finally, "I think I should take you back to your hotel. Ivor wouldn't approve of the lateness of the hour."

"I'm flying to Hamburg at noon."

"You and your hangover."

She blinked at him. "Am I drunk?"

"A reasonable facsimile thereof."

"Don't use such big words," she said querulously.

"Okay. You're pretty close to plastered."

"It's all your fault."

"Yeah?"

"I have no idea what to do about you."

"Welcome to the club," Seth said wryly.

She gave him a big smile. "You're really cute, though."

Lia, sober, would never use a word like cute. "Thank you," Seth said solemnly.

"But I sure don't like your family." She swallowed the last of the sticky green liqueur, licking the rim of the glass. "Every now and then it hits me, what your mother did. The pain she caused because she was afraid I'd sink my sharp little claws into her money...aren't you absolutely furious with her?"

"Yes," said Seth, not liking the way the conversation had turned.

"Yes," Lia mimicked. "Is that all you can say?"

"You think I'm totally unfeeling?" Seth said violently. "I can hardly bear to think about it. About you, alone with a new baby, thinking I didn't even care enough to pick up the phone—for God's sake, Lia, give me a break."

Lia looked at him owlishly. "I pushed a button there."

Seth scowled at her. "You're cut off. Black coffee from now on."

"Ugh—at this time of night?"

"In that case, it's time to leave."

She wrinkled her nose. "I'm in the mood to seduce you. 'Cause the only time I'm not confused is when we're in bed together."

"That goes for me, too."

"I love what we do in bed," she said chirpily.

Their neighbors at the next table were unabashedly listening. "So do I," said Seth.

"Why are we sitting here, then?"

Seth dealt with the bill and got up, tucking her shawl around her shoulders. She lurched to her feet. "Ouch," she said, "I wish they'd turn off the strobes, they're making me dizzy."

Seth, wisely, didn't suggest that lager, Riesling and crème de menthe might have some connection to dizziness. He put an arm firmly around Lia's waist, steered her toward the door and quickly flagged a taxi; she was in no shape to walk. In the back seat, she put her head on his shoulder and fell instantly asleep.

None of the malleable women he'd dated had ever drunk too much. Neither had they played their guts out in front of two thousand people; or made love with Lia's generosity and wild abandon.

By the time he got Lia to her hotel room, she was paper-pale. "I sh—shouldn't have had the crème de menthe," she muttered and headed for the bathroom. Seth turned down the bed, found her deliciously lacy nightgown under the pillow and briefly held it to his face. He wanted to see her wearing it; then strip it from her body. But tonight wasn't the night.

When she next made love with him, she was going to be wide-awake and fully aware of what she was doing.

He wrote her a quick note, propping it up on the bedside table. Then she emerged from the bathroom, sagged into his arms and said muzzily, "Your eyes are the same color as crème de menthe. Turn off the light and come to bed with me."

Seth made a soothing and noncommittal noise in his throat as he pulled her evening dress over her head. Her silk underwear made his head swim; swiftly he unclasped her bra and slipped the nightgown on. As he eased her down on the bed, he noticed with huge tenderness that her dark lashes were already drifting to her cheeks. After peeling off her stockings, he covered her with the blanket. "Sleep well, darling Lia," he said.

But Lia was already asleep.

At nine o'clock the next morning, a knock came at Lia's door. She peered through the peephole, already knowing who it would be. "Good morning, Seth," she said pleasantly.

His jaw tight, he thrust a newspaper at her. "Have you seen this?"

"Yes. Don't worry about it. It happened once before and the fuss died down in no time."

On the front page of the tabloid, beneath a color photo of Rosnikov kissing Lia, were inch-tall headlines insinuating that the cellist was the father of Lia's child. "Don't worry about it?" Seth snarled. "My daughter's being subjected to the gutter press and all you can say is don't worry about it?"

"This is Austria. Not New York. No one at home will see

it," Lia said reasonably, wishing her headache would go away. Not that she didn't deserve the headache. She was never going near crème de menthe again.

Trying to change the subject, she added, "The reviews of the concert were good, weren't they?"

"Lia, I won't tolerate this kind of gossip about Marise."

"Why are you so upset? It's my problem, not yours."

He felt as though she'd punched him, hard. "Marise is my daughter, too—don't you think it's about time you admitted that? I'm going to meet her, Lia. Whether you want me to or not." Allan, his father, might have allowed Eleonore to walk all over him. He, Seth, wasn't about to let Lia do the same. Marise was too important. Too essential, he thought, and wondered where that particular word had come from.

"We'll see," Lia said, her jaw a stubborn jut.

"Don't try and stop me," he said very quietly. "You'll regret it if you do."

"Are you threatening me?"

"I'm telling you the truth."

"You're forgetting that Marise has a say here," Lia pointed out. Poking the tabloid with one finger, she added, "In the meantime, you're blowing this way out of proportion."

"It's untenable—a seven-year-old's name smeared on the front page of a cheap rag."

Her nostrils flared. Her temper rose to meet his. "So what am I supposed to do? Marry Rosnikov just to keep the newspapers quiet?"

"Marry me, instead," Seth said.

The words echoed in his head. What in hell had possessed him to say them? He didn't want to marry Lia. He didn't want to marry anyone.

"No, thanks," she said.

Did she have to answer so promptly? Did he mean so little to her that a proposal of marriage didn't even make her blink? "So much for that idea," he said sarcastically.

"Oh, come off it," she flared. "If I'd said yes, you'd be clocking a four-minute mile to the airport right now."

That she was probably right only infuriated him all the more. "That's precisely where I'm going...I'll call you on the fifteenth and we'll set up a meeting with Marise. Who, I sincerely hope, will remain ignorant of all this garbage." He tossed the tabloid onto Lia's bed.

"I protect her from as much of the world's garbage as I can," Lia snapped. "But I'm not omnipotent, Seth. The world exists, and all children have to lose their innocence." Her face suddenly changed. "As you did," she whispered, resting one hand on his sleeve. "I'm so sorry, I wasn't thinking."

The last thing Seth wanted was sympathy. He picked up her hand and let it drop by her side. "I hope Hamburg goes well," he said coldly.

"I'll say hello to Ivor for you."

Her cheeks were bright pink with temper. Seth planted a very angry kiss full on her lips, feeling heat rip through his body straight to his loins. Then he turned on his heel and left the room, shutting the door with a definitive snap.

He ran down the stairs at a reckless speed and strode through the lobby into the spring sunshine. He'd had more than enough of Vienna. Manhattan, he thought. That's where he was going next. Home, where he knew which way was up.

CHAPTER ELEVEN

"LET's go see the daffodils, Mum."

"Sure," Lia said, smiling fondly at her daughter. Marise was wearing her new yellow boots and slicker, her brown curls tucked under a sou'wester. Lia took her own slicker off the hook and grabbed an umbrella before they walked outdoors.

She took a deep breath. Wet soil, new leaves and the promise of spring. If only she could simply enjoy it.

But she couldn't. She had to tell Marise about Seth.

He wasn't going to go away. Not this time.

Trying to calm her nerves, Lia waited until she and Marise were kneeling down picking some of the daffodils that bloomed among the birch trees. Rain pattered on the umbrella. "Marise," she said, "I have some big news for you."

"Did I pass my math test?"

Lia laughed ruefully. "You aced English, that's all I know. This is about something else."

Marise had always been sensitive to shades of feeling. She buried her nose in a wet yellow trumpet, her green eyes wary. "You're not sick like Mary Blunden's mother, are you?"

"No, I'm fine—I was talking to Mrs. Blunden yesterday and she's getting out of hospital very soon, so that's good news. This is about something else. It's about your father, Marise."

Marise's dark lashes, so like her mother's, dropped to hide her eyes. "What about him?"

"Years ago, when I realized I was pregnant with you, I wrote and told him about you. He never answered my letters."

"He didn't want me," Marise said with irrefutable logic.

"That's what I thought at the time. But I was wrong. Some-one took the letters before he could read them. So it wasn't his fault that he never got in touch with me."

"How'd you find that out?" Marise asked with a touch of belligerence.

"I met him again, by chance, when I was at White Cay. Then I saw him last week in Vienna. He showed me proof about the letters. I couldn't let you go on thinking he stayed away from you on purpose because he didn't care about you— that's not true."

"Oh," said Marise. Methodically she started shredding the petals from a daffodil. "Will he come to my school? So the other kids can see I've got a real dad?"

Lia's heart clenched. Feeling her way, she said, "Would you like him to do that?"

"Mmm...I'm the only one in the whole school who doesn't have a father somewhere. The kids tease me sometimes, and call me names."

Lia could imagine all too easily what those names might be. "You've never told me that before," she said with careful restraint.

"What was the use?"

What indeed? Lia snapped off a white narcissus and added it to her bouquet. It would seem the decision had been made for her: she had to allow Seth to meet Marise, for her daughter's sake. "I expect he'd go to your school," she said. "He really wants to meet you."

Marise sat down hard on the wet ground. "I won't know what to say to him."

"He may not know what to say to you, either. Not the first time. But, providing you're willing, he'd like to keep on seeing you—he's based in Manhattan, so you could get together quite often if you wanted to."

"All three of us."

"Sometimes I wouldn't be there," Lia said casually.

"Are you going to marry him?"

"No." With a nasty clench of her stomach, Lia remembered how Seth had asked her to marry him, and how quickly she'd brushed him off.

"What's his name?"

"Seth Talbot."

Marise now looked frightened. "He'll change everything."

Lia could have denied this. But within appropriate bounds, she'd always tried to tell her daughter the truth. "He'll change some things, yes."

"Does he look like me?"

Lia had been prepared for this, and had gone on the Internet for a photo of Seth. She'd zoomed in on him, and printed his image in full color. He was standing in his office in a pinstriped suit, the Manhattan skyline in the background. His thick blond hair looking encouragingly untidy; his eyes were a startlingly clear green. "That's him," Lia said.

"He's awfully big."

"He's tall, yes. But he's not mean, not like Tommy Evans. He'd be good to you, sugarplum."

Tommy Evans was the local bully. "His eyes are like mine. If he's so great, why don't you want to marry him?"

"You have to be in love to get married."

Marise frowned at the photo. "Am I s'posed to love him?"

Her daughter had a penchant for asking difficult questions. "Love isn't instant—it takes time. Perhaps you could start out by liking him. We could meet him in Stoneybrook, at the café here—you always enjoy their tuna melt sandwich."

Marise looked even more frightened. "When?"

"I'll call him when we go back to the house. How about Saturday for lunch?"

"I—I guess so. Can I tell Suzy about him? And show her the photo?"

Suzy was Marise's best friend. "Sure you can," Lia said and passed over the photo, watching as Marise jammed it into the pocket of her slicker.

"Can I go see Suzy now?"

"Just for a little while. Then you have homework to do."

Motherhood, so Lia had already discovered, meant accepting that her daughter might possibly tell Suzy more about her feelings than she'd tell Lia. They walked through the woods to the adjoining property, where Suzy lived, talking about anything other than Seth, Marise clutching a bouquet of daffodils for Suzy's mother. Then Lia went back home. Not giving herself time to think, she picked up the phone and dialed Seth's private line at work.

"Talbot," he barked.

"This is Lia."

Seth's heart did an Olympic high jump in his chest. "It's only the fourteenth."

"I talked to Marise today. We'll meet you for lunch at the Maplewood Café in Stoneybrook. On Saturday. Would noon give you enough time to get there?"

A lump the size of a small mountain had lodged itself in his throat. "Yes," he said, "I'll be there."

Quickly she gave him directions. He said choppily, "Does she want to meet me?"

"She's scared. Wary. But she'll be fine."

"Not half as scared as I am," Seth said.

"You'll both be fine."

"Last time I talked to you, you were hellbent on keeping me a thousand miles away from her—what happened?"

"She wants you to go to her school. So the kids know she's got a real dad just like everyone else." Lia's voice faltered. "They've been calling her names, Seth—I didn't know anything about it until today."

Seth's expletive hung in the air. "Children can be crueler than any adult ever thought of being."

"Will you do that for her?"

"Sure I will." It wasn't the best time for Seth to realize he'd do anything for Lia's daughter. He said abruptly, "How was Hamburg?"

"Once I got over the hangover, it went well."

"Whenever you look into my eyes are you going to be reminded of crème de menthe?"

"Time will tell."

His voice hardened. "I notice you're not suggesting we meet at Meadowland."

It would have made more sense, giving them all some much-needed privacy. "No...I'm not ready for you to be here yet."

"Have I got to earn the right?"

She flinched at the bite in his voice. "I don't know. I just don't know."

Quite suddenly he'd had enough. "Saturday at noon," he said brusquely. "I'll get there a bit early so I don't keep Marise waiting."

Lia said stiffly, "That's a good idea. Goodbye, Seth."

"Bye."

She plunked the receiver back in its cradle and stared at the raindrops weeping down the windowpane. Three days from now she'd see Seth again. But she wouldn't be able to touch him, or speak to him privately.

She'd be sharing him with Marise.

Marise's fingers were cold in Lia's as they walked into the café with its cheerful decor of ruffled curtains and checkered tablecloths. Seth was sitting at the table by the window that offered the most privacy. He got to his feet as he saw them come in the door.

Lia threaded her way across the room, smiling at a couple of acquaintances. He said easily, "Lia...nice to see you," leaned over and kissed her on the cheek. Then he hunkered down and smiled at Marise. "Hello, Marise," he said softly. "We should have met a long time before this...I'm sorry we didn't."

Marise gazed at him with her big green eyes; they were, Lia saw, giving nothing away. "Mum told me about the letters. Why did somebody do that?"

It didn't occur to him to lie. "My mother had very definite ideas about the woman I should marry, and your mother wasn't it. So she destroyed your mother's letters to me."

"Just like in a book," Marise said. "She was the villain."

"I guess so."

"The kids at school tease me 'cause I don't have a father."

Seth grimaced. "I'm sorry about that, too. Very sorry."

Marise glanced up at her mother. "Can I have a tuna melt sandwich and a chocolate milkshake?"

"Sure," Lia said. "But we'd better give Seth the chance to read the menu."

He'd practically memorized it while he was waiting for them. "I'm going to have a chicken burger with fries and coffee."

"Fries are bad for you," Marise said primly.

"Marise..." Lia said.

"They are. Miss Brenton said so in health class."

"Miss Brenton is right," Seth said. "But sometimes I break the rules. Do you ever break the rules, Marise?"

She wriggled in her seat and said with killing politeness, "That's a secret between me and my friend Suzy. Do you have a best friend?"

"A good friend of mine lives in Berlin. He introduced me to classical music a couple of years ago."

"So you don't see him very often," Marise said crushingly.

"Not as often as I'd like."

"Suzy lives next door."

That seemed to be the end of that particular conversation. To his huge relief Seth saw the waitress approach. They all gave their orders, then into the silence Lia said, "Seth loves to swim, Marise."

"I can do the backstroke," Marise said.

"Where do you swim?" Seth asked.

"We have a pool at home."

Lia smiled. "I won the Finlandia competition last year. Sibelius paid for our pool."

"When you do the backstroke," Seth said, "it's hard to see where you're going."

"Not if you look over your shoulder."

Lia said easily, "Here comes your milkshake, Marise. You're getting pretty good at diving, too."

"I don't have to hold my nose anymore."

The conversation labored on, relieved by the arrival of the food. It was horribly clear to Seth that Marise wasn't giving him an inch...and why should she? For years his absence had caused her grief. Intertwined with grief, he'd be willing to bet, was anger. He was turning into a child psychologist, he thought mockingly, as he tucked into his fries.

Marise was eyeing them. He said mildly, "Help yourself if you want a couple, Marise. Lia, did you tell me you're doing some recording soon?"

"The week after next. Until then, I have eight whole days off...pure luxury."

"You work too hard," he said roughly.

"You never do," she said, raising her brows.

She was casually dressed in jeans and a ribbed sweater that

clung to her breasts; he did his best to keep his eyes on her face. "I've been known to. Do you have to work hard at school, Marise?"

As a kid, hadn't he always hated grown-ups who asked dumb questions about school?

"Sometimes."

Lia began describing some of her daughter's English compositions, doing her best to oil the wheels. Seth, she could see, was trying as hard as he could to reach Marise in some way; it wasn't his fault he wasn't succeeding.

She was finally beginning to understand how deeply the lack of a father had marked Marise. What a mess this all is, she thought wretchedly, and started describing the competition Marise had won for a poem she'd written about raccoons. Marise said nothing.

Dessert was ordered, arrived and was eaten. Lia said brightly, "Well, I guess we should get going. Suzy's coming for a sleepover tonight."

Seth had hoped lunch might end with him and his daughter taking a little walk down the pretty main street of Stoneybrook; but now he knew better than to suggest it. He said, "Perhaps next time you could come to Manhattan with your mum, Marise? Have you ever gone to the Children's Museum?"

Marise nodded, staring down at her plate. "It's a neat place," she said in a small voice.

"Let's work on that, then," Seth said. He leaned forward, gently lifting her chin. "I know this is difficult for you—it's difficult for all of us, but especially for you. I'll do the very best I can to be a good father to you. But it'll take time for us to get used to each other. To trust each other."

"Will you come to school sometime? So the kids can see you're real?"

He fought back the sting of tears. "Of course. Anytime you want and as often as you want."

"Okay."

The child looked as though she, too, was on the verge of tears. Seth pushed back his chair, paid for lunch and led the way out of the café. On the sidewalk he said calmly, "Lia, I'll talk to you soon. Bye for now, Marise."

Then he watched as Lia drove away. Marise didn't wave.

He was exhausted, he realized, getting behind the wheel of his beloved red Porsche. It was easier to merge two corporations than to make contact with a seven-year-old who didn't want to make contact.

Would he ever reach her?

Lia, he was almost sure, hadn't been pleased when he'd suggested she bring Marise to Manhattan; certainly he'd given her no chance to argue.

Too bad, he thought heartlessly. If he wanted to make contact with Marise, didn't he also want more from Lia?

If only he knew what.

He was going back to his brownstone and spending the evening listening to Lia's CDs. If that was a maudlin and generally useless thing to do, so what?

The dazzling pyrotechnics of a Paganini violin concerto were rollicking through his living room when the phone rang. He picked it up. "Seth Talbot."

"Good taste in music," Lia said.

"The best." Discovering he was grinning like a mad fool, he added, "What's up?"

There was a short silence. "I didn't want you blaming yourself for what happened today," she said stiffly.

"What didn't happen, you mean. I'll admit to feeling god-awful as I drove home. It'll take time, Lia. That's all."

The silence was longer this time. Then Lia said in a rush, "Would you like to spend next weekend at Meadowland?"

Once again, she'd taken him completely by surprise. Wishing he could see her face, he croaked, "You mean that?"

"Yes."

"What made you change your mind?"

"I can't keep you and Marise apart—it would be wrong of me to even try. I never realized how desperate she was for a father figure…I feel so guilty, Seth."

"I'm the one who should feel guilty."

"No, you're not. Your mother should."

"Good luck," he said.

In a low voice Lia went on, "I watched you today with Marise. You were trying so hard to reach her, yet you never overstepped her boundaries. You'll make a very good father."

For the second time in one day, Seth felt the prick of tears. "Thanks," he said gruffly. "I wish Marise agreed with you."

"Maybe if you come here, it'll help."

"Marise and a big wad of guilt—are they the only reasons you're inviting me?"

"I—I don't know."

"Come clean, Lia."

Sounding thoroughly exasperated, she said, "Every time I see you, I see more layers. More depths. When I was partway plastered, I said you confused me. You still do. But you also intrigue me—I want to know what makes you tick. I shouldn't even be telling you this, my tongue has a nasty habit of running away with me…but I really like you, Seth."

Something moved in his chest, physically, as though a weight had been lifted. "I like you, too," he said huskily.

"Since we're Marise's parents, it's just as well, don't you think?" she said, a new lightness in her tone.

"So are we going to stop fighting?"

"Providing you always do what I tell you."

"What are the odds on that?"

"Extremely low," she said cheerfully.

"I wish you were here right now," he said. "I'd take you to bed. Show you how much I like you."

Her heart was triphammering in her breast. "Obscene phone calls are illegal."

"Chicken."

"Yep. But Seth, at Meadowland we won't—"

"Then I'll have to inveigle you to my brownstone. My bedroom has skylights and French doors onto a roof garden."

"Does it have a bed?"

"You do go for the essentials. When should I arrive on the weekend?"

"I won't be able to spend much time with you," she said hurriedly, "I have to practice for the recording sessions."

"That's fine," he said equably. "What time?"

"How about Saturday morning? As early as you like."

He was supposed to be in Texas on Saturday morning. "Nine-thirty," he said promptly.

"The coffee'll be on." Her voice suddenly faltered. "I hope…I mean, I wish…darn it, I don't know what I mean."

He felt precisely the same way. Although he, unlike her, wasn't about to admit it. "I'll see you Saturday," he said and put down the receiver.

How could one woman and one small girl make him feel so ludicrously unsettled?

Dammit, he was still in control of his life.

Scowling, he cut Paganini off in the middle of the adagio and substituted Louis Armstrong. First thing Monday morning he'd get on the phone to Texas.

By two o'clock on Saturday afternoon, Seth was beginning to wonder why he'd come. Meadowland was beautiful, a beguiling combination of unkempt woodland and wild gardens, the house itself welcoming, comfortable and pleasantly cluttered. It was the nanny's weekend off; Lia had greeted him at the door, holding a mug of coffee in front of her like a bulwark. She looked strained and tired, he thought, and forbore to say so.

Marise was polite and as far away as the rain forests of Borneo. As difficult to reach, too, Seth thought, striving to hit the delicate balance between showing her he cared, without pushing her too hard. Then, as he was sitting out on the patio in the afternoon sun, he overheard his daughter's raised voice from an open window overhead. "But I want to go for a swim, Mum."

"I can't stop yet, Marise—I've got the rest of the sonata to go through."

Sulkily Marise said, "You'll be forever."

"No, I won't. I'll be another hour."

"An hour's forever."

"Why don't you ask your father if he'll go for a swim with you?"

"I bet he doesn't have a swimsuit."

"Ask him."

"I don't want to!"

Lia sighed. "Then you'll have to wait for me."

Five minutes later, one of the French doors opened behind Seth. Marise trailed across the slate patio stones toward him. He looked up and smiled at her. "Hi, there. What's up?"

She was industriously chewing on her bottom lip. "Do you want to go for a swim?" she mumbled.

"Love to. Give me a couple of minutes to change—why don't I meet you out here?"

Her face had lightened perceptibly. "Neat."

He ran upstairs, wondering if he was a fool to regard Marise's request as a small victory. Throwing on a T-shirt and his blue trunks, he went back to the patio. She was already there, wearing a bright pink swimsuit and laden with an assortment of inflated toys. "Let's go," he said.

He unlocked the gate to the pool, threw his towel over the chair and peeled off his shirt. "Last one in's a rotten egg," he said. "Or don't kids say that anymore?"

But Marise was gazing in fascination at his chest. "Who did that to you?"

The scar over his ribs was still an angry red furrow. "I—it was an accident."

"Sometimes Suzy and I watch cowboy movies. Did a bad guy shoot you?"

"Yeah…he did."

"Was there a stagecoach?"

Seth sat down on the edge of the pool and patted the cement beside him. "It was in Africa."

"Wow," she said, "were there lions?"

Striving to censor the truth yet hold her interest, Seth began to talk. She kept interrupting him with questions, her little feet splashing in the pool, and gradually Seth shifted into telling her about some of the children he'd met on his third world trips. She edged a little closer to him, laughing at some of his jokes, big-eyed when he did describe a near-encounter with a lion, and how he'd once followed a small herd of elephants. She said with a contented sigh, "You tell good stories."

Feeling as though he'd been awarded the Nobel Prize, Seth said, "Lots more where those came from. Should we go for a swim now?"

"I can show you my backstroke," she said with a shy smile.

"I'd like that," he said with huge understatement, and slid into the water.

From the upstairs window, where she'd been trying to concentrate on a Beethoven sonata, Lia watched father and daughter cavorting in the water. She'd also watched them sitting side by side talking to each other, Seth's blond head bending to Marise's brown curls, Marise's face lifted confidingly to Seth's.

Change, Lia thought. So much change.

Seth and Marise were beginning to forge a relationship. She was happy about that, of course she was. But she wasn't blind to the consequences. Her daughter would, from now on, be shared between herself and Seth.

Don't be an idiot, Lia scolded herself. You already share Marise with Nancy; and love isn't something to be measured out in small doses.

If only Seth weren't so barricaded, so guarded. Sometimes it seemed to her that only in bed was he truly himself.

It had been a long time since he'd held her in his arms.

Seth had hauled himself out of the pool, swiping his soaked hair out of his eyes. As the sun gleamed along the long line of his spine, Lia felt desire uncurl in her belly and lazily stretch its limbs. Then he reached down and lifted Marise out of the water, carefully putting her down beside him. She was laughing at something he'd said.

Father and daughter, side by side. Grabbing a tissue, Lia wiped her eyes and turned away from the window. The score was a blur of black notes. How was she supposed to work when her world kept shifting beneath her feet?

She did work for another couple of hours, partly to give Seth and Marise more time together. After hanging up her violin, Lia went downstairs and the three of them had dinner together, then watched The Lion King on video. When it was over, Lia said, "Bedtime, honeybunch."

Marise said craftily, "You could both read me a story."

"I'll read one chapter and your father another," Lia said firmly.

Which is what they did, in Marise's pretty yellow bedroom. Seth read his way steadily through his part of the story, keeping his eyes on the page; he was finding his participation in an obviously much-loved ritual almost unbearably moving. When it was time to say good night, he contented himself with patting Marise on the shoulder. "I'll see you tomorrow," he said.

"We could go and see Suzy," Marise said, giving a little bounce on the bed. "She thinks it's awesome that you're here."

"I'd like that. Night, Marise…I had a great time with you today."

Leaving Lia to kiss Marise good night, he ran downstairs, grabbed a jacket and hurried outdoors. The stars looked very close. New leaves were rustling gently in the breeze. His mother hadn't believed in coddling her only son, and he couldn't imagine her sitting on his bed and reading about the adventures of a mouse called Stuart Little. His throat felt clogged; his shoulder muscles were tightly bunched.

As a boy, he'd been surrounded by money and the things money could buy. But Marise was by far the richer.

Seth set off down the driveway, walking fast. Too much had happened today; not the least of which had been spending several hours at Lia's beloved Meadowland. All day, with one part of his brain, he'd been achingly aware of her nearness.

It was going to half-kill him to sleep alone in the guest bedroom under the eaves.

Half an hour later, he headed back to the house. Its lights shone gold through the lacy network of branches. It would suit him just fine if Lia had already gone to bed; he'd had enough emotion for one day. He didn't need to add sexual frustration to the list.

As he went in the front door, Lia called to him from the kitchen. Reluctantly he crossed the hall. She was standing by the stove, in faded jeans and a baggy blue sweater, her hair tied back with a ribbon. "I made hot chocolate—want some?" she offered.

"Think I'll pass, and head upstairs—it's been a long day."

She put down her mug and in a low voice said, "Will you come to bed with me?"

As had so often happened, she'd rocked him to the roots. "That's not in the cards—not with Marise here."

"She's sound asleep and I'll lock my bedroom door."

He raked his fingers through his hair. "What's up, Lia?"

"Please, Seth…come to bed. We can talk there."

She still looked tired, her mouth a vulnerable curve, her eyes full of uncertainty. Any opposition he might have felt melted away. "I locked the front door," he said matter-of-factly.

She switched out the kitchen light; from upstairs, the hall light beckoned. She headed for the stairs, aware in every nerve of Seth padding behind her. She'd lit two candles in her bedroom; as she closed the door behind him, shadows flickered over his face. She had no idea what she was going to do next.

Seth put his arms around her, drew her close and pressed her face to his chest. She leaned against him. His body heat seeped through his cotton shirt; the heavy stroke of his heart felt immensely comforting, and slowly all the accumulated tensions of the day slid away. "Where's your nightgown?" he asked.

"Under the pillow."

He edged her over to the bed. His face intent, he slowly undressed her, his fingers lingering on the slope of her shoulders and the lift of her breasts, smoothing the long curve of hip and thigh as he drew her jeans down her legs; and all without saying a word. Finally he slipped her white silk gown over her head.

Her whole body felt liquid; she swayed toward him. But Seth was in no hurry. He took off his own shirt and jeans, tossing them on the rattan rocker. Then he drew her down on the bed beside him. Only then did he kiss her, a lingering kiss with none of the frantic hunger of their other couplings.

Catching his mood, Lia edged one thigh over his, linked her arms around his neck and surrendered. Slowly and surely he drew her deeper and deeper into a place lit with golden sunlight rather than with the whip of fire. Heat, yes, that melted her bones and bathed her in intimacy. A warm light that dazzled her. But instead of being caught up in a desperate drive to completion, she was surrounded by caring and sensitivity. By gentleness, she thought in wonderment.

Engulfed in the slow, sure currents of yearning, she sighed his name, her lips buried in his shoulder, then moving to caress the hard curve of his ribs. She twisted gracefully in his arms, her breasts to the tautness of his belly, and felt him slip inside her, silky and hard.

As she made a small sound of delight, Seth began to move with long, slow strokes. She moaned softly, her hips moving with him. His eyes were trained on her, molten with what she could only call tenderness. Like the green leaves of spring, she thought. Tender, vulnerable, opening to a new life.

Her heart opened in response even as her body gathered to its crescendo. Her breath was rapid in her throat, her hips pumping to bring him closer and closer; yet still her gaze held his. His own eyes had darkened to a forest-green; the thud of his heartbeat was like a primitive drumming. Caught in its rhythm, she rushed toward him, her tiny cries like the echoes of faraway music. He groaned deep in his chest. Together they fell, entwined as one.

Lia lay very still. Her cheek was pressed to his breastbone, his arms wrapped around her as though he never wanted to let her go. Like the slow unfolding of a leaf, emotion filled her heart. I'm falling in love with you, she thought. Oh, Seth, I'm falling in love…

She closed her eyes, and knew her own words for the truth. For now they were enough; and too new to be shared. Feeling utterly peaceful, she let herself drift off to sleep.

CHAPTER TWELVE

SETH had to leave right after lunch on Sunday, to prepare for a business trip to Venezuela. Marise unaffectedly hugged him goodbye, then skipped off to play in the shrubbery. Lia, tongue-tied, watched him put his leather overnight bag into the back seat of his red Porsche.

She hadn't told him she loved him; the thought terrified her. But when would she see him again? "That's a very jazzy car," she said.

He straightened and grinned at her. "You can drive it. Anytime."

"Flat out?"

"It's the only way. I've got a suggestion, Lia. Why don't you stay at my place this week while you're doing the recording? I'm away until Saturday, you'd have free run of the place."

She could see where he lived: perhaps learn more about the guarded man she'd fallen in love with. "I'd like that."

He hadn't expected her to agree so readily. Giving her the extra key, he said, "Make yourself at home. Perhaps Marise could come up next weekend?"

"Sure."

He might as well push his advantage. "My father would really like to meet her."

Lia's eyes clouded. "Your father lives with your mother. I don't want your mother anywhere near Marise."

"I'm not suggesting you invite my mother."

"I'll see," Lia said, her lips set mutinously.

Seth scribbled Allan's personal number on his card. "My father wants to mend, not to destroy," he said, lifting his hand and tracing the smooth hollow under her cheekbone. "If Marise weren't cavorting in the forsythia bushes, I'd be kissing you blind. See you Saturday—late afternoon."

He put the car in gear, beat a tattoo on the horn for his daughter's benefit, and drove away.

Six days passed, four of which Seth spent in the Venezuelan oilfields, with a side trip to Peru to check on a project his foundation had started in Lima two years ago. He was glad to get home, he thought, as he climbed the steps of his brownstone near Central Park. Everything looked the same: the polished brass door handle, the elegantly proportioned windows and the dark oak door. But inside, he knew, Lia and Marise were waiting for him.

He hadn't talked to Lia since he'd left Meadowland; since a lovemaking so different in quality that it had both disarmed and dismayed him.

Too emotional. That was the catch. The e-word, he thought with a rueful smile, unlocked the door and stepped inside. But the first person he saw wasn't Lia or Marise. It was Allan, his father, who came around the corner, his shirt rumpled and far from clean. "Seth!" he exclaimed. "We weren't expecting you for another hour."

So Lia had invited his father, Seth thought in a rush of gratitude mingled with another, deeper emotion he didn't want to name.

"Plane was early," he said prosaically. "How are you, Father?"

Allan gave him an atypically boyish grin. "Wonderful," he

said. "I've spent the day with Lia and my totally charming granddaughter—took her on a tour of my favorite bookstore. She talked the ears off me."

Seth blinked. "What's that on your shirt?"

Allan glanced down. "Fingerpaint," he said. "We're in the kitchen, why don't you join us?"

"Lia's there, too?"

"She's a lovely woman, Seth."

Seth grunted something indecipherable and followed his father into the ultramodern kitchen. The granite counters were covered with sheets of paper that had been smeared in every shade from pink to bilious green. The warm odor of choco-late chip cookies filled the air. Marise looked up. "Hi!" she crowed. "Come see my painting, can you guess what it is?"

"Mmm…an orchid?" Seth hazarded.

She giggled. "It's a flamingo—look, here are its wings."

"Ah," he said, "I see. Hello, Lia."

She was standing by the counter, wearing a T-shirt that under a riot of musical notes announced that Musicians Score. As always, he was struck first by her beauty. The shiny fall of her hair, the luscious curves of her cheekbones, now deli-cately flushed…had he forgotten anything about her?

"Can I have a cookie?" he asked.

Laughing, she passed the plate. "You sure can."

Effortlessly he was incorporated into the chatter and warmth. If Allan looked different, so too did his own house, Seth realized. Cluttered. Lived in. In a way that he'd never managed on his own.

A family kind of clutter.

He kept this thought to himself.

An hour later, they walked three or four blocks to a trattoria Seth frequented; on the way, to his annoyance, they ran into a media crew conducting a survey. Although Marise was entranced by the cameras and questions, Seth hurried her past them. "I'm starving," he said. "The last time I ate was in Miami. Did I tell you about the dog at the airport?"

Deflected, Marise skipped along beside him. "Was it a Dalmatian?"

"It was a Scottie with very short legs," he said, and took her by the hand to cross the street.

"Is it another story?" she asked hopefully.

"I believe it might be."

"I like the way you tell stories," Marise said. "What am I s'posed to call you?"

Seth stopped dead in the middle of the street. "You could try Dad. If you felt like it. Or Seth is fine with me."

"Dad's best. What happened to the Scottie?"

He tried to gather his wits; her small hand curled in his, her astonishing acceptance of him as her father, had thrown him for a loop. "We're nearly at the restaurant," he said. "Why don't I save it until we're sitting down?"

Allan went ahead with her; Seth turned to Lia, realizing how quiet she'd been. He said softly, his hand at the small of her back, "How are you?"

"I missed you," Lia said. It was true. She had missed him, unrelentingly, day and night. She'd also, when she'd seen Marise hold his hand a few minutes ago, fallen a little more deeply in love with him.

"I'd like to be making love with you right now," Seth said.

"That, too," she said, tossing her head.

"So why else did you miss me?" he rapped, his smile fading.

"I'll tell you later," she said and walked across the charming patio of the trattoria to one of the brightly painted tables.

Yes, he thought, you will, and sat down at the table. But that evening, once Marise was settled in bed, Allan said edgily, "Seth, can I have a word with you? In private."

Lia stood up, stretching lazily. "I'm going to have a leisurely bath and go to bed early," she said. "I'll see you both in the morning."

She was avoiding him, Seth thought. Had been ever since he'd arrived home. What was going on? Not that he was likely to find out with all these people around.

Trying to tamp down his frustration, he watched her leave the room. He needed to touch her. Hold her in his arms. That way he'd find out what the matter was.

Meanwhile Allan was pacing up and down the faded antique carpet. As soon as Lia shut the door behind her, he said jerkily, "I've left your mother."

"What?"

"She was furious that I was planning to come to Manhattan to see Marise. Absolutely furious. Forbade me to even think of it. One thing led to another…and for the first time in years I didn't back down, Seth. I held my ground."

"Good for you," Seth said warmly.

"She told me if I came to Manhattan today, she'd never speak to me again. So I said she was right, she wouldn't, because I wouldn't be living with her anymore…I've moved into a suite at the Ritz-Carlton." His smile was wry. "To say she was taken aback is putting it mildly."

"I'm proud of you, Dad," Seth said, noticing absently how easily the diminutive slipped off his tongue.

"Thanks, son," Allan said huskily. "She's not an easy woman, your mother. But I've never told you about her background—she didn't want anyone to know, least of all you, so she swore me to secrecy years ago. Now that I've left her, I don't feel bound by that promise any longer…she had a terrible childhood, Seth. Unrelenting poverty coupled with violence. Her father was a migrant worker, and when he hit the bottle, which was frequently, he also took out the belt and hit whichever kid was nearest—she ran away from home when she was fourteen, got herself a menial job and never saw him again. Never trusted anyone again, as far as I can tell. Even me, who loves her. But for the sake of that skinny little girl picking grapes when she should have been in school, I've forgiven her a great deal."

Shaken, Seth said, "I didn't know any of that."

"Maybe I should have told you long ago, despite Eleonore's wishes to the contrary. But somehow the occasion never arose."

Seth asked several questions, learning more about his parents' difficult marriage in half an hour than he had in all his thirty-seven years. Allan finished by saying heavily, "Not even for Eleonore will I shut myself off from my granddaughter. Not for anyone."

"Marise is a sweetheart."

"As is her mother."

Seth didn't want to talk about Lia. "You look tired, Dad, and I know I'm wiped. Worked my guts out all last week. Shall we hit the pit?"

"I'm glad we had this talk, son. Long overdue."

"I'm glad, too." Seth gave his father a rough hug and watched him leave the room. His head was whirling, from a combination of jet lag, information overload and too much emotion.

He craved sleep. But more than that, he craved Lia. Who was sleeping in the guest wing next to her daughter.

She might as well be in Venezuela.

Seth was up before anyone else in the morning. He went downstairs and settled himself with his coffee in the breakfast nook that overlooked the garden. As was his habit, he skimmed through the newspapers first, to get an overview of what was going on in the world.

On the seventh page of the second section was a large colored photo of himself, Lia, Marise and Allan. "Family Out-ing," the caption read, giving his and Allan's names. Lia d'Angeli was listed as Seth's companion, Marise as her daughter. His eyes and his daughter's had been printed an identical, startling green.

Companion, thought Seth, feeling his temper rise. What kind of word was that? The caption hadn't needed to say anything else. The point was made. Lia as mistress, Marise as illegitimate child.

Himself as the father who didn't care enough to put things right.

Goddammit, he wasn't going to put up with it. Vienna had been bad enough. But Vienna was on the other side of the Atlantic. New York was where he lived, the headquarters of his company. They'd hit too close to home this time.

No more.

It wasn't an opportune moment for Lia to wander into the kitchen, rubbing her eyes. She was wearing a long silk robe streaked with blues and reds, belted around her waist; her hair was a loose tangle down her back. She sniffed the air. "Coffee," she said. "You're an angel."

He said flatly, "Are the others still in bed?"

Her eyes snapped wide. "What's the matter?"

"Are they?"

"Yes. Why?"

He thrust the paper at her, jabbing at the picture with his finger. "I won't have this, Lia. I won't have Marise subjected to any more gossip and innuendo. We're going to get married and put an end to it."

She took the paper from him, reading the caption. Frowning, she said, "Marise has already told everyone at school that you're her father. So this doesn't really matter."

He surged to his feet. "It matters to me. And it should damn well matter to you."

"I've lived with the fact of my daughter's illegitimacy for

seven years," she said steadily, reaching up in the cupboard for a mug. "And don't you dare tell me how I should feel."

He snatched the mug from her and banged it on the counter. Pulling her against the length of his body, he plummeted to find her mouth. Shock made her, momentarily, rigid. Then she opened to him, digging her nails into his shoulders and kissing him back with searing passion. Flame tore through him; he cupped her breast and jammed his hips to hers.

Then, as roughly, he pushed her away. "How soon can you get married?"

"Are you asking me to marry you or telling me I'm going to marry you?"

She looked magnificent, her cheeks the same bright red as the pattern in her robe. "It's not up for negotiation," he said.

"That's what you think."

"Yes, Lia, that's what I think."

Her back to the counter, her hands clasping the smooth edge, she said, "Do you love me, Seth?"

"No."

"So how can you say we're getting married?"

"I like you, I admire and respect you, and I sure as hell lust after you. That's not a bad start."

"It's not enough."

"Then you're a starry-eyed romantic."

"Don't make fun of my feelings!"

His eyes narrowed. "What are you getting at?"

"I've fallen in love with you," she said evenly.

He opened his mouth to argue with her. But something in her stance and her clear gaze made the words die on his lips. "When did that happen?"

"I realized it the last time we made love…at Meadowland. Maybe it happened a long time ago in Paris, who knows. It doesn't really matter. The fact remains that I won't marry you if you don't love me."

"Love's the most abused word in the language."

"That's your opinion—it doesn't happen to be mine. I deserve a husband who loves me, and Marise deserves parents who love each other. End of discussion."

"My father loved my mother," Seth snarled. "Much good it's done him."

"My parents loved music, their careers, each other and me. Not necessarily in that order. We can do it all, that's what I'm trying to say."

"You're a deluded optimist."

"I'm a realist. After all, we both love Marise. That's a start—a wonderful start."

He did indeed love his daughter. "It is wonderful. But it's not the start of anything. For me it's all there is."

"I won't compromise, Seth—I want the whole nine yards," she said, her chin tilted. "A husband who loves me and who loves our child."

She wasn't playing hard to get: he knew her too well for that. So it was up to him to change her mind. Short of throwing her over his shoulder and lugging her to the nearest registry office, Seth had no idea how to begin. "Corporate mergers are a piece of cake compared to you," he said caustically.

"I should hope so," she said, her dark eyes full of defiance.

"You look as though you could chew me up for breakfast and spit me out before lunch."

"I have to have my coffee first," she answered with a glint of amusement.

Seth stepped closer, slipping his arms around her waist. Her body felt deliciously warm and soft, all voluptuous curves under thin silk. "If only we could go to bed together," he muttered.

"Sex is no substitute for love. Not in my books."

Surprising them both, he laughed. "When it's sex with you, it comes darn close."

Swiftly she reached up, fisting her hand in his hair and

dragging his head down, then hungrily sealing his lips with her own. The kiss slammed through him. Feasting on all the sweetness of her mouth, he pulled her closer.

Footsteps clattered on the stairs. Lia shoved Seth away and hurriedly straightened her robe. "It's Marise," she gasped.

Seth was in no shape to face his daughter. He turned to the counter and busied himself pouring Lia a mug of coffee. Unfinished business, he thought savagely. Welcome to fatherhood, Seth. The trouble was, Lia was going home to Meadowland tonight, then to Prague later in the week; while he was leaving for London and Malaysia first thing in the morning.

The wedding date wasn't set. She'd won this round.

CHAPTER THIRTEEN

THE cab dropped Seth off in front of Rudolfinum, the neo-Renaissance concert hall on the banks of the Vltava in Prague. It was pouring rain. He ran for the entrance, his black shoes splashing through the puddles.

He was late. He'd be lucky if he made it for the intermission.

He hadn't planned to come to Prague. He'd planned the exact opposite. To keep his distance from Lia for a while. Let her cool her heels, come to her senses and decide to marry him.

The usher led him through the well-dressed crowd mingling during the intermission to the best box in the house; Seth had achieved this by pulling any number of strings at once. The door to the box closed behind him. He hung up his raincoat and sat down in the plush seat. His trousers clung damply to his legs. His hair was wet.

But he'd made it in time to hear Lia play.

The audience as well as the orchestra were filtering back to their seats. The stage was high-arched, backed by an array of gleaming organ pipes. Seth's box was in full view of the podium. Would Lia see him?

When she was playing, her focus was too strong for her to be distracted. He hoped.

He hadn't made love to her since that night at Meadowland.

It felt like forever. Wasn't that why he was here? To make love to Lia?

He was here to change her mind on the subject of marriage.

He had a reputation as a perennial bachelor; in the early days of his career, the gossip magazines had used up considerable ink trying to pair him off with one glamorous beauty after another, all to no avail. Yet now he was determined to marry a woman he didn't love, a woman who was, moreover, resisting him every step of the way.

Did he want to marry solely for Marise's sake?

Hadn't he been avoiding this question all week?

A panel in the wall swung open and directly across from him Lia walked out on the stage. The audience broke into spontaneous clapping. As she acknowledged the applause, looking around her, she suddenly saw him.

Her steps faltered. Even from his perch, Seth could see shock flash across her face. Then it was gone, erased as though it had never been. She took her place by the podium and smiled at the conductor.

Her dress was scarlet, strapless and slim-fitting, her lips the same uncompromising color. Her hair was drawn back with two sparkling clips; with a clench in his gut Seth noticed she was wearing the earrings he'd given her. Just before the conductor raised his baton, she looked directly at Seth.

Intimate. Intense. Challenging. How would he describe that look? It had gone straight through him, he knew that much.

As she raised her instrument to her chin, the orchestra played a single chord. Then the violin began its restless, lonely searching, lyrical and melancholy. Seth sat stone-still. Although the Nielsen violin concerto had long been one of his favorites, tonight it was as though he'd never heard it before. Lia was playing for him alone, he knew she was; as the minutes passed, she released all her love, passion and pain in a glorious outpouring of music that shook him to the core.

The final chord filled the sumptuous hall. A roar of applause broke out. Feeling as though he'd been stripped naked in full view of every soul in the hall, Seth got up, left the box and sought out the house manager in his office. "Would you see that Lia d'Angeli gets this note?" he said, passing over a sealed envelope with a banknote discreetly tucked beneath it.

"Certainly, sir. My pleasure."

Seth thanked him and took a cab through the unrelenting rain back to his hotel in the Old Town. The next move was up to Lia.

Either she came to him of her own free will, or not at all.

He had a shower, changed into casual slacks and a sweater and poured himself a drink. The post-concert reception, he knew, could take a while. All he had to do was wait. When had he ever sat in a hotel room in one of the most beautiful cities in Europe and waited for a woman to come to him?

Never.

The minutes ticked by. He flicked through the channels on the TV, trying to attune his ears to the various languages, then giving up in disgust. It was nearly midnight. Shouldn't she be here by now?

The phone rang on the cherrywood desk, making him start. Seth snatched it up. "Yes?"

"It's Lia. I'm in the lobby."

"Suite 700. Take the elevator to the top floor."

"I'll be right up," Lia said and put down the phone.

But for a moment she stayed where she was, gazing blindly at the elegant Art Nouveau decor. She knew what would happen if she went to Seth's suite. Was that what she wanted? If not, why was she here? Gathering her skirts in her hand, she walked swiftly toward the elevator.

Just as she raised her fist to tap on the door of his suite, Seth opened it. Instinctively she took a step backward, and saw his jaw harden. "Lia," he said, "come in. Did you get soaked in the rain?"

"The taxi driver very kindly held his umbrella over me, and then parked under the awning of the hotel," she prattled. "He loves Dvořák, so we had lots to talk about."

"You probably made his night. Would you like a drink?"

"No, thanks. Not after what happened in Vienna."

"Were you pleased with the concert?" he asked, cursing himself for making small talk as though she were a casual acquaintance.

"Yes. Were you?"

So the small talk was over. "How could I not be," he said, "when you played only for me?"

She didn't bother denying it. "Another way of telling you I love you."

"You think I'm so thickheaded that I wouldn't realize that? I heard you. Heard love, desire and tears."

"I was pleading my case." Her red dress swishing softly as she moved, she walked closer to him, resting one hand on his sleeve. "Perhaps too strongly. But I can't make myself into another kind of woman, Seth. I am who I am. Impatient. Passionate. Uncompromising. Can you not love that woman?"

"I've never in my life fallen in love. Had no use for it."

"So I'm the same as all the rest?" she flashed.

"You're utterly different—but I can't make myself fall in love to order!"

"Won't, you mean."

"Can't is what I said."

"Then I won't marry you."

"What is this," he demanded, "a battle of wills to see who comes out on top?"

"As it stands now, we're all losers. You. Me. And Marise."

"Now you're fighting dirty," he grated.

"Did you expect any different?"

In spite of himself, he lifted one hand to trace the soft

curve of her cheek and the jut of bone above it. "I want to go to bed with you."

Unconsciously she swayed toward him. "I want that, too," she whispered.

His heart was juddering in his chest. "Suits me a lot better than arguing."

"No more words, Seth," she said with sudden fierceness. "Take me to bed. Make love to me, make me forget everything but your body."

He lifted her off her feet, carrying her across the thick carpets to his bedroom with its imposing four-poster bed; there, he laid her down on her back and flung himself on top of her, hauling his sweater over his head. "You drive me out of my mind," he muttered, then plunged to ravage her mouth. Her tongue laced with his, her teeth scraping his lip, a small pain that only served to inflame him. She was writhing beneath him, mouth and hands so hungry that he lost all restraint. Throwing himself sideways, carrying her with him, he yanked on the zipper of her dress and tugged it down the length of her body.

Her bare breasts, the slide of silk over her hips…would he ever have enough of her? She was fumbling with the clips in her hair, tossing them onto the floor so that her hair spread like dark satin on the pillow. Her irises, so dark he could lose himself in them, were blurred with desire.

Fiercely he took from her, giving no quarter, feeling her nails rake his back, her teeth nip his shoulder. She was his mate, meeting him in every way that mattered, hunger for hunger in a primitive dance. Tasting, teasing, arousing, he traveled every inch of her body, making it his own.

She was his.

But he didn't love her.

When he entered her, she arched and bucked, her fingers like manacles around his wrists. He plunged, deep, deeper, groaning her name as he fought for breath.

The climax ripped through her, leaving her breathless and spent; his whole body pounding his own release, Seth dropped his head to her shoulder, feeling sweat cool on his bare back.

He had no memory of how he'd gotten out of the rest of his clothes. Or where they were. Not that it mattered.

He turned on his side, burying his face between her breasts. This was what he wanted, Seth thought dimly. Lia in his arms. What more could there be?

He'd left Malaysia very early that morning after three days of intense meetings. With the suddenness of a small boy, Seth fell asleep.

Lia lay still, listening as Seth's breathing settled into a smooth rhythm. For the first time after making love to him, she felt less than fulfilled. Physically she was satiated; that was a given. But her soul felt empty, she thought unhappily. At the moment of climax, she'd wanted to cry out how much she loved him; and hadn't done so. He didn't want to hear those words from her, because he didn't share them.

How strange to feel lonely when Seth's arm was draped over her hip and his breath was wafting the curve of her breast. Yet lonely was how she felt.

She waited another few minutes before slipping free of his embrace. He muttered something in his sleep, reaching for her. Paralyzed, she crouched on the bed. Only when his breathing had steadied again did she scramble to the floor. There were two fleecy robes in the bathroom. Belting one around her, she went to sit in one of the window seats, upholstered in embossed brocade. The lights of Prague twinkled through the leaded panes. Like diamonds on black velvet, she thought, fingering the earrings Seth had given her.

A church spire lanced the darkness. Several streets over, the river wound its lazy way through a city where she'd always felt at home, so permeated was it with music.

But now she felt exiled. In playing for Seth, she'd given

him her heart; yet she'd failed to reach him, or to change him. Dropping her head to her knees, Lia let the slow tears course down her cheeks.

She wept in silence until she was drained of emotion. Getting up, she went to the bathroom, washed her face and walked slowly back to the bedroom. Her dress was lying in a crumpled heap on the floor. Red as blood, she thought with a superstitious shiver, and picked it up. Her underwear was on Seth's side of the bed, tangled in his trousers. Moving as quietly as she could, she got dressed.

But as she reached for the cold sparkle of her hair clips, she bumped the side of the bed. Seth stirred. "Lia?" he muttered. "What are you doing?"

Frozen to the spot, she watched him rear up on one elbow. He reached for the bedside lamp and switched it on. Blinking in the light, she said, "I'm going back to my hotel."

He swung his legs over the side of the bed, running his fingers through his tousled hair; he was instantly awake in a way that frightened her. "You're running away," he said. "Just as you did in Paris."

"It's too late for that," she said bitterly. "Because of Marise, I'm tied to you." She dropped the clip into her evening bag. "I have to fly to Basel in the morning—a final concert before I go home."

"Why are you leaving now, in the middle of the night?"

The truth, she thought. Why not tell the truth? "I can't do this," she said, despair thinning her voice. "I love you. To be with you like this, knowing you don't love me—it's too painful. It tears me apart."

"You came to my hotel. Knowing what would happen."

"I didn't know how I'd feel afterward—how could I? Tell me, Seth, why did you come to the concert?"

"I couldn't stay away. I needed to touch you, hold you in my arms. It nearly drove me crazy having you stay in my house last weekend, knowing I couldn't take you to bed. Couldn't even kiss you the way I wanted to."

"There's more to making love than the physical," Lia cried. "Do you know how I felt tonight? Why I couldn't go to sleep? I was lonely. Horribly, desperately lonely. I can't separate making love with you from being in love with you. It's that simple. And that complicated."

He said in an ugly voice, "So if I don't fall in love with you, I don't get to go to bed with you?"

"You make it sound like I'm blackmailing you! I'm just trying to protect myself."

He stood up and walked over to her, unselfconscious in his nudity. "Come to bed with me now, Lia...you need to sleep. I don't know what we're going to do any more than you do. But surely we can work something out."

His body, as well-known to her as her own, towered over her, pulling her to him as effortlessly as a magnet attracts metal. "I can't, Seth," she whispered. "It hurts too much. You're giving me all the gifts of your body—but you're holding the rest back."

"I'm not holding anything back—it's not there to give."

His words were like a death knell. "I'll stay out of your way when you come to Meadowland to see Marise," Lia said tonelessly, "and Nancy can deliver her when she goes to Manhattan to stay with you."

"Marise is a highly intelligent child. You think we can behave like a couple of strangers without her noticing? You told me she deserves parents who love each other. I'm not so ambitious—as far as I'm concerned, she deserves parents who can be in the same room together."

"Stop!" Lia exclaimed, covering her ears. "I'll do the best I can, for Marise's sake—I promise."

"Then marry me," Seth said harshly.

Knowing she had to get out of here, Lia said nastily, "I see how you got to the top—you're ruthless, you don't care about other people's feelings. I'll clear it with Nancy when I get home, and you and Marise can work out how often you want to see each other. Dammit, where's my other shoe?"

"Under the bed," he said, bending to retrieve it, then passing it to her.

She took it gingerly and shoved her foot into it. "Good night. Sleep well."

She looked like a firecracker about to explode. She also looked like a woman on the edge. "Lia," he said hoarsely, "I can't help the way I was brought up. That night when I overheard my mother telling Dad about the abortion—it killed something inside me. The ability to love. I can't give myself to a woman, it isn't in me."

Her eyes were dark as woodland pools. "You're saying I should take you as you are?"

Grateful for her understanding, Seth said, "Yeah, I guess that's what I'm saying. I'll be faithful to you, I'll be the best father to Marise that I can possibly be…but that's as far as it goes."

She remembered how her violin had wandered through a desert of notes, searching for a place to rest, only finding it after long struggle; and shook her head. "You already love Marise. Your father and you are mending years of neglect." Her lips curved gently. "And you love music. How can you say you're unable to love?"

He didn't smile back. "I'm talking about you, not Marise or my father. I've lived with myself for a long time—I should know by now what I'm capable of."

He looked so adamant. So unmovable. "You're letting fear run your life," Lia accused.

Flicked on the raw, Seth said, "I wish it was as simple as that. It's not. It's a blankness—an emptiness. A lack. Hell, I don't even know how to describe it."

"So tell me about it," Lia said fiercely. "Make me understand."

Why not tell her? What did he have to lose? Seth sat down on the edge of the bed. "I was eight years old, a year older than Marise. I'd sneaked down to the library that night to get a book—I used to read in bed till all hours—when I heard my father coming, and hid behind the big leather couch. He sat down at his desk and started going through some bills. Then my mother came down the hall, talking to one of the servants. Dad called her in and held out a piece of paper, asking what she'd had done at the private clinic she always went to."

He paused, lost in memory. His mother had been wearing a black cashmere sweater and a strand of pearls; as a boy, he'd thought it was weird that a pearl could come out of an oyster. "She said she'd had an abortion," he went on, ironing any emotion from his voice. "I'll never forget the shock on my father's face. He asked if there'd been a medical reason. No, she said, she simply didn't want another child. Then my father asked if it had been a boy or a girl. A girl, she said indifferently, as though she was talking about a dress she'd discarded. My father was crying, tears sliding down his face—it terrified me. *A daughter,* he said. *Eleonore, you know I've always wanted a daughter.*"

Seth rubbed his jaw, trying to lessen the tension. "I didn't know what abortion meant, but I knew my mother had done something terrible. Then my father said, *How could you have done that?* My mother rarely lost her temper, control was too important to her. But she lost it then, screamed at my father that she'd never bring a little girl into the world, threw a priceless crystal statue at one of the cabinets—there were shards of glass everywhere—and stormed out of the library. Eventually my father got up, staggering like an old man…he went down the hall and I heard his bedroom door close. That's when I ran upstairs to bed."

"Seth, that's a terrible story," Lia faltered. She reached out her arms, her one urge to comfort the little boy he'd been and the man he'd become.

He struck them down. "Don't," he said in a voice scraped raw, that long-ago dissonance of terror and incomprehension swirling in his head. "This wasn't a bid for sympathy."

"I didn't think it was." Lia made one last try, letting the words pour out. "Seth, I talked to your father last weekend—on Sunday, after you'd left. He told me a little about your mother's upbringing, how violent it was. Despite my parents' careers, I had such a happy childhood, filled with music and the constant undercurrent of knowing I was loved. I can't imagine a childhood like Eleonore's. It made me understand her a little—perhaps even begin to forgive her for the harm she did to me. Couldn't you do the same?"

"Forgiveness isn't the issue. I wanted you to understand why I'm not into marriage, that's all. My father loved my mother. He gave her his soul and she trampled all over it. So I learned very young that love means betrayal and heartbreak."

"It doesn't have to!"

"A barrier slammed down that night, against knowledge I was too young to comprehend and emotions too terrible to bear. It's still in place. It always will be."

It was the finality in Seth's voice that destroyed Lia's last vestige of hope. Her whole body felt ice-cold. Picking up her wrap, she clumsily drew it around her shoulders. "Thank you for telling me," she said helplessly. "I'd better go…I'll see myself out."

Seth made no move to stop her. Feeling as though her own heart was breaking, Lia hurried out of the bedroom.

CHAPTER FOURTEEN

SUMMER had arrived at Meadowland. The flower beds were a riot of color, birds were nesting in the trees and the swimming pool shone turquoise in the sunshine as Lia and Marise frolicked in the deep end.

Lia should have been happy. Marise was out of school. She herself had only two summer festivals to attend and a benefit concert at Carnegie Hall; so she was able to spend hours of precious time with her daughter. The vegetable garden was flourishing and they had a bumper crop of strawberries.

Marise had spent a lot of time with Seth; he'd gone to her school closing, and the last three weekends had taken her to his summer home on Cape Cod, where he'd introduced her to sailing and ocean swimming. He'd also dropped in at Meadowland twice with Allan, occasions that had sorely tested Lia's composure.

Not once had he mentioned marriage; it was as though he'd forgotten both his proposal and her refusal. Certainly he never mentioned the night a little boy had hidden in the library of the big stone house by the sea. Instead he treated her with a courtesy that scoured every nerve in her body; he might as well have been in Paris as standing in her sun-dappled kitchen.

Marise loved him, and he loved Marise. That much, she knew.

He'd never love herself. She knew that, too; and ached every moment of the day from the knowledge.

Marise splashed her. "Mum, watch me dive all the way to the bottom! Dad taught me how."

With a start Lia came back to the present, to her daughter heaving her lungs full of air, then kicking herself deeper and deeper into the water. When Marise surfaced a few moments later, red-faced and sputtering, Lia said, "Great, Marise— you're a way better swimmer than last year."

"Dad's teaching me all kinds of neat things." Marise put her head to one side, trying to get water out of her ear. "Why don't you ever come to Cape Cod with us?"

Lia should have been prepared for this question; and wasn't. "It's better that you make your own relationship with your father, Marise." She sounded like a self-help book, she thought in disgust.

"Hasn't he asked you?"

"He has a lot of catching up to do…seven years, honey-bunch. You don't need me around for that."

Marise's chin, so like her mother's, had a stubborn tilt. "You'd like his house in Cape Cod. There's two kids next door for me to play with…I'm going to ask him to ask you next time."

"You mustn't!" Lia gasped, swallowing a mouthful of chlorinated water.

"He said I could ask him anything I liked."

Cursing Seth inwardly, Lia said weakly, "This is different."

Marise was batting at the water with her fingers; her eyes looked more turquoise than green. She said in a rush, "I wish you and Dad would live together. All the time."

"Oh, Marise…"

"You could get married." Marise's smile was artless. "In the garden. I could be the bridesmaid. There's lots of flowers out now, you wouldn't even have to buy a bouquet."

Lia bit her lip. "Sweetheart, it isn't that simple."

"I don't see why not. Dad's really nice," Marise pleaded, a catch in her voice. "He could live here—he likes it here, he said so."

Lia stared at her daughter, one word overriding all the rest of the words tumbling in her brain. Selfish, she thought. She'd been utterly selfish the past few weeks. Acting as though marrying Seth only affected her.

Marise now had two parents, something she'd always longed for. Why wouldn't she want her parents safely married? Most of her school friends had a mother and a father who lived in the same house, slept in the same bed, came together to parent-teacher interviews. Ordinary. Normal. Of course Marise wanted the same.

Lia said with attempted briskness, "I promise I'll think about everything you've said, sweetie. Now we'd better get out and get dried off. I want to make strawberry jam before supper."

"Okay." Marise gave a gap-toothed grin. "I'll beat you to the end of the pool. Then I can help hull the berries."

By nine o'clock that night Marise was sound asleep in bed, her fingers still red-stained, and Lia was standing in the kitchen gazing at the neat row of jars filled with ruby-red jam. They'd taste wonderful in February, she thought absently. What in heaven's name was she going to do?

Behind her, the phone shrilled. The number that came up was Seth's. With a superstitious shiver Lia picked up the receiver and said hello.

"Lia. How are you?"

Confused. Unhappy. Terrified. "Fine," she said.

"I wondered if I could pick Marise up tomorrow morning? She's been asking to go to the IMAX, and there's a show on tomorrow evening about whales. I could bring her back the next day."

"Sure," Lia said. "Come early, she'll want you to have a tour of the garden."

"See you around ten, then."

She opened her mouth to say she needed to talk to him, but the connection was already cut. Saying a very rude word, Lia slammed the receiver back in its cradle and wiped the sticky spots of jam off the counter. Nancy was on holiday. Quickly, before she could change her mind, she picked up the phone and arranged to have Marise play with Suzy tomorrow morning until about eleven.

That way, she'd be alone with Seth.

But only for an hour.

The traffic was worse than Seth had anticipated, and it was 10:25 before he turned into the long driveway to Meadowland. As always, its serenity tugged at his heart. Lia couldn't have chosen a better place to bring up Marise, he thought, and steeled himself for the inevitable meeting with Lia.

He hated them. He spent every one of them being painstakingly polite to her, when all he really wanted was to kiss her senseless.

He couldn't do that. Not in front of his seven-year-old daughter.

He parked by the front door, ran up the steps, knocked on the screen door and let himself in. "Marise?" he called. "Are you ready?"

Lia walked out into the pool of sunshine on the worn pine floor. "Hello, Seth."

She was wearing yellow shorts and a loose white shirt, her hair in a ponytail; her feet were bare, her toenails painted neon-orange. Her slender legs, delicately tanned, made his head swim. Then his heart gave a nasty jolt in his chest as he noticed how tense she looked. Tense, guarded and unhappy. "What's wrong?" he demanded. "Where's Marise?"

"I sent her over to Suzy's for a few minutes. I need to talk to you."

His pulse was now thudding in his ears. "Is she all right?"

"Yes...I've made coffee. Come in the kitchen."

The windows were open, the curtains flapping lazily in the breeze. "What's up, Lia?"

She poured his coffee, indicating the cream and sugar on the counter. "If you still want me to, I'll marry you."

This time, his heart gave an actual lurch in his rib cage. "You'll what?"

"You heard."

She was standing braced against the counter, her arms folded over her chest. Keeping his own distance, Seth said carefully, "What made you change your mind?"

"Marise. She really wants us to get married. She wants a normal life, Seth—two parents under the same roof. It was selfish of me to think only of my own needs, blinding myself to hers."

Seth said, even more carefully, "Are you still in love with me?"

"Of course. It's the forever kind of love and I'm stuck with it."

There was as much emotion in her voice as if she was discussing the grocery list. Feeling the first twinge of anger, Seth said, "If it weren't for Marise, you wouldn't be marrying me."

"You got it."

She was now gazing out the window as though he wasn't even there. Her face, normally so expressive, looked blank. As if she'd gone into hiding, he thought, unease adding itself to anger. "How soon do you want to get married?" he asked, keeping his eyes trained on her.

"As soon as possible. There's no reason to procrastinate."

"You sound so cold-blooded," he burst out.

"You're the one who started this farcical idea of marrying me to stop the gossip."

"But now it's segued into giving Marise what she needs." He hesitated, knowing he was on the brink of a momentous decision, wondering if he was making a disastrous mistake. "Why don't we try for two weeks from now? Does that fit your schedule?"

"I'm playing at Carnegie next week. Otherwise I'm free until early August."

He could shift his trip to Australia to later in the month. "Do you want a big wedding?"

"No!" she said, looking hunted. "A small one. Here."

"We have to let the media know. Or else we're defeating the purpose," Seth said sharply.

"Afterward. We'll let them know afterward."

"This is all wrong, Lia—we sound like we're planning a funeral, not a wedding."

She shrank away from him. "I don't know how else to do it."

"When we tell Marise, you could try looking happy at the prospect of marrying me," he said with brutal truth.

But even that didn't rouse her. "I will," she said. "I'll look after my end of it, and you look after yours."

He wanted her fighting him, he realized with a cold thunk in his chest. The old Lia, fiery-tempered, not giving an inch. Eyes glittering, face lit with passion.

That's what he wanted. And that's what he wasn't going to get. He said, sounding like a robot, "We'll sleep together after we're married. That's nonnegotiable."

"Naturally. Marise is quite old enough to know that Suzy's mum and dad sleep in the same room."

So once again he was back to Marise. "I'll see about getting the license."

"I'll ask the minister of our local church to do the ceremony. Do you want a ring?"

"Yes," he said, "I do. What about you?"

"I guess so. It'd look better."

"So this wedding is all about appearances."

"Well, isn't it?"

He said flatly, "I think I hear Marise."

Through the open window he'd heard someone dump a bicycle on the porch. As the screen door slammed shut, he watched Lia gather herself: as though she were about to play in a concert, she was going inward, he thought, connecting to all her resources. Then Marise came running into the kitchen. "Hi, Dad!" she crowed and flung herself at him.

He swung her up and over his head, laughing at her, wondering if he'd ever get over the wonder of her existence. "Hi, there. Ready for the movie?"

"All my clothes are packed, and Robert."

Robert was the large, rather dilapidated bear that traveled everywhere with her. "Good. I've told your mother I'll bring you home tomorrow afternoon."

Lia said easily, "Marise, we have some news for you. Big news that we hope will make you very happy." As she glanced over at Seth, she was smiling. "Why don't I tell her, Seth?"

He tried to loosen the tension in his jaw. "Go ahead."

"We're going to be married, Marise. Your father and I."

Marise looked from one to the other of them, her eyes huge. "Will Dad live with us?"

Finally Seth found his voice. "Sometimes I have to travel for work, just as your mother does, and sometimes we could spend weekends in Manhattan. But most of the time, I'll be living here."

"Like a real dad?"

"I'll do my best," he pledged, his throat tight.

Marise threw her arms around her mother. "I won't mind sharing you. Not with Dad."

There were tears sparkling on Lia's lashes. Suddenly tired of pretense, Seth put his arm around her, pulling her close. "We could get married in the garden," he said.

"Can Suzy come?" Marise asked.

"It'll be a small wedding," Lia said, giving Seth another of those brilliant, fake smiles.

"It'll be perfect," Marise warbled and started dancing around the kitchen. "Why don't you come with us to the movies, Mum?"

Seth felt a tiny shudder travel the length of Lia's body. She said calmly, "I have to practice for the Carnegie concert, sweetie. Maybe next time...you should get on your way. I packed a few sandwiches, Seth, and some juice."

"Thanks," he said. "Want to put them in the car, Marise?"

As his daughter skipped out of the kitchen, he turned Lia in his arms, ignoring her resistance, and kissed her full on the mouth in an impressive mixture of anger, frustration and desire. "There," he said, "that feels better."

She'd been rigid in his embrace. He added, baring his teeth in a smile, "I'll tell you one thing—it won't be boring, being married to you."

Then he strode out of the kitchen to join his daughter.

Four days later, Seth was one of the crowd taking their seats in Carnegie Hall. This time he wasn't in a tuxedo heading for an exclusive box seat; he was in casual clothes, sitting quite far back and to one side on the parquet level, along with a thousand other listeners.

He didn't want Lia to see him.

Above his head shone the circle of lights that memorialized the wedding band Andrew Carnegie had given his wife. An ironic touch, Seth thought, with his own wedding due to happen in just over a week.

He hadn't gone to bed with Lia since the night in Prague; he'd invited her back to his brownstone tonight, but she'd refused. She was icily polite with him when they were alone, and overly animated when Marise was around. He wasn't sure which he disliked more. But if his fiery, argumentative

Lia were to return, she wouldn't be marrying him. He couldn't have it both ways.

He'd gotten what he wanted, at the cost of driving Lia underground to a place where she was unreachable: he felt a million miles away from the woman who would be his wife in less than ten days. Was this why he was here, to try to reconnect with her in some way?

Pretty pathetic, he thought, and settled in his red plush seat to read the program.

Last night had been even more pathetic. Unable to sleep, he'd prowled around the house from midnight to three in the morning, rearranging books that didn't need rearranging, doing a wash that could have waited another day. Running from his own questions.

Why couldn't he fall in love with Lia?

That was the only question that mattered. To which he always came up with the same answer: the barrier that had slammed down when he was eight was firmly locked in place.

He was still behind it, Seth thought as the orchestra tuned up; and it was from behind it that he watched his beautiful Lia.

She wasn't his. Not really.

Because he didn't love her.

As she walked onstage in a shimmer of black silk, Seth forced himself to pay attention. But at the intermission, he got up and left the massive brown brick building on the corner of 7th Avenue. Thrusting his hands in his pockets, he walked east on 57th, then north on Madison toward his brownstone.

Lia had made at least three mistakes in the first movement of the concerto; although she'd recovered each time with lightning speed, he knew the critics would savage her the next day.

He felt responsible. Him and his ultimatum.

But how could they call off the wedding? Marise would be devastated.

He let himself indoors and ran upstairs, hoping against

hope that Lia might have left a message on his machine during the intermission. She hadn't. And although he stayed up until well past two, she didn't contact him. He even got up early the next morning, praying that she'd share with him her feelings about two very lukewarm reviews.

At nine-thirty, when Seth was getting out of the shower, the doorbell rang. He dragged on a pair of jeans, tried to subdue his wet hair and took the stairs two at a time. But when he pulled the door open, it wasn't Lia standing on the step. It was Eleonore, his mother.

Seth's face froze with shock. "Mother—is something wrong?"

"Are you going to invite me in?" she said tartly. "Or keep me waiting on the front step?"

"Sure…come in. I've got fresh coffee on, would you like some?"

"For heaven's sake, put some clothes on, Seth."

"I wasn't expecting you," he said dryly. "Make yourself at home, I'll be right down."

When he came back, Eleonore was sitting ramrod-straight in the living room in a very expensive chair made by a Finnish designer. She said irritably, "This chair is astonishingly comfortable—I can't imagine why."

He passed her a paper-thin porcelain cup of coffee. Eleonore took a sip and put the cup down on a leather-topped table. For once, she seemed to have nothing to say. Seth said casually, "You got my invitation to the wedding?"

"Yes. To the fiddle player. I thought you were against marriage."

"I am. Marise wants us to get married…so we are."

Looking out the window, Eleonore said stiffly, "Will your father be there?"

Seth nodded. "He and Marise hit it off right away."

"You know he's left me. He'll never forgive me. The child

all those years ago. And now keeping his grandchild a secret from him the last eight years."

"You could meet Marise, if you wanted to."

"I never thought he'd leave me!"

In the morning light coming through the tall windows, Seth could see his mother had aged in the last few weeks. Or was it simply that she'd lost some of her formidable self-control? "It came as a surprise to me, too," he said.

Eleonore bowed her head, twisting her fingers with their array of diamonds. "I—I miss him."

"He's changed," Seth said. "He'll never take orders from you again."

"I realize that, Seth," Eleonore snapped. "I'm not in my dotage yet."

"So what are you going to do about it?"

Eleonore fiddled with the diamond-studded bracelet of her watch. "I'm afraid to contact him. He might say he wants a divorce. That he's finished with me."

"He told me about your childhood, how—"

"He had no business telling you that!"

"Yes, he did," Seth said forcibly, "because it helped me understand you. You were never loved as a child—not as you should have been. You were beaten and abused instead. So you've been protecting yourself from love ever since. Refusing to give anyone else what you'd been so brutally denied."

But wasn't he speaking of himself? For years he'd been protecting himself in just the same way.

"Love's a trap," his mother retorted. "Let it in, and it destroys you."

"The lack of it is destroying you now," Seth said. "I can see it in your face."

Eleonore's mouth thinned. "How dare you talk to me that way."

But both of them had heard the quaver in her voice. "Phone

Dad," Seth said gently. "I don't think he's ever stopped loving you…why don't you see if I'm right?"

"If you're wrong, then I'll make a complete and utter fool of myself."

"If you don't get in touch with him, then you're a coward," Seth said grimly; and once again knew he was talking to himself.

"After I ran away from home, I swore I'd never be afraid of anyone again," Eleonore said haughtily.

Seth held out the portable phone. "Prove it to me."

"It would seem I've misjudged you, Seth—you've inherited more than your share of my pushiness."

"I believe you're right," Seth said, and punched in his father's number. After passing his mother the phone, he walked out of the room.

He had a phone call to make, too, he thought. To Lia. Although he had no idea what he was going to say.

He could start with *I'm sorry.* For hiding behind the past. For allowing it to dictate his life. For hurting her.

Five minutes later, Eleonore joined him in the kitchen, where he was gazing sightlessly into the garden. She said stiffly, "Your father and I are meeting in fifteen minutes on the steps of the Metropolitan Museum. We're going for a walk in Central Park, then he's taking me out for lunch."

"A date," Seth said naughtily.

She sniffed. "I guess I should thank you."

"I guess you should." He grinned, picked her up and whirled her around; she was lighter than he'd expected. "Have fun. Eat big globs of whipped cream. Don't forget to tell Dad you love him."

"Seth, put me down!"

She looked so scandalized, Seth started to laugh; and saw, to his great satisfaction, that Eleonore was smothering a smile. "Do you want me to call a cab?" he asked.

"I shall walk," Eleonore announced. "Years ago, your father used to give me a single yellow rose every month on the anniversary of our wedding. I might buy him one. On the way."

Seth kissed his mother on both cheeks. "I think that's a fine idea," he said thickly.

Staring at his shirtfront, she said rapidly, "I did a terrible thing—the abortion, I mean. But when I was a little girl my mother went through pregnancy after pregnancy, and each one dragged her further down...I should never have destroyed those letters, either. It was very wrong of me."

Her eyes were wet. Seth said huskily, "Sometimes tears can be more precious than apologies, Ma."

She looked him right in the eye. "I've wasted a great deal of my life, Seth. Don't do the same. I'd prefer to be called Mum, not Ma." Then she marched out the front door and down the steps.

Her advice was stunning in its simplicity.

All he had to do was take it.

CHAPTER FIFTEEN

As Seth went back inside, his cellphone started ringing. He took it out of his pocket, afraid it might be Allan saying he'd changed his mind.

"Seth?" Lia gasped. "Oh, Seth, is that you?"

His heart closed with terror. "What's wrong? Lia, what's the matter?"

"I'm in a terrible—just a minute."

He heard garbled voices in the background. Then she came back on. "I don't know—"

"Marise—has something happened to her? For God's sake, Lia, answer me."

"I would if you'd stop interrupting! Marise is fine, she's staying at Suzy's. Seth, I was so upset by the reviews that I left my violin on the back seat of a cab." Her voice wavered. "My priceless violin. My Strad."

In a great surge of relief that it was only a violin, Seth said, "Where are you?"

"I'm in another cab. Going to a pawnshop. That's where the first cab went after it let me off." Quickly she gave him the address.

"You're not to go there on your own—that's a really rough area of town. Stop the cab now, Lia, and I'll catch up with you."

"No way! I could never replace that violin, its tone is gorgeous. Indescribable. Plus it's worth a ton of money—I've got to find it."

His fiery Lia was back, in full force. "Give me the address of the pawn shop, I'll be there as soon as I can. Wait for me there—that's an order."

"Huh," she said, sounding slightly less upset. "It'll depend whether I get the violin back or not."

He was stuffing his wallet in his pants pocket and going out the door as he spoke. "My car's at the garage. I'll have to take a cab. Hell's teeth, Lia, don't put your life at risk—it's only a violin."

"Only?" she repeated incredulously.

"You're a thousand times more important to me than any violin—do you hear me? I can see a cab, I've got to go."

He flagged the cab down and tersely gave the address of the pawn shop. "An extra fifty bucks if you can get me there in fifteen minutes."

Settling back in the seat, Seth punched in Lia's number on his cell phone. An impersonal male voice said, "Your party is unavailable at this time. Please try again later."

Cursing under his breath, Seth jabbed the numbers again, only to get the same recording. She'd turned her cell phone off.

Or had someone done it for her, against her will? Had she run into trouble at the pawnshop?

As the cab whipped across two lanes of traffic, Seth was thrown sideways in the seat. Two words were drumming through his veins. Too late. Too late.

What if he was too late? What if something had happened to Lia?

He couldn't bear to lose her. His life would be meaningless without her.

Bathed in a cold sweat, he tried her number again. He could get to hate that guy's voice, he thought viciously, not as much as blinking as the cab squeezed between a garbage truck and a bus. Where was Lia? She had to be safe. She had to be.

In exactly thirteen minutes, the cabbie drew up outside a seamy little shop on an even seamier street. "You want me to wait?" he asked. "This don't look so great."

"Yeah…I'll be right out."

Seth ran for the door, which was weighted with heavy metal bars. He went inside and knew instantly that Lia wasn't there. He said to the proprietor, a man of indeterminate age who looked as though he'd been exposed to every vice humanity was capable of, "A woman was just here, looking for a violin. Where did she go?"

"What's it worth to you?"

"If I had more time, you and I could have a fascinating discussion on that subject." Seth banged his fist on the counter. "Tell me where she went."

"Okay, okay." The proprietor named a street in a nearby Puerto Rican neighborhood. "Some fella bought the violin. Real quick turnaround."

"If she's not there," Seth said pleasantly, "I'll be back. You'd better hope she's there."

The cab was still waiting. Seth gave the new address, bracing himself as they screeched around corners and edged through gaps that looked far too narrow. The vehicle jerked to a halt near the end of a street. "This is it," the cabbie said dubiously.

Seth got out. Over the racket from a construction site and the shrill voices of kids playing on the street, he heard, unmistakably, the sound of a violin. He said to the cabbie, thrusting some money through the window, "Another fifty if you'll wait."

"Sure thing." The cabbie leaned back, tipping his hat over his eyes.

Seth ran down the street. The passionate lilt of a Spanish dance echoed among the buildings, with their rusted fire escapes and cluttered sidewalks. He rounded a pizza joint, and saw Lia standing in front of a blue metal Dumpster, wearing a flowered skirt and a scoop-necked T-shirt, her beloved violin tucked under her chin. A small crowd surrounded her: men, women and children, stamping their feet, dancing and singing.

Briefly he sagged against the nearest wall, his breath rasping in his throat. She was safe. She hadn't been mugged, raped, murdered or kidnapped: any of the dreadful fates that imagination and terror had been conjuring up in his mind.

Who else but Lia would play her heart out on a windy street corner for people who probably couldn't afford even the cheapest of seats for one of her concerts?

Straightening, he walked toward her. She saw him coming, gave him a gamine grin and, with a grandiloquent flourish, finished the dance. The crowd burst into cheers and clapping.

When he reached her, she was still smiling. "Hi, Seth," she said. "I got my violin back."

"So you did." Holding her gaze, Seth got down on one knee on the grimy sidewalk. Her toenails were now painted a vibrant pink, to go with her fuchsia-colored shirt.

A fascinated silence fell, in which he heard, like faraway birds, the cries of the street children. He said formally, "Lia d'Angeli, I love you. *Te quiero. Te amo.* I've loved you ever since that night in Paris eight years ago. I love you with all my heart and all my soul. I loved you yesterday, I love you today, and I'll love you for all our tomorrows."

Lia had lowered her violin. She said blankly, "You're kidding."

"I've never been more serious in my life."

"Then you've lost it."

"Stop arguing—or I might change my mind."

"But you said you'd never fall in love."

"I was wrong, I was a fool. *Bufón. Idiota.* I came to my

senses this morning." His voice cracked. "Tell me I'm not too late. That you still love me and you'll marry me, be the bride of my heart."

A satisfied sigh emanated from the crowd. Lia was now blushing. "You've fallen in love with me—you're sure about that?"

He grinned, shifting his knee. "I'm as sure that I love you as this sidewalk's hard. Try not to keep me in suspense too long, huh?"

"You deserve to be kept in suspense," she said severely. "I've been very unhappy ever since I agreed to marry you."

He reached for her hand and raised it to his lips, kissing it with all the love in his heart. "I swear I'll do my utmost to make you happy every day of my life."

Her blush deepened. "What made you realize you loved me?"

"My mother came for a visit this morning. She was all shook up…different than I've ever seen her. She actually said she was sorry for what she'd done, she had tears in her eyes…and when she left, she was planning to buy my father a yellow rose. If she can do that, I can smash the barriers I've been hiding behind. I have smashed them. But then when you phoned, I thought something terrible had happened to you, and that I was too late. That I'd never be able to tell you I love you."

An elderly woman in a long black dress, a black headscarf over her hair, sighed softly, *"Te amo."* A young man put his arm around his heavily pregnant wife. Lia gave a sudden rich chuckle. "The audience is on your side, Seth."

"I need all the help I can get."

She pulled him to his feet. "I long to be your wife, *querido*. To be your beloved."

"Finally we've got it right," Seth said, kissing her passionately and at some length.

It was Lia who broke free. Her eyes were blazing with happiness, her hair swirling in the wind. "I think they deserve an encore," she said, and launched into a fierce flamenco dance. As the elderly woman lifted her arms, clicking imaginary castanets, Seth began to dance with her.

Had he ever been as happy as he was right now?

The dance ended as wildly as it had begun. Seth bowed to the black-clad woman. Lia said breathlessly, once the applause had died down, "This gentleman had bought my violin from the pawnshop, for his daughter."

The little girl was gazing up at Seth with big, dark eyes that were very like Lia's. "We'll buy her another violin," Seth said.

"And I'll give her lessons," Lia promised.

"In the meantime, dearest Lia, I have a cab waiting to take you home," Seth said. "I wish it was a pure white steed."

She put her violin back in its case, gave the little girl's father her card and wrote down his phone number. Then, hand in hand, she and Seth started off down the sidewalk. Lacing her fingers with his, Lia said, "A cab is fine. A steed of any color would take longer."

"Are you in a hurry?" he said innocently.

"Yes," she said, "I want to go to bed with you."

Abruptly he turned to her, tracing the soft line of her lip with his fingertip. "I'm so sorry I caused you pain—I was so convinced I couldn't fall in love."

"Just as well," she teased, "at least it kept you from falling in love with anyone else."

"Maybe, deep down, I knew you were waiting for me."

"Oh Seth, we're going to be so happy!"

"I suspect my mother and my father will come to the wedding. Together. I'll warn her not to call you a fiddle player."

"If she does, she might find out that I'm more than her match. You've forgiven her, haven't you?"

"Forgiven her. Let go of that night in the library. Opened

my heart to the most beautiful woman in the world. It's been quite a morning."

Lia laughed. "Here's the ultimate test—Marise's idea of a flower girl seems to involve throwing daisies and snapdragons at all the guests. With Suzy egging her on. Can you handle that?"

"Sounds like fun. How about in the fall we host a very big party at the hotel in Paris where we met?"

"That sounds like fun, too."

"But first things first," he said firmly. "Bed."

The cabbie was still behind the wheel, snoring loudly. Seth took the opportunity to kiss Lia again. Then he tapped on the window, and they climbed in the back seat. Seth gave his address. "No rush this time," he said. "I found her. The woman I've been waiting for all my life."

"I should get an extra big tip for that," the cabbie drawled.

"You will," Seth said.

Twenty minutes later, the cabbie drove away looking very pleased with life. Seth unlocked his front door, then picked Lia up, violin and all, and carried her over the threshold. "Getting in practice," he grunted, locking the door behind him.

"So that's why you want to take me to bed—just to stay in practice?" she asked, wide-eyed.

"I'm taking you to bed because it feels like forever since I've had my arms around you. Because you're gorgeous and sexy and I love you to distraction."

She laughed, a cascade of pure delight. "I love you, too, darling Seth. And you know what they say—practice makes perfect."

Seth cupped her face in his palms, such a wealth of love in his eyes that Lia's heart melted in her breast. "You're perfect already," he said.

To marry a sheikh!

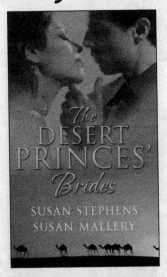

The Desert Princes' Brides

SUSAN STEPHENS
SUSAN MALLERY

The Sheikh's Captive Bride by Susan Stephens

After one passionate night, Lucy is now the mother of
Sheikh Kahlil's son and Kahlil insists that Lucy must
marry him. She can't deny her desire to share his bed
again, but marriage should be forever.

The Sheikh & the Princess Bride by Susan Mallery

Even though beautiful flight instructor Billie Van Horn
was better than Prince Jefri of Bahania in the air,
he'd bet his fortune that he was her perfect match
in the bedroom!

Available 19th December 2008

www.millsandboon.co.uk

M&B